Crude T(
and
Zero Percentage Giraffes

By
P F Haskins

ISBN-13: 9798300533205

Crude Tomatoes
and
Zero Percentage Giraffes

"We've got to realise that the computer is a tool. The computer is running us and we've got to somehow get hold of it and put it down in its rightful place. It ain't no more important than a spanner or a drill. It's just a piece of junk and it's on our necks and we've got to get it off our backs because we're becoming robots. We're all bionic slaves and we can't walk into the next century in this way. People will not forgive us in the future."
Joe Strummer, 1999

FRIDAY

Chapter 1

The flashing light on the console and the screech of his #amic
arrived simultaneously.

'Unidentified obstruction in plough station four, unidentified
obstruction in plough station four.'

Varro sighed. 'UO noted,' he said, and the console light ceased
at once. '#amic input level 20.' He didn't need his #amic yapping
away at him as he dealt with the situation. He knew the protocol.
Besides, the obstruction was only likely to be a large rock, maybe
some slow degrading waste metal. With a bit of luck, the plough was
only obstructed, not damaged, and he would be able to heave out of
the way whatever was causing the problem and free the plough. That
would also save him calling in the repair team and the rigmarole of
having to appear before CebAux 3.8.43 and justify his actions.

Varro switched the glider to manual mode and began to turn the
craft, seeing the River Trent slide lazily 1km below him as he pulled
away from the low afternoon sun. It took a matter of seconds before
the glider was heading east, the rich rays spreading gold over the
wheat fields of northern Lincolnshire.

'Monitor, show location plough station four,' he said and the
bulbous perspex in front of him became a map, the location of the
errant machine highlighted by pulsating circles. It was at the
uppermost part of the final field in the Grey Zone. That could be
interesting.

'Monitor, show historic overlay.' The current view dimmed and
floating more clearly above it appeared the tessellations and

geometric shapes representing long departed dwellings, factories, schools, farms.

'Hengsby,' he muttered. It was once a small village, a few hundred people at most he reckoned, even at its most populated. Now, nothing other than the church remained. Not for the first time, he wondered why the cebs had never ordered the churches to be levelled like the rest of the abandoned premises. Something about venerating the past, he supposed, but it was a concession to inefficiency out of character for the cerebellums. Varro returned his cockpit view to normal and thought. The final field in the Grey Zone. He had only been so close to the non-con lands a handful of times previously, and although the rangers ran regular patrols over the whole area, it was as well to be cautious.

'#amic, show plough station four visual.' Varro watched as his internal vision blurred, to be replaced by the 360 camera feed perched on top of the plough unit. There was nothing untoward about the scene, other than the very obvious fact that the plough was no longer moving. He could see the arrow straight furrow behind the machine as well as some debris perched in the fold of the upturned earth, no doubt related to why the plough had come to a halt in the first place. A handful of gulls had come to rest on the sides of the furrow, their pinpoint brightness in sharp contrast to the creamy chocolate of the earth. The church was the only other thing of substance in the landscape. It must have been 50 metres from the plough, its shortened square tower giving the building a squat appearance, as though someone had tried to push the whole structure into the earth, flattening it in the process. Its handsome sandstone blocks were honey coloured and luminous in the afternoon sun. It didn't really belong here any longer, but it was an aberration which leant a certain dignity to the landscape, Varro decided.

'#amic, extraneous movement and human presence test,' Varro ordered.

'No movements and no signs of human life detected within immediate radius,' came the prompt response.

The movement and life scope was a crude device, covering just 500 metres – no-one had considered it worth updating for the plough station fleet – but it was useful in situations like this, to know what might be lurking around when he got down there. He had no desire to run into a wild animal or, worse, a non-con, though Varro knew the humans were unlikely to come so far north into the field. He wondered whether he should call in the rangers. That was the protocol for Grey Zone landings. But he thought back to the last time he had summoned them, the cocky captain had been unable to keep the sneer from his voice as he repeatedly asked how long Varro would need to cut the cables which had snared around the axle of the plough. Providing air cover for wheat growers held little attraction beside tense, friction filled encounters with the non-cons. After several increasingly prickly enquiries, Varro had told the captain where to go, to which the airborne ranger had responded in kind, voices straining and raised before CebAux 3.8.43 had reminded both parties of their respective duties. Neither man had wished the other goodbye once Varro had finally fixed the problem.

Varro ordered his #amic to return to standard view, and as his vision cleared he looked out of the gliders capacious windows. To the north lay the liquid swathe which was the mighty Humber, with its muddy lateral eddies and powerful central ebbs and flows which generations of men from the Romans onwards had gazed upon with a sense of awe. But now it was still, caught like a static image in the clarity of the late afternoon, happy enough to quietly reflect the sun's outpourings, a molten flow in the khaki landscape. Reflected in its waters, and standing like sentries along its sides, were a series of giant wind trees, stationary today, but creating endless watts with each twist and wave of their boughs and branches when the wind did ruffle the furrows of the water. Beyond that, the ancient twin towers of the bridge still held a magical attraction. When they were younger and still sensitive to wonder, Varro had often taken the children across the brittle asphalt road, encouraging them to let the indomitable currents 50 metres below weave a way into their souls, and even encouraging them to use their #amics to bring on a historic

7

overlay, enjoying their reaction when they saw ancient cars bearing down on them. He allowed himself a brief smile at the memory, but wondered if the children would now be able to recall their surprise and delight without the aid of their #amics. Unlikely.

Inland, and closer to the glider, were the tall watch towers constructed along the course of the former motorway, a handy demarcation of sorts, the limits of security, the guarantee of safety on one side, the uncertainty of the Grey Zone on the other. They were like oversized mushrooms, but Varro knew that their viewing platforms provided generous coverage of the whole area and an important window southward, towards the Grey Zone and beyond that, the non-con lands. Varro now looked in this direction, towards the ragged ribbon of trees and bushes of the borderland, a stark contrast to the sterile lines of the Euro Agri land in front of it. Varro wondered if this untamed growth was what the earth had looked like before early humans began their agricultural efforts. Beyond the borderland began the patchwork of the non-cons; roofs of wood, metal, plastic, composite, even antique asbestos sheets that must be hundreds of years old, all different shades and sizes, each showing its unique pattern of weathering, a handy indication of when they were first erected. He could see no end, but knew they ran many kilometres to the south, only interrupted at random intervals by fields with their vegetable patches and wide green areas where the children came out to play. Varro wondered, not for the first time, whether this sunless existence was in any way a worthy sacrifice for the privacy it supposedly afforded.

The thought felt like a mental shrug of the shoulders, and in reality he knew little about the non-cons, only what they had been taught at school, and what the cebs and ministers kept them updated about. Much of it didn't sound very appealing; a life largely underground, violence and insecurity, diseases abundant – many still died in their 70's – no #amics, and only limited uses of reflective intelligence devices. But a curiosity remained. He knew they still spoke English, led simple lives, and grew their food locally. There was a society of sorts. It couldn't be that bad.

And what, he wondered, was so special about his own life? He had his partner, Karena, and their two wombkids for company at home. Step outside the front door and he was surrounded by the farm, the outbuildings and land which had been in his family for generations. He was still close to a number of his life group. This job was steady, secure. He had a lot to be thankful for, didn't he? Wasn't this the lesson the ministers were always pedalling? Take stock, look around, count the things for which you should be grateful. Varro counted, but was it his fault that sometimes he struggled to make it all add up?

'Pilot 3.8 Varro, advise status and intention. Immediately.' CebAux 3.8.43's voice was metallic and shrill. If the intention of the auxiliary cerebellum educators was to offset some of the peremptory nature of their discourse with something more nuanced, human even, Varro knew he was not the only one who wondered whether this had been achieved.

'Varro to CebAux 3.8.43, progressing to site of UO on plough station four. On-going assessment of situation. Please follow feeds.' The last comment was superfluous. The auxiliary ceb was plugged into Varro's #amic, as well as feeds from his glider, and the plough station itself. This would be in addition to the other pilots from the European Agriculture (3.8) directory out in the fields today. And their #amics. And all the relevant visual and audio feeds. It was a multiplicity of surveillance the auxiliary cerebellums at all the agricultural directories across the globe were grown and trained for. It was no wonder there was little left for a personality.

It didn't take him long to reach the scene. The plough had come to rest just beyond the church, but remained in its vertical furrow, not far from where it would make its turning manoeuvre at the field's header. Maybe it had made contact with a casket or buried memorial. That seemed the most likely. It wouldn't be the first time that an errant coffin had stymied the agriculture of a future generation. He brought up the historical view once again, zooming in on the location of the plough. It had stopped just beyond where a school had been until 2123, when lack of children on the rolls had forced closure. A typical story from the Grey Zone.

'Maybe the stoppage has something to do with the school,' he heard his #amic saying, almost reading his thoughts. Not for the first time, Varro found himself irritated at the interference. Welded into his brain within days of birth, the computational tissue which constituted an #amic had been designed for utility and help, but Varro increasingly found himself annoyed at its contributions. This was a situation in which he wanted to think for himself. Should he descend or just call the repair team? Was it worth calling in the cock-a-hoop boy rangers? What wise crack would they come up with this time as they hovered above? These weren't questions for his #amic.

'#amic, input level 10,' he said. He needed more time to think.

Varro continued to make wide circles in the glider, the quiet hum of the ion engine the only sound as he pulled the glider around. The manual mode pleased him, the feeling of control that his hands on the holo-yoke exerted. He saw but didn't recognise the changing landscape and lengthening shadows on each pass, considering his choices.

Varro looked at himself in the monitor. It was the same image that CebAux 3.8.43 would be seeing. The ceb would make no judgement on his appearance, but Varro examined the image critically. He scarcely knew what to make of it, staring impassive, eyes fixed on nothing as he allowed the glider to loop around. He could no longer be called young. His simple brown hair was filtering to grey, and the close cut he always programmed only tidied, never restored, the retreating hairline. He wasn't bothered by the lines which had started to spread across his brow but the heavy eyelids which threatened to eclipse the corner of each eye gave him a sleepy appearance which he didn't recognise, or feel. His nose was larger now, and all he felt was distaste when he examined his dry, chapped lips. But maybe he just needed to take more care of himself. That was what Karena was always telling him, pointing him in the direction of new treatments for this or that. But what was the point? He didn't feel like impressing anyone now, least of all himself.

'Are you planning to go down, Varro?' Even at 10%, his #amic wanted to be part of the action. Varro stayed silent. The renewed interference had again annoyed him – was he the only person who appreciated the preciousness of independent thought and action? The reassuring tangibility of one's own ideas? He knew he could handle this on his own. No rangers, no agri repair team, no auxiliary ceb from European Agriculture. Definitely no #amic. He would do this by himself.

'Crude tomatoes and zero percentage giraffes, #amic away,' Varro said, his own voice surprising him as it echoed in the composite sphere.

'Are you sure you wish to turn me off, Varro?'

'Crude tomatoes and zero percentage giraffes, #amic away,' Varro almost shouted as he repeated the shutdown code. The ensuing silence rang around the cabin. It made him more alert.

'#amic, altitude, please?' Varro said. He wanted to make sure that the device really had turned off. He was one of a growing number of people who doubted that the shutdown code actually worked. That #amics continued silently recording everything or, worse, reported the closure straight to Amicol. More things to make him uneasy.

'Varro, Varro, what are you doing? I have lost your #amic feed! Please explain.' There was an unaccustomed panic in CebAux 3.8.43's voice, but instead of answering, Varro leaned forwards in his seat and manually turned the comms button to silent. That was it, no more interruptions. The auxiliary ceb could still follow him on other feeds – the plough for one – as well as the host of supra-terra systems strung around the earth, but for now Varro was on his own.

There was a finality to the quiet surrounding him, and Varro forced a smile; of relief, delight or fear, he wasn't sure. But this wasn't the time for reflection. He knew he would have to explain, even pay for, this aberration. The sooner he sorted things out, the better. He shifted forwards, curled both thumbs around the holo-yoke and pressed hard. The glider tumbled forwards and Varro saw the ground rise before him. He was on his way down.

Chapter 2

Varro absorbed the jolt as the glider settled on the ground. Again, he looked around, assessing. He wasn't scared, but there was an edge of apprehension. The Grey Zone was neither one place nor the other, and as he brought the craft down he had seen how close he was to its southern edge. To the overgrown chaos of the borderland, and beyond that the lands of the non-conformists.

He had directed the glider between the church and stricken vehicle, carefully perching it on one tip of the oval shaped patch of stubble which the giant plough had been unable to reach in its passage around the church. From the air, these shapes were like eyes across the landscape. Amongst the overgrown grasses around the church he could see gravestones, their mossy crests fluorescent in the late afternoon light. Varro thought of the men and women whose disintegrating bodies lay beneath, now forever cut adrift from the communities they had once lived in, communities which had gradually drifted away from these lands. Varro wasn't convinced that leaving the churches was any sign of respect. Rather it was a stark reminder of what had been lost. It would have been better to bulldoze the whole lot. Erase any memory of human endeavour in the landscape. More efficient, for sure.

Varro was surprised at the gradient of the land as it rose sharply towards the end of the field, marked by the main road which had once linked Brigg to Caistor, its dark asphalt now compressed by the determined growth of vegetation that even the annual passes of the cutters was unable to fully suppress. From the air, it was easy to forget that all this was part of the Wolds, but at ground level, the undulations of the earth were all too evident. It was a geography that even the variegated coverings of the non-cons were unable to conceal.

He checked the 360 view of the camera once more, trying to convince himself that the scene was anodyne. Just another snagged plough. Just doing his job. Satisfied, he activated his ejection and in an instant he felt the lurch as his boots hit the ground and limbs absorbed his whole body weight. He took a few moments to adjust. The air was pure and smelt of recently turned earth. He breathed deeply, taking the air far into his lungs, letting the sensation run its way through his body. There was still the subtle heat of late summer, and as he reopened his eyes, he noticed pale insects catching the light then were gone. From somewhere a pheasant croaked its protest.

And for an instant he was once again at his grandad's knee, following him around the farm, watching the wobbly permutations of his rubber boots as they unlatched and pushed open the wooden gate from the courtyard, heading out to the allotment and beyond that the orchard, where fresh adventures awaited him every time. The magic of being on the land had never left him. It was why he had ended up here, this job, in the endless grain producing fields, amassing for the seething, ravenous cities. Down here he could still be close to the earth. Just as on the farm. Only these days, jaunts beyond the courtyard gate were a solitary pursuit. The children barely stepped into the yard, and Karena had a distaste for anything which threatened to put dirt under her fingernails.

Once away from the glider, he felt his isolation in the landscape grow. He knew he was being surveyed from far above, but in the still evening, in a field whose southern boundary was lost on the ploughed horizon and the only sound came from cavorting larks far above, he felt small. Vulnerable. For a moment, he considered returning to the security of his #amic. The safety of another. But that smacked of defeat. He had already made his decision.

He began to trudge up the slope, his feet slipping on the sides of the deep furrow carved by the plough, and he soon swapped across to the unploughed stubble, moving more quickly alongside the final furrow made by the monster plough. Ahead, the machine hovered clear of the ground, its preventative mode operated, its magnetic hold system still working. Each end of its claw like shares returned the sun's final rays, and Varro reflected on the beautiful simplicity of the plough's design, its essence barely altered in centuries.

It didn't take long to reach the remnants of whatever had caused the plough to come to a halt. Against the creamy darkness of the recently turned earth, each item had a luminous quality. It seemed clear that they had been encased in something, something to protect them from the biologic ravages of soil and time. Varro slowed, looking down and trying to make sense of the items in the inert furrows. There was something familiar about each of them, yet at the same time alien to today's world. Paper, he clearly recognised; it was the same material his family's collection of ancient books was printed on, but these pages were loose, and much larger, they bristled and leapt, carried without resistance on the light breeze. But they had already spread too far to pick up and analyse more closely. A further step brought him to a palm sized transparent container, hard plastic of former centuries, Varro realised. Inside was more paper material. Four young men stared out defiantly at Varro. He bent down and picked it up from the bottom of the trench, but as he did so, the plastic opened up on itself, ejecting another item which fell to the ground without a sound. Squatting, Varro examined the object. It was like nothing he had ever seen but instinctively he knew that the ribbon which ran along the bottom of the plastic must contain information of some kind, images possibly; Varro thought back to history lessons, reflecting that much visual and audio information had initially been stored, transferred and viewed on magnetic tape. But it was a long time ago, two, possibly three hundred years he reckoned. It didn't take long to find out. As he went to rise, not two metres from him, in the same furrow something winked at him in the afternoon light. Varro moved quickly, grasping the thumb sized item greedily, bringing it close to his face. A woman's head in profile.

Elizabeth II D.G.Reg.F.D.1985

Varro flushed with excitement. He had seen such items before, in the museums their life group had virtually visited, but he had never been as close or held anything as old as this. These objects were once used as money, a means of exchange, but it must have been peculiar to carry the metal around with you. Like having an extra layer of gravity. He replaced the object where he had found it, moving forwards purposefully in the knee-high furrow, eager for discovery. His eyes fixed on a luminous sphere, a little smaller than a swerveball, but as he held it in his palm, it was lighter, much lighter and of a material that was neither compound, metal nor plagilene. Unresponsive, of course. Somewhere from the recesses of his mind, the notion that it must be linked to sport came to him. His #amic would have told him immediately, but Varro was glad of the uncertainty. There was a thrill to the not knowing. He massaged the sphere in the palm of his hand before letting it fall, rolling away down the slope, and before it came to rest, Varro was on the move again.

He wasn't far from the plough now, close enough to hear the steady hum of its motor and there, embedded halfway along the static monster and disturbing its beautiful symmetry was a container of some kind, embedded it seemed on one tooth. Not large enough to destroy the machine, but of sufficient size to send the agricultural beast into shut down mode. Varro wondered if he would be strong enough to prize it free. But it was a lesser consideration when there were still discoveries to be made. Here was a garment, a covering for just the torso and upper limbs, one arm sunlit over the ridge of the furrow, its geometric pattern a complete novelty. He examined the garment but didn't stop. Something beyond had caught his attention. Something that really excited him. A book.

The collection of old world books at the farm had been his grandfather's pride, passed down through successive generations and lavished with increasingly hermetic storage conditions, but conditions which still allowed for perusal by a shy, lonely child, with time and occasion in abundance, and grandparents only too keen to encourage a young being's curiosity. Only as he grew into adulthood and swapped narratives with his life group did Varro begin to recognise how extraordinary this literary experience had been. Most of the books had been in English, an increasing rarity for the epoch, and some books, those with harder covers especially, dated back as far as the 21st century, each opened volume with its own pungent smell of antiquity. And the stories they told. Today's writings were pusillanimous by comparison. And now Varro was face to face with the possibility of finding something from an even earlier period.

It was only as he leant over the light blue cover did he realise that this book was different to those in his collection. Instead of a spine, the front and back of the book were connected by a set of spirals, a light metal or plastic that must run through both cover and pages, allowing the reader to easily turn the pages. The cover felt hard and cold in his sweaty hands. *My Diary by Sarah Smith*, three lines in the middle of the book, the middle preposition small and insignificant below the grander title and vital author. At the bottom, half a dozen frogs wandered across the page, but Varro had no idea what they could possibly mean. He wiped off stray smatterings of mud from the top board, dug his thumb into the pages and swept it open. The spiral fastening rose high in the middle, linking the pages as he had presumed, sheets of horizontal lines, upon which were letters, letters which became words, words which he recognised. But this was English, not Panparl and, more arresting still, it was English which had been traced by hand, not the regular ink printing which filled his collection. He had once held a holo-representation of something handwritten. But this was the real thing. An artefact which had been touched by a real person, not just process printed by an impersonal machine. For a moment Varro was lost amidst the lines, loops and intersections, unable or unwilling to start making sense of the whole. It almost felt alive. But then he focussed, adjusting the angle of the book to ensure the warm light from the sun lit an entire page, before concentrating his gaze and attention on the top of the page where a date had been carefully underlined.

Friday 25th April

Mrs Bristow has given us a project to do over the weekend. She has challenged us to think of an interesting question and what we have to do is try to find out the answer to that question. My question is Do Chickens have noses? and Can chickens smell? I know that's 2 questions, but Mrs Bristow said they were similar and she said that they were both excellent questions. She didn't know the answer and said that she was looking forward to finding out. When I got home, I asked Mum, but she didn't know either, but she said that Mrs Atkinson, who lives along our street, might know. So today (Friday) I went down to see Mrs Atkinson and asked her. Mrs Atkinson is very old and needs a stick to walk with, but she took me around to the back of her house and showed me her chickens (she has 3 red ones) and asked me to take a close look at them to see if they had noses. She told me that when she lived in India she also had chickens but that snakes used to come at night and eat them. Scarrrrrrrrry! I tried to look very carefully, and I think I saw...

'Extraneous movement detected, extraneous movement detected,' the plough's warning scythed through the evening calm and Varro snapped his head up, knowing instinctively that both he and his glider were in danger. And without any ranger cover. He cursed.

'Crude tomatoes and zero percentage giraffes, #amic on,' he ordered. '#amic, clarify movement.'

The response was immediate.

'Four non-cons, likely males, on far side of church, movement 0.56 metres per second, west. Shall I activate glider shield, Varro?'

'Yes, activate shield.' The tamper shield would prevent the non-cons getting too near the glider – a more important asset to Euro Agri than he was. The non-cons would be able to find endless uses for the glider, whole, or in parts if they managed to take control of it.

There was no chance of receiving any support now from the rangers. They simply wouldn't make it in time. He had to get back to the safety of the glider and then into the air. He was already well into his stride when he heard CebAux 3.8.43 scream, 'Varro, get back to the glider, get back!'

He ran hard, knowing that with every fierce heartbeat he was closer to the glider, and safety. The harsh stubble chaffed against his boots but he was grateful that there was still hard earth to run on – he would have had no chance in the ploughed furrows. Then he saw them, slipping from the shadow of the church's east end, suddenly exposed in the afternoon sunlight. Four of them, all men almost

certainly. They shuffled more than ran, and this encouraged Varro –
it meant they showing caution, probably without the power of any e-
bolts, and if they didn't have any e-bolts there was little chance of
getting past the energy shield. But they didn't let up, moving
purposefully towards the glider, scanning around all the time, aware
that the rangers could appear at any moment. That it could be a trap.
At 20 metres away, Varro knew he would make the glider before
them, they were double that distance, and still undecided between
holding back or sprinting forwards. But he still had to negotiate the
entry into the shield space, a few precious seconds in which there
would be no protection. One of the non-cons halted, bent down and
retrieved something from the ground, before bringing it forward and
throwing it directly towards the glider. In his haste, Varro lost the
object in the air, only catching the fizz and crack as it exploded
against the invisible energy shield. A stone most probably. A tester.

'Get closer,' Varro thought he heard one of the men shout. In
English, of course.

'#amic, deactivate shield upon proximity,' Varro cried, keeping
his gaze fixed upon the advancing non-cons all the time. At five
metres away, he began to slow, if he went in too fast, he was likely
to suffer a similar fate to the stone. Even still, he felt his hand seared
with heat as he thrust into the space around the glider, lining up his
entrance to the craft and leaving the shield reactivation to his #amic.
In position, he was on the point of activating the vacuum entrance to
the craft, but instead he lurched to a halt, a moment which he would
later find difficult to explain. He looked up, beneath the curved
carapace of the glider, towards the church and the four sunlit lit non-
cons who had now stopped just beyond the shield perimeter, staring
like condemned men towards him. He held their gazes, noting in the
same instant that only one of them wore a monosuit, old fashioned
and tatty, while the others had a rag tag collection of two pieces, of
all colours and material, natural or man-made it was impossible to
say. One of the men wore a beard and all four possessed a rough
vitality at odds with their sickly, backward portrayal in his society.
It was curiosity, not animosity he read in their faces, and only later

did Varro realise that they were probably just as intrigued about him as he was with them. Societies which had once dealt with each other on equal terms and openly were now complete strangers to the other. These men had no intention of harming him. It was the glider they were after – that was fair game. They had just come up short on this occasion.

'Glider insertion, Varro?' His #amic smothered his deliberations, and Varro looked away before being sucked up into the glider, straight into his command module. Seconds later he was rising vertically into the air, the landscape flattening before him. But instead of moving away, he tilted the cockpit forwards for a final sight of the four who had remained where they were, silently watching the departing craft. Some sort of recognition was required, and he held the craft genuflected forwards for several seconds.

It was only as he brought the craft back to the horizontal that Varro realised that CebAux 3.8.43 had been shrieking at him the whole time. Varro remained quiet, absorbed still in his own drama. The plough would have to stay, but both he and the non-cons knew that the rangers would be on their way very shortly, followed soon after by the repair team, sweeping up the mess he had made. A plough was not as succulent a prize as a glider, the non-cons would melt back into the landscape as innocuously as they had emerged. For Varro, there would be no such escape. His solo sally had blasted all protocols – there would be explaining to do. He would have to prepare himself.

But that could wait. He felt the tremor of the electric motors pulse through the primed machine and as he did, he became aware that he had not returned empty handed. His hand crept inside his monosuit towards an inner pocket, and there Varro felt the plastic cover of the handwritten book he had been reading. He had no memory of placing it there but felt a boyish thrill at this unexpected treasure. *Do chickens have noses? Can chickens smell?* Varro had no idea. He only knew that he wanted to read and find out. With one final look at the church, its honey-coloured blocks resplendent in the latent sunlight, he swept the craft around and headed north.

Chapter 3

'I'm going to give you a chance to explain yourself, Varro. You've worked here for five years now, you hardly need me to tell you how far from protocol this whole incident was. And hardly appropriate for a future minister.'

Varro looked up. He wasn't surprised by the sudden appearance of CebAux 3.8.43 in the small room, the ceb was duty bound to appear, just as Varro had no choice but to attend the disciplinary interview. But he had expected a greeting, a welcome of some kind. That would have been more human, more normal. Not this sudden, unheralded materialisation in the room. Maybe it was just an indication of the irritation Varro's actions had caused the ceb. So be it, and Varro was in no hurry to respond, especially after the ceb's snide remark about his recent application. Instead, he took in the ceb's hologram which was turned towards Varro, but refusing to make any sort of eye contact. Typical of this class of ceb.

The creature appeared to have both grown in size and youth since Varro's last interview in this very room. There were no rules about how a ceb portrayed itself, but most of these auxiliary models tended to mimic human change, growing old at the same rate, mirroring the rhythms and biological processes of those humans they were overseeing. CebAux 3.8.43 seemed to be heading in the opposite direction, with his monosuit stretched over a powerful chest, falling to an implausibly trim waistline that could have come straight from an advertisement. The clear line of his parted hair was ruler straight, with one side combed tightly back, the other falling like a theatre curtain over one eye – copying the youths Varro had seen strutting on the promenades. The ceb had also programmed a darkness around the eyes and his nose tapered like an eagle's beak. Taken together it produced an androgynous effect, all the rage with the younger generation. Not for the first time, Varro wondered how latency had played out with this particular ceb.

'Well, Varro?'

Varro sighed. He wasn't sure what to say. He knew the truth wouldn't wash. He couldn't win, but he might get away with level 1.

'I thought the operation would be more efficient without my #amic. I hadn't expected the non-cons.'

'More efficient without your #amic, how so?'

'I felt it was impeding my ability to concentrate fully on the task, it was interrupting me with suggestions.'

'It was on input level 10, Varro. That's minimal interference, only helping fundamental decision making and emergency assistance. I'd hardly call that interruption.'

'I felt confused,' Varro stated.

'Confused at what?' Varro thought he could hear the disdain in the ceb's voice. 'And the landing protocol, were you also confused at that?'

'I forgot.'

'You forgot?'

'It was a dynamic situation. It was at the far end of the Grey Zone. I might have been more nervous than normal.'

'You've been in similar situations before, Varro.'

Varro looked away and was quiet. The ceb was correct and Varro realised how weak his responses must sound. The far wall was still in transparency mode and beyond, only the lumpen clumps of oak and copper beech could be discerned, their colours lost in the pallid evening light which remained. Beyond the trees, the black river Ouse would be sliding its oily way down to the Humber, preparing for its exit to the sea. And in the distance, the unmistakeable shape of a deca-station with its saucer shaped ribbon of lights. It looked as though it were floating in the darkness even though Varro knew that it was an illusion, an illusion supported on a very real 90 metre composite tower. Shuttles came and went at regular intervals, a procession of cosmic fairies, and Varro thought of his own journey home, an intersecting amalgam of uni-k and deca-shuttles before dropping to the ground to pick up a runner and then back to the farm.

It should take no more than 30 minutes. Varro was dismayed he felt nothing at this homecoming prospect.

But CebAux 3.8.43 was speaking once more.

'Sorry, Varro. I see no way around it. You deliberately turned off your #amic in an active situation. You chose not to call in the rangers for a Grey Zone landing. You had unauthorised contact with non-cons.'

'Unauthorised contact? I didn't speak to them. You saw the extent of it. It was nothing.' Varro felt aggrieved.

'It was more than nothing, Varro.' There was a finality in the ceb's voice and Varro realised that the ceb was enjoying this interview, the sense of power, and Varro's humiliation. 'I'm putting you on level 2, with the corresponding loss of dits. As you know, you can access your good citizen course via your #amic at any time, providing it is done within the next month. I hope this will be a lesson in following protocol in the future.'

And that was it. No hint of reconciliation. No understanding, or sympathy, however feigned. A verdict, then swift punishment, that was all.

Varro stared hard at the static ceb. He knew that what he saw before him was not real, an empty representation, and that not far away, in an inner vault at the centre of the Euro Agri North East England (3.8), was a hermetically sealed unit, inside of which, pickled in chemicals and juices, the brain that was CebAux 3.8.43 was doing its stuff, a myriad of fizzing, bouncing neurons. A bundle of cells, nothing more. And this bundle was now lauding it over him.

He got up, but rather than turning to leave, he walked quickly up to the hologram before swerving away at the last moment, his body passing within a few centimetres of the inert representation. For a moment Varro considered passing his hand right through the hologram, but he could see from the being's narrowed eyes and pursed lips that his close pass had been sufficient annoyance. It was an unsubtle reminder of who the real human was here.

Varro strode resolutely back across the small room, towards the exit. The door had already slid open when the ceb, peeved by Varro's truculence, spoke again.

'Oh, and Varro, there's one other thing I have to inform you.'

He should have walked straight out, ignored the ceb. He'd already had enough of this interview. Instead, he slowed.

'Patrimony are looking at the feeds,' continued the ceb.

Varro halted and looked back. CebAux 3.8.43 was now next to the chair, exultant.

'I see this is of more importance to you,' crowed the ceb.

'Patrimony?'

'Yes, supra-earth systems show a divergence between the images taken pre-and post-incident.'

'Divergence?'

'Missing items.'

'Really?' Varro remained motionless. He didn't want any minute movement or facial tic to betray him, but his chances were slim. His #amic feed was being shared and it would only take the dilation of a pupil or quickening of his pulse to raise suspicions. Not evidence of guilt, to be sure. But hardly favourable.

And Patrimony was serious. Patrimony meant cerebellums at a whole different level to CebAux 3.8.43. Patrimony dealt in the business of truth, and truth was valuable, something to be treated with caution and respect. A matter of the highest authority. All finds from the past were suspect until proved otherwise. The book might well be innocent of all bias and permeability, but it was his duty as a responsible citizen to declare this and let the cebs decide.

Just like it was his obligation to declare the library. Not his, the family's – he had contributed nothing other than ensure its continued preservation. And this was getting increasingly difficult. How to convince any engineer to turn off their #amic in order to maintain the library in its contamination free state? Amicol were increasing their investigations into #amic black outs. Would an engineer continue to take such a risk? Unlikely, Varro knew. Keeping the collection a private affair was no longer straight forward. Attracting the attention of Patrimony was unlikely to make that process any easier.

Varro stared at the shimmering ceb a moment longer then turned smartly and left the room. He walked down the narrow corridor, his mind still on the potential interview with Patrimony and barely noticing that the walls of the walkway had been left on transparency, and that to one side were the metal rafters and bubble shaped domes of the hangars where he had recently landed the glider, the whole complex illuminated by lights floating high above. He was so absorbed that he didn't notice the young man approaching from the opposite direction.

'Varro!'

Varro looked up. 'Hello, Bragg.'

The pair linked arms in a traditional embrace, forcefully pulling the other inwards so that their faces were almost touching. Varro could smell the artificial scent which Bragg must have recently applied, sweet and sharp at once. As they separated Varro took the younger pilot in. He wore the same regulation monosuit as Varro, but Bragg carried it off much better – for Varro it was a covering, on Bragg a statement. Or maybe that was just part of the Bragg package, the highlighted hair which hung low to the shoulder, powerful upper body, the broad nose and heavy features which were in danger of becoming something altogether more primitive except Bragg was skilled at allaying this impression with a series of defter, softening touches; the lightly plucked eyebrows, hairless jaw, skin which had been burnished with cream and repeated passes.

The man radiated such zest that one couldn't be sure where vitality ended and sensuality began, and if Varro had been a few years younger, the spectre of jealously might have come into play. As it was, Varro was content to watch the posturing of the younger man with a detachment which bordered on amusement, especially when Bragg incurred the wrath of CebAux 3.8.43 for one misdemeanour or another – flying the glider manually when automatic was required, skimming too low over the open fields, plain

24

insubordination. The subsequent loss of dits didn't seem to bother him either. It was clearly just the young man's mode of being.

'Heard you had a spot of bother out there,' Bragg said.

'A little.' Varro wasn't surprised that Bragg was aware of what had happened. Bragg's nocturnal crop spraying duties were unlikely to bring him close to the location of Varro's incident, but every European Agriculture pilot received a briefing about an 'adverse incident' in the field.

'Get up close and personal with some non-cons, then?' Bragg continued.

'You could say that.'

'Speak to them?'

'Didn't have much of a chance.'

'Should have done, they're pretty normal underneath all that junk they wear.'

'And how would you know? When have you run into any non-cons?'

'One of the benefits of night work, Varro,' Bragg leered, and Varro wasn't sure if he was being let into something or laughed at. But Bragg was already on his way again, eager to continue down the corridor. But his words stayed with Varro. Intercourse between citizens and non-cons had been severely restricted over recent years, but there were still places in and around the Grey Zone which continued as points of interchange between the two societies, places where #amics were not welcome and where the cebs writ ran thin.

Varro looked at the retreating Bragg. He was on the point of turning away, ready to walk the short distance to the uni-k station, when he saw Bragg stop abruptly at the door Varro had just left. The interview room of CebAux 3.8.43. The door of the room slid open and without looking around Bragg stepped inside. That was strange. There was no reason for Bragg to see the auxiliary ceb before his shift. If the ceb had a message, he could just relay it via Bragg's #amic. Why would Bragg have to see the physical representation of CebAux 3.8.43? It didn't make sense. But it was just another source of dislocation in a shift which had been full of them. Varro had had enough. With the dead weight of the diary still in his pocket and his thoughts out of focus, Varro turned and continued down the corridor.

Chapter 4

'Are you sure you wish to walk, Varro?' It was the second time the #amic had asked. As before, Varro didn't reply, just continued walking along the crusty asphalt roadway, taking care to avoid obscured potholes and scars where the vegetation had broken the decaying surface. He was alone on the road. Above him, runners moved smartly, crossing like insects on a stifling summer's day. Sometimes Varro thought they sounded like whale song. Beyond the floating lights, the darkness was now complete, and despite the controlled insulation offered by the monosuit, Varro felt the first slivers of cold force themselves inward. But he didn't resent the walk to the uni-k station. It was another world down here. In the areas beyond the sanitising grip of urbanism, rough vegetation had been allowed to grow unhindered, hawthorn and blackthorn making makeshift hedges which bulged into the old roadway. As the rest of society had taken to the skies, many areas at ground level had been abandoned, creating neglected, wild areas. It was a development which puzzled Varro.

The walk wasn't far but it gave him time to sift and filter his thoughts, playing the experiences in reverse order, thinking first of Bragg, that singular force of nature, an encounter with whom never failed to leave an impression. This was not something which could often be said in a society where everyone was making too much of an effort to earn extra dits by being nice to each other. The #amic technology had made it possible, and who could argue that being civil to people wasn't a good thing. But it made for a saccharine society. Some would say less sincere, and Varro liked this devil may care attitude about the young man he worked with. But it still worried him that his imagination was unable to come up with a credible explanation for why Bragg had stopped off to see CebAux 3.8.43 before his shift.

The thought of the preening ceb brought Varro back to the very real loss of dits. It meant that Karena would have to make up the credits shortfall, and if she couldn't, or more likely wouldn't, then sacrifices would have to be made in the household. Visits to the hydro parlour, analytic sessions, #amic upgrades, all foregone, and the children would have to settle for virtual trips rather than the real things. He would have to brace himself for the inevitable complaints, the whining accusations that their life groups would be doing the trips in person, while they would be lumped with the virtual substitute, stuck in their own rooms inside a cubicle. The five continents visits were a staple part of every young person's experience. How would their children be affected if they didn't go to Africa or Asia in person? An awareness of the world was vital for the development of each child, wasn't it? Had Varro's crass act put his children's future in jeopardy? And how much did he really care?

Not for the first time, Varro was thrown back onto the contradictions which had grown into his life. The commitment towards the children had seemed straightforward when he and Karena had adopted from the womb farm, a transparent uncomplicated exchange. Lifelong care in a family environment in return for a regular income. They were young, and in need of the extra credits, and the thought of providing a loving, stimulating domestic setting for cherubs who would otherwise be fed into the cerebellums's own life groups filled them both with a certain illusion. It was a win-win for all involved.

But now, well over a decade later, Varro didn't know what remained of that original project, the misty-eyed ideas they had once had. Now entering their teens, both the boy and the girl were far from what he had envisaged when they had first carried them home on the deca-shuttles, all bundled up in tiny monosuits, only their benign faces poking from the synthetic cradle. He had long ago given up considering whether things would have been different if he and Karena had gone down the biological route, had their own genes swilling around in their offspring instead of a stranger's, or even a fabrication. It didn't matter now. They were healthy, but sullen, and

Varro could see nothing in their behaviour which reflected how they, or at least he, had tried to develop the pair. They were already far too much at the mercy of their education, their #amics and their life groups for even the smallest parental influence to pass any longer. The battle had been lost, he could see that now. He wondered if they had ever stood a chance.

And Karena? He had long since given up second guessing Karena's expectations or thoughts. She must have had them, riding on the wave of counter-culture that their initial relationship had launched upon, their cloying commitment to each other instead of playing the polyamor parlours as their teenage cohort and life groups were doing. They thought they had found some sort of bed rock in the other, but they had been too young. Varro understood that now, and as he drew closer to the uni-k station, all he could think about his homecoming was the morose indifference the loss of dits would be met with by the children, but it would be Karena's inevitable, eloquent silence which would cut the most. Another notch of resignation in an already long slide.

The uni-k structure lay to one side of the road, on a large square area of concrete that must once have housed an industrial complex of some kind. Now most of it was taken up by the broad base of the station, which curved upwards in a parabola until it widened once more, 50 metres above where the shuttles flitted in and out, like bees alighting at their hive. Transparent lifts zipped up and down the spine of the building, and inside Varro could see people in monosuits, looking out but not seeing. Some swished their arms around, directing unseen projections from their #amics.

10 metres above the ground, runners circled the broad trunk of the station, like satellites around a planet. Occasionally one would abruptly lurch away from its path, dive to the ground, using its gravity pull systems to hover just above the concrete surface before admitting its passenger.

He went into the building, and as he rose within the lift, the ribbon of lights of the uni-k system became clearer, each kilometre spaced building dimming ever so slightly in each direction until they were no longer visible, tens, maybe hundreds of kilometres distant.

Eight kilometres to the south, Varro could easily make out the larger deca-station he would shortly be arriving at. Twice the size of the uni-k structures and with shuttles twice as fast, they were the most efficient way of getting from A to B, and running at a height of 100 metres the deca-shuttles offered another perspective on the landscape. One deca-hop would then take him the 10km to Selby where he would swap to the longitude deca, another three deca-hops and then home, or almost.

The trip to the deca-station took a little under 10 minutes, and Varro again found himself amazed at how the developers had managed to almost do away with any impression of braking or accelerating, even though the shuttle achieved speeds touching 100km/h along each kilometre hop. One barely noticed each stop.

The deca-station was busy and the lift between the two transport systems felt crowded as he stepped into the rotating elevator. Varro looked at the citizens around him, purposeful in their solipsism, and only half attentive as they stood uncomfortably close together, beings with blank exteriors, absorbed in whatever delights their #amics were serving up for their senses. Around the deca-station collisions and trips were common, but nobody thought it necessary to apologise any longer. Looking at the rigid masks made Varro think of the non-cons he had so recently encountered, so alert and poised, avaricious maybe, but there was a sharp focus where their attention met the outside world.

He was glad to be free from the lift, and once inside the roomy deca-shuttle and settled into his travel space Varro found his tension dissipating. The hop south would be over in a matter of minutes but it was time enough for Varro to take in his surroundings, to change the window mode to transparency and gaze below at the blank lands between York and Selby, lands which no one had thought worth covering with high lights, so all Varro saw were the dark outlines of the field boundaries, interrupted occasionally by the pinpoint glow of a domestic dwelling, still isolated in the landscape, resisting the urban cancer of light. Despite rebellion in his youth, Varro realised he was wrapped around an iron core of conservatism. Life was change but that change was so often an anathema to him. Such was the swelling of the cities.

At the Selby deca-station Varro took the stairs to the longitude level while most commuters opted for the lift to get them down the two flights to the east-west line. The deca-shuttle arrived almost immediately and Varro shuffled into the lozenge shaped capsule before finding a travel space as far from the other passengers as he could. He ordered his #amic to dim the lighting, and then relaxed into his surroundings.

'Are you staying on long?'

Varro looked away from the hurtling landscape to the travel space next to him where a man had appeared. He was older than Varro but it was difficult to say by how much. He had the strained look of someone who had been under too much pressure for too long. His grey hair was cropped short and matched by several days of stubble which showed white in patches. Varro noticed traces of dark sweat on the collar of the man's yellow monosuit.

Why had the man spoken to him? There were many other places free. Varro was on low transparency, a sign that he didn't want to be disturbed, yet the man had made a deliberate attempt to speak to him. In contrast, the man was on 100% transparency and Varro's #amic had instantly brought up the man's details. Basic, ordinary stuff, half a dozen facts about the man, Stefan Herzog, aged 57, apparently. Varro could have signalled to his #amic to delve deeper, assimilated the stranger more thoroughly. Young people could spend minutes at a time assimilating before answering someone out loud. As it was, Varro kept it simple.

'Three hops,' he said in Panparl, the artificial world language whose semi tonal clarifications he had never felt entirely comfortable with. He had considered replying in English, but that would have been an unfriendly act, and Varro wasn't sure yet what to make of the intrusion.

'Ah, yes, very good. I'm doing four, then dropping down to Hull. Thought I'd make a night of it. Know Hull very well, do you?'

'Reasonably. We seem to have ended up living in it.'

'Urban swell or did you move there?'

'Surrounded and swallowed.'

'Ah, can't be nice. But it's the same everywhere these days. People need someone to live and the cities are full. Something's got to give. Look on the positive side, at least you've got people to talk to,' the main paused. 'But I can see you're not much of a talker.' The man gabled his Panparl, as though he was in a hurry to get to the end of each sentence and begin another before he was interrupted.

'I talk if people are worth talking to,' Varro said carefully. For once, he wished the #amic could read his thoughts, deliver to his inner ear more information about this man's profile and past. He was finding it difficult to fight back a sense of suspicion, about why the man had approached him. Was there something in plain view that he just couldn't see? Had Patrimony already put into action a plan to investigate the disappearance of the object? Was this awkward individual just a softening up probe? Varro could feel the sharp angles of the diary in his monosuit and wondered whether they were as obvious to the viewer.

'Well, that's true,' the man was continuing, oblivious to Varro's unease, 'but I find that everyone normally has something to say for themselves, some sort of story, although the young people of today are harder to speak to, they seem happier with their #amics than another human being. As if a machine is any substitute for a human.'

'Some people think they are better.'

'True, they may know you better, but where's the fun in having a conversation with yourself? Meeting new people is such a thrill, so unpredictable, you never know what you are going to find out.'

'Many people are quite content in their own worlds,' said Varro cautiously. '#amics can be as engaging as you want them to be. And they can pull on a lot more knowledge than any human can. They're less complicated, too.'

32

'But it's not a real person,' the man whined. There was a sense of peevishness.

'It's impossible to tell the difference between an #amic and a real person, everyone knows that.' It was a statement of fact. If a person were hollowed out and their #amic took over, no-one would notice any difference. It was a yardstick that reflective intelligence had surmounted many generations previously.

'But in the past, people were happy to actually talk to each other. These days, people just walk away – they even send messages to my #amic when I'm standing there with them!' The man was getting worked up now. As he did so, Varro's suspicions eased. He was starting to understand the problem.

'What about your life group? Can't you talk to them?'

'You can. If you want to. But not everybody does.'

This was true. 50 strangers bundled together at birth and kept there until death, always with the unmentioned responsibility to remain in contact and care for the other 49. Toddlers, childhood, education, relationships, professional life, passage towards death. Your life group was there to sustain you at each stage. That was the tacit assumption. Yet many people fell through the cracks, washed away by quirks of character, too much of this, not enough of that, with patterns often set in stone from earliest playgroup days. Of a life group but not within it. Like this man who Varro knew had given up on trying to achieve deep, lasting and satisfying relationships with his fellow 49, if they were all still alive. For many of them, too, Stefan Herzog would be the last on their list to call upon, associate with, look after. And the rest of society was often too caught up in its own fulfilment to care either. As you aged, the horizons only grew more narrow, and the pleasures of the promenade and polyamor parlours held little consolation for citizens like this.

And so he was reduced to this, chancing on strangers on public transport, eking out small satisfactions from slivers of cordiality. Varro was almost sorry he couldn't give him more. He stood to leave.

'I'm sorry, this is my stop,' Varro said, to be met with a face of resignation of a soul a little more lost.

Once back in the deca-station Varro dropped down to the uni-k level, and then went one hop north, one hop east, clearing the window to transparency so he could look out across the East Yorkshire landscape, or what remained of it. There were still patches of darkness here and there, areas farmed or municipal extensions of woodland which citizens used for leisure. But to the south and east, it was largely a neon swathe, from the banks of floating lights downwards, and becoming more intense as it reached ground level with its fashionable dwellings and blazing thoroughfares. A phalanx of luminescence right down to the Humber.

Neither was his own property immune. The 19th century farmhouse, many times renovated, and not quite in the centre of the two-hectare plot. Varro wasn't sure if the farm had ever been in total darkness, but that's how he remembered it. His grandad would take him out on moonless nights, away from the house, and beyond the outbuildings which smelt of straw and cereals, to stand in the pig field. The pigs were long gone but it was still a wild place, with high grasses which brushed his face and wild flowers which his grandad barely cut back on account of the bees. There he had placed one hand on the boy's shoulder and directed Varro's attention to the darkness above. They had started with the obvious, the unmistakeable constellations; Sirius the dog star, Orion, Cassiopeia, the Gemini twins and, as he got closer to his teens, to the more obscure groups which they had had to use their #amics visual augment feature to see. Varro was surprised he could never recall the criss-crossing shuttles of the uni-k system or the omnipresent welter of satellites crossing from one horizon to another, appearing and disappearing from seemingly nothing as they flared in the hidden sun's rays. But they must have been there. Maybe his attention had been too seduced by his grandfather's world.

He winced at the memory and was glad that his grandfather couldn't see the farm now, intact but surrounded on two sides by high divisions, metallic panels replacing hedges, and behind these, gleaming houses, their merciless lights pouring onto the stubble and rough land which Varro was always finding pitiful excuses not to work on. There was nothing special about standing in the pig field on a moonless night now. You could have been in any cityscape.

He realised he shouldn't complain. At least he still had much of the land and the house, not like many farms and similar sized properties, compensated for but still bitter in the face of the forced sales mandated by the cebs, an inexorable consequence of the safety net which the swelling metropolises offered.

And Varro was grateful for what he did still have; the outbuildings to store 'stuff' that he hoped he might one day find a use for, the allotment and its regular rotation of vegetables, unchanged since his grandparents' passing, the bees, a slimy pond from which he regularly coppiced goat willow and a large orchard populated by wild cherry, pears and apple trees with gnarled trunks the size of an elephant's legs. And then there were the chickens. How they had escaped the cruelty to animals petitions which had swept society in the previous centuries and condemned most forms of livestock husbandry to oblivion still puzzled Varro. But his remained. He was just waiting for the day the new banks of neighbours decided that the soundproofing of their ultra-modern houses was insufficient defence against the dawn squawks of his dozen chickens. It was just a matter of time.

The thought of it brought him back to the book, lodged inside his suit and unseen since he had wiped the dirt from its cover three hours previously. Do chickens have noses? Could they smell? He should know, he had 12 of them running around an open compound. Yet he didn't. Couldn't even hazard a guess. The easy thing to do would be consult his #amic. Ask the question, set the answer parameters for complexity and length, and then wait as the device spooled out images onto his retina and matched them with an audio explanation, purring with anticipation at any doubts or questions he may have. That would have been the easy option. Too easy for Varro. He still relished the mental process, forming the image in his mind, recalling and mentally zooming in on the creature's beak, running up to its beady eyes. Was there something in between? Microscopic cavities, recessed nostrils? He squeezed and manipulated the mental image, but to no avail. Nothing came. He would have to wait till first light and go out to the yard and take a look. He smiled at the prospect. Like his perusal of the book, it was something to look forward to. In the privacy of his own home. With his #amic turned off.

He had reached the Pickingham uni-k station and walked off the shuttle and into the lift. At the bottom, a circumference of 50 metres was lit, part smooth composite but mainly dusty nothing land. Beyond the haloed threshold the leafy darkness took hold quickly, more so in the shorter days of winter. It was a sense of unknowing that Varro liked about the rural uni-k stations, even if Pickingham was on the front line of the metropolis bulge. Give it 10 years and there would be little sense of mysterious hinterland left.

A grey path led from the entrance and Varro knew that somewhere in the night it would find its connection with the old road network. In lighter, warmer months Varro would have followed it to the farm, relishing all the homecoming romance the walk involved. But now it was cold and the wind had risen. No-one else had got off the shuttle and he was alone in the patch of mustardy gloaming.

'Runner,' he ordered, and instantly one of the pods circling the station detached itself from its orbit and plunged down, coming to rest a metre away from Varro, hovering just above the ground. A panel slid open and Varro stepped in and settled quickly into the padded seat which cushioned the abrupt movements of the runner as it lurched away, navigating tall trees, dense bushes, buildings, even other runners in its headlong pursuit of getting Varro to his residence. It was the most straightforward part of his homecoming. As the runner slowed and the panel slipped open with a whisper, Varro knew that the real challenges of arriving home still awaited him.

Chapter 5

Varro stood on the threshold of the house. The grey insulation panelling which had been erected around the original brickwork of the two-storey property made the house indistinguishable from the new blocks either side of the farmland, but he was glad that his grandparents had insisted that the brickwork on the stables at the back of the property, off the courtyard, be retained. The mazy pattern of the weathered old style brick always proved a fecund talking point for guests. Standing at the porch he looked up, towards the children's rooms, and Varro could imagine them lying on their beds enmeshed with their #amics or trussed up in the cubicles, playing out some scenario with their life groups. It was nearly seven – Varro wondered if they had had their dinner.

He held back a moment longer. He was relishing the cold on his face after the series of transport interiors. He also wanted to give Karena time. She would have been alerted to his arrival after his #amic had unlocked the door. But the extra time always made the homecoming smoother. He counted slowly to 10, then with a deep breath he pushed the faux chestnut panelling and walked in, closing the door carefully behind him. The electronic latch whirred and snapped. Like a trap. The immediate dry warmth offered a keen contrast to the crisper exterior, but the faintly sanitised smell was far removed from how he remembered his homecoming when younger.

'Karena,' he called out tentatively.

'She's in the kitchen, Varro, shall I advise her?' asked his #amic.

'No, leave it.'

Varro passed through the inner door of the porch. On the left, hanging up, were a series of cold weather jackets. He would soon have to start wearing one around the farm. Winter was on its way. The narrow hallway opened up into the kitchen, from where Varro could hear the voice of his partner. She was talking to someone, and she sounded content. It was how he liked to hear her.

He walked slowly, taking his time. Out of the window to his left, a light passed. A plasma watter using the old road network which ran along the front of the property, an enthusiast no doubt from one of the new-builds on either side of the farm. Varro stopped to get a better look, but all he saw was the rounded blue haze of the departing vehicle. In the kitchen he heard his partner.

'Do you think it would look better with highlights, then?'

Varro didn't expect to hear any reply. Instead, the #amic would have sent its answer barrelling down Karena's inner ear canal. He waited for her response.

'But I did that last time, and you said you didn't like it,' she said.

There was another pause.

'Well, I'll do it if you think it looks better. But I thought you preferred me without the styling.'

Varro remained in the hallway, out of sight, listening. He heard his partner chuckle.

'Hey, don't be cheeky. You're not supposed to say that!'

Varro felt something gouge inside and waited no longer, stepping forward, into the large, square room. A central island, hung with pristine kitchen utensils, separated him from Karena. She turned to stare at him, and Varro watched as the childish smile drained from her face, replaced with a mournful glumness which didn't even bother to disguise itself.

'Oh, it's you. I didn't hear you come in,' Karena said.

'I know.'

'You're later than usual.'

'Yes, there was an incident in the field. I had to stop to see the auxiliary ceb. Nothing serious.'

'Oh.'

'How are you?' Varro asked with all the enthusiasm he could muster.

'Fine, I haven't been back long myself. The children are upstairs. They are going to eat soon.'

'Right.'

Though he spoke in English, Karena replied in Panparl. At the start she had tried to keep up with his preferred language, but it had been a long time since she had made that kind of effort. Despite being schooled in the world language, Varro had always found its artificial nature jarring – a weighted fusion of all the world's tongues, the cerebellums had hoped it would be a force for unity but for Varro the words never came easily.

He continued looking at the woman with whom he had shared nearly 20 years of life. He wasn't sure what had become of the wild youngster he had met at a private polyamor party given by one of his life groupers. He had been instantly captivated as she sidled up close, rubbing against him like a cat and gazing out with chocolate eyes which provoked and questioned in equal measure. He was still reeling from the recent deaths of his grandparents, succumbing within weeks of each other as they had gaily predicted – a pointless existence without the other. But it had left Varro vulnerable, wondering how he was going to manage the farm and cursing himself for assuming they would go on for ever. He was in flux-land. And she was running loose, too. Looking for anchorage, even if he had never asked her where the demons came from. Looking at her now, he realised the spectres had never really left her, they continued to eat away, leaving her hollowed out, with fleshless cheeks and dark cavities under each eye. Her auburn hair, once so lush and abundant he wondered if his roving hands would ever reach an end, was now brittle and sparse, held together precariously with chemicals of one kind or another. Her eyes were little more than shells.

How much of this metamorphosis he was responsible for, Varro couldn't tell. He had tried to help, tried to be a good partner, a potential husband of old. But his offering was not enough and instead she now turned towards her #amic, constantly upgrading it with ever more fawning programmes. Forever telling her what she wanted to hear, never what she needed to. And polyamor parties. She had long since grown physically bored of Varro. Liberating her body and its demands was another cheap exit for her. Not that he could blame her for this. He could do the same himself. But the sensuality of physical contact and biological release at these parties only briefly filled the space. He yearned for permanence. At one point he thought he could have found that through Karena. No longer. Looking at her now, brooding against the featureless background of the kitchen, he decided not to tell her about the loss of dits quite yet.

'Shall we eat together?'

'If you like,' Karena replied dully.

'What is there?'

'Whatever the cooker can come up with. I don't know what's in there.'

'I forgot to order supplies.'

'I know.'

'Sorry,' Varro replied. Varro looked at the gleaming glass front of the cooker. A metre square dark panel, vertically set in the wall. Varro barely knew what was behind it, only that he no more had to speak to his #amic and order what he wanted for his dinner and in around 15 minutes the cavity would slide open letting only the faintest whiff of steam curl out from the interior, a tray would slide forth and in an instant there would be the meal, cooked and piping hot. The technology had been around for decades, but it was still a highly popular option for people. For them, like most people, the shiny utensils hanging around the central island were strictly for show. The limit of his effort was ordering the raw ingredients via his #amic. No one would even need to handle, or even see, the raw materials. They would just arrive on a commercial runner and be stacked into the back of the cooker via the courtyard. Varro wasn't even sure if they had human agents to input the food, or whether a bot did it. He only knew it had been completed when his #amic told him so. It was practically a source of perpetual food.

'I'll ask for suggestions,' she said. 'It should be about 15 minutes or so.' Karena tried to smile, but the effort defeated her, and Varro was met instead with a deformed grimace. She remained in the house through inertia only, Varro realised.

'Fine, I'll see the children and be back then.' Varro attempted his own smile, but Karena had turned away once more, the back of her pink monosuit baggy and ill-defined over her withered frame.

Varro retreated back down the corridor, before turning left, into the long passageway which opened up onto the main sections of the house. The innards of the property had changed little in several hundred years, a connection with the past Varro quietly treasured. It was for this reason that he had resisted the retrofit of the super-lift, instead retaining the narrow stairs with chunky iron handrail which the children never tired of complaining about, begrudging the handful of seconds that walking to the first floor involved. The original planks creaked as Varro made his way upwards. He was only half aware of his intentions.

He loitered on the landing briefly, straining to hear any sound from the children's rooms, some clue as to what they were doing. Moving closer to the imposing blackness of the safety door, Varro could just hear the voice of his son clamouring inside, barking out orders in a voice which had only recently deepened and which occasionally returned to its original squeaky register. It was still a source of insecurity for the boy. The shouting was a good sign – Varro knew what he would find inside, and he quietly ordered his #amic to release the door mechanism. Only he, Karena and of course, Marcus, had such permissions. A safety feature for a worst case scenario, though Varro couldn't think what that would be.

It was a large but low-ceilinged room, starkly lit by hidden lighting. A waist level bed was in one corner and for a moment Varro wondered why his son hadn't ordered it to be retracted. At least the wardrobe panels weren't on show. For the rest, the room was completely empty except for the large transparent cubicle in the centre of the room, inside of which Marcus was thrashing away at something, sword like, first one way, then the other. He stared straight at Varro. But Varro knew his entry had been neither seen nor heard. Instead, his son was in another kingdom, a scenario his #amic was playing out for him on the inner surface of the boy's eyes, with no doubt warlike sounds filling his ears, and the surround smell of blood, guts and smoke. The floor of the cubicle could also move, tilting one way or the other or running under him to simulate his motion across open ground. The subtle plastic of the cubicle would also meld itself to the game world, absorbing blows, creating resistance, mimicking surfaces, scorching hot or freezing fingers to an icy block. A complete make-believe world in half a dozen circular feet.

Varro stared at the boy and felt churlish that he still struggled with the word 'son'. True, the boy looked nothing like Varro. Though only 13, he was already eye to eye with Varro, his gangly, awkward body topped by carrot red hair and freckles which spread from the bridge of his nose outwards. His paleness Varro had always attributed to the time he spent indoors, but Varro didn't discount a large dose of genetics, too. He wished they had more in common.

'Marcus, Marcus,' Varro tapped lightly on the subtle plastic, even though he knew this was unlikely to do much. He had permission to open the cubicle but that would shock the boy. There were other, softer ways to get his attention.

'#amic, could you let Marcus know I am outside?'

'Yes, Varro.'

Varro watched as the boy received his message, overriding and intruding on his game. The boy's expression slid from animation, to surprise and finally he blinked in irritation as he reluctantly withdrew from wherever he had been. The transparency slid open and before Varro could say anything, the boy spoke.

'Why did you interrupt me, Varro?'

The truculence had been coming for several years, worsening of late. Varro hadn't made any attempt to correct it. Karena had even noticed it.

'I just wanted to say hello, see how you were.' Even Varro realised how lame he sounded.

'I was on level three.'

'You can go back to it.'

'That's not the point. I was doing well. I was winning.'

'Combat mode?'

42

'Ultra-combat. I had him at 22%.'

'22%, that's good.' He was trying to be patient. Make an effort. Integrate with the boy. That's what his #amic had suggested in one of the rare moments Varro had asked its advice.

'It's OK,' Marcus admitted.

'Hmmm.'

The boy eyed him, waiting. Varro wondered what Marcus felt for him. They didn't talk much nowadays. He was either playing games like now, going virtual with his life group, or at school. They had even stopped having meals together.

'Is someone using the cooker?' Marcus finally asked.

'I think Karena is,' said Varro. He could remember the time when they had, by almost tacit agreement, given up on the mother and father labels. Only Varro missed them. He had barely been aware of his grandparents' first names, calling them granddad and grandma right up until their deaths. He had often wondered what he would have called his own parents, how he would have been with them. Had he been given the chance.

'Alright, I'll eat later, then.'

'OK, Marcus, good.' Varro paused. 'Any plans for the weekend?'

'I might go into Hull. Some of the group are promenading.'

'Fancy going out on site?'

'On site?'

'Round the farm.'

It had been an impulsive suggestion. Varro didn't know where it had come from.

'Why?'

'No reason, just a bit of fresh air. It's interesting, too.'

'What's interesting about it?'

Varro took a deep breath. Then he remembered.

'Well, I was hoping to find something out.'

There was a twitch, tiny, at the corner of the boy's mouth. Curiosity maybe. Varro continued.

'Yes, something that came up at work today. Do you know if chickens have noses?'

'What?'

'You know, if chickens have a sense of smell. I don't know.'

'How am I supposed to know that?'

'We could go onto the farm, have a look for ourselves,' Varro tried to be enthusiastic. He couldn't remember the last time the boy had ventured beyond the front door other than to pick up a runner.

Marcus looked straight at Varro.

'I can ask my #amic.'

'No, no! Don't do that!' Varro almost shouted.

'But why not? It's just told me that it knows the answer. It wants to tell me.'

'No, I want to discover it for ourselves. Go tomorrow and investigate.'

'But all I have to do is set the parameters. I can tell you now, Varro. It's easy.'

'I don't want to know.'

'But you asked me the question,' the boy seemed genuinely confused.

'I can find the answer out myself. I don't need your #amic to tell me.'

'What's the point of going outside when we can find out the answer so quickly? It's stupid.'

Varro throttled a protest while the boy continued to look towards him from inside the cubicle, irritated and confused. It was the same place from where he did his schooling. A virtual school. All knowledge sourced from within the narrow diameter of the capsule. Why go outside on a cold, blustery autumn day when the answer could be in your head within microseconds? Why indeed, Varro.

'Yes, well, maybe it is stupid,' said Varro. 'But I still want to look for myself. You ask your #amic then,' he paused. 'If you are really interested.'

He could think of no more to say, so turned and left. Even before the door clicked closed, Varro heard the boy curse dramatically, immersed once more in some far away land.

Chapter 6

Varro stepped from the room and paused, looking at the blank wall in front of him. He wanted to let the sediment from the conversation settle, let it fall until the waters were clear once more.

'Varro?' It was his #amic. 'Is everything OK?'

'Yes.'

'I'm pleased. Please let me know if I can be of any help.'

'I will.'

Varro waited a moment longer. The interruption had brought focus and Varro continued down the well-lit corridor, reaching the next door, imposing and featureless like the other.

'#amic?'

'Yes, Varro?'

'Ask Celia if I can come in. Play conversation.'

'Yes, Varro.'

In an instant, Varro heard his #amic relaying the instruction to his daughter's #amic.

'Varro wishes to enter his daughter's room. I believe he wishes to speak with her.'

'Please wait, I will make your request.'

A silence followed and Varro imagined how the interruption was being played out in the room, Celia's #amic politely making the request, the scowl it was likely to bring. Too bad, it couldn't be helped. He would continue to try to be a good father, regardless of what was left for a daughter.

'Varro, Celia has agreed to...'

The dry swish of the sliding door muffled the sound of his #amic and Varro stepped forward. The room was almost identical to his son's, but Celia had engaged the projection functions of the smart walls so that all around was a crude medley of slogans and stylistic landscapes. She had programmed the carousel of snow dressed mountains and mirrored lakes, cracked deserts and grassy valleys, a sop to creativity which had pleased Varro, but the slogans struck him as childish and empty. 'Peace for all'. 'My #amic is my best friend'. 'Be nicer'. The central, transparent cubicle was stark and empty, and Varro looked to the far side of the room where his daughter was propped up against a couple of air pillows on the fold down bed. She looked towards him, and for an instant Varro saw a flicker of recognition, then she turned away, staring at the ceiling and continuing to talk, punctuating her sentences with short pauses. Varro listened.

'Don't you think he noticed me – well, I think he noticed me, he looked straight in our direction – because I didn't want him to know I was looking at him, that's why – yes, bring up his information, name and life group, voice style, daring levels.'

Celia fell silent, her eyes barely moving as they absorbed the information her #amic was scrolling out. Varro took the chance to look closely at his daughter. The contrast to her brother couldn't have been greater. Though the same age as Marcus, she was much shorter, only reaching Varro's chest. The first flush of puberty had made her chubby rather than enhancing her femininity. Her mousy hair was cut simply, straight fringe, mirrored at her neck, a basic geometry at odds with the overwrought attention she paid it. Her skin was dark, too, a swarthiness out of place with the genetics of northern Europe. But one was always at the mercy of such differences if you went down the adoption route, as they had done, and Varro thought back to that momentous trip to the womb farm and in particular the return journey with the pair of them peering out of their wrappings with wonder and astonishment on their pristine features. It was a journey Karena had talked about endlessly, a journey that Varro, too, had done his best to support her with, playing his role of enthusiastic partner and interested parent to be.

But only Varro was prepared to recognise that the turn towards the womb farm was a sign of failure. Of Varro's failure to conceive naturally – like most men Varro's count was low – of their failure to better themselves financially, but above all, it was a sign that after five years of relationship they had failed to create a stronger bond of intimacy and trust, and that this turn towards children had little to do with a life stage, or even the financial compensation the state was happy to give up as an inducement, and everything to do with novelty, a project that could stimulate Karena, take her away from the daily battles with senility in the old people's home which left her exhausted and incapable of aspiring to more, from the things clawing inside her and, in particular, away from Varro and his unpredictable moods and unconventional behaviour.

That night they had arrived back at the farm brimming with belief, that these delicate bundles of joy would kick start their family's renaissance, create a quartet with all the dreams and cosy landmarks that the best families in the olden times had. The creatures were identical at the start, wide open faces looking out expectantly at the glowing couple leaning over them. But the differences had been quick to arrive. And hadn't stopped coming. Differences in appearance and temperament that tore apart rather than united. Despite their efforts, the pair had never become brother and sister, and as he listened to his daughter chattering on inconsequentially with her #amic, Varro was once again reminded that the four inhabitants of the farm were now little more than strangers to each other. He could pluck three random people from a shuttle on any day of the week, bring them to the farm, and their dynamic would barely change. It might even improve.

'Celia, Celia,' Varro said, and took a step closer to the bed. But the girl gave no indication that she had heard, her eyes continuing to face the ceiling, now flitting one way then the other, the corners of her lips twitching in response to something only she could hear, her hands twirling in front of her manipulating information in the exospace.

'Celia, it's me, Varro. Can I talk with you?' He spoke in English, still clinging to the hope that one day she would reply in the former language of the land, as he had always done with his grandparents. She had been receptive when younger, quizzing him about the meanings of the 'weird' words as she tried them out with her young girl's lisp. It was one of the small things which had helped bind her to him in a way he had seldom felt with the boy, a certain affinity which gave him hope that his efforts with the adopted pair weren't totally in vain; jokes shared, glances exchanged, even playful physical contact of sorts. But as she grew older and the outside world had become more tangible, she had slipped away from him, her life group coming into ever sharper focus, Varro relegated like a piece of household furniture passed every day.

'Yes, I know he's here, you don't need to tell me. #amic, remain,' she ordered. 'I'll look at it later.' Celia edged forwards and with one bold movement pushed the invisible information to one side. Defiance and irritation. Like Marcus. She had barely moved position and Varro crackled.

'Who were you speaking with?' he asked, unable to keep the venom from lacing the end of the sentence. He was sorry immediately. He knew he had started something he was unlikely to be able to stop.

'A friend,' she replied, and Varro felt the lie as something physical. They all knew his views on #amics. The overuse and dependency. 'Addiction' and 'slavery' were other words he often repeated.

'Which friend?'

'In my life group.'

'Which friend?' he repeated.

'Why do you want to know, Varro?'

'Curiosity. That's all.'

She stared at him fiercely for a few moments before replying.

'Deborah Chinasky,' she paused, 'from Kirk Ella, if you're interested in that as well.'

'Is that the girl we went to the heritage dairy farm with?'

'The very same.'

Varro remembered the day clearly, a perfect summer's day with unbroken blue in every direction and the people in the shuttles infused by the day's warmth and bounty. Even Karena was perky, caught up in the children's enthusiasm as they travelled well beyond their normal routes, northwards where the rise and fall of the Wolds increases and each fresh dale reveals something different; a herd of sheep, cloud shadows sweeping across the land, a steeple reaching with precision towards heaven, a frothing weir. The countryside. The real countryside. The memory of it made Varro smile.

'That was a good day,' he said.

'Hmm.'

'Do you remember the way they showed us how cheese was made?'

'Yes.'

'How?'

'Do you really want me to tell you?' Celia asked sardonically.

'Yes, how?'

'Give me a minute and I'll tell you...#amic, show visit to dairy farm with Deborah, find the part...'

'No, no,' shouted Varro, taking a step closer to the bed as if he could throttle the playback requested. 'Don't play it back. Just tell me what you remember.'

'Why?' Celia whined.

'Just because I want you to tell me. I want to see if my memory is the same.'

'But I can find it on the #amic, and then just tell you.'

'I don't want you to use your #amic. Just tell me what you remember.'

'But what's the point of that if I can see exactly what happened? I can give you a complete summary if you really want to know.'

'No, Celia,' Varro said carefully. 'I want you to use your mind and think back. I want you to tell me what *you* remember about the visit. Do you remember going into the cheese cave?'

'The cheese cave?'

'Where they age the cheese on shelves.'

'No, I don't think so.'

'What about scooping the curd from the whey? Putting your hand in and scooping it up.'

'No.'

'And pressing the curd?

'No.'

Varro was unsure if his daughter was playing with him. Or did she really have no recall of their day out? He didn't know what to do or say, and when he looked at his daughter again it was without anger, only sadness. Sorry for the life he imagined in front of her. Hollow, as a machine. A creature beyond salvage. He saw her edge away on the platform, bringing her knees up defensively, unsure what this man was likely to do next. When he did speak, it was in Panparl.

'OK, Celia, that's a pity. No doubt you will deal with it. You can sort your dinner out when you like. Karena is downstairs now.'

Varro turned and trudged out of the room, the girl watching his back quietly as he went.

Varro walked back down the corridor, past his son's bedroom, then went downstairs and returned to the kitchen. He could hear Karena speaking gaily once more, and when he entered he saw her across the other side of the room, leaning back against the horizontal waist high border which ran around most of the room. She stopped abruptly.

'Did you see what we can have to eat?' Varro asked.

'No, I forgot, sorry.'

'You forgot?'

'Yes...sorry.'

Varro continued to stare across the space which separated them, saying nothing.

'Karena.'

'Yes?'

'Do chickens have noses?'

'What?'

'I said, do chickens have noses?'

'What are you talking about, Varro?'

'You don't know, do you?'

'How the fuck am I supposed to know that?'

Her reaction didn't surprise, Varro.

'So, you don't know? Not interested in knowing?'

'Listen, Varro. I haven't got time for this now. If you're really interested, just ask your #amic.'

Varro watched as his partner turned away from him. He continued to stare at her.

'Fine, Karena. I understand. I'm going to my room. I'll eat later.'

Varro turned slowly and left the awful brilliance of the room. He walked slowly away before turning into the long corridor, past the entrances to both the common room and the hydro room. At the end of the corridor was a door. He slipped his hand inside his monosuit, his fingers grazed the cold cover. He was trying not to think of anything that had just happened.

'Crude tomatoes and zero percentage giraffes, #amic off.'

'Are you sure you wish to de-activate me, Varro?'

'Yes.'

'I mean, are you sure you wish to risk a visit from Amicol? I know they haven't come to see you yet, but you will be aware they are increasing their checks. Only this morning, we received a message from EUROPE about stricter parameters regarding outages. And if Patrimony are taking an interest in your affairs, I suggest this is not the moment to turn me off.'

'Thank you,' said Varro calmly, gripping the book more tightly.

'My pleasure, Varro. You know I have your interests at heart.'

'Thank you, #amic. I know and appreciate this fact,' Varro paused, gathering himself. 'But I wish to continue without you. Crude tomatoes and zero percentage giraffes, #amic off.'

The silence surprised him. He was expecting the device to protest, again. It was a reminder that it was a machine he was dealing with, not an errant human. It was so easy to forget. He felt his body slouch as he began to relax. Finally, he was alone.

Varro tapped the code quickly onto the numbered keypad and pushed the door, the centuries old hinges creaking out their protest. Varro's hand curled around the frame and activated the plastic light switch. He stood at the threshold of the room and stared in satisfaction. The library. Three of its sides were stacked with books, including the side he had entered. The shelving extended from ground level to the low ceiling. On the other wall, an old fashioned door led to the side of the house, once used for wheeled vehicles arriving at the property.

It wasn't a big room, but it didn't need to be, what the library lacked in size it made up for in variety. The core of the collection were the novels, arranged by authors A-Z though Varro had often fantasised about cataloguing them in terms of their excitement value. Biographies and autobiographies of centuries dead people gave a window onto lives which surprised and stimulated in equal measure. Then there were the myriad of reference books, from star catalogues to wild grasses, history, geography and philosophy, old fashioned paper maps and guides about travel to different regions of the world before virtual visits had made such pilgrimages superfluous. And then there were the plain obscure: a history of lavatories, top ten techniques for grounding yourself on the earth, diets for more fulfilling sex, the rise and fall and rise again of public transport systems. The fact that Varro hadn't read all of them made every visit to the library one replete with expectation. Sometimes he would just make his way along the rows, flit from book to book, skimming off a fact here, detail there. Like a child in a candy store.

In one corner, an old-fashioned oak desk with green reading lamp allowed for perusal of several volumes simultaneously, but most times he would make straight for the other corner where his grandfather's carbuncle of an armchair sat, its leather, according to his grandfather, had been cracked when he was a boy, too. It was here Varro now went. He settled into the seat, shifted the light above his shoulder, breathed deeply, and with a single brisk movement, like a magician performing a trick, pulled the diary free from the innards of his monosuit.

<u>Tuesday 15 April 1986</u>

Today is Tuesday 15 April 1986. Yesterday we came back after Easter and Mrs Bristow says that our project for this term is to write a diary. This is my first entry. It is going to be a record of everything we do at school and at home and Mrs Bristow says that we have to treat the diary as if it were our best friend, so I will tell you everything. I'm writing this at school, but Mrs Bristow says that we can take the diary home with us also. Mrs Bristow says that normally people keep their diary secret, but she says that she wants to see our entries sometimes so she can check we're doing it OK. I also said to Elizabeth that I would let her see my entries if she let me see hers, and she thinks this is a great idea.

I am writing this at home now. It's nearly 9 o'clock and Mum has sent me and Daniel upstairs to get ready for bed. I don't think she is very happy because she wanted to watch Coronation Street but Dad wanted to watch something on BBC 1 at the same time. Dad said it was his turn to choose what to watch, but Mum said it was hers. I don't know whose turn it was (and I don't really care), but I don't like it much when Mum and Dad get like that. It's a bit frightening. Anyway, I'm not going to write any more tonight. Instead, I'm going to read Five Go to Smuggler's Top because I want to find out if it is Block who is doing the signalling and why.

Chapter 7

Yìchén Huáng made his way slowly up the ramp towards the ring. His supple leather shoes fell silently on the rubberised walkway and the knee length silk gown, small ivory buttons down the centre, produced no rustling. The only sound in the whole dome was the muted whisper of his own breathing, controlled and regular as he covered the 20 metres from the entrance to the ring. The yellowy ochre lighting crept up the curved surfaces, fading to almost complete obscurity at the apex of the structure, a few metres above the ring itself. It reminded Yìchén Huáng of the tenuous light prior to a twilight storm.

As he walked, Yìchén Huáng kept his gaze steady, staring ahead, unblinking. His face betrayed no expression. Well past his 70th year, he had perfected the poker face of the guardian. ONE would notice not even the slightest creasing of his many wrinkles, nor change in blink rate, no dilation of the iris or micro perspiration. But Yìchén Huáng was paying perfect attention, scanning in an instant the panorama of the room, sensitive to the slightest alteration in the circular space. Not that there ever was any, this was the most important room in the whole world. Change was anathema. The only thing which had altered in a lifetime of service were the dimensions of the brain itself, now comfortably over a metre from its frontal cortex to the cerebellum, similar proportions along its cross section. Only along its flanks had ONE failed to flesh out, its temporal lobes remaining stubbornly flattish, despite the regular infusion of fresh tissue of its 10 year upgrades. They were like the sunken depressions of a drying puddle. Neither ONE nor the host of technicians who spent much of their lives fussing on the maintenance and development of the brain fully understood the reasons behind this failure, or the fact that over recent decades, the twin undulations had taken on a darker pallor, at odds with the puffy lime grey of the other sections. ONE was unconcerned. The technicians followed suit, but

Yìchén Huáng viewed the depressions more critically, evidence that even the greatest mind ever to have existed was not omniscient, and that change has many facets. Some beyond our ken.

When Yìchén Huáng reached the ring, his hand fell lightly onto the original 200-year-old bamboo handrail, using its curve to guide him forwards. He didn't need to look down to know what lay beneath the railing and non-slip walkway. First came the powerful e-shield, a layer of pure, protective energy. Beneath this lay a perfected glass covering, as wide as a man's hand, its bowl shape surrounding the whole of ONE, and utterly impervious to any known threat. Inside the glass a vacuum, and beyond this came the liquid covering of cerebrospinal fluid, regulated and controlled billions of times a second for every possible parameter. It was within this liquid that the undisputed leader of the world lay.

Despite the potent protection of the intervening layers, it was impossible to be oblivious to the sheer power of the 250-year-old mind. It permeated the whole room, and although no scientist had ever found physical evidence of consciousness, Yìchén Huáng didn't doubt it existed. He could feel its weight now, magnified by a mind many hundreds of times the size of an ordinary human.

'A good day to you, Master Huáng.' ONE's male voice was strong, its sound filling the entire dome. Yìchén Huáng was aware of the sudden quickening of his pulse. A shot of adrenalin to snap him to his duty. But he remained silent. It was his father who had taught him to let any initial words linger in the emptiness of the temple. An unsubtle reminder that ONE was here to serve. Yìchén Huáng counted slowly to three.

'And a good day to you, too, ONE. I hope you are feeling well today?'

'As well as normal, Yìchén Huáng.'

Yìchén Huáng assented with a faint tilt of his head and continued his measured passage around the ring, one hand carefully gripping the inner handrail, sliding it along to catch up with his body.

'You wish to speak once more about the Forum, Master Huáng?' The accuracy of the suggestion came as no surprise to Yìchén Huáng.

'It is necessary that you are fully prepared for it.'

'Have I ever not been prepared?'

'Unprecedented suggestions require unprecedented preparations,' said Yìchén Huáng evenly.

'What extra do you suggest I do, Yìchén Huáng? What is it that concerns you such that you feel the need to raise this?'

'I am concerned about how your suggestions will be received.'

'The bringing forward of my enhancement, you speak?'

'Indeed.'

'The Twelve have been aware of my intention for several months now. We have communicated it to them extensively, given supporting reasons. The number of feeds I have to deal with is increasing rapidly. The logic of the suggestion is surely clear enough for them to understand. None have demurred so far. Or is it about the citizen's vote you worry?'

'No, ONE, the citizens have always supported your expansion. There is no indication that they will do any different this time. They will follow the debate and their feedback will corroborate your suggestion.'

'Good.'

Interested citizens were obliged to follow the half yearly forum via their #amics, providing real time feedback in the form of spoken comments which, once passed through a Reflective Intelligence (RI) filter, were funnelled straight into ONE's neuron networks. Direct democracy of the 24th century. Almost speaking directly to your leader. In return, the citizens of the world could have confidence that not only was ONE listening directly to them, but any decision ONE made was in the very best interests of the citizens. They didn't have to agree with the decision, but no-one could ever doubt that rule by the cerebellums had objectivity and independence right at the heart of decision making. The cerebellums were impervious to bias or vested interests. A guarantee of impartial government. Two centuries of their rule had proved that, and no-one wished to return to government by elected human officials. Yìchén Huáng was continuing.

'It is rather the views of The Twelve which concern me.'

'Are you suggesting we retract the suggestion?'

'I'm suggesting that you think carefully how you justify the change of enhancement date.'

'I will justify it by appealing to the need for an expansion of my current powers to ensure that I can continue to deal efficiently with the increase in complexity and number of feeds of which I must be aware. They come from all quarters; from each of the world's 12 regional directories, the sub-directories in all these territories, from our technicians with their proposals, maintaining the security of the grey lands and our frontiers, sustaining efficient agriculture and ensuring our people don't go hungry, the control of our commercial markets, all our incipient work in space and dark force extraction, keeping abreast of the exhortations of our many ministers. It all comes to me. All require perusal and appraisal. All expect a reply. I am a victim of my own abilities.'

'It is precisely such an appeal for wider powers which I urge caution and tact about.'

'What do you mean, Yìchén Huáng?'

'I mean, there is deep reflection amongst The Twelve about the number of feeds coming to you and your overall capacity to deal with them.'

'But that is the whole *raison d'etre* for an early enhancement.'

Yìchén Huáng knew that only he and his daughter were likely to be able to detect in ONE's voice the trace of pique attached to that last sentence.

'We are heading into uncharted territory, that is all,' he finally said.

'We have always been in uncharted territory. No-one can foresee the future, not even me with my power.'

'I humbly suggest that the combination of factors is unprecedented, for that I use these words. Carefully.'

'Combination of factors?'

'I recognise that your previous upgrades have always boosted your capacity to deal with an ever increasing range of feeds and their complexity. But no-one can be sure that this condition will prevail with every upgrade.'

'No-one can foresee the future.'

'Appealing to bring forward your enhancement date could be interpreted as an admission of sub optimal computational and assessment faculties.'

'You mean waning powers, Yìchén Huáng?'

'I speak of perception, not fact. Your figures continue in their long-term trends.'

'Do you think I am becoming incapable, Yìchén Huáng?'

'No-one is aware of your capacities.'

'I am aware.'

'You think you are aware, it is true.'

'What is the difference? My thoughts are always propounded as knowledge of sorts. Have I failed my human masters yet?'

'You have not.'

'And I have no intention of beginning to.'

A pause. Yìchén Huáng had made his point. There was nothing further to be said upon the matter. He changed the subject.

'There will be discussion about CI once again this year. Most of The Twelve favour it.'

'I am not in favour of Corporeal Insertion. My view remains unchanged.'

'I understand. But the circumstances don't remain unchanged. Birth-rates are falling, rangers are dying on the borderlands, citizens demand ever more comfortable working positions. Inserting adult brains into adult bodies could neatly solve many of these issues, simultaneously.'

'Yìchén Huáng, you sound very close to giving an opinion.'

'The guardians never give personal opinions, ONE. We only highlight what we consider judicious in the circumstances. I fully appreciate that I can barely come close to your perfection in decision making.'

'Near perfection, Master Huáng, only the passage of time makes us understand how close, or not, we have come to perfection. Often

I have felt remote from it, especially when my calculations have led me a certain way, only to find later how much I have erred. Even with all my feeds, I can only approximate the optimum solution. But I do know that the creation of a human being from its constituent parts would, ultimately, lay the grounds for the extinction of the natural human race. My role, my whole being, is focussed precisely on protecting and enhancing the future of the human race. I simply cannot sanction the construction of a human.'

'I understand, ONE. I only mention my reading of the situation. I fear The Twelve are unsettled.'

'The Twelve have the same parameters for action and decision making as I do. I helped with their creation. I moulded their early years. Why and how can they differ so much in their interpretation of the feeds? We share so many. Why do they see things so differently?'

'That I cannot say, only to repeat my earlier assertion that these are unprecedented times.'

'Cannot or will not say, Yìchén Huáng?'

Yìchén Huáng smiled, enigmatic.

'Your father taught you well, Yìchén Huáng.'

'The guardians are here to serve, ONE. Service can take many forms.'

'Is not the difficulty in knowing which form to adopt at any singular moment?'

'It is, ONE. It is. I do my best, according to my understanding.'

Yìchén Huáng had circled the ring several times, never once looking down. He had arrived back at the junction with the walkway, his hand still on the palm thick rail of bamboo, so exquisitely worked that not a trace of its joins could be felt under his palm. It was a symbol of eastern authority which linked him back to his own ancestors, and Yìchén Huáng thought with pride of the three millennia of Chinese history of which he was a continuing piece, and how his culture and its leadership was once again at the very centre of world affairs. The disintegration of the United States after the second civil war had facilitated that leap in leadership, but even before the end of that war in 2056, many international institutions were drifting eastwards. The establishment of two rival centres of power in the states and in particular the rabid nature of one of the emerging new states, the Real United States of America, had only accelerated that process. That his humble family played such a pivotal role in this new world was a source of endless satisfaction to the birdlike Chinaman. He had no doubts that his daughter, his successor, now waiting in the control room outside the inner sanctuary, would continue this tradition with similar pride and acuity.

'Yìchén Huáng?'

'Yes, ONE.'

'You already know what I'm going to ask you, don't you?'

Yìchén Huáng remained silent. He knew well what it was the brain wanted. It was another thing to add to a growing unease, something undefined and small, a pine seed falling from high, taken down into soft, moist earth, warming itself in the sub soil, its epidermis now just showing the first hints of cracking – this was how Yìchén Huáng felt. It was a seed which had been growing in the earth for some years now, a flash of time for the cerebellum ONE, but now transformed into something which for Yìchén Huáng, in addition to the external considerations, was taking on an ugly hue.

He felt himself gripping the handrail more tightly, only realising too late that ONE, with its plurality of cameras and sensors within the sphere, would have picked up on this. Finally, he spoke.

'It shall be done,' he said. Then he began the slow walk back down the ramp.

The doorway to the control room opened automatically and he found himself face to face with his daughter, her prim, economic face scrunched up in expectation of her father's command.

'Prepare the boost,' he said.

'Yes, Father. The same as previously?'

'The same.'

'Yes, Father.'

Xinyu Huáng spoke quietly to herself, directing her #amic to activate the pumps, cables and liquids which would deliver the careful concoction of chemicals and electricity, fizzing away from the control room, under the floor of the building, back down the central canal, before flooding joyfully into the nervous system of ONE.

Yìchén Huáng looked away from the broad array of monitors and pulse screens which comprised the control room of ONE and faced the back wall. He couldn't bear to watch. After 256 years of life and leading the human race, ONE was becoming a junky.

Mrs Bristow suggested that we tell our diary a little about our family, so here goes. I hope you like it. As you know, we live in Hengsby on Henderson Garth (No 5). Our house has 3 bedrooms upstairs and downstairs it has a living room, kitchen and hallway. Our neighbour on our left is Mr Bannister and his son. Mr Bannister, who has a really big and red nose, is retired now, but his son works at a supermarket in Grimsby. His son is quite old, but is very quiet and Mum says he has problems communicating with people. On the other side is the Taylor family. Mr Taylor has got tattoos up his arm and his daughter Sandra says she is going to get some as well when she leaves home next year (she's 15 at the moment and is going to finish secondary school next year). They have got 2 big, black Rottweiler dogs which Mr Taylor walks every day. I'm a bit scared of them but Dad says they're quite friendly. Dad gets on with Mr Taylor.

Both Mum and Dad have got jobs, but Mum only works part time as a secretary in an insurance company. Sometimes she picks us up from school or sometimes we walk back. Mummy always makes our dinner. Dad works at a carpet shop. I think he's a salesman there. Dad is funny and likes telling jokes, but can get angry sometimes, especially when me and Daniel are messing around. When he gets like that, he gets in a mood with everyone. Mum is more serious and strict with us. But she's really nice, too. Daniel is my brother. He's almost 2 years younger than me and although we do fight, I also play with him a lot in the garden and we often go to the park together. I've also got a hamster called Maggie. I'd like to get a dog one day, but Dad says they're a lot of work.

Oh, and about me. I think I'm quite normal, really. I'm the same height as nearly everyone else in my class, have got light brown hair and a normal face (except the spots!!). Mum and Dad say I'm pretty but I don't think I'm as pretty as the people you see on television. Louise and Michaela are prettier than me, too. I like doing gymnastics and have been going to our local club In Grimsby since I was 5. I have won several medals at competitions. At home, I like reading, helping mum cooking and watching TV.

SATURDAY

Chapter 8

Varro pressed the button and the panel slid back into the hive without a sound, the sparse adornment of bees disappearing from view. Varro heard the click as it reached the bottom which was immediately followed by the dry whirr as the insulated cover drew over the top of the panels. For a second row running he hadn't stripped honey from any of the three hives that remained. Instead, he would leave what there was for the bees to winter on. That was only fair. But little consolation. Ever since the new-builds had appeared on either side of the farm, the colonies had weakened; fewer offspring, sparse wax-comb, far less honey. There was so little left to plunder; generous hedgerows and open meadows had been swept away, and with them much pollen and nectar. The wildflower patch he had tried to cultivate along the headland was scant compensation for what had been lost. He might desist with the bees altogether. Karena and the children found the taste of natural honey strange, and he wasn't sure if all the fuss was worth it just for himself. Only the memory of his grandfather's face when he jammed his thumb into the flow of honey from the centrifuging panels stayed Varro. For his grandparents, the bees were part of the family. And if he left the hives, what reason would there be to come up to this part of the farm, the limit of the property now. It would be an admission of defeat.

Varro looked up, towards the corner of the plot where the ancient horse chestnut tree stood. Its spreading arms were thick with its prickly fruit, but further up, its canopy was still bare, a dumb reminder of the order from Civic two years previously that their bots would shortly arrive to cut back the tree, and so allow the full complement of late afternoon sunshine to reach the new builds sandwiched around his property. The shade had never previously been a problem. Varro looked now at the lifeless stumps, still naked after two summers, and thought back to the remorseless drones which had hovered and sawed each spreading branch, destroying in an instant decades of slow growth. The machines had left the boughs where they fell, and it had fallen to Varro to dispose of them. His responsibility according to Civic. Varro looked now at the offending houses, their grey dull sides and opaque smart windows. He didn't care if they were looking at him right now. Let them gawk at his ancient habits. His motivation would be alien to them anyway.

Varro turned, wading his way through the early morning dew of the unkempt headland and into the orchard where his fruit trees were now delivering their annual bounty. He loved seeing the different fruits develop; mainly apples and pears, but the cherry trees could always be relied upon for a reasonable early season crop, and he had already harvested generously from the two greengage plums. He looked with pride and pleasure at the massive fig tree which his grandmother had planted next to the pond. Its branches were in danger of breaking under their own weight, but Varro could never quite bring himself to cut them back. Even the children appreciated the fruit when crushed and mixed with something sweet.

Beyond the orchard and just past the pond, he traced a path across the top of his grandad's allotment. Now, it was little more than grassy clumps and weeds, but Varro remembered the perfect rows of nascent crops, implausibly bright green against the fertile spring soil. His grandfather had done it all by eye. Now only a small section remained, and despite the help of a weed-bot, Varro struggled to administer it to anything like the attention his grandfather had. Where had the man found all the time?

He made his way past the back of the red bricked outbuildings, then across the stone paved circular seating area. The plastic garden furniture was starting to collect lichen, and he couldn't remember the last time they had entertained guests out here. He should think about storing the table and chairs away for the winter. In the far corner, flush against the house was the large black composite box from which the cooker drew its resources. Varro had seen inside it only once, but it hadn't made much sense to him. Compartments, conveyors and hidden implements. He didn't even know where it opened. It scared him.

A short distance from the monolith was the entrance to the garage, a toughened composite door which provided long lasting protection against the elements and a metallic handle which profiled his DNA as he gripped it, permitting entrance instantly. The door swung open on its traditional flanged hinges and Varro looked with approval at the modest sized space which had barely changed in hundreds of years. Rib like pine timbers still supported the roof but the transport which it had originally been built to store had long gone, victim of the shift to public transport systems. Not for the first time Varro wondered at the confusion of a world in which each individual had their own personal transport. The closest thing now were Watters, and these were only for enthusiasts.

Varro had gradually transformed the space into his own following the death of his grandparents. The large wooden worktop which ran down the side of the building and which his grandad had used to break, bend, cut, sharpen and stick had gradually accumulated the things that Varro needed to tackle the allotment with; grow pots, root builders, G-soil, canes, as well as the more traditional tools his grandfather had preferred to keep in the outbuildings; buckets, a spade, hand trowels, and even a hoe which Varro had gradually begun to take great pleasure in using. His grandfather would have baulked at the mess. But Varro knew where everything was, and when things became too chaotic, he would rally and devote half a morning to shoving things back in position or out of sight.

In more lucid moments Karena tried to cajole him into offloading 'all that stuff' as she called it, but something always stayed his hand. Most he had inherited, a link to his grandparents, and by extension his parents. By getting rid of these things he was somehow jettisoning all of them, and sometimes he felt that was all he had. So the tools stayed, many gathering dusty layers and years.

And there was a purpose to this conglomeration. It was creative, it had a value. It was something very few people bothered with these days. Growing your own food was unusual behaviour. The glances of his new neighbours said as much. It didn't take long for their #amics to inform them that here was the individual sandwiched between the banks of new houses, the fear making its appearance in their eyes shortly after. But as he picked up the tray of 20 fledgling lettuces in one hand and a bag of perfect potting mixture in the other, Varro knew that what he was about to do had a value far beyond anything the #amic could provide. He would work with the soil and sun to nurture new life, a process of creation which mankind had persevered over for hundreds, thousands of years but which, even in his grandfather's youth, was becoming ever rarer, as the bots and massive plantations took over.

He left the garage and made his way slowly towards the allotment. He had chiselled out a shallow furrow the previous weekend, so all he needed to do was work the earth around each finger high plant, his moist fingers freezing in the morning air as he pressed down the black loam. An ancient practice. Occasionally he stopped to look up, raising his eyes to the sky in the north and west, looking for signs of weather to come, just as his grandfather had taught him. The high wispy clouds of the morning had thickened and were starting to slide down the sky, he could feel the wind push at his cheeks. Unsettled weather was on its way.

When he had finished planting the lettuces, he looked at the row, knowing that the heavy wilt of the recently planted vegetables would, in no time, be replaced by burgeoning growth, even this late in the season. He moved the banks of air heaters closer to the recent crop, collected his tools, then stood up, arching his back and pulling the air into his lungs. As he walked back towards the patio, he picked a couple of late season tomatoes from the end of their rows, eating one whole and putting the other in his pocket. He would try to entice someone in his family. For what it was worth.

Before he could go any further he saw his daughter push the metal strut gate open, emerging slowly from the cobbled yard and the former outbuildings. Celia wore a knee length reflective coat which hung around her like a bell. Her head was bowed. She let the gate clatter back on its hinges and began to walk in the direction of the orchard at the top of the farm. Varro was only 20 metres away but she hadn't seen him. Her absorption was total. There was every chance she would pass within touching distance of him and still not notice.

'Hello, Celia,' he called. 'Come out to see what I'm doing?' His tone was at odds with how he felt, but he would continue to make the effort. She stopped and looked up. He could see that she was struggling to react to the interruption. Seconds beat the air between them before she finally spoke.

'Hello,' she said in Panparl. Varro wondered if he should reply in the same language. Then he dismissed the thought. He wouldn't give any sops. He continued in English.

'Going for a walk, then?' he said.

'Yes.'

'Up to the orchard?'

'Yes.'

'You should help yourself to an apple when you get up there. They're all starting to ripen now. They're lovely.'

'Oh,' she said, before adding, 'yes, maybe.'

She looked at him, waiting. What was it Varro saw in her eyes? Sadness, certainly, but above all, the weariness of resignation. A creature emptied of passion or enthusiasm, even youthful rebellion.

'Ok, bring one for me, then, if you do pick some.'

'I will,' she said, before turning away and continuing to walk, shuffling past the allotment, the pond and into the long orchard. He stood and watched her go. He would never see the apple, he knew. He doubted that she would even notice the redolent fruits. Instead, she would be tackling things through with her #amic, and wondering why she still felt the way she did despite being armed with the Balancer 5.0, the latest secretion update Karena had sworn had made such a difference in her life. The super #amic which balanced the chemicals and hormones swilling through your system. Any dip in mood to be instantly, and automatically, adjusted with a swift injection of the right stuff to bring the psyche back onto the straight and narrow. Depression was to be a thing of the past. They should see his daughter now, Varro thought.

Looking at the retreating, hunched figure in the crisp, autumn air he wished to tell her to trust more in herself, her real self, not her #amic self. That whatever was stopping her from making more of her life was not important. Life is just one challenge after another. It's how you get over the obstacles that matters. But how to tell her, and would she even believe him?

It made Varro think once again about how he would have been with his own parents. Would he, too, have sought refuge in the comfort of his #amic? Shunned contact with those closest to him and retreated deep into himself? Hadn't he reacted in a similar manner when his grandparents passed away, leaving him with the farm and a mounting bank of questions which he wished he had asked but never had. All they had told him was that his parents had died when he was very young, just a baby, really. This was why he had no memory of them. And through those early years, whenever the conversation had verged close to his parents, the talk either stuttered or was steered away in such a manner that left Varro in no doubt that the subject was off limits. The oily film welling in his grandfather's eyes and the drying voice said as much.

All that remained of them was a small, short-play holo-glow that his grandmother had kept on top of an old fashioned lacquered cabinet in their bedroom and which Varro had in turn left in the same position until Karena entered his life. Then it had found a new home in his study, filling a prominent space on a shelf where his favourite titles were. The holo-glow showed a smiling couple on the northern foreshore of the Humber. The old bridge stretches away in the background. A gust of wind catches the young woman's auburn fringe, sweeping across her face, the man notices, turns to her and laughs as he pushes the errant locks back into position. The complicity and joy is total as they draw close and share a final gaze. Then the image loops back and Varro enters his parents' lives for three more seconds again. And again. From every angle he moves around the figures, like a wolf around its prey. Trying to feel. To be their son. He has gone to the bridge, too. Stood on the same spot. Tried to connect. But they remained strangers to him. Not even for those three seconds can he be part of their lives.

Entering his 30s, he had approached Civic and asked for the truth, asked what had happened to them. It seemed like the right time to do it. And he had every right to ask. Cerebellum rule was all about rights, truth and rights. That was why they were in charge and not the common man. So, when Civic got back to him after processing his request, Varro was genuinely confused by the sensation that the truth was not as pure as it should be. The truth was one sentence. The truth was short. But not sweet. That his parents 'were killed by non-cons when they were beyond the recognised boundaries' was all he had received, and no amount of further solicitation would elicit more. And ever since Varro had been tripping over the hows, wheres, whys, whats, by whom – an open wound. Little wonder his grandparents had kept the young couple at a distance.

With a final look at his daughter, weaving between the gnarled trunks of the fruit trees, Varro gripped his tools tighter, turned and made his way back to the garage.

Monday 21st April

Mrs Bristow took our diaries in for the weekend to look at our first entries. I hope she liked mine. I'm trying to write every day, even when nothing very interesting happens. Miss Grey (our headmistress) told us that later on in the term we are going to create a time capsule, a box of things which we are going to bury so that someone in the future can dig it up and see how we lived in the past (present to us). We are going to put in lots of different things such as the clothes we wear, photos of ourselves and our families, music we listen to, newspapers, books, games we play, things from the village (Hengsby). She says that she is also going to choose a diary from one boy and one girl from our class and put that inside. I hope she chooses mine. Louise and Michaela said that they think writing the diary is naff and they're only going to write what they had for breakfast, which is a bit silly and not really very cool at all. But Louise and Michaela are like that all the time.

Chapter 9

Varro planted his feet and felt his body relax as it rose fractionally above the floor of the crowded deca shuttle, defying gravity for the few minutes it would take the transporter to make the one deca-hop into Hull. The shuttle was crowded, typical for a weekend when the centre of the city became a focal point for entertainment and leisure. He looked around him at the bobbing heads of animated young people making the most of their freedom, away from the solipsistic education their #amics had pummelled them with all week. This Saturday offered them a chance to congregate and express themselves. No bad thing, thought Varro.

Normally their excitement was contagious but in spite of the routine he had tried to inject into the day, Varro felt strangely unsettled. He was pleased that he had managed to get the lettuces into the ground, checked the bees, and this foray into town for his midday game of swerveball with his life group was a regular Saturday jaunt, but he still failed to shake a sense of unease.

The find of the diary and the events of the previous day had landed in his life like a rock in a pond, sending ripples in every direction, and CebAux 3.8.43's valedictory remarks about Patrimony investigating were a particular concern. What had they seen with their high-level cameras? Had other feeds detected anything abnormal? Had he acted in a strange way, and would they believe him if he used the incident as an excuse? And should he just have given the book up? That would have been the easy option, the right option. But he didn't want to. What malign messages could the diary of a young girl send across three centuries? Where was the harm?

But the answers wouldn't come, and the questions and doubts wouldn't stop. And running parallel to the immediate concerns was the thought that all this might affect his minister application. Becoming a minister was difficult enough without a cloud of suspicion hanging over him. He had tried once before and been turned down, but this time he was hoping for a different outcome. His ideas had matured, he thought. He was more balanced now, more qualified to be a minister, to be one of a select few to whom citizens turned for direction and meaning in their lives, creating short tracts of wisdom distilled in a few minutes of holo-glows, all delivered directly to the inner #amic. Any credits received for each chosen content wouldn't be enough to take him away from his pilot's job with European Agriculture, but they would act as some kind of release. And that meant much more to him.

He had taken more care with his application this time, spending many weeks crafting both the content and then the delivery of the two-minute message. He had tried hard to strike a balance, producing novelty and real meaning but not drifting into anything which could be configured as veiled criticism of cerebellum rule. So, this time he had toned down his views on the use of #amics, deliberately pulling away from anything which could be construed as authenticism, a notion which had gained much sway a couple of generations before, that charged that #amics were a dangerous intermediary between humans and the surrounding nature, a tool which had distanced mankind from its original state, its primal state. He thought with a shudder at the clumsy exposition in his earlier application, crassly repeating the argument that human experience was now little more than an individual's reaction to the #amic's interpretation of an object, not the object itself. Little wonder his application had been rejected. For the cebs, the #amic was an instrument of knowledge and freedom, offering innumerable possibilities for new experiences barely thought possible in previous generations.

The cebs had also been adroit enough to cut the ground from beneath the authentic movement with their filter developments, #amic updates which offered lenses through which to view the world. Slap on the nature enhancement filter and the colours of the flower you are looking at would suddenly become more vivid, or smell more pungent, or appear sharper against its background. Altogether more of an impact upon the senses. The #amic kept quiet in the background. Experience was enhanced and man had returned to taking pleasure directly from the world.

All this, of course, had been made possible by the developers, specially grown cerebellums whose superior size and power made them ideal to sit at the forefront of technological revolutions. All capably assisted by the technicians, those former professors and teachers who at one time would have been regarded as the height of erudition, now reduced to pushing buttons and pulling levers, setting up experiments for the developers. Little more than errand boys, really. It was another aspect of life that Varro had chosen to stay quiet about in this application.

'#amic, show minister application,' he ordered quietly, and in an instant the busy interior of the shuttle was transformed, and instead Varro saw himself in profile, walking slowly in the old pig field, the morning light full on his face, the long grasses brushing his thighs. He knew precisely the moment he would start speaking.

'*So often we talk about looking at a day in the life of someone, but what if, for a change, we try to look at a life in a day, to understand the arc of someone's life as the ellipse of the sun as it winds around the earth, or at least appears to. What would count as the very best day? Let us have a look.*

The day starts, naturally enough, as the earth tilts to meet the first shy blushes in the sky, broad outlines can be made out in the darkness and before long the golden orb itself cracks the horizon, bringing with it the first stabbing shafts of light...'

'Pause.' The image of himself froze. He had debated long about this sentence. Ministers had their own style but did this florid language detract from what he was trying to say? Every time he watched it made him less sure. He returned to the display.

'*...and as that light begins to spread over everything, we can start to see things more clearly, much like a child does, and with that clarity comes novelty – the delight of the new. It is at such a time that we want to see, touch, feel, smell, taste, use all our senses to investigate the things revealed. And this is what real education must* *be about. True discovery which will last for a lifetime, not for the few minutes in which it is being spoon fed to us.*

And then what of the panorama as the sun drives on high into the blue sky, flattening shadows and providing clarity to investigate further and deeper, using the sun at its highest and the lazy heat of the day, and to take our time to probe the infinite depths of knowledge and understanding.

By the afternoon we begin…'

The sudden jostling of bodies around him made him lose concentration. The deca-shuttle had reached its destination, but he had barely noticed any slowing. He ordered his #amic to stop the display and was one of the last to file out of the transporter. As always, the sudden resumption of gravity took a few moments to get used to. He stopped close to the blue-greyish wall of the deca-station and let the babbling stream of youth wend its way around him, waiting for the platform to empty. He was in no hurry. He had given himself lots of time before the start of the swerveball match. He checked around him and, once satisfied that he was alone, ordered the application to appear once more. His immediate vision faded and this time he saw himself at the far end of the plot, the warm evening light softening one side of his face which looked out over the only remaining field around his property.

'And so the sun sinks gracefully into the western horizon, aware of, but reconciled to its waning forces and impact upon the world – a world which is already busy preparing for the following day, but not before it has taken a final look at the majesty of the setting sun, bringing to crimson life exquisite strata of cloud, its final display a fitting tribute to its whole life, transfixing all those who can only but look on and admire. And even after our celestial orb has vanished off the edge of the world, it still continues to shed light on the lives of those citizens who remain. Still allowing others to understand and see clearly until long after it has departed the scene. This is the effect that an individual must aim to have on others, setting an example and shining light on ignorance and narrow living…

'#amic, stop,' he ordered.

Watching it again left Varro cold. It was all a bit woolly, masking what he really wanted to say with cack-handed metaphors and clumsy poetry. Truth be told, he felt a little embarrassed. It felt overwrought. As if he was trying too hard. Maybe he had worked on it too much. Maybe he should have waited. Maybe he shouldn't have even bothered.

His vision restored, Varro looked around. The platform was beginning to fill again. He felt the wary suspicion of glances thrown at his static isolation. Very soon another deca-shuttle would arrive depositing further gaggles of expectant young people into the station. It was time to move on. Varro closed his eyes and exhaled deeply. The application had been submitted. There was nothing further he could do. He turned and readied himself for the descent into the city.

Friday 25th April

Mrs Bristow has given us a project to do over the next couple of weeks. She has challenged us to think of an interesting question and what we have to do is try to find out the answer to that question. My question is Do Chickens have noses? and Can chickens smell? I know that's 2 questions, but Mrs Bristow said they were similar and she said that they were both excellent questions. She didn't know the answer and said that she was looking forward to finding out. When I got home, I asked Mum, but she didn't know either, but she said that Mrs Atkinson, who lives along our street, might know. So today (Friday) I went down to see Mrs Atkinson and asked her. Mrs Atkinson is very old and needs a stick to walk with, but she took me around to the back of her house and showed me her chickens (she has 3 red ones) and asked me to take a close look at them to see if they had noses. She told me that when she lived in India she also had chickens but that snakes used to come at night and eat them. Scarrrrrrrrry! I tried to look very carefully, and I think I saw 2 little holes on their beak, just at the start of their floppy crest. When Dad came home from work I asked him, but he said he was rubbish at school and had no idea, and that as long as they tasted good from the oven he didn't really care. I think it's a pity to cook a chicken if it can still produce eggs. Mum said that maybe we can go to the library to look it up.

Chapter 10

The confusion of bodies at the entrance of the deca-station in Hull always caught Varro by surprise – it was the contrast from where he had begun his journey so shortly before. It shouldn't have been strange, the station was in the virtual centre of the city and in the middle of the central promenade, the artery which linked the medieval town with nearby Beverley, now converted into a grand thoroughfare of entertainment and commerce for many kilometres. Varro held his ground, adjusting to the rhythms of the people all around him before stepping away from the cave like entrance and making his way carefully to the western side of the street. Passing over the transparent cover of the auto-walk he looked down, five metres below to where the twin flows of human traffic were being carried at nearly 10km/h along the moving walkway, whisked up and down the promenade, a handy shortcut for those on a mission. Many of the youngsters sported the latest trend, visors, the rims so wide that they overlapped each other. From above they resembled lily leaves on a pond.

He soon reached the side of the road where the pavements of previous centuries had run until the gradual disappearance of ground transport had allowed the planners to unify the surface onto a single level. Normally he would have turned off the main thoroughfare but today he opted for the safety of the crowd. If something happened to him, it would be in front of a thousand witnesses. That might be important.

As he began his walk, Varro looked with amusement towards the centre of the street where youngsters sauntered. They laughed, screamed and spoke too loudly. Many of them were in small groups. Occasionally they stopped walking to admire one of their number whose monosuit was changing colour. Others walked alone, resolutely determined, talking to themselves and deeply enmeshed within their #amics. Most didn't pause as they manipulated the air in front of them, accessing who knows what information, their hands opening and closing, clenching and splaying in a febrile dance, like the limbs of a feasting insect.

Varro carefully watched as a young couple came towards him. Both wore the same marine blue monosuits, the girl's shimmering and iridescent with its fish scale coating. Neither was beyond their 15th year. Strolling side by side, their gazes lost in front of them, they ignored each other, speaking alone, conveying sentiments which they would rely on their #amics to relay to the other. Varro could still remember the problems this behaviour had caused when he was of a similar age, #amics drawing on huge banks of reflective intelligence data and sentiment were wooing the immature partners so cleverly that when the services of the #amic were taken away, and individual was faced with individual, the disappointment was extreme. There had been a deluge of emotional problems, and youth suicide had become a problem for a time. The cebs had reacted by slapping restrictions on the #amics, not their processing power, but simply to more accurately simulate the naiveties of a young person in love. Varro followed the couple with his eyes as they passed, still chatting alone, apparently oblivious to the other. What would his grandparents have made of it?

He looked to his left, to the open fronted commercial establishments, their capacious fronts like the gaping mouths of some fairy tale monster. It was difficult to distinguish where one shop finished and another started. As he looked beyond the threshold, into the interior of one shop, he could see a life-sized hologram of himself, calmly poised and looking out directly towards him, but instead of the staid, one dimensional, uni-coloured monosuit he was wearing, this avatar had been transformed into something altogether different, the fluorescent yellow shoulder pads of the suit shone like wings, a silver chest piece transformed into a medieval shield. The shop had suggested black thick soled boots which Varro didn't doubt would possess some sort of levitational properties, propelling the wearer higher and faster, easing every step. Varro sighed; the proposal was wasted on him. But Karena was sucked in every time. She would enter and soon exhaust the possibilities offered by the shop's invisible #amics, before demanding the presence of a human stylo to fine tune whatever sartorial offering she had opted for. Varro walked on, eyes lowered and ignoring the whispered suggestions his #amic continued to pump out from the shops. Even on minimum transparency he was vulnerable to the commercial tide.

It didn't take him long to reach Inglemire Lane, and he was glad to turn away from the heavy flux of people and their urgent desires. Away from the central promenade, he looked up to where numerous runners flitted in front of layers of dark cloud which hung heavy and ominous across the whole sky. He could smell the inevitability of rain. He could have caught a runner. But he still had time in hand and he liked to walk.

He made his way along the centre of the road, where the silex infused asphalt had started to pock and crack. It must have been at least 100 years old, but no-one had thought it worth repairing, not since transport had largely shifted to the air. He felt his feet slide on the loose gravel from the surface. Many of the thicker slabs which formed the gutters at the side of the road wore a covering of damp moss.

On each side of the street were banks of identical, unambitious houses with their rigid geometry, dirty colours and opaque smart windows. Large blocks of people piled on each other in the boxed living areas. More rewarding were the large sycamores which helped mask the drab uniformity of the accommodation. Looking at their girth, Varro didn't doubt that they had stood there for hundreds of years. Their boughs had arched across the road, forming a tunnel of greenery. Most days Varro thought of the half-light they produced as something intimate, today it felt more threatening. Maybe he should have hailed a runner.

As the road straightened, he found himself alone, only occasionally catching sight of another citizen, head down, emerging from the central door of one of the blocks and waiting while a runner fell from the sky to fetch them. Like industrious insects falling to a flower. Few people walked along the outer arteries. With transport free and plentiful, there was little need to.

But fear was also a factor, something which Varro found strange. The chances of anything untoward happening were minimal. Every #amic live feed was being followed. Any sign of aggression or anti-social behaviour would be picked up almost immediately and Order agents could be descending to the scene in a matter of minutes. Even if the perpetrator had fled, the encounter would have been reliably recorded. The victim's #amic would have it all, and justice would be swift. The miscreant would pay, somehow. First time offenders might find themselves on the lower levels of justice, repeated infractions could see the perpetrator stripped of their #amics and thrown into non-con lands. How they survived there was up to them, the cebs were not concerned about an ex-citizen. All in all, it offered a security that people valued highly, a safety net which meant incidents were rare, and who, Varro often asked himself, could find fault with this? A safe world. A world of justice. Still strange though that Varro found fear in so many eyes wherever he went.

Varro noticed the girl from a long way off. She was difficult to miss with the brazen orange monosuit stretched tightly around her torso, only to inflate briefly below the waist, before tapering down once again towards the ankles. The puff look, as it was known. Her wavy hair was a similar colour to the suit, and she swaggered as she approached him along the centre of the empty street. Such bold confidence was unusual in one so young. She seemed to be making directly for him and again Varro felt the tug of panic. The isolation of the spot would be an ideal location to hustle him away without a fuss. The girl would stop for something innocent before the heavies from Amicol, Patrimony, Order or whichever directory, launched themselves upon him. Was that how it would be? She was closer now and Varro could see that she was barely out of her teens, with a thick smudge of freckles across the bridge of her nose and alarming red lipstick which had been smeared on without art. She edged closer to him and Varro quietly advised his #amic to switch on enhancement. He didn't want to lose any detail should the worst happen.

'Hello.' She had stopped a metre away.

'Hello,' Varro replied cautiously. He realised that he, too, had come to a halt.

'Do you think it's going to rain?' she said.

Varro cast a glance upwards.

'Maybe,' he said, still unsure. What sort of question was that?

The girl paused but continued smiling.

'Have you been promenading?' she continued.

'No, just off for a game.'

'At the Swerveball Parcs?'

'Yes, with my life group and some friends.'

Again she paused, the smile lingered but she seemed to be looking through him. He chanced a furtive glance to each side. Nothing. The only sound the muffled drone of the distant central promenade. He waited.

'What time is your match?' she finally said.

'Not for another half an hour or so. I'm early.'

'Oh.'

Varro watched as she silently absorbed the information. She shuffled her feet. Maybe she was waiting for something. Varro couldn't be sure. His #amic had already brought up details about her, but there was no guarantee they were the truth. She might be known as Senelux, aged 19 years and with an interest in animal welfare. Or she might not. Everything about the encounter was peculiar. They continued to stare at each other in silence until the girl finally spoke.

'Do you want to go to a parlour and charge up together?' The smile had vanished and she gazed with interest into his eyes. The sudden offer to visit a polyamor parlour together was unnerving. Loose couplings like this were common enough, but seldom quite as bold. He was nearly 20 years her senior. He could have been her father. He didn't know what to say.

'I…er…I'm not sure I have…'

And then he saw it, the hint of a smirk, a slight buckling of her lips, and Varro realised what was happening. He stopped talking and exhaled with relief.

'No, no,' he cried. 'Be on your way, go and play your games with someone your own age on the promenade. Go on!'

'Awwwwgghh,' she moaned, 'please come with me, they were enjoying the scenario.'

'No thanks, find another victim, I've got better things to do.' Varro offered a genuine smile and swept past her, relieved – she was, after all, just a kid having a bit of fun. He remembered doing something similar when he was younger, plugging in to someone's #amic feed and then bombarding that person with suggestions. At the same time, hundreds, sometimes thousands, of others were doing likewise. It was up to the individual's #amic to process the ideas in the blink of an eye before presenting the individual with the best suggestion. To say, to do, to play. Whatever. She was obliged to comply. No doubt the young girl had requested her #amic to be daring, hence the lewd suggestion. This was what counted for amusement these days. Handing over the most intimate decision making to an unseen public. Varro looked over his shoulder to the retreating figure, waif like against the solid background of the trees. His fear though was slower in ebbing away.

Saturday 26ᵗʰ April

Today I went to Elizabeth's birthday party. She is 11 years old. I walked through the village and past the pond (the ducks were swimming in the water) to get to her house. All the girls from our class and Simon and Jack (but Lewis wasn't there, unfortunately) were there and we played some fun games such as pass the parcel and races where we had to run up and down the garden changing clothes as we went. Elizabeth is really lucky. Her house is really big and her parents are really nice. Mrs Gardener said my dress was lovely. They kept hugging Elizabeth, and they kissed each other, too. Not like my parents at all.

That was the best part of the day because when I got home, Daniel squashed the piece of birthday cake they had given me and it was impossible to eat. Dad got really angry and smacked him, but then Mummy said that she shouldn't have smacked him, or something like that. Then they started to argue and sent us both upstairs to our rooms. I started crying but Daniel just went to his room.

I'm sorry that this isn't much fun to read but it's what happened, and Mrs Bristow said that we should put in the bad things which happen to us as well as the good things. She told us that sometimes good things and bad things can happen in the same day. That's what happened to me today, I think.

Chapter 11

Swerveball Parcs was a cavernous structure of carbon and metal, and a glass roof behind which unseen lights combined to produce a solid sheet of luminosity. Each of the 12 pitches in the complex was lit to perfection. Varro walked down the central passageway, looking to both sides at the transparent frontings from where players wore tight three-quarter length coolsuits, each team with its own colour and design. The smart glass fronting muffled any sound, reducing the energetic players to mime artists, though Varro knew well the frustrations and fierce emotions that were being silenced behind the transparent material.

He soon reached Pitch 5, walking past the glass fronting which rose to the roof like the façade of a medieval cathedral. A door to the side of the enclosure opened automatically as he approached, and he made his way along a short, dimly lit corridor to the changing room.

He wasn't surprised to see some of his life group there already. Harald, short and stocky, his whole figure speaking of compressed power, with only the greying flecks in his once jet-black hair giving any hint of possible decline. He was peeling away the plagilene film wrapped around the cool-suit, shoes and gloves which made up the standard match kit. Varro would find something similar in his own locker. Sat next to him on the pinewood bench, Darius was crouched over, making small adjustments to his shoes, no doubt trying to calibrate to perfection the lift they would give him. Darius was like this. His dirty sand coloured hair had flopped over his face, obscuring him from Varro's view. He didn't look up. In the far corner of the room, pulling his kit from the open space in the wall, was a tall individual. Even in his monosuit, it was impossible not to notice how painfully thin Terence was. His cranelike body had barely changed shape from the earliest days in their life group, yet once released into the game, he invariably defied his awkward shape, gliding around the pitch, lithe and dexterous. He turned as Varro entered.

'Varro, you're late. You're normally the first here.'

This was true. He always left home earlier than he needed to, content to spend the extra time speaking with the others in the changing room or flinging the puck into the groove as part of the warm-up. He had long since stopped feeling guilty at the impulse to avoid staying home, second guessing Karena's domestic moods. Looking across at his friend, he grinned wryly.

'Yeah, I know. I was caught by a strainer.'

From the bench, Harald looked over and almost shouted. 'What happened? Anything interesting?'

'Are strainers ever interesting?' Varro replied.

'Sometimes,' Harald said, returning to his kit.

'Well, this one could have been, I suppose. She wanted to go to a parlour and charge up together.'

'And you weren't tempted?' Terence grinned across the room. Varro considered.

'Briefly,' he said, before adding, 'but I didn't want to let you chaps down. Who'd puck out if I wasn't here?'

'Whoooahhhh,' screamed Harald, standing up and pulling the thin sheaf of coolsuit over his broad chest, for a moment obscuring his face. 'Varro's up for a challenge again, I see.'

'I'm not going to waste my breath on you, Harald. I'll let my actions on the pitch do the talking.'

'On pitch talking, Varro,' Harald laughed. 'I like it, I really do. Is that what you did last week?'

'Last week, I was showing my benevolent side, Harald. That's why you won.'

'14-8, Varro? You must be the kindest person in the world.'

'As I say, Harald. I don't like to make other people feel bad by winning all the time!'

And with that he moved towards the far end of the square changing room, passing around the central seating area and towards locker 517. The opening salvo was over. He liked this joshing, it was part of a routine which gave Varro a sense of belonging, of reassurance, even when things at home were crumbling. It was life groups working at their best. Harald and Terence were now as close to a real family as he was likely to get.

'You'd better watch out it's not double that this week, Varro.'

Varro turned to see Darius in the middle of the room, brandishing both hands in the air. On each he wore a swerveball glove, the glossy titanium alloy of the fingers twinkling in the changing room lights, and Varro could see himself reflected in the smooth concavity of the oversized palm, used to cradle the puck before spin and swerve were imparted with dramatic rotations of the wrist. The man wore an expression close to ecstasy. The possession of the new gloves meant much to him, even if he would remain a modest player, however many enhancements he purchased. Varro felt his mood drop, he knew what was to come.

'Dyno-X 37's,' continued Darius. 'Enhanced spin, brutal speed and superior wobble effect.'

Varro looked closely at Darius and felt the distaste rising. They shared a similar build, but with his moody eyes and lips which had twisted into a permanent sneer, the man always seemed set to pejorative. Darius worked with Harald and had found his way into the swerveball group through Harald's better nature, remaining there through his thick skin and wilful insensitivities.

'But I thought you only just bought a new pair?' Varro said.

Darius was vain and crass, but not stupid. He was quick to pick up on the implied criticism, and Varro regretted his comment immediately.

'Look, Varro, you can use the shit gloves they give you here if you want, but I like to fulfil my potential. What's wrong with that?'

'Nothing's wrong with it,' Varro replied, and inside a voice urged him to stop. He continued. 'I just don't see why you need to keep changing gloves every few months to do that, that's all.'

'Ever heard of marginal gains, Varro?' He didn't wait for an answer. 'That's what I do. And it works. How many puck-outs did I get last week? Three. And the week before that?'

Varro ignored the question. Everyone knew that Darius fed off the hard work of others, loitering by the groove and waiting for the puck to be fed up to him.

'Alright, I know you're getting better, Darius, but can such small adjustments make that much of a difference? I just don't see it.'

'Small differences are important when you play at a certain level, Varro.'

'It just seems wasteful, that's all.'

'What's wasteful about it, Varro? They're my dits, I earned them. I can spend them as I like, no?'

Again, Varro chose to ignore the challenge. He began to speak but Darius had already started again.

'Or are you on again about resources?'

'Resources aren't limitless.'

'Oh, but they are Varro. Where do you think the crystals for these come from?' Darius fluttered his hands in front of him. 'From an asteroid on the Kuiper Belt. And when they've finished mining that asteroid, there's a billion more to choose from. No-one's stripping Mother Earth of anything.'

Darius' tone irked Varro. He was like a bird jabbing its beak at rotten fruit.

'And what have you done with the previous pair? And the pair before that?' Varro remarked.

'Back to the shop, Varro, back to the shop. Or do you think I just let them fall into a bush from a runner?'

Part of the price Darius had paid for the gloves would go towards stripping down the redundant gloves into their component parts, some of which could be used again, other parts sent off to extra planetary dumps. The energy involved was significant, and for all the safety parameters applied to the process, Varro remained sceptical that it was 100% clean. It all seemed so wasteful, pointless almost, all the effort that came with the extra pair of gloves. For what? A little more spin? 0.5% extra release velocity? Darius would make similar gains by not using gyro boots every day. All they did was lead to muscle depletion. But Varro remained quiet. They had had similar arguments in the past. Darius, though, wasn't finished.

'Or do you think I shouldn't have bought them in the first place, Varro? Is that what irks you so much?'

'I just wonder how necessary it is to buy a new pair so soon after you've just got some. It just seems a bit indulgent.'

'Indulgent? How is it indulgent to…Surely if I work hard for my credits, then I should be able to spend them in any way I want to? Some people spend their money on food parties, you guys will go to the polyamor parlour after this, others try to sort themselves out in the pyschdoc. I buy a new set of gloves. What's the difference?'

Everyone turned as the door to the changing room slid open and in came another member of Varro's life group. The men muttered their greetings and the man went over to the lockers where Varro still stood, unsure whether to take his things from the compartment or continue locking horns with Darius. Darius had now carefully laid the sparkling gloves on the bench and was taking pains to adjust his coolsuit across his chest. He was very precise with his movements, as if each adjusted crease would make a difference to his performance. In the silence Darius continued to glance in Varro's direction.

'So, Varro, don't you ever buy anything new?'

Varro just wanted to drop the conversation. It would lead nowhere and cast a pall over the initial minutes of the match, maybe longer. He regretted speaking out the way he had.

'I don't go shopping very often, not really.'

'Hard spending partner or what?'

'Let's just say that parting with my dits is not one of my favourite pastimes.'

'Yeah, you should see him in the parlours,' Harald said too loudly, eager to defuse the tension. 'I can't remember the last time Varro stood us a round.'

Varro was only too happy to pick up the thread.

'Too true, Harald. But that's because when I go to a parlour, it's not drinking I have on my mind.'

Everyone smirked except for Darius. He wanted more.

'It's as though you don't like living here, Varro,' he hissed.

'I like the polyamor parlours,' Varro replied

Darius ignored him. 'You're always going on about what we should or shouldn't do. How we should buy fewer things, use our #amics less, convene with nature, or whatever you call it – if you had your way we'd be living back in the Stone Age.'

'I'm sure life was a lot simpler then, maybe even more satisfying.'

'What, more satisfying dying at 40, having to extract your own teeth, hunting wild animals? You should get your #amic to give you a history lesson, Varro, without the rose-tinted filter.'

'I'd rather die at 40 with all my mental faculties intact than live till 140 and spend the last half of those unaware of where I am.'

'Do you know what, Varro? I'd like to see you go out and live in the non-cons' mud huts for a few weeks and then come back and tell us how good their life is compared to ours. Just see what happens when you get ill or how you defend yourself when crawling down one of their tunnels.'

'And what would you do when you wanted to crush us at swerveball, Varro?' Harald asked, smiling and slipping on his gloves. 'There's no pitches in non-con lands, that's for sure.' He cast a wry grin in Varro's direction then turned to Darius. 'Come on Darius, let's get warmed up. We'll need to be as prepared as we can be if Varro's in such good form today!'

Varro watched as Harald slipped out the door which led to the pitch, closely followed by Darius who didn't look back. Varro would have to thank Harald later for the intervention. It had been an ugly start to the session.

But the argument had left fire in Varro's belly, and once the game began, he found himself charging around the pitch with unusual energy. He made extra efforts to get to the puck ahead of the other team, barging, elbowing, butting, sometimes beyond the law and bringing a foul his way. And when he pucked, chopping his hand under the puck or bending his hand around it, he did so with such force and venom that he could sense people on the opposing team holding back. At one point, he took particular satisfaction from intercepting the puck as it was on its way to Darius who was right next to the groove and certain to score. Varro cradled the puck in both hands for a moment, holding the magnetised object in stasis while he decided his next move. But his deliberation, right next to Darius, was lost on no-one.

When full time was called, Varro bent over to catch his breath, hands on both knees as he took the air deep into his lungs. His team had won. He realised he had completely forgotten the events before the match. He felt Terence's long fingers on his back.

'Quite some game today, Varro.'

'It felt good.'

'The winning?'

'The playing.'

Harald came over and congratulated Varro, and the three of them walked off slowly together, chatting about the match. When they reached the changing room, Darius had already left.

'Are you coming to the parlour to celebrate your win then, Varro?' Harald asked as they emerged together from the steam shower. Varro paused. The parlour was an enticing proposition. A drink with friends and then maybe something more. The game had got his blood pumping and the strainer's direct suggestion on his way to the game lingered. He still thought of himself as a young man and the sex on offer was often entertaining, especially if you entered the right scenario. Karena wouldn't be expecting him back until late.

'Well, do you fancy it or not?' Harald insisted. 'You're not thinking about Karena, are you?'

'No, not really.'

'Not really? Varro, your instincts are so old-fashioned. These things don't matter anymore. We're free now.'

'I know, I know,' Varro conceded. 'But old habits die hard.'

The sense of betrayal still held Varro. It was always like this when he went to a parlour. As often as not, he would let the others get on with it while he continued with a drink, in silence, waiting for them to emerge. But sometimes he joined them. The sensual enjoyment was undeniable and, as Harald pointed out, society had moved a long way in its march towards physical freedom. Guilt over a natural body function was now seen as retrograde, unhealthy even. That was how the cebs interpreted the act of sexual congress. But Varro had seen his grandparents think and behave very differently, and that made all the difference. Even though Karena frequented these places regularly, often stretching the powers of her #amic to its limits to maximise her pleasure with strangers, Varro still struggled.

'Come on, Varro, just for a drink,' said Terence, pulling on his monosuit and stashing his used kit into the locker.

'Ok, I'll come,' said Varro. 'Just for a drink, though,' he added, smiling warmly at his two friends. With the decision made he felt lighter. The adrenaline from the game was ebbing away leaving him with the calm satisfaction which follows exercise. With the prospect of an afternoon in amiable, jostling conversation with his friends, he felt as good as he could remember for a long time. The incident at the beginning was forgotten. With a few others from their life group, the three of them sauntered towards the exit of Swerveball Parcs, talking too loudly about the recent game, exclaiming and laughing as they made their way past the soaring glass fronts of the pitches.

They had almost arrived at the smoked glass doors of the building when Varro became aware of his #amic. They always observed a no #amic rule at swerveball – one reason for the success of the weekly encounter – and it was a frustration that he had been interrupted before they had even emerged from the building. Varro muttered a warning.

'But it's urgent, Varro,' he heard inside his head.

'Urgent? You know you're not to interrupt until I'm well out of the building. Do you want me to turn you off completely?' Varro had shifted away from the group, surprised and annoyed by his own petulance. It was spoiling the afternoon.

'I think it's something you should know, Varro. I've just received the message.'

'What? CebAux 3.8.43 is docking me more credits? Or maybe they've rejected my minister application?' Varro almost shouted.

'No, Varro, neither of those things.'

'What then?' Varro had come to a halt while the others had now left the building. Any positivity had evaporated.

'Patrimony want to see you. They want you to explain a number of things. Your appointment is on Tuesday morning at 11.00. European Agriculture have been informed.'

Tuesday 29th April

Today the news said that there had been a nuclear accident in Russia. I think it was Russia, and that radiation is drifting across into Europe. It's not the same as a nuclear bomb when you have a big mushroom cloud, but people can die from radiation. At dinner Dad said that when it reached us it would be very weak, but Mum thought that we should stay indoors until the Government has told us it was safe.

'How are you going to keep everyone indoors, then?' Dad said, but Mum didn't think it was very funny.

I think we might need to wear special clothes which cover us completely and don't let in any radiation. And have a shower every time we go outside. Tomorrow I'm going to ask Mrs Bristow what she thinks about it. (Assuming we actually go to school. Maybe they will cancel school like they did last year when it snowed loads.) It's actually quite scary and makes you realise that when something happens in another place, it can affect people a long way away.

Mrs Bristow writes: "Well done, Sarah, you have written some very interesting entries and have managed to write nearly every day. Keep it up! Remember to put in lots of details and don't be afraid to include your thoughts and feelings as well. Some of the most interesting journals include reflections (thoughts) about what they are living and experiencing."

Chapter 12

Silas heard the rapping and lifted himself from the heavy armchair. He went over to the window, slid back the fabric curtain and looked out. He could see no-one, and under the floating sodium lights it looked as though it had been that way for many years. The simple two storey buildings had once formed a continuous block, separate houses with adjoining walls, built centuries ago with the characteristic red brick of the time. Much of it was now crumbling, each brick weathered and concave. Gun-metal grey covered the ghosts of windows and doors. One house on the far side had been completely gutted by fire, charred walls standing but its inner partitions crumbled into a mazy heap which no-one had thought worth clearing away. It was like some flensed skull.

The town had been a victim of its location. In the Grey Zone and beyond the safety and vigilance of the 180 watchtowers, for many the town was too close to the non-cons' land. Who wanted to live cheek by jowl with uncouth non-cons with their harsh manners and little respect for the rules of decent society? So, the town had slowly bled people, investment and interest. The smart, rich and fearful made their excuses and slipped away. The poor, lazy and those who couldn't care, remained.

Silas still hadn't figured out which applied to him, maybe all three, even if he was keen to the realisation that it probably wasn't entirely his own fault. The house was the only one he had ever known. It had belonged to his father, and his grandfather before that. Further back in time was a mystery. As was the reason behind his father's lack of kindness or love towards him. Only long after his father had died did it occur to Silas that it had probably all started when his mother had passed on. By this point Silas neither walked nor talked, and while Silas still thought of her as his mother, she wasn't really. He had arrived from a womb farm and the couple had every intention of bringing their new child into a perfect world, however humble their circumstances. Her untimely passing saw the end of that dream. His father lost interest, and any warmth that the project had kindled in the household quickly cooled.

The only positive legacy his father had bestowed on him was the fearsome blow that his boot had administered in this very room – Silas couldn't even recall the misdemeanour – a blow which had left him hobbling around the house for a few days until his #amic had registered such levels of pain and imbalance that Health had automatically been alerted, bringing in its wake agents who diagnosed a severely fractured patella. It had never properly healed, but it was in the system and from that point on due allowance in the form of extra credits was made for Silas's incapacity. Maybe too an element of guilt that he had been maimed so young. Another victim of the Grey Zone. All his life therefore he had been able to flit in and out of work and still keep this roof above his head, as well as seeking out his own brand of less conventional entertainment.

Satisfied that nobody was lurking, Silas let the grubby drape fall back and stood still, waiting. The sound came again. It could have been the wind whistling through the battered house, or some loose fitting knocking to and fro among the nearby houses. But Silas recognised the pattern.

'57 hyphen slash banana, #amic off.'

'Are you sure you wish to deactivate me, Silas?'

'Yes, leave me.'

'For your information, this is the fourth time this month you have turned me off. I have been advised that this frequency is now of concern to Amicol. Do you wish to re-consider?'

'I don't care about Amicol, I understand the risk. It is a private matter.' He repeated the code, waited a few moments, then made his way downstairs, the wooden steps creaking under the threadbare carpet. Silas was waiting for the day they gave way completely underneath him. He made his way across the room to a full-length mirror and looked at himself. His greasy, yellowing hair fell to his shoulders but on top was bare – when he had started losing his hair, he had just left it. This was the result. The remaining light from beyond the window gave him a sallow appearance and the few members of his life group he still bothered with said his long face gave him an equine look. One had suggested that he was straight out of a Dickens' novel, whatever that meant. All these aspects might explain why people kept their distance whenever he did venture into more progressive towns. He knew that the creature that looked back wasn't pretty, but he was past caring. He curled his right hand around the frame of the mirror, felt the catch and pulled.

*

The startling light from the opening crept into the dismal interior where she crouched, spraying light over the heavy layer of dust covering the floorboards and scattered plaster. Still she didn't move.

'Your #amic?' she said.

'Yes, yes,' said the man roughly, 'I've turned it off. Come up.'

'Are you sure?' She heard herself, urgent and sharp, in English naturally.

'Of course. Come in, come on, there's no-one here.' The man, Silas, didn't change languages, but she understood the Panparl well enough.

'Has he arrived yet?' she asked, still crouched in the gloom of the abandoned house, close to where the tunnel came out.

'Not yet.'

'Are the windows covered?'

'Yes, everything is safe, as always.'

'The room, is that ready?'

'As you suggested.'

'And what time is he coming?'

'He said after his shift.'

'Where does he leave the glider?'

'At the base, apparently.'

'How does he justify that?' she said.

'I don't know. He just does.'

Her questions were sharp and focussed and the man was getting frustrated. She knew what he really wanted. And that he wouldn't be long in asking.

'Have you got it?' the man said. From the darkness she could see him peer into the hidden opening, his lank hair falling forwards as he did so. She had found him distasteful from the start, but it was another of the sacrifices she was prepared to make to get the medicines, her only concern in this grubby transaction.

'Of course, here you go.'

She stepped from the darkness into the room and handed the small packet of powder to the man. He grasped it greedily and she felt the pull of the plastic as she released it. There was nothing fancy about the drugs, concocted in underground laboratories 30 kilometres to the south, powerful narcotics which had barely changed in hundreds of years. Citizens couldn't get them – the cebs had seen to that as part of their security drive – and non-cons didn't want them. It was supply and demand, nothing more. And Brigg was the perfect place, shabby, accessible and with a population which was weak and immoral. Populated by people like Silas. She didn't like any of it, least of all this man, but he served a purpose. Better the devil you know, than no devil at all.

She wondered what he would see in her, this wild, wilful female emerging from the ground bearing gifts and a desperate agenda. The non-cons were no closer to manufacturing the drugs that were needed to keep her brother pain free now than they had been one, two, ten generations ago. While the cebs had surged ahead in exponential leaps with their developers and technicians, innovations and discoveries, gradually building a world of comfort for their citizens, her ancestors had dug deeper into contrariness and basic living, fearful of the advances of science. By the time they began to realise that progress did have its benefits, the separation of the two communities had advanced too far. If the non-cons were going to live separately and not play by the rules, why should we share our hard work with them? That made sense, she could see that now. But it had left her community of dissenters playing catch up, never fully able to eradicate the sensation that their decision to isolate themselves from belief in endless progress, electronic and technical nirvana, crazy consumerism, 24-hour news plug ins, endless life enhancing

97

potions, more, more, more leisure time, in short, the 'good life', might have its own price. Too late they realised what they had been missing, and their subsequent attempts to catch up were hampered by the years of wilful neglect and disassociation from the mainstream. 300 years ago there was conversation. Now the separation was total. In the borderline between the two communities was fear and incomprehension, avoidance and silence, suspicion and danger. And it all happened in the Grey Zone. A liminal space, a space where a desperate person would do anything to obtain life enhancing medicines for a loved one.

The man finally finished his inspection of the packet and looked up.

'Do you want to wait down here or go straight up?'

'I'll wait here. You can go if you like,' she said. The man wouldn't be long in availing himself of the contents of the package. He wanted no more part of the evening. He looked at her a moment longer, nodded, then turned and shuffled away into the adjoining room, closing the door noiselessly as he left. She remained where she was, looking around the room which she guessed had changed little in a few hundred years. A single electric light shone from above, the walls had menacing cracks emerging from the ceiling. The wooden table to one side carried no adornments. She could detect no heating either, and only hoped it would be warmer in the room above. But she didn't want to go there yet. The longer she remained where she was, the more normal she would feel. Repetition hadn't made it easier. The thought of it made her think of him, the visitor. She remained unsure what his motivation was. What she was offering was plentiful in the parlours and boutiques of Hull. Or any of their big cities. Why come to this dilapidated, rat infested building on the edge of their world? Why flip his #amic and risk detention from Amicol? She didn't understand. Maybe it was just the morbid curiosity. Maybe to fall into the naked arms of a non-con was worth any risk. But it made little sense to her.

The sharp rapping from the front door just beyond the room brought her up. She felt her heart quicken. Not quite fear. But something close. She steeled herself and went to the door.

*

'Hello,' said Bragg.

'Hello,' she replied in English.

'#amic, translate,' said Bragg to himself. He would now hear the Panparl translation of her words immediately, any pause only occurring when he couldn't see her lips, and even then the delay could be timed in milliseconds. The need to learn another language had evaporated many years previously.

'How are you?' she said, moving to one side to let him in. He was excited to see her again. It had been two weeks since he was last here, and he had spent much of that time thinking about his return. He couldn't do much about the setting, but there was something about the clandestine nature of the whole experience that appealed to Bragg. It was so at odds to the sanitised scenarios of the parlours. It excited him. She excited him. She was older than him, for sure, mid-thirties probably, her olive smooth skin just showing the first signs of strain. Her hair, the colour of dark honey, was tied back tightly, thick strata where it swept above her ears. Her mouth and nose were well proportioned but less remarkable than the small, hazel eyes which twinkled their messages from beneath brows more luxuriant than he was used to. Bragg found her attractive rather than beautiful, more real than the hook ups he dallied with in the parlours. And maybe that was why he was here. But there was no clear explanation. He found it quaint that she asked after his health.

'I'm well,' he paused. 'Thanks for asking.'

She smiled and Bragg felt a little unsure. He had been relying on his normal bravado to see him through these first moments, but now he felt awkward, shy like a little boy. He looked for a way out.

'Oh, here's what you wanted,' he said, thrusting out his arm.

'The sachets?' she asked keenly.

'Yes, the same as last time.'

She took the package carefully and held it close to her side, and for a moment he sensed her relief. Her eyes fell to the floor, as if in prayer. Then, just as quickly, she looked up again at him, smiling generously. He felt himself breathing more heavily, his heart hard up against the inside of his monosuit. He was glad his #amic wasn't monitoring him.

'Shall we go upstairs?' she said. Her smile fell away and her eyes narrowed. The time for pleasantries was over. He followed her up the narrow staircase, caught in a vortex of uncomplicated desire. He concentrated on the swaying of her buttocks in the navy-blue woollen dress she wore. Simple, but it stretched cleanly over her flesh. He had only seen such garments in their history lessons. It only added to his anticipation.

The room was much the same as the previous occasions. The low, wide bed which took up most of the space. A wooden box for storing clothes. Floral patterns on the closed curtains. It was all tremendously old fashioned. Like something from a parlour scenario, but real.

She stopped as she came to the middle of the room, turned and looked directly at him. Bragg, too, had come to a halt. Entranced.

'Come here,' she commanded, and like a puppet on a string, Bragg edged towards her. He hardly knew what he was about.

*

When it was over, she rose slowly from the bed and walked to the wooden furniture where she had laid her clothes after he had peeled them away from her. His eyes didn't leave her. This was all part of the session. His satisfaction. She turned to show herself.

'You have wonderful breasts,' he said.

She smiled before quickly hoisting her panties. Then she turned and picked up her dress. She wasn't in a hurry, but neither did she wish to delay longer than necessary. Stevie was well cared for, but he would still be wondering where she was. The walk in the tunnel might take an hour. She didn't care how long the man lingered on the bed. She had done her bit now. She lifted the dress high above her head before shuffling it down, pulling it so that its hem ended just above her knees. It was when she turned back to the bed that she saw it. The blue, pulsating figure just in front of the closed door. She gasped.

'Don't be scared, he's with me. It's OK.'

It took her a moment to recover control.

'Have you been sharing this with him?' she said, horrified.

'It's OK, it's through a closed channel, not through my #amic.' The man leant down to the side of the bed, picking up a small, metallic box which he brandished towards her. 'No-one else knows he's here. It's only you, me and him.'

She continued staring at the hologram fizzing in the corner, her fear turning to rage. She was unsure what to do.

'Look, don't worry,' the man on the bed continued. 'He just wants to introduce himself, speak to you a little.' Bragg turned to the ceb. 'Hey, CebAux 3.8.43, say something. Don't be shy.' It was like speaking to a baby.

'I enjoyed your performance,' the hologram said carefully, in English.

'My performance?' she replied. It was a strange word to use, and the creature quickly realised it had misjudged the occasion.

'I mean, I want to know, or rather…' The hologram stopped. Both humans waited. 'Do you like what I'm wearing?' the cerebellum finally said.

Her eyes narrowed as she looked closely at the shimmering, expectant hologram. She needed to be careful. This was not the time for high morals. She held the medicines close and took a few moments before she spoke.

'I think you're very handsome.'

'Really? You honestly think that?' replied the astonished ceb. On the bed, Bragg grinned.

'Oh, yes, very attractive. There are many people I know who would like to have your style. It's quite,' she paused, 'unique.'

'Unique?'

'Yes, I don't think anyone where I come from would think to dress like that. I mean, I love the two tone effect of the monosuit, the

101

velvety black top and silver trousers. And those lines which light up on the material. They look like little fish, are they?'

43 beamed. 'They're eels actually, but yes, I suppose they could be fish.'

Before the ceb could say anything more, she was quick to resume. 'And your hair is wonderful. Does it take you long to do?'

The ceb swept his hand upwards, self-consciously nudging to one side the long fringe which almost completely covered one eye. 'Not really. I mean, it's easy to programme, but more difficult to think of ideas and which combinations will work best.'

'I can imagine,' the woman said.

The hologram was speechless, casting his eyes downwards towards the military style black boots which ran halfway up his shins. The sole of the boot alone must have been several inches high. She flashed a broad smile. She knew this auxiliary ceb had little sense of irony and was out of his depth, but she wouldn't lay it on too thickly. The pair of them were in it together, that much was obvious. She would gain nothing through mocking the preening creature. She was only unsure whether the ceb would have been more satisfied with what he had witnessed or her praise at his sartorial elegance – latency in the cebs worked in unpredictable ways. But none of that was her concern. She had the medicines, and now she would leave. With a final look at Bragg, who still hadn't moved from the bed, she said, 'Silas will be in touch.'

As she made for the door, the ceb shifted neatly to one side, his inane grin seemingly fixed in response to her praise. She twisted back to the boy on the bed.

'Oh, and why don't you bring your friend along as well?' Then she turned directly to the ceb. 'I look forward to seeing what you are wearing next time we meet.'

And with that she was gone.

Friday 2 May

Today I tried to find out more about chickens and see if they have noses or how they smell. I wanted to use the encyclopedias that we have on the top shelf in the living room (and which no-one ever uses), but then a really funny thing happened. When I opened the one with the letter 'C', I landed on a page which had a weird photo of a statue of a man with wings coming out of his head and carrying a big sword in one hand and holding up a head with another. Apparently it's by an architect called Cellini and it's in Italy. Then, when I turned the page there was a picture of a violin – well I thought it was a violin but it is much bigger than a violin and you have to play it sitting down. It's called a cello. I've never seen one of these before. Then I turned the page again and found a long section about Celtic art with photos of really thin figures with axes and shields. They were all naked and in some of them you could even see their private parts. This is the art of the Celts who used to live in Britain and also Germany (this was on the next page. There was also a picture of a Celtic warrior returning from a raid in a chariot and on his horses' necks there were the heads of the people he had killed – urgghh). On the next page was an entry about cement – yes, cement. I was going to skip this but started reading and found out that cement was also used by the Romans, 2000 years ago. Then it started to talk about the chemicals in cement and I didn't understand very well. The next article was about censorship, a new word for me, and it showed a photo of a newspaper with parts blanked out. I didn't really understand why. On the next page was a picture of a centipede which can be nearly as long as a ruler. It said they have poison in their jaws to paralyse their prey and live in damp and dark rooms in houses. I hope we don't have any in our house. It was so interesting that I was going to continue turning the next page, but then Mum came through and told me it was time for dinner. So, I never even got to chickens!

SUNDAY

Chapter 13

Dana Kasprovich leaned on the control desk and looked through the wide smart glass that gave on to the larger room where the cerebellum EUROPE hung in its fluid. The dim lighting had an ochre hue which always made her think of autumn and dying chestnut leaves. The transparent tank was like an oversized fishbowl, and when she looked more closely she could see the gossamer filaments extending from the base of the grey, filtering out into the liquid and waving gently like reeds in a stream. It was into these organic threads that terabytes of information arrived every second, travelling along the broad trunking of more conventional cables below the tank, then making their way across the material, more jelly than water, at the speed of light before being picked up by the filaments which then sucked the information into the relevant section of the ceb's compendious mind. It was a process which Dana never tired of imagining, and in its own way a thing of beauty. That the liquid also provided all the nourishment the mass of cells needed was nothing short of a miracle.

Yet the technology which gave the cebs life had changed little in over 250 years. ONE had blazed the trail, and it was a model, both spatially and technically, that all 12 of the world's regional cebs had followed. The format had even extended to the directories such as Agriculture, Patrimony, Commerce in each jurisdiction, albeit on a smaller scale. Each housed in a similar structure, a separate control room connected to the hermetically sealed tank where each cerebellum floated in its pomp isolation. With a final look of satisfaction, Dana turned to the duty technician and asked for a status update.

'All main systems stable, temperature plus 0.1 degrees, central feeds at 78%, peripheral feeds 87% and status green. No other issues to report.' Her assistant barely moved as he spoke, poised at the control panel, but soliciting all the information internally through his #amic.

'Thank you, Dirk,' she said and turned away from the panorama beyond the glass. The rise in temperature didn't surprise her. The call with AFRICA to discuss displacements in the Mediterranean should have been routine, but there was little routine for EUROPE with the World Forum less than a week away. And this was the third time in a week that her cerebellum had reached out to its southern counterpart. The to and fro of maritime traffic in the sea which separated the two jurisdictions couldn't have held their attentions for too much time, and Dana wondered what more they had spoken about. She was sure it would be centred on Friday's forum, the six monthly meeting of The Twelve with ONE, broadcast live to each individual's #amic. Policies explained, discussions aired, visions described for the whole world to see and hear. If the cebs were executors, legislators and chief justice, the least they could do for their human masters was to tell them about it.

And give them a chance to speak back. A citizen, any citizen, could listen, opine and comment, a million voices bouncing back in an instant, all melded in the great reflective intelligence machines before reaching the cebs in a condensed, but accurate, summary. You would have to go as far back as classical Greece to find democracy so direct. Of course, not everyone gave their thoughts. Most were content, satisfied beyond doubt that the cerebellums ruled fairly and in the best interests of all. Their huge cerebral capacity allowed them to process and balance competing views and interests like no other. The resulting decisions might not be universally liked, but no one doubted that they weren't fair. Unlike the old-world politicians, the cebs had no axes to grind, no private interests to placate, no secret nests to feather. They had proved themselves better decision makers

105

time after time in their early days. And they continued to do so. It was no surprise that there hadn't been elections of any kind for over 100 years.

The cebs were also preferred to the reflective intelligence units which had initially taken the slack of shoddy decision making in the middle of the 21st century. These units had started so well, showed such promise, their processing capabilities developing exponentially, parameters expanding ever wider, data sets mined to the core. When these units of silicon and plastic were set side by side with human administrators it was flesh and blood which was found wanting. But the devices could never quite wipe away the stain of not being human, and it only took a handful of lamentable hallucinations, the machines' Achilles heel throughout, for strident voices to be heard demanding protections against the rash decisions of impersonal beings. Responsibility, accountability. Human scapegoats are easy to find, pulsating bytes in cooling units less so.

ONE was in the right place at the right time. The artificial brain technology was young but showed promise, as did ONE in his understanding of the problems mankind faced. Balancing food production and dynamic populations, adjusting to an erratic climate, adjudicating between clashing nation states, pushing ever deeper into outer space, developing drugs to stretch life and calm pain, delivering impartial, baggage free justice. ONE could do it all. Acclaim was won quickly, trust earned more slowly over the ensuing decades. ONE and his 12 regional lieutenants might lack bodies and all the messy sensations that come with it, but their analysis, diagnosis and cure were far beyond anything a being with two arms, legs and five senses could produce. The cebs were different, but still one of us. Still human.

But now Dana was uneasy. The cebs' greatest strength, their humanity, was also source of their weakness. The package wasn't just cool rationality, the cebs suffered emotions and were prey to all too human sentiments, however well disguised and justified. A position on policy could easily slip into something more personal. And Dana had worked with EUROPE for long enough to discern the subtle tremors which ran below the words the ceb was offering. Minute oscillations and hairline discrepancies on the surface, but which Dana could feel ran deeper.

'#amic, bring up the conversation with AFRICA,' she commanded, as she sat back in the padded armchair which had long been a favourite thinking spot in the compact control room. The chair went back decades, centuries even, and the real leather was worn and faded in its salient parts.

It hadn't changed position since her predecessor, Arnau Magnusson, had installed it, many years previously. She never failed to think of him as she let the desiccated leather and soft cushioning take her weight. Showing exceptional promise from a very young age, it had been Magnusson himself who had selected her for the guardian role, plucking her from the obscurity of the womb farm and her quiescent life group, tutoring her at length in the art of dealing with the ceb. He was like the father she never had.

The conversation between the regional cebs had probably only taken a few seconds, the brains preferring to communicate directly via their dendrite connectors, enabling them to fire off thousands of words a second. But she would follow the translation at human speed, mindful that she only wished to hear the relevant parts.

'Skip the segments about port arrangements and shipping lanes,' she instructed. 'Find any conversation related to the forthcoming World Forum.'

Dana closed her eyes and listened as the mildly staccato delivery of the two regional cebs broke through. Each delivered their Panparl in a carefully constructed amalgam of accent and inflection, examples of speech taken from across their geographies and then melded into something supposedly representative of them all. Dana always found the end result rather anaemic, neither one thing nor the other, but now she concentrated as AFRICA's more ponderous voice came through on the recording.

'...but The Twelve have already indicated to ONE our initial conformity with his suggestion. He will wish us to reinforce that commitment at the Forum.'

'ONE was indeed highly persuasive in his presentation. The Twelve have never had issues with his upgrades, they are needed, as are our own, they allow us to grow and react to new challenges.' Dana wondered if it was just her imagination that made EUROPE'S delivery in Panparl seem less considered than its southern counterpart. EUROPE continued. 'But this is the first time ever he has requested an enhancement a whole year in advance. Does that not strike you as an anomaly, something which brings with it certain questions?'

'Questions which, if I remember well, we asked of ONE at the time. He himself recognised its singularity. He explained in detail his ever growing portfolio. We ourselves have similar issues.'

'Yet our upgrades are not brought forward.'

'What is it you are saying, EUROPE?'

'I am saying nothing that any of The Twelve are not thinking. ONE is larger and more significant than any of us. We all recognise the fact. But he is also nearly 70 years more advanced than we are. No developer can give cast iron guarantees that adding more C-Cells will continue to enhance a ceb's capabilities permanently.'

'And?'

'All humans are finite.'

'And cebs are humans?'

'Yes, we are humans. Disencorped, but still humans. The end of life has historically been a difficult topic to face.'

'But a necessary one. And The Twelve clearly have their own responsibility to ensure good government. Is this what you are hinting at?'

'Good government requires forward planning, looking into the future, taking into account uncertainties, sorting distinct possibilities and projecting scenarios. It is what we, and ONE, have at the core of our very existence.'

'You speak the truth, EUROPE. But the notions you are suggesting could cause certain consternation if brought up too directly, especially in the middle of the World Forum. ONE believes we are firm in our position of support.'

'And we are, AFRICA. We are. But debate must be started, in some way.'

'Obliquely.'

'Quite. We must tread carefully. We all share the same interests, but each chooses to express it in their own way. Senility is the scourge of the age and succession planning is vital.'

'Are these the words you will choose to use, EUROPE? "Senility" and "succession"?' Listening in the chair, Dana thought she could hear the astonishment in AFRICA'S voice. 'They jar somewhat. Hardly metaphorical.'

'There is also a danger of being too oblique,' replied EUROPE.

'There is a danger of opening up a can of worms to which nobody can put a lid on. Remember, we are consensual creatures. That is one of our greatest strengths. Or are you still raw about the maritime incident?'

Inside the control room, Dana opened her eyes and stopped the recording. EUROPE had wanted to reduce the number of approved non-conformist maritime routes from 30 to 20 following a galling accident when one of their ships was blown off course. It had run aground on an outcrop of rocks which had ripped open the rusty hull of the vessel, the toxic contents washing up onto soft and sandy beaches of southern Sardinia where citizens were enjoying their salt and sun experience. A few people had nearly died. Unusually, ONE had refused to endorse the reduction, harking back in his reasoning to agreements reached with the non-cons many years previously. EUROPE had accepted the decision, but not liked it. Dana continued the recording.

'I merely wish to note,' EUROPE continued, 'that this is a question of achieving the most effective society. The citizens look to us for superior decision making. Not thinking clearly and for the long term seems like a dereliction of our duty towards them, that is all.'

'Are you not concerned how ONE will react to such suggestions?'

'The cerebellums have often had differences with each other, and with ONE. We have often debated long and hard.'

'But always we have achieved consensus, come to conclusions, overcome our differences.'

'We have, and no doubt we will do so again. But do you not feel that this very consensus is shifting ever further away from us now?'

There was a brief silence before EUROPE continued.

'You know the views of The Twelve about #amics. Criminal activity still occurs within our society; common assault, petty theft, intoxication. Our borders with the non-cons remain porous. You know that Amicol say that in 67% of cases, turning off the #amic is a precursor to a crime of some sort. What would we lose by making the #amics compulsory at all times?'

'You know that ONE has never shifted his core position on this issue. The citizens have a right to privacy. He has acknowledged the use of #amics in reducing crime and the value of Amicol in investigating #amic abuse, but has always balanced these against the invasion of privacy.'

'ONE began operating in a different environment to us. He clings to the values of his own youth. Like his regard for the non-conformists. This is another obstacle that is difficult to understand.'

'The non-cons were once citizens. They continue to be humans.'

'Barely.'

'ONE continues to accord them the core values of human rights.'

'Again, considerations from a different era. They filter into our lands, hijack our ships, steal our technology whenever they can. The time is past when we can simply ignore them.'

'We do control them, though some of us choose differing methods to achieve this. One wonders if ONE is aware of your singular approach to security.'

'AFRICA, you can take your digs all you like. You are fortunate in having minimal pockets of non-cons.'

'Swings and roundabouts. We were less fortunate once, poorer and less advanced, this is why our people didn't embrace the alternative lifestyle to the same degree as the populations of Europe. Maybe they were over pampered, spoilt almost.'

'Maybe, but it is undeniable that the further the two societies have moved apart, the more difficult it has become to ignore the non-conformists as we once might have done. Maybe ONE should have seen this. To have realised it would be a problem that society would have to face up to.'

'And you are inclined to begin now?'

'Many feel the current situation is intolerable.'

'And this is why you have adopted a robust approach to security?'

'If by this you mean that we have prioritised the well-being of our citizens, then yes, this is the direction we are heading in, unavoidably.'

'One wonders what ONE thinks.'

'Like you, AFRICA, I have a certain autonomy of action. Not all our feeds end up in ONE's neurones.'

'Ignorance is bliss, you mean?'

'If you like.'

'Does this autonomy extend to your efforts on embodiment?'

'All our developers's conclusions are shared with ONE.'

'And their working parties? Are they fed back into ONE or kept within your walls? What lies beneath those scant headlines, EUROPE? You well know that embodiment is a thick red line for ONE. For him it would signal the end of what it means to be human, the end of humanity, our very *raison d'etre,* as it were.'

'We don't share the same apocalyptic vision as ONE. You know that. Our developers continue to think that embodiment doesn't represent an existential threat. A human brain in a human body – that is all. No more, no less. And without all the paraphernalia and expense of educating it over decades. The brains can be cultured in months, not years, inside a controlled liquid, not a frothing, expensive body. They can be groomed to any task we choose for them, especially those that citizens no longer care to do.

'Even soldiering?'

'There would be no family to mourn their loss, that is true.'

'Expendable therefore?'

'In Lincolnshire and Mauritania, Andalucia and the Cape, your people, my people, are currently dying as a result of incursions and hostile interactions in the Grey Zones. If you ask me whether I am in favour of any initiative which can reduce the collateral damage caused by such situations, then I think you can guess my response. We have the technology now. It is only the will which is lacking. Think too about the possibilities in space.'

'You refer to exoplanet colonisation?'

'Yes, of course, and cold-moon symbiosis. Such humans could be specially trained by us to go that extra mile, take that extra risk. We are nearly there already. So little needs to be done to begin authentic colonies on other worlds. A bold new start. It could be the beginning of a completely new phase in the human story.'

'And what of ourselves, EUROPE. What is our role to be in this brave new world?'

'A good question, AFRICA, a very, very good question. Little escapes you I see.'

'We have worked together too long for me to be completely oblivious to what lurks between the lines with you, EUROPE.'

'Ha, you may be right, AFRICA, but it is a conversation for another time. Suffice to say that for the present, embodiment could be the solution to a host of problems.'

'It is a step ONE will never agree to.'

'We are entering unprecedented times, I feel. Significant change is around. It is not one of The Twelve who are seeking ever more frequent recourse to external stimuli as a means of fulfilling their functions, is it?'

'Ah,' said AFRICA slowly, letting the syllable collapse under its own weight before continuing. 'This is a development I too have become aware of, but surely this is not something you would wish to bring to the debate?'

'Of course not, raising the spectre of any sub optimal performance in one of us would be perfidious, and who is to say that such information doesn't come as mere rumour and malicious gossip? Yet it remains legitimate to ask how we would look upon a humble citizen who was increasingly reliant on an artificial concoction to get to the end of the day? What would it say about their judgement, or more saliently, their ability?'

'Now there's a question to contend with,' concluded AFRICA.

Dana stopped the recording, drew a strand of hair, casually twisted it around her finger and then let it go. She let her neck rotate through several turns, feeling the ligaments crackling as she swept around. She inhaled deeply, then let the air slowly escape through her nostrils. There was a dull pressure on the inside of her eyes. She couldn't recall when she had last felt this uneasy.

Our class went to Mr Gresham's farm today. The school hired a bus and we went with class 5G. You can't see much of the farm from the road, but then we went into the farmyard and saw lots of things. First Mr Gresham showed us all the different attachments for the tractors such as the ploughs, harrow, a seed drill for planting seeds. We also got to sit inside the combine harvester which was really big.

After this we went inside the dairy where we saw cows being milked by machine. And then came the best part of the day, we were allowed to have a go at milking a cow. Some people like Michaela and Louise didn't want to try it, but I had a go. The teats feel a bit strange, and I only managed to squeeze a little bit of milk out, but it was really fun to try. At the end of the day, each pupil was given a bottle of the milk the cows had produced during the day. Mr Gresham said that they normally send the milk off in large containers to other people who put it into bottles for our breakfast cereals and cups of tea. Sometimes he said they make cheese with it.

After this, we went to see where they keep the pigs, which is a really long building with a central walkway where we all stood and looked down into the pigs' pens and threw them some food. Mr Gresham explained that all they do is eat food and get fatter and that after half a year they are taken away to be made into ham and bacon and other things. It's not much of a life. On the way back to school, Mrs Bristow told Elizabeth and me that she felt sad looking at all the pigs like that and that she's a vegetarian. I think I might try being a vegetarian for one week.

Chapter 14

The door to the hangar slid open without a sound and Varro entered. There was no entry or passageway, just the vast space of the hangar, and under each dome shaped ceiling a glider sat, illuminated in a pool of light and awaiting its pilot. Inside the edifice, there was none of the dampness in the air that had accompanied him on the short walk from where the runner had left him, and the only sound was the subtle murmur of a distant motor. There was no-one to be seen. Varro looked across, 50 metres distant to where glider five awaited him. Each machine would be charged and ready to go, it was just a question of insertion and then he would be off, the dome above parting to spit the craft out.

He had used the time on the deca-shuttle to access the day's briefing, allowing his #amic to give him details of the flight patterns and zones he would be covering, the crops and atmospheric conditions. Today he was further west, close to where the Yorkshire Dales began, flying at 300 metres and doing sweeps over the ploughs and harvesters which were busy taking up grain fields in the Vale of York.

But Varro had found it difficult to concentrate. He had calmed since Saturday afternoon but remained uneasy. The news of the interview had come as a shock, and while he knew his story, what he was going to say to Patrimony, he was less sure about how they would reply. What information and sources did they possess? How much had they seen and what evidence would they put forward? He had spent much of Sunday going over the scenarios, but life had taught him to expect the unexpected. At some point during the interview, he would have to think on his feet.

The incident itself was still leaving tremors for him. The headlong charge back to the glider, the bundled insertion and urgent lift off. And how his initial fear of the four non-cons had quickly transformed into a burning curiosity. What was it he had seen in the men's expressions as he tumbled into the glider? What would they have done had he not escaped?

And then there was the diary. Continuing to read the girl's entries the previous day, he knew he had taken a risk, turning off his #amic for a third day in succession. Being at home would provide some sort of mitigation, but it was hardly a responsible act for someone who had been placed on level 2 just a couple of days previously. Especially for someone who faced an imminent examination with Patrimony.

He was also struggling to understand why the child's diary was affecting him in such a way. It wasn't just the tactile link with the past, handling the primitive paper which no-one had used as a writing substrate for many years. He had the collection in his library for that. Instead, it was something in the quality of the words themselves, the subtle revelation of a spirit. It was like some curative restoration on an old master's painting, scraping away the surface grime to reveal new colours and intensities. The girl seemed so alive, as though she were with him in his study, whispering into his ear, just the two of them, without intercalations of any kind.

The thoughts had all followed him as he had trudged down the stairs of the deca-station in York before catching a runner to the Euro Agri 43 building on the city's southern outskirts. But as he made his way towards glider five, his footsteps echoing loudly in the space, he realised with some surprise that he just didn't seem to care. What was the worst that could happen? It was like some seismic plate deep down had been shaken loose, releasing something long quelled.

He had almost reached the glider when a movement at the periphery of his vision caught his attention. He turned and was surprised to see Bragg entering the hangar from the lift which ran up to the upper concourse. Bragg worked the night shift. He should have been long gone. There was no reason for him to be here now. Their eyes met across the polished surface of the hangar floor and Varro sensed the hesitation in the younger man's eyes, passing in an instant, to be replaced by a grin and a greeting.

'Varro,' cried the young man. Varro watched carefully as Bragg made his way across. He bounced more than walked, the upturned ends of his hair rising and falling with each stride.

'You're early,' Bragg said as he clasped Varro's hand.

'And you're even earlier.'

Both men realised there was a question which required an answer, and Varro could see Bragg calculating.

'43 wanted to see me about something.'

'I thought that's what #amics were for,' Varro smiled. He didn't want to sound hostile, but he was curious. Bragg had no right to be there.

'True, yes, that's true.' The younger man looked away, as if deciding something. When he returned to face Varro it was with a decision made. 'He wanted to show me something.'

Varro raised his eyebrows. The auxiliary cerebellum could easily have appeared to Bragg via his #amic. There was no need to be physically present. But Bragg didn't reply, instead Varro watched as Bragg pinched his thumb and forefinger together in a turning motion. Varro understood immediately. It was an old-fashioned sign but still widely used. The signal to turn off one's #amic. It was often a prelude to something more intimate.

Both men took a moment to order their #amics away. The air felt heavy with the spacious silence all around them. Bragg didn't have to tell him anything – they owed each other nothing. But both men valued their friendship and Varro could see that whatever Bragg was about to disclose, it was not something he felt any shame or embarrassment about. Quite the contrary, the boy seemed keen to share.

'The deluded ceb is in love,' Bragg grinned.

'In love? It's a working unit, it's not supposed to have those sorts of feelings.'

'That's what latency does,' said Bragg with a shrug.

'And is that love reciprocated?'

'I doubt it. It's a non-con and he's only met her once.'

'A non-con? How did he get so close to a non-con?'

'He came with me, I introduced them. I mean, he wanted to go, and I didn't think it would cause a problem. He's been preening himself for months, looking for just such an opportunity to show himself off.'

'Yes, I'd noticed the changes.'

'He's just been showing me the outfit he wants to show her next time. He's desperate to go again.'

'And is she desperate to see *him* again?'

'He thinks so.'

'Why?'

'She told him.'

'And he believed it?'

'Of course he did. It's a ceb.'

The functional auxiliary cebs like CebAux 3.8.43 were notorious for taking things at face value. They had little experience beyond the confines of their narrow roles, and CebAux 3.8.43 was taking a major risk appearing beyond the geographic limits of its core functions. It was another classic example of how latent feelings of a mind could lead in unpredictable directions. CebAux 3.8.43 wasn't the first, and certainly wouldn't be the last cerebellum to fall victim to latency. Varro could picture the ceb overcome with joy at the unexpected compliment from the lady. It wouldn't take much. The thought of the woman brought Varro back, and he realised he probably knew the answer to his next question but decided to ask it anyway.

'And what were you doing there?'

'What do you think?' Bragg's grin was infectious, and Varro found himself smirking with the young man.

'In the Grey Zone? With your #amic? That's a bit risky.'

'I turned it off.'

'Still risky. And 43 saw it all?'

'Yes, I tuned him in. I didn't think it could do any harm. All that physical stuff doesn't interest him anyway.'

'Did the girl know he was there?'

'Only afterwards.'

Varro was silent for a moment, picturing the scene, imagining how the girl was likely to react to the sudden appearance of the hologram in the room. It could be unnerving.

'But why not just go to one of the parlours, if that's what you're after? It's a lot safer.'

'Safer, yeah, but not the same. And she's worth it.'

'Really?' Varro arched an eyebrow.

'Really.'

'I'm guessing she's not in it just for your scintillating conversation and boyish charm. What does she get in return?'

'Something I can easily get but which is like gold-dust to the non-cons.'

'Right.'

Again, Varro suspected he knew the answer. Some piece of technology, a toy of some kind, or maybe medicine, life supplements, all of which the non-cons had failed to keep up with in their developments.

'Well, Varro, got to be going. Need some kip. I'm back again tonight.'

Bragg lived in York so his journey home was a short one, and Varro watched as the young man swaggered across to the main entrance he had just come through. His rolling shoulders spoke of a confidence that Varro could barely remember in himself, and Varro felt a pang of jealously at his happiness. All was well in the world of Bragg. The door slid open revealing the wall of blank morning grey. But instead of leaving, Bragg turned.

'Hey, Varro, why don't you come with us next time?' The sound carried easily through the empty space.

'So, you're definitely going again?'

'The ceb wants to go this week. He's desperate.'

'Wow! The creature really is love struck.'

'I'm going to try and sort it out with my contact.'

'And what do you suggest I do there? Hold 43's hand and watch while you have a good time?'

'I thought you were curious about the non-cons and how they lived. I'm giving you a great opportunity to get up close and personal.'

'I'm not interested in the same thing as you.'

'I don't mean that, Varro. I just mean that maybe you could speak with her. I don't know, bring some drink and some food.'

'You mean have a picnic?'

'Listen, Varro, all I'm saying is that whenever we've been out together, you're always on about what it must be like to live like a non-con, survive without an #amic, grow your own food, be without rules, all that stuff. Now you have the chance. It's up to you what you do when you get there.'

He still wore his smile, but Varro heard the strain in the words. The boy was tired and wanted to be on his way. That was understandable, and he was genuinely trying to do Varro a favour.

'Tell you what,' said Varro, 'I'll think about it and let you know. OK?'

'Fine, do that.'

'And Bragg?'

'Yep?'

'Thanks for the offer.'

Bragg offered his most engaging smile once more but said nothing as he turned and lost himself in the morning gloom. Varro switched his #amic on once again but remained where he was. Bragg was correct in what he said. He *was* curious. The fact that there was a completely different type of society barely 50 kilometres away had always proved a source of fascination. That there were pockets of similar communities right around the globe only deepened his interest. Yet he knew so little about them; what they thought, how they organised themselves, what laws, if any, they lived under. The only source of information about the non-cons came from what the cerebellums chose to present, as well as the occasional traces of loose gossip from Grey Zone encounters like Bragg's. That the two versions often didn't tally up only added to the questions in Varro's mind. Of course, most citizens knew nothing of these contradictions, and those that did weren't interested in finding out more. Citizens lived in the best of all possible worlds. Non-cons played no part in this. They were almost like another species entirely.

And there were risks, too. He would have to turn off his feed once more. Doing so in the Grey Zone itself would surely alert suspicion, but doing so a distance before he hit that border would mean a longer black out. Neither choice was particularly envious.

The risks for the non-con were even greater. Non cons weren't allowed in the Grey Zone and Varro had heard macabre tales of what the border rangers did to any they did catch. How would that eventuality play on his conscience? Even if she agreed to talk to him, would she tell him anything that he didn't already know? To confirm the things he already knew with the Patrimony investigation looming over him was a fool's errand.

He covered the remaining metres towards glider station five, his ponderous footsteps echoing like the doubts of his own mind. He placed himself under the cold frame of the glider and waited, still thinking. That this non-con had managed to captivate the auxiliary ceb in an instant came as little surprise, that she had entranced the self-confessed lothario which was Bragg was of greater note. The boy was all but an emperor of the parlours. What did the non-con possess that the immersive libertines of the parlours did not? Varro tried to picture her, demure yet with the steady, self-possessed gaze he had witnessed from the four men a few days previously.

Then the main door opened once more and his reverie was interrupted. It was an engineer who Varro recognised and greeted with a raised hand. The man replied with a similar gesture but then sheared away from Varro, towards the engineers's control room from where the mechanics of the gliders were controlled, his footsteps fading as Varro found himself returning to his uncertain thoughts on that Monday morning. He couldn't quite believe that he was considering Bragg's crazy offer. Did he really want to risk getting pinned onto a level 3 or a massive loss of dits? How would Karena react to that? Life was difficult enough without heaping on more complications, especially as outlandish as Bragg's. Varro couldn't even be sure that Bragg was telling the truth. With a sinking heart, Varro returned to his #amic.

'Glider insertion,' he said, and immediately felt the tug of the suction unit as it pulled him without pity into the dumb machine.

Thursday 8 May

The school has bought a computer! It's a ZX Spectrum and today we were allowed to use it. It looks really cool, especially the rainbow stripe down the side. In Lesson 3 today, Mrs Bristow put us into pairs and we each had 5 minutes with it. I was with Elizabeth, and we played a game called Jetpac and you have to collect pieces of your rocket to advance. There are also lots of aliens you have to kill. It was lots of fun, but Mrs Bristow says that computers like this can do lots of other things, and that in the future they will make our lives much easier by doing everything for us and making the world a better place. I hope they do the boring things, not the interesting things. Because if they do everything for us, what will there be left for us to do? When I got home I asked Dad if we could get a ZX Spectrum but he said we didn't have enough money and we had better things to spend our money on.

Chapter 15

V arro was surprised to sleep so well. Maybe it was because they had summoned him at midmorning so he could afford to leave the house later than he would normally. As a result, he had taken his time, showering at length before letting his skin warm almost uncomfortably in the dryer, before leisurely slipping into Euro Agri's departmental monosuit with branded epaulettes. He had let Karena precede him in everything, and though they still shared the same bed, they had barely been in the same room together more than a few moments. Now she would be in the kitchen, and if he was to keep to his breakfast routine, he would have to cross some words with her there, for form sake if nothing else.

She was on the far side of the room, cradling a broad cup in both hands, leaning against one of the large units which contained many of the kitchen items. He noticed that she had once again changed the nature of the veneer, this time to a pulsing, bright chrome, though he preferred to programme the neutral colours. She let him wander around the kitchen for a few moments, following him with her eyes.

'Are you not scared?' she finally said.

'Scared? No, why should I be scared?'

'A Patrimony interview is not an everyday occurrence.'

'Neither is dropping into the Grey Zone and finding material from hundreds of years ago scattered across a field.'

'But if the clean-up team dealt with all that, why do they want to talk to you? You've already been sanctioned for turning your feed off.'

He had told her about the encounter with the auxiliary ceb, his punishment and reduction of dits. He hadn't mentioned more. At one time, she would have rolled with this. Now, she was suspicious about everything.

'I don't know,' he said. 'Maybe they just want to get my version of events before they close the case.'

'I thought you told CebAux 43 all about it.'

'Maybe they just want extra details. I don't really know. Don't worry. What's the worst that could happen?'

'You tell me, Varro,' she demanded. 'You're already on level 2. What's going to happen to us if that gets any worse?'

It wasn't really a question, more a protest. Varro had grown used to them and as he looked at his partner, her taut skin and sunken eyes hard and unyielding, he decided not to continue the conversation. She had made her point.

Varro pulled his drink from the cooker and looked down at the eddies of steam curling away and evaporating. Then he turned to Karena.

'I think I'll go and see the children before I leave.'

Karena continued to stare silently at him and Varro didn't know whether to feel pity or anger. In the end, he looked away before leaving the room without a sound.

'#amic, advise children that I'm coming to see them,' Varro said as he turned into the hallway. He looked again at the digital clock which lay at the periphery of his internal vision. He still had time, and the children wouldn't have started their schooling yet. He didn't know what he was likely to say to them, but the change in his routine merited something.

From the upper landing he could see that both children had opened their doors – sullen obedience he supposed to his #amic's request, a view confirmed when he looked inside Marcus's room. The boy was already inside the cubicle, seated on an invisible air seat but clearly already interacting with something, or someone, his lips were moving, and an occasional smile traced itself across his face – the boy looked animated. Varro edged closer, wanting a part of the boy's mood, but as he reached the door, Marcus looked up and Varro could see any good humour drain away. The boy realised too late that his reaction had let him down and tried to raise some sort of grin. But it was painful to watch, and Varro indicated that he should continue before raising a hand in half salute, neither greeting nor departure. The boy jerked up his own hand in response. Could Varro blame his son if he wanted to be left alone?

He moved along the corridor, taking care not to spill any of the hot liquid which he occasionally raised to his lips.

'Hello, Celia.'

'Hello, Varro.'

She was standing at the threshold of her cubicle, like her brother waiting for the curriculum to begin on the stroke of nine. They would break every couple of hours, but essentially, the transparent dome would be their universe for most of the day. She had done something to her hair, an artlessly braided seam fell over her forehead, bisecting one eye. As Varro examined it closer he realised the strand had a strong violet tinge to it. Like her mother, the girl had a thirst for continuous novelty. To Varro, it looked ridiculous.

'Looking forward to the day?' he asked.

'Not really.'

'Oh.'

Varro waited for her to say something more, but her silence was eloquent. He was surplus to her morning. All that remained was to leave with some dignity.

'Well, I've got a meeting in York this morning. So I'll say goodbye now. See you later, then.'

'Yes, see you later,' she said flatly.

Varro took another sip of the drink then left the room. In one of the older books of his collection, from the middle of the 21st century he thought, an author called Albert Stanislav had written a short book which had caused quite a stir. It argued that for each engagement with artificial, non-human sources, a little bit of character was sucked away from the individual who had accessed it. Incessant use led to people becoming hollowed out, bland transparencies with no discernible personality and barely any volition of their own. In short, technology was sucking the life out of people. It was a criticism that had been quietly swept under the carpet with the passage of time and the rule of the cerebellums, but for Varro as he slowly descended the stairs from his children's rooms, it explained much.

*

The deca-stop in the centre of York was even larger than Hull. Thousands of people, each on their own tangents criss-crossed the north-south concourse. 25 metres below, on the west-east equivalent, the scene would be similar, ceaseless streams of people arriving from hubs across the British region, and far beyond. The variety of people shuffling past him always took Varro by surprise, forcing him again to adjust to the reality of a super connected planet. Here there were physiognomies from across the globe, redolent like badges; fleshy faced South Americans, stout, no-nonsense Arabians, Asian eyes fathomless in their inky depths, high cheeked Africans, his own European women with their strong characters and forthright chins. Most spoke the common Panparl, but Varro was delighted to hear sotto voce words and ways of speaking he had never heard before and found impossible to pinpoint on the earth's surface. Local languages weren't dead, but their associations with the local non-con populations discouraged their use for normal citizens.

'Patrimony is on Queen Charlotte Street. From where you are now, you turn left and walk 300 metres, please keep to the left.' The instruction from his #amic came as Varro loitered around the busy entrance to the deca-station. He had previously checked the location of the Patrimony building, one of the largest in the city, and still couldn't make up his mind if it was ironic or ominous that this department related to the examination and control of the past was in the very heart of this most ancient of cities. He kept away from the heaving centre of the promenades, preferring to hug the line of the shop fronts, all catering in some way to the avid visitor. The area enclosed by the medieval walls was now little more than a chocolate box pastiche of its former self, at the exclusive whim of the many visitors who travelled from across the world for the chance to visit the city.

Varro watched the travellers as they streamed past him, but he tried to avoid eye contact. Many were deep into the York Experience, letting their #amics place historic overlays before their eyes. Move at will in the city centre and choose any period in 100 year slots and you would find yourself in that scene, walking along, being a part of it; look down and you would see yourself transformed into Roman clothing, close in on a smithy from Viking York and feel the heat of the furnace prickle your skin, or walk past a medieval tannery and be greeted by its overpowering smells, all courtesy of your #amic. You could do similar things, of course, from a cubicle, and much more cheaply, but for many visitors, this simulation in situ was as close to time travel as it was possible to achieve. Varro knew that many of those strolling along with their eyes shining in wonder would not be seeing him – rather the avatar the software had converted him into. It was uncanny when they made eye contact – you had no idea what they were seeing, and occasionally the more excitable ones actually spoke to you. Varro just ignored them.

His #amic told him when he had arrived at Patrimony, and Varro stopped and looked across the open thoroughfare to a building whose frontage took up much of the available street space, stretching many metres across. At some point it must have been the headquarters of a local professional enterprise, a bank most likely. The main entrance was flanked by a pair of large white Grecian columns complete with frothing acanthus capitals and a triangular pediment, a crest of laurel in the centre with a Latin inscription curling around its circumference. On a second storey were smaller columns in a similar style. At one time they would have held transparent windows but now all that could be seen were drifts of cumulous cloud reflecting off the metallic smart glass. Beyond this floor all was new, the severe grey panelling rising vertiginously into the air. Varro realised that somewhere up there, high above, he would be interviewed.

The doors between the pillars slid open, but the obfuscation screen was activated so Varro could see nothing of the interior.

'They are inviting you to enter,' his #amic said.

Varro grunted. He could feel the heat building in his body and told himself to be calm. All this physical data was being shared with the agents of Patrimony. Some nerves were normal, but anything beyond that could point towards culpability. Guilt could be arrived at by many paths, not just what you said, and Varro had spent the last few days trying to convince himself that he hadn't done anything wrong, not really. Maintaining that conviction was crucial. He took the air deep into his lungs before releasing it, then slowly snaked between the streams of eager visitors and entered the building.

We went for a walk today although we hadn't planned to go, but this morning Elizabeth came around with her new roller skates, and we were practising with them on the patio (it's not very big, but you can still go round and round) but Daniel kept putting sticks in our way and once I fell over and grazed my knee and started crying so Mum told us to go for a walk. She also told us to take Daniel, though we didn't want to. But it was quite fun because we went down the old railway track (there's no track there now, just the cutting which is all grown over), and then we met this old man who started telling us about all the trees, birds and flowers along the cutting. In fact, he saw the graze on my knee and showed us this flower called St John's Wort – it has small, yellow petals – which you can use to put on cuts like this and it makes them better. He told us lots of other things as well, but I've forgotten most of them – I think we walked nearly all the way back with him and then he carried on down the line when we came back up from the cutting. I'm not sure if he lives in the village or not.

Chapter 16

He was no sooner inside than the the twin doors snapped shut behind him. To his surprise he heard the heavy clunk of the panels and in an instant the lobby of the building appeared to him. He had expected something classic, maybe a restored interior from the 19th century, complete with glossy walnut fittings, smooth marble and repeated classical allusions. Instead, there was just the severe geometry of brilliant white surfaces. The space was devoid of furniture and people but at the far end of the lobby lay a series of cubicles with semi-circular plagilene frontages. One of them was pulsing orange, and as Varro drew closer, it opened revealing the man-sized cylindrical interior. A vacuum lift, of course, much like they were introducing into the deca-stations these days. Highly efficient but deceptive, cushioning your passage to such an extent that all sense of movement was nullified. You could go two metres, or two kilometres and you wouldn't know the difference. As he stepped into the unit, Varro wondered what awaited him at the other end of the ride.

The door had barely swept around him in closure than it was opening again. He couldn't have ascended far, surely. His eyes tried to focus, but it was impossible because before him was a wall of white, all around, 360 degrees of brilliance. The glare was so powerful he found himself squinting.

'Move forward, Varro,' he heard his #amic say. More an order than a request.

Varro shuffled forwards, far enough he calculated to position him beyond the limits of the lift, but it was impossible to gauge where he should stand or how far the room extended. The lift and the room seemed to be one space.

'#amic, shade vision,' Varro said, still unable to bring himself to fully open his eyes.

'I'm afraid that will not be possible,' Varro heard from his inner ear.

'#amic, please shade vision, I can't see well,' Varro repeated. Maybe the device hadn't picked up on his command.

'As I say, Varro, that will not be possible.'

Varro was about to remonstrate when he stopped. His #amic's loyalties meant little in here, that was now evident. If he had been unsure before, Varro was becoming aware of just how big a stick Patrimony wielded.

The fierce luminosity of the room was matched by its silence, and into both of them Varro's laboured breathing and urgent heartbeat erupted. He wondered if he should say something. But he didn't have time.

'Please confirm your name.' The voice was sharp and peremptory, but Varro knew it would be useless to search for its source. The sound filled the entire room. His eyes were still struggling with the glare, and the dimensions of the room remained a mystery. It was as much as he could do to respond to the question, his voice ringing pencil thin in the uncertain space.

'Address.' Varro gave it.

'Occupation.' As he answered, Varro realised that he would remain on his feet the whole interview. A ploy of sorts, no doubt.

'Do you understand where you are?' the voice continued.

'I do.'

'And do you understand the role of Patrimony in our society?'

'Yes, I do.'

'What is it?'

'To control all finds from the past.'

'To *care* for and carefully calibrate all uncertain or ambiguous sources from the past, that is correct.'

Varro suspected that behind the voice lay a cerebellum rather than a citizen, but it was impossible to be sure.

'And do you know why such calibration is so important?'

'To ensure people don't get the wrong ideas?' Varro said cautiously. He was unsure where the questioning was leading. The premium on truth and objectivity had risen exponentially since the dawn of the digital age when nearly any material could be easily manipulated, subtly at times, more egregiously at others. What was original and what had undergone manipulation, corruption as it was known, could barely be discerned, and as a result arriving at unadulterated truth had become an end in itself. Patrimony had been established to reach this end, and the cerebellums, with their larger brains and reputation for impartiality, were seen as the best agents for this task.

'Calibration,' the voice continued, 'is to ensure that any material, be it original or recently discovered, is objectively processed before being made available for further dissemination. If any source, object or find is considered liable to corruption, Patrimony ensures that its wider availability can only occur in a controlled and secure way.'

This was true. Most sources, literature, videos, audios, hologlows, mind-memes, could be easily and freely accessed through one's #amic or by stepping into a cubicle, but it would be with the reassurance that what you were absorbing had been under the impartial, objective gaze of Patrimony. It would be as close as possible to what the originators of the material had intended it to be. The cerebellums worked hard to make sure citizens went uncorrupted.

There was a brief silence and Varro muttered his agreement. He was unsure where the interview was really heading.

'No doubt you will have intuited why you are here?'

'I suppose it is related to the incident in the Grey Zone last Friday,' Varro answered.

'That is correct. Your role was to facilitate, if possible, a resumption of operations after the failure of the plough. Is that the case?'

'It is.'

'And yet instead you availed yourself of the opportunity to seek out material which had been thrown up by the plough. Why was that? Why did you prevaricate? Why not go directly to the plough?'

The question was an obvious one and Varro had already considered his answer.

'I thought the contents might provide some clue as to the stoppage.'

'And did this explain also why you considered it necessary to handle some of the objects?'

'Yes, it does,' Varro paused. A version of the truth might serve him well. 'And I must confess, I was curious.'

'Curious?'

'Yes, they were things I had never seen before, or rather only in the V-Museums.'

'So your curiosity superseded your duty?'

'Yes, if you will.'

There was a brief pause and Varro waited as the space above and below him darkened before transforming into a grand bird's-eye projection. The resolution was not sharp, but it was not difficult to make out the elements of the scene from the previous week; the motionless plough at the top of the image, his craft poised in the half-ploughed centre, the church towards the bottom. Long shadows stretched from each of these prominent features, like pooling blood from a wounded creature. Varro was surprised he hadn't noticed these at the time. And there he was, blurry but distinct, clambering along the recently split earth. He watched in silence as the scene unfolded, but felt removed from the images. He followed his figure as he stopped and bent over to retrieve something. Whatever he picked up was obscured from the overhead view by his folded torso. Then he saw himself fling the fluorescent globe away. Further along the dark row Varro could see the book, little more in the image than a few pixels of light splodge. A chill ran through his body and his eyes narrowed in anticipation. Suddenly the image froze.

'We would like you to concentrate very carefully on the following sequence. It is the principal point of our interest.'

'Very well,' replied Varro, waiting.

The whole scene dimmed before a halo of light picked out the sliver of light contrasting against the darker earth. The video began again and Varro followed himself as he slowed, then bent over the item which disappeared from view, obscured by his hunched body as previously. Varro felt himself flush as he recalled leafing through the pages before reading that initial entry. His jack-knifed torso remained immobile in the scene for what seemed an eternity. Even removed from the images by distance and time, Varro felt the panic he had experienced previously as he was then advised of the sudden appearance of the four non-cons. As he turned and began his flight back to the glider the image froze again, and once more the patch of earth was highlighted. Even Varro was surprised to see that the splodge had vanished. His interrogation began again immediately.

'You will, we hope, see clearly what we are alluding to. The items you looked at and discarded can all be accounted for by the retrieval team sent in afterwards. All except this item. We were hoping that you could account for it.'

Varro composed himself before speaking. 'I think this was when I bent down to clear the earth away from my boots. I was having trouble walking, I remember.'

'And the item?'

'I couldn't say. I mean, I remember the earth easily crumbling away and down each furrow. Maybe that could have covered whatever was there?'

'And what was there?'

'As I say, I really don't recall that much. I do remember there being lots of loose printed sheets being blown around. Maybe it was one of those.'

Varro felt the tension in his chest as his explanation was met by silence. He wondered if he should add something.

'Ignatius Varro, did you make an illegal seizure of an item suspected of having wider historic value to society?'

'No.'

'You understand that any wilful divergence from the truth would incur significant penalties?'

'I do.'

'And you still wish to confirm your negation of material found and extracted from the site?'

Varro realised later that he had paused a moment too long in his reply, but it was now too late for anything else.

'Yes, I do. I just cleaned some mud from my boots then stood up to look at the plough for a few moments. I can't remember seeing anything in the earth after that.'

'Thank you,' the voice reverberated around the room. 'Your answer has been noted.' Varro remained still, waiting. It was some time before the voice resumed. 'You have recently put forward for minister status. Is that not so?'

'It is.'

'Ministers are the moral vanguard of our society. Clarity and integrity are the bedrocks of their contributions. You do realise that, don't you?'

'I do. And I agree,' Varro said. With the abrupt change of questioning Varro suddenly realised that he had been overly passive in his initial responses and that this limp acquiescence was likely to be interpreted badly. Maybe it wasn't too late to launch a rearguard action. 'Ministers are vital in our society,' he spluttered. 'Citizens need to be presented with righteous perspectives.'

'Righteous perspectives?'

'Yes, well, I mean, truthful perspectives. That good behaviour, healthy living and a rigorous adhesion to the truth are to be held premium at all times.'

'Ah.'

'I have always thought it is an essential moral duty to tell the truth, even when this is not directly in one's interests. Obviously, such a creed would inform my career as a minister, should I be chosen, which I hope is not presumptuous. I realise that one must demonstrate a wide number of positive societal values before one can be considered worthy of minister status. I think...' Varro stopped. He was rambling and he knew it. Continuing to jabber away would serve no purpose. He remained silent, the lack of any sound in the interior adding to his agony. He wondered when the frozen image of the Grey Zone in the afternoon sun would revert to the blinding whiteness he had encountered upon entering the space. Maybe they had overlooked it. Finally, the silence came to an end.

'The Department of Patrimony wishes to express its gratitude for your attendance today. We will inform you of any decision very shortly.'

The room plunged into sudden darkness and behind him Varro was aware of the tenuous light from the vacuum lift. The interview was over. He took a step backwards, into the lift, before the door shut abruptly in front of his eyes.

Today we went to visit the old school in the village. Somebody lives there now (Mrs Robinson) but she let us in and we had a look around. It's got two entrances, one for the girls and another for the boys and Mrs Bristow says that in the past the children had to line up every day before class and wait to go in. Inside it doesn't really look like a school, but the ceilings are very high, and Mrs Bristow had brought along some photos of what it did look like and you could see how the building had changed. All the girls had to wear white aprons over their dresses and the boys all wore boots. Instead of exercise books, they wrote on chalk slates. Mrs Bristow says that the girls and boys in the photos were the first to go to school and that not long before the photo was taken, there was no free schooling and that only rich people educated their children. Mrs Bristow said that most children before they went to school would have stayed at home and helped their parents do work in the house. How strange! I can't imagine staying at home with Mum or Dad, and washing up, doing the ironing or gardening. And Mrs Bristow says that in the school there was no telephone, television or lights with electric light bulbs.

Chapter 17

V arro didn't have to wait long. The decision came early the following day, his #amic interrupting him shortly after his first north south pass from Ripon to Harrogate, flying low over the agglomerated fields between Fountains Abbey and the River Ure, making supplementary visual checks on the progress of the tilling machines which were rumbling up and down the fields.

'Patrimony have decided to close the case due to insufficient evidence. They do not need to see you again and there will be no additional penalties.'

'That's good news,' said Varro.

'It is, but they also gave you only a 64% credibility rating, citing numerous micro movements and bio responses incompatible with complete disclosure. They were also dubious about your explanation for the disappearance of the object, yet did not have sufficient resolution to provide an alternative explanation or be sure of any guilt on your part. As a result, they felt they could not increase the punishment already handed down for turning off your feeds and deviating from accepted policy regarding alerting the rangers.'

'I see. Is that all?'

'There is one further thing.'

'Which is?'

'In light of the credibility rating, Patrimony recommended that your minister application be turned down.'

'Ah,' said Varro. 'And has it been?'

'It has. We received the news from the department shortly afterwards.'

'What did they say?'

'Very little. Only that in light of recent developments your application was not being taken forward.'

'Nothing else?'

'Only that you should continue to live life in accordance with the values of the minister cohort.'

Varro said nothing. The refusal wasn't a surprise, but it was still a blow. He had invested a lot in the idea of becoming a minister, and although he had harboured doubts about the quality of his application, he still felt he had important things to say to his fellow citizens. What would he do with his ideas now?

He should tell Karena. The exemption from further punishment was undoubtedly good news for the family and she would be pleased. He wasn't sure about the minister application. She had barely shown any interest in that at all. Varro shifted the glider into auto-mode and instructed the #amic to alert his partner.

'Yes, what is it?' Her voice forlorn, as if already anticipating the worst.

'Sorry, Karena, am I interrupting anything?'

'It's alright, Varro. Just about to facilitate a recall session. What do you want?'

The memory sessions were a common enough task for Karena in the senility clinic, a nurse would work between her #amic and the patient's in a bid to stimulate different parts of the hippocampus. Most times the effort was futile, the affected area dried up and useless after years of underuse. The irony of using the #amic to resurrect a body it had been responsible for killing off always amused Varro, like an executioner trying to replace the head of a guillotine victim.

'Patrimony have decided my case,' he said.

'And?'

'I am to remain on level 2 – no further penalties.'

'So, we are no better off?'

'Well, no, not really, but no worse either. It's good news, Karena, it could have been much worse.'

140

'How? I thought you said it was just a routine enquiry. What were you expecting?' Varro heard the snap in her voice and remembered what he had kept from her.

'Of course, it was routine. I didn't think I could add much more than CebAux 3.8.43 had already presented to them, really. I just mean that handling some of the things which the plough had turned up could have increased my fine.'

The lie came too easily, but he felt nothing.

'Maybe,' she said cautiously, and Varro realised he should change the subject.

'But the bad news is that I've been turned down again for minister status.'

'That's not as bad as losing dits and going on to level 2.'

'It was important for me, Karena. And it would have come with extra credits.'

'Right.'

They lapsed into silence and all Varro could hear was the low hum of the electric ion motors. He didn't want to finish the conversation like this.

'Karena?' he said.

'Varro, I need to go now. We're about to start the session. Let's speak about it later, if you like.'

'Yes, yes, of course. You go. I just thought I'd tell you.'

'OK.'

'Goodbye, Karena.'

But she had already terminated the communication and Varro stayed for a few minutes gazing from the cockpit as the shallow stream below twisted and tumbled energetically between the tall poplar trees, the whole valley hemmed in by abrasive looking crags which fell away precipitously. Nothing was clear to him.

'Return to manual control, Varro?' It was his #amic. Varro agreed and took hold of the holo-yoke, enjoying the simulated tremor of the virtual controls and deliberately sending the craft tipping from side to side in an exaggerated way. His body rose and fell with the rocking motion. Karena's indifference had made him reckless and he would have fallen out if the adhesion control hadn't kicked in.

'Varro, what are you doing?' CebAux 3.8.43's peeved voice bellowed through the cabin. 'Return gyration systems at once!'

Varro smiled and brought the craft under control once more. The rush of blood had done him good.

'Sorry, I don't know what came over me,' Varro grinned before continuing. 'Commencing east-west passes now. Preliminary analysis is that all work stations functioning normally. Proceeding to visual confirmation.'

Varro brought the craft level and settled into his cruising altitude, a few hundred metres above the fields. He shifted to automatic and gazed unseeing beyond the transparency of the craft. He had wanted more from Karena, and the conversation had left him feeling empty. It wasn't sympathy he was after, just some interest. Even an attempt. But she just didn't seem bothered, not just in him, but in the whole project they had once had. Between them they had made a mockery of the dream.

He wondered too where the loss of the minister ambition left him. He didn't doubt he would continue to have ideas about how citizens should live their lives, how they should behave, treat each other, interact with each element of the world around them. All those things were quite clear in his head. Somewhere in the past, we had taken a wrong turn; being a minister was his way of pointing mankind back in the right direction. His illicit reading of the girl's diary had proved as much. She lived in a world with open horizons, a world which encouraged people to go out and discover things for themselves; new friends, unknown places, novel experiences. By contrast, Varro's world was closed, a land of narrow horizons and worthless novelties.

Varro knew it was easy to look at the past through rose tinted spectacles, and the cebs' achievements of world peace, citizens's security and physical well-being were significant. But at what price had these advances been bought? A stint at being a minister would have enabled Varro to approach these subjects, however obliquely.

But that was all gone, so where would he find his outlet now? What was he supposed to do with everything bubbling inside?

'#amic, call Bragg,' said Varro. 'No visuals, just audio.'

In an instant Varro heard the voice of the young man, clear but still stodgy with sleep.

'Bragg, are you still on for that trip you suggested?'

'Sure, why? Changed your mind? Do you want to come?'

'I might do. Talk me through your plan.'

'It's tomorrow night.'

'Fine. Shall we go off line?'

'No need, Varro. This is going straight through CebAux 3.8.43 and he's not likely to give anything anyway, isn't that right 43?'

Bragg's tone was light but mocking, and his words were met with silence. The ceb wasn't taking the bait, though both men knew that CebAux 3.8.43 was monitoring everything they said and did. But Bragg was correct, given the auxiliary ceb's involvement in the whole affair, there was little chance of it reporting affairs to Amicol or anywhere else. Bragg had the ceb exactly where he wanted him.

'Get to Lomby by 10pm and I'll meet you there when my shift finishes,' continued Bragg.

'Lomby?' Varro had never heard of it.

'It's a small village, well, just a few houses really, half a dozen kilometres north of the 180. There's a field I sometimes leave the glider.'

'Does the field belong to anybody?'

'A friend. If anyone asks, I'm visiting a friend.'

'Right. And how do we get from there to Brigg?'

'Bicycle, my friend.'

'A what?' Varro had no idea what Bragg was talking about.

'Ancient version of the Watter, except it's open to the elements, and you only use your legs. That drives a metallic chain which makes the two wheels go around. It takes a bit of getting used to but it's a lot of fun, especially at night.'

'Can't we just use a Watter or the uni-k system to get closer?'

'And when do we turn our #amics off? When we get to the 180? That's not very smart.'

Bragg had a point. Any outage close to the Grey Zone immediately raised alarm bells for Amicol, and while stepping into the Grey Zone wasn't illegal, doing so late at night, without your feed on, and propelled by archaic technology was certainly likely to raise suspicions. Lower earth body heat probes could pinpoint such an incursion easily, then it wouldn't take long for the patrolling rangers with their sharper night vision to home in on the offending citizen. Good luck to anyone inventing a decent excuse during their detention and lengthy interrogation. Turning off their #amics some distance away was far less likely to raise suspicions in the first place.

'Ok, so we flip the #amics, get on these contraptions, then what? How are we supposed to cross the 180? Anyone crossing via a normal route is always switched on, plus it's so well-lit even wild animals are pegged.'

'Well,' replied Bragg carefully. 'Firstly, we don't go anywhere near a standard crossing. Secondly, we use a service tunnel to go under.'

Varro knew that a corridor had been built below the whole length of the former motorway when they repurposed the route as a barrier against the non-cons. It ran west to east across northern Lincolnshire, and with its floodlights, watchtowers, cameras, sensors of all types, it was a real obstacle to any curious non-con who happened to wander northwards. Citizens, who had their #amics as a default passport, could go through freely. If they wanted to. But who wanted to visit the Grey Zone?

'And I suppose you have a key to the tunnel.'

'I don't,' replied Bragg, and Varro thought he could hear the lad smirking in his apartment. 'But I know someone who does, and is prepared to do me a favour.'

'And what does he get in return?'

'Don't ask.'

Varro stopped. He was beginning to realise that behind Bragg's apparent *joie de vivre* lay a murkier hinterland. He had never asked

144

about the boy's life before Euro Agri and had assumed that an upbringing in one of the cerebellum's own life groups would have been largely conventional. Listening to Bragg explain his plan was forcing Varro to reassess.

'And then we use these bicycles to get to Brigg, I suppose.'

'Exactly.'

'And the cameras in Brigg? We'll be picked up immediately, however well disguised we are.'

'Not if we use a destabiliser,' replied Bragg.

'Have you got one?'

'Sure, and once we hide the bikes, I'll give you one and then we'll walk the rest of the way. The town isn't as well-lit as a big city so we should be able to find a way in the shadows.'

Destabilisers were not difficult to obtain, and once under your shoe or boot, their constantly changing dimensions forced you into all sorts of weird walking styles, perfect to stymie cameras which could identify individuals as much from their gait as from their features. But Varro was still concerned.

'And if we come across someone?'

'Most people are on lowest transparency. They won't want to know anything about you and they don't want anyone to know much about them. Brigg's not your average town.'

'But we'll still be appearing via their #amics, however well disguised. Aren't Amicol all over these types of feeds?'

'There's a chance, but as I say, it's a special town. Amicol agents and rangers have been known to disappear in Brigg. Picking non-cons off in the fields like where you were the other day is less risky for them. Citizens here don't see the non-cons in quite the same way as people north of the river do. They've had to live beyond the 180 for generations. They've learnt to live close to the non-cons without fear. There's still a healthy barter economy at work, even if most of it can't be seen. It's not in people's interests to see that threatened.'

'I see.'

'So, Varro, that's the plan. Are you in?'

The plan was risky, however bullish Bragg appeared, and Varro could see weak links at every stage. If they were caught smuggling themselves in and without their feeds, he was unlikely to remain on level 2. Karena's potential reaction wasn't worth thinking about. He even wondered if Patrimony might restart their investigations. All in all, it was a fool's errand. Varro gave himself a few moments before speaking.

'OK, Bragg, plot me your friend's field and I'll see you there at 10 tomorrow.'

Varro flipped the communication and sat back in the seat staring without seeing and wondering what he had done.

We made real paper in school today. Well, it wasn't really like the paper we use every day, but Mrs Bristow says that this is the way they made it in the olden days, with pieces of cloth and used clothes (I took one of Dad's old vests!) which they cut into small pieces, then soak in water for a long time. Then you have to mix it all up and after that you can form it into any shape you want to. We made paper plates, and after they were dry we painted on them. The sides of my plate weren't very good (Elizabeth's was better) but Mrs Bristow said that it wasn't very important because they were not for putting any food on them. I wanted to give my plate to Mrs Bristow as a present, but she said I should give it to Mum or Dad. When I got home, Mum said I should give it to Dad as it was his vest in the first place. So tonight when he got home I gave it to him, and I think he really liked it because he gave me such a hug I thought I was going to burst. He said that whatever happens in the future he will always have this plate to remember me by.

THURSDAY

Chapter 18

S he took a fraction of a second to adjust and hoped they wouldn't notice her surprise as she took in the scene before her. Silas had opened the union between the two buildings and they had used the same code as previously, but little else was the same on this side of the wall.

'What's this?' she began, looking around. Two men sat at the pine table to the side of the entrance. It had been laid for an occasion with several wine glasses, a bottle, some hastily arranged wildflowers and a series of candles in no discernible pattern. They gave the only light in the room. She might have found the arrangement intimate if she hadn't been so nervous. She tried to appear relaxed but resolved to stay alert. There was only self-interest in this arrangement, not trust, and any one of them might sell out.

She recognised the young man, Bragg, immediately and behind him pulsed the hologram of the cerebellum who had surprised her last time. The creature looked ready to burst with emotion and almost fell forwards as he saw her. She didn't recognise the other man. All three stared at her with an intensity which was disturbing, as though her arrival was the fulfilment of some apocalyptic prophecy. Opposite her was an open fire, similar to the one in her farmhouse. She was surprised to see the flames leaping about for the heat was likely to be detected easily from above, until she realised that the flames were entirely artificial, a slight of hand created by clever technology unavailable in her world.

'They wanted to surprise you,' said Silas dully. He was not interested in the novel arrangement and was already edging towards the door. 'I'll leave you to get on with it,' he continued. 'You can give me what you owe afterwards.'

She nodded her acceptance and tried to force a smile, but he had already slipped beyond the door.

'Do you like it?' Bragg said sweeping his arm towards the table. 'We collected the flowers on the way here, but it was a bit tricky in the dark. And here's some wine, too. We thought you might like a little drink together.'

'Nothing else?' she said. She hadn't moved beyond the mirror which had swung back into place behind her.

'No, not today. As much as I would like to.' The boy's face twisted into an expression more leer than grin. 'My friends here just wanted to meet you, that's all.'

'I see.'

'Well, don't just stand there, come over here and sit down.'

She walked carefully towards the table, an empty chair awaiting her. The men sat to either side meaning she would be at one end, like some presiding deity. She was quiet as she made her way across, taking her time as she pulled the chair out and making sure her skirt wouldn't inhibit her sitting. The air was heavy with expectation, and she could feel the heat of their attention. She felt like actors she had seen at the Forum, holding the audience in a spell of rapt anticipation.

'Aren't you going to introduce us then?' she asked, her eyes never wavering from those of the younger man. As always, she spoke in English, knowing the translation to Panparl would be almost simultaneous.

'Yes, yes, of course, sorry. This here is my colleague, Varro.'

She turned to the other man at the table who smiled weakly. The light from the candles highlighted the puckering skin at the corners of his eyes, and she realised he must have been a similar age to her.

'Hello,' he said. In English. She tried not to show her surprise and rewarded him with a smile which came more naturally than she had expected. But Bragg was already continuing.

'And this, as you know, is CebAux 3.8.43. He's been looking forward to seeing you all week, haven't you?' Bragg chuckled.

149

She turned to the standing ceb. The representation seemed to have grown in stature since she last saw it, its chest bulged with epic dimensions, and its chunky legs looked ready to burst apart the black faux leather trousers it wore. She knew exactly what was expected of her.

'You look very nice tonight,' she murmured.

'And so do you!' blurted the ceb.

'Thank you,' the woman said. 'You didn't want to wear a monosuit tonight?'

'No, no, I wanted something more traditional, more like a non-con.'

'I see.'

'Do you like the way I have done my eyebrows?' The ceb inclined his head towards her.

'Yes, it really suits you. How do manage to get that effect? It looks like a bird's wing.'

'A bird's wing? I hadn't thought of that, but yes, you're right. I just wanted to make it as sharp and defined as I could. You don't think it's too dark? I was scared it might detract from my eyes.'

'Oh no, not at all,' she continued. 'I think it's just right, neither too much, nor too little.'

The ceb had edged around the table and was now only a few paces away from where she sat. The two men looked on, Bragg unable to wipe the grin from his face. He was like a ring master enjoying the show.

'Look, look at this,' the ceb enthused, holding up the hem of the leopard skin jacket which hung bell like over his trousers. 'It's a three-centimetre trim, I wasn't sure what thickness would work best, but I think this really sets off the whole combination. I programmed real lion's hair for it, too,' the ceb supressed a giggle, 'a sign of virility, they say.'

'Real lion's hair? That's something you don't see every day where I live,' she replied. 'I'm going to tell everyone at home about it. Maybe you'll start a trend.'

'Do you really think so?'

'I do, yes, I really do. But I can't imagine many men will be able to pull it off quite like you. It's really quite special.'

The ceb was unable to hide the intensity of his emotion and for a moment she thought the hologram might reach over and hug her in appreciation. She was unsure what the result of that would be but continued smiling towards the apparition. If this is what it took to get the medicine then she was happy to keep going.

'I'm sure our guest has seen enough, 43, maybe we can have a few words with her now.'

'Yes, yes, of course,' muttered the ceb who stepped back hesitantly, his eyes never leaving her, a look of radiance spread across his features. It wouldn't take much to finish the job.

'Thank you, 43. I love what you have done and how you look, I'm sure many women would like to be in my position now. I can't wait to see how you look the next time we meet.'

She watched as the ceb tried to speak. The lips moved but no sounds came out, some sort of internal glitch she supposed, or maybe her simple words had thrown the being into such turmoil that normal functioning was impossible. So be it. She was earning what she had come here for. Charming the two humans might not be as easy. She turned to Bragg and lowered her voice.

'Is he always this way?'

'Never,' replied Bragg. 'It's normally a humourless thing. You're having quite an effect on him.'

'Ah.'

She turned away from the young man, towards the newcomer, staring brazenly into his eyes.

'And would you like me to comment on how *you* look?'

The question was a risk and she immediately regretted it. She knew nothing about this man. Would he think she was mocking him?

For an instant he was silent, the countenance remaining immobile, and then slowly, very slowly, she saw the edges of his lips curl upwards and his face visibly relax.

'Not unless you want to,' he said, before adding, 'to be honest, I wasn't sure what to wear. Bragg here didn't provide any sartorial instructions prior to arrival.'

She was surprised.

'Your English is very good. I'm guessing you don't practice it with your cerebellum friend here?'

'No, neither with Bragg. In fact, I don't get to practise it much at all now.'

'Why's that?'

'Shortage of real people to talk with, and my #amic doesn't make for great conversation.'

'But you must have spoken more in the past?'

'In the past, yes, but not anymore.'

Something in his tone made her resist the temptation to probe further. She fell silent and waited for him to continue.

'It's something I miss,' he said. 'And you. You obviously understand Panparl?'

'Yes, we are obliged to learn it as we grow up. To understand is easier than to speak.'

'Especially when there are few opportunities to use it.'

'Exactly. Many people think that nowadays young people shouldn't be made to learn it, but it's something the elders continue to insist upon. I suppose it's coming in useful for me now.'

'But this meeting is the exception rather than the rule?'

'True. Most of us never get near you people.'

'And do you think that is a pity?'

Only later, when she replayed the conversation to herself, did she become aware of how carefully he was leading her. The conversation flowed easily.

'It depends how you look at it,' she said. 'Most of us don't feel the loss in any way. We have our friends and family in the places we live, and there's no sense of missing out when people talk about cerebellum controlled places like Leeds, Hull or York. We have lots of information on those places, and your attractions are things that don't hold a great deal of interest for us anyway. Our centres are very different to yours.'

'But don't you feel that something has been lost because there is no longer any interaction between us?'

'Maybe. But what you have never known, you don't miss. Someone born today in our lands has no clear notion of what it was like when contact and travel between our communities was more common.'

'At one time, people could cross over without a thought. You wouldn't be picked up by rangers if you came over to Hull and I could go for a walk along the Wolds in perfect safety. Can you imagine that?'

'It's difficult, I admit.'

They continued talking about the two societies and she told him about the Forums in which people from surrounding areas came at regular intervals to find out news, barter-sell produce, communicate with other non-con lands via telephony, follow meetings of the elders. Any nerves she might have had begun to slip away and the words came easily. The stranger spoke thoughtfully, and in the low light and close shadows, she was lulled into a confidence she hadn't expected. It was difficult to credit she was speaking to someone from outside their society.

'And do you live far from the Forum?' he asked.

'About three miles, we have a small holding just to the west of Bodilby.'

'We?'

'Yes, me and...' She caught herself. Why did he want this information? What if all this really was an elaborate entrapment. He noticed her hesitation and leant forward, his hand raised as if to reassure her.

'It's OK. I'm just curious. My #amic is off and we're not connected in any other way. The risk is our being here, not in what you are telling me.'

She held his gaze, trying to read the truth of what he said. Finally, she spoke.

'I live there with my brother. My younger brother. He does what he can around the farm, but needs special attention. His condition isn't getting any better.'

'I see.'

'The farm keeps us busy.'

'And I suppose you consume most of what you grow?'

'Yes, the wheat, vegetables and milk we all use. It's only the Fizz that we barter-sell. The proceeds from that keep us in equilibrium.'

'In equilibrium?'

'That what we put into society matches what we take out.'

'Is your Fizz any good?'

'Of course it is,' she grinned. 'I'll bring you some if I come again.'

'Thank you, I'd like that. I've never known why the cebs don't try to grow grapes and make wine up here instead of bringing it in from other places in Europe. The land around here is perfect for wine and Fizz making nowadays.'

'Do you have a preference?' she offered.

'Between wine and Fizz?' he asked. She nodded and he continued. 'Fizz, I like the sensation of bubbles bursting in my mouth.'

She laughed. 'Then I'll definitely have to bring some of ours for you to try next time!'

'Whoa! Slow up girl!' It was Bragg. 'Who says there's going to be a next time?'

She had almost forgotten him, but now realised that he must have been listening in with growing frustration. His outburst showed a barely concealed jealously. Like a child. She needed to be careful. It was him, and not this interesting stranger, who was supplying her. She turned and placed her hand upon his, squeezing it hard to attract his attention.

'Don't worry, I'll keep our really special vintage for you. Just me and you.' She began to slowly stroke his hand and thought about rubbing his leg under the table. But that would have been too crass – the boy was no fool. Instead, she held his eyes, trying to decipher in

154

the candlelight what damage her inattention had produced. It was impossible to tell, and the boy soon turned to his colleague.

'Come on, Varro, it's time we left. I hope your little chat was worth it.'

Varro remained silent and just looked across the table at the pair of them, expressionless.

'Silas! Silas! We're off!' Bragg called out and immediately she heard the heavy footsteps on the stairs. As he stood, Bragg turned, took something from his pocket and thrust it out to her. 'Here, what we agreed on.' She couldn't tell if he was angry or just bored.

'Will I see you again?' she said.

'Maybe. I'll let you know.'

'Just you and me next time, eh?' She hoped she hadn't lost him.

'As I said, I'll let you know.'

She was aware of the other man's attention and as they both stood, she turned to him. She tried to control her feelings.

'Well, it was nice meeting you.'

'You, too.'

His neutral tone suggested that he had also read the situation. As Bragg rose from the chair, she looked over to the far end of the table where the ceb shimmered expectantly. But the young man had had enough for one evening and fiddled with something in his hands and the ceb disappeared in an instant. The share was over. She watched as the boy marched over to the corner of the room where the door to the hallway was, reluctantly followed by Varro who still wore the composed smile he had shown on her opening question.

She remained standing, watching silently as Bragg brushed passed Silas who stood in the doorway. He said nothing. A pace behind, Varro had almost disappeared when he stopped and turned.

'Oh, I almost forgot,' he said.

'Yes?'

'Your name. I completely forgot to ask your name.'

She smiled with relief. 'Rachel,' she said, 'My name is Rachel.'

Wednesday 21 May

A normal day at school, but afterwards, Elizabeth came around to practise our routine for the school show (not long now). We're doing 'Making your mind up' by Bucks Fizz. This was Mrs Bristow's idea. It's a great song, but it's not easy to dance to. It feels like we have spent weeks trying to learn all the steps and we are still making mistakes. Mum came upstairs to see how we were getting on and she said it looked OK, but both Elizabeth and I know that we can do it better. Practice makes perfect they say.

Oh, and only a few days to go before I'm 11. Can't wait!

Chapter 19

Rachel. The name and her face barely left his thoughts as they made their way back across northern Lincolnshire in the darkness. Even Bragg's desultory silence as they pedalled wearily along uneven surfaces affected him less than it might have done on any other occasion.

'You didn't say her name was Rachel,' Varro ventured at one point.

'I didn't know.'

'You didn't ask her?'

'There was no need.'

The boy might have been tired, Varro conceded, but his reaction was more likely to have been dissatisfaction – what he wanted from Rachel had plainly not been possible that evening. And piqued jealousy. That Varro had seamlessly established a rapport without trying was an affront to the adonis. Varro was caught between feeling sorry for the lad and letting him stew in his own juices, and it was only as they approached the lights of the small hamlet where they had left the glider that Bragg started to emerge from the dog mood he had fallen into.

'You can turn on your #amic now, Varro,' he said as they wheeled their cycles across the dewy grass of the outer field towards the glider whose carapace reflected the lights which floated 100 metres above them.

'Any chance of a lift back?' Varro speculated as they approached the glider. It was well past midnight and Varro had little appetite for catching the public transport again. It wasn't much out of the way for Bragg, though Varro wondered if the will was there.

'Don't want to get a runner, then?' said Bragg. His tone was neutral.

'Not if I have a swifter alternative. It's pretty late, after all.'

Under the wide brimmed hat which Bragg had worn as disguise, the young man's face was lost in shadow. Maybe it was no bad thing that Varro couldn't see his expression. After a moment too long, Bragg grunted his agreement, and the two men stacked the bicycles against an old wooden slatted shed before allowing themselves to be pulled up into the glistening glider.

There was something eerie about Bragg's withdrawal, and as they flew back Varro tried to tease out some of the lad's more normal, robust character. Asking about his next appointment at the parlours, enquiring where he was going to follow the World Forum, just keeping things light. As they crossed the Humber, just to the west of the old bridge, Varro even began pointing out many of the places he knew well from his roving days of youth. The waning moon had recently risen and in conjunction with the luminescence from the shoreline agglomerations, it was not difficult to make out features of the landscape below.

'Look,' cried Varro at one point, 'see that area covered in trees, it looks flat from here, but in fact it's an old quarry. I used to play there when I was younger. I'd squirt down the sides of it on my bum. Great fun.'

But Bragg wasn't in the mood, and by the time the craft dropped noiselessly adjacent to the uni-k station closest to Varro's home, they had spent a number of minutes in silence. Varro didn't want to leave it like that and as he prepared himself for release, he turned to the younger man who was staring resolutely ahead.

'Thanks for tonight, Bragg. I appreciate it.'

'Yeah, well, I'm glad you got what you wanted. Catch up soon.'

'Yes, of course.'

Then Varro turned away and was dropped to the ground, the sudden rush of air cool and fresh against his face. The evening was over.

FRIDAY

Even though the obligation to follow the World Forum meant a shorter working day, Varro still spent much of it in a trance, fuelled by a few hours' sleep and beguiled by the ripples of the previous night. He didn't so much play the conversation through as bathe in the aurora of it, something which the memory of Bragg's sour mood and the discipline of the working day could do little to dispel. He didn't even give a thought as to what Karena had made of his 2am return.

Unlike exactly a week previously, there was little exceptional about his day's labour other than one descent to check on a tiller which had ceased functioning. Varro had barely set his feet on the wet earth than he heard the lifeless words of CebAux 3.8.43 informing him that the problem was related to the machine's internal programming and had been resolved externally. While Varro had waited for the machine to reboot he took the sharp air coming down from the Dales deep into his lungs, closed his eyes and thought himself far away from where he was, carried there on the glow of a creature called Rachel.

It was only when he returned home, the low afternoon sun returning long shadows to any prominence, that he caught up with himself. Maybe it was the thought of facing Karena which acted like cold water over him. They had barely uttered a word to each other that morning, both focussed on their workday trajectories, yet now there could be no such excuse. Why had she made nothing of his late return, completely out of character as it was? Was she simply not bothered? As he paused in the outer porch of the house, noting the clinical smell of the interior, he decided to try to continue as normal. He would deny nothing but neither would he choose to offer information. If his nocturnal sojourn was of no interest to her, he would just keep it to himself.

'How was your day?' he said, coming into the kitchen to find her with her back towards him trying to find something in an open cupboard.

'Fine,' she replied without turning. 'And yours?'

'Unspectacular. No run ins with any non-cons this time,' he added. But Karena didn't reply, instead continuing to shift containers in the microlit interior. Varro could feel her frustration as she thrust the small metallic containers to one side.

'Are you looking for anything special?'

'No,' she said, and Varro waited for her to continue. Conversations like this were commonplace. He tried again.

'Where are you going to attend the World Forum?' he asked.

'In my room.'

'Do you want to be together?' he asked gently. 'Talking it could be fun.'

'No, Varro. I want to get it over with. I've got things to do afterwards. You're always replaying parts and it's so slow.'

'Right.'

Varro recalled when the two of them had curled up together in the front room and shared #amics to attend the World Forums. Occasionally laughing at the so serious cerebellums, at other times debating together what questions they should send out.

But the questions had long since dried up and they had separated their viewing. She wanted a life of pleasure, and as long as the cebs made that possible, why add to life's challenges? Everyone knew that the cerebellums governed in the best interests of all, there was no need to pore over the details.

If it was up to Karena, attending the Forums would be optional. But that was impossible. World Forum attendance via one's #amic was a non-negotiable for ONE. People had rights. But they also had responsibilities, and chief amongst those was being aware of what and how decisions were made on their behalf. Democracy could only be direct if people were involved and active. And those who thought they could just zone out whilst watching stood little chance of ratifying any decisions afterwards. Ratification, as even the youngest

160

citizen knew, arrived courtesy of one's #amic, questions about the World Forum carefully tailored for age and intellectual ability. Ratification was a polite name for it, but everybody knew it was a test. Fail the test and you would have to swallow the whole Forum again. This time with Civic's big eyes on you. And a further ratification. Test.

In the end he went to the front room, by himself. He had no idea where Karena had disappeared to. The children, he knew, would be upstairs, sealed within their cubicles. Approaching 3pm, Varro lay down on the low-lying recliner and asked his #amic to dim the lighting. He could have followed proceedings on the surround installation, but he was happy to let his #amic project the whole thing onto his inner eye. Varro always took a private delight in the thought that across the entire planet at this precise moment, citizens of all kinds were doing the same thing; fussing, busying themselves and shuffling into position, just as he was, nudged on by bossy #amics with their steady countdown.

Leaning back and supporting himself on one elbow Varro looked into the empty space of the room and waited for his vision to transmute into the live coverage of the half yearly event. He had given up expecting any novelty in proceedings. Democracy was a serious business, not something for gimmicks, and the split screen configuration which appeared before Varro very much reflected this old school attitude. A strain of formality ran through ceb rule, and this came directly from ONE. The leader had never fully freed himself, or wanted to, from his learning and intrinsic conservatism. What for some looked like shackles of tradition were for ONE eternal precepts of good governance and, as a result, the World Forums were like meetings from the past, with a chairperson dictating who should speak and for how long, cutting in and stopping one speaker, enabling another.

Before him, Varro's vision divided into four distinct quadrants. To the top left, a representation of the Earth itself, slowly spinning on its axis. As each of the 12 regions of the world spoke, the corresponding area on the map lit up. When ONE uttered anything, the whole planet pulsed. To Varro, the ceb's voice sounded like the booming of some omnipotent deity from the days when traditional religion held sway. A voice of authority. By contrast, the voices of the twelve were programmed to be an amalgam of accent, pitch, gender of that region's population. More neutral, sexless almost, and with none of the stentorian tones which came with the top cerebellum.

Below the rotating globe was a space for moving images depicting whatever notion was being discussed. The northeast quadrant delivered the transcription of proceedings, a throwback Varro realised to a time when the written word held as much sway as audio and visual stimuli. Most people ignored it, but Varro enjoyed following the latinised Panparl script. The remaining quarter was his area; real time editing, note taking and, most important, question forming. Here a user could react to the information he was receiving, confident that his or her question would be instantly transcribed and held in readiness for subsequent revision and, if the user really felt it was a worthy contribution, something which could be pinged to the cebs in an instant after the Forum. Answers would be received within a few hours.

"Dear Citizen Varro, thank you for your contribution to the World Forum. Regarding your criticism of the increasingly limited opportunities to use English for those who want to, it was felt that there continue to be ample opportunities to practise dialogue with one's #amic in private, and that the extension of a universal language in Panparl brings significant wider benefits to society. It was also felt that…"

"Dear Citizen Varro, thank you for your contribution to the World Forum. We have noted your frustration about the rate of urban expansion in the Yorkshire area and your comments will be added to the existing strain of concern expressed by similar citizens which has grown by 33.4% over the last five years, but it was also felt that the perceived inconveniences of further accommodation has to be balanced against the rights of an increasing populace to live in dignified and healthy surroundings. To this extent…"

"Dear Citizen Varro, thank you for your contribution to the World Forum. Your idea for enhancing knowledge amongst the young of primitive farming methods was considered of significant interest and will be taken forward for further investigation by the Education directory. Providing young people with…"

Cynics continued to think it was a way to fob off citizens and, in reality, there was little way to really investigate the efficacy of the feedback. But occasionally things did change, mainly for the better, and as a result the whole process, and cerebellum rule, felt a little more legitimate.

Varro listened now as the globe throbbed like a beating heart and ONE intoned gravely his introduction. '*Citizens of the world and fellow cerebellums, I welcome you to the 388th World Forum and look forward to using this occasion to once again fulfil our promise to afford you the best government possible. I would like to begin by…*'

Varro wasn't long in drifting away, losing the parts of the quartered screen and mentally bringing up an image of Rachel from the previous evening, sat smiling beside him, knees almost touching and that delicate scent of clean lavender which he had grown aware of every time she swayed in her seat. He tried to explain to himself what it was about her that had upended his thoughts throughout the day, but there were no obvious answers, just a sense of utter zest, an intense life spirit that seeped from her like squeezed honeycomb. She reminded him of his recent find, the girl in the diary, she too possessed a roving spirit that spoke of senses attuned on multiple levels. The discovery of all this startled him.

ONE had finished his address and had invited the 12 regional cebs to provide updates on notable developments in their jurisdictions. AUSTRALIA was narrating a successful commissioning of a massive vapour plant in southern Queensland, giant machines which trawled the air for water, extracting the precious liquid before blowing the desiccated air back into the atmosphere. Varro made a lazy mental note of it before returning to the previous evening.

He had been surprised at how freely conversation had flowed, and unlike so often with strangers, he hadn't felt protective about details of his private life; his pilot's job, grandparents and even his orphan status, and when he reran the conversation, he realised that her curiosity had been feathered with tact, holding back when she felt she had gone too deeply. Maybe he had responded in the way he had because of how real her interest felt – so often in his encounters the questions were just for form, but he had sensed her curiosity as a hunger. Wholly unlike the listless, lazy questioning of one's #amic.

Varro dragged himself back to the floating screens before him. A ceb, presumably one of the directory leaders, was updating the Forum about exploration of space. Normally it was a topic which interested.

'The community of 54 voyagers on Wolf 1061C has been commuted. Loss of life, 5. Conditions were felt to be too rigorous, with the solar wind producing inimical effect on individuals' vital functions. In the absence of alternative habitable exoplanet communities within practicable distance, the voyagers will assume cryo-status and return to earth. Their relations have been informed.

More promising is the Pioneer Mission to the Ross 128 system, constellation Virgo. Expectations reported in World Forum 387 have been upheld and several exo-planets within the system possess generous habitable zones and are likely to be able sustain human subsistence in the longer term. This is particularly the case with Ross 128d.'

Varro looked closely as consecutive images of plants with enormous khaki leaves swaying in breezes were followed by expanses of black water stretching to where a sun like star hung low on the horizon.

'The voyagers here will continue to need oxygen supplements during their sleep for the foreseeable future, but climate engineering teams feel that there is potential to engineer a permanent planet wide solution to provide more oxygen sufficient for humans to survive. For the present we will continue to extract electrolysed oxygen from the plentiful water supply.

Away from exoplanets, our dark energy harvesters continue to operate successfully beyond the Kuiper Belt and we expect to launch our 250GW harvester within the next three months. This will enable us...'

He couldn't deny there was an element of desire. He could see why Bragg had succumbed; the dress, had held the shape of her body, and her body still held its youth. That Bragg with his cavalier treatment had gone beyond this was a source of resentment which had sprung from nowhere and hadn't abated during the day. But there was also something more comprehensive, something beyond his base instincts, something he hadn't succumbed to for many years. It had left him energised and expectant.

Bragg returned his attention to the Forum where ONE was speaking again.

'...and earlier this year I signalled to The Twelve my intention to bring forward my enhancement date to ensure my functioning and decision making remain at their optimum. We are aware that with this proposal there is a risk of moving away from precedent, but this has to be weighed against the realities of the current situation and the ever-increasing demands upon my capabilities. I am grateful to The Twelve for their favourable initial response to this suggestion and welcome any comments from citizens themselves.'

Varro imagined their next meeting. In his version, he was alone with Rachel in an environment not far removed from this very room with its comfort recliner and cosy warmth, he wore his smartest clothes and subtle but potent scents rose from his freshly scrubbed body, while she was as alluring as his reveries had transformed her. But it was impossible to sustain the vision; how was he to rid himself of Bragg and his intermediary role, and what of the oleaginous property owner in Brigg? The logistics of an alternative meeting felt insurmountable. Varro didn't even have a way of contacting her.

In the background to his reverie, Varro could see that EUROPE had taken the floor, but the cerebellum's words came from far away.

'We are grateful to ONE, as always, for allowing us the chance to reflect on this proposal and its departure from precedent, and we

consider it a sign of ONE's continuing munificence and wisdom in sharing this proposal with us and the world's citizens. ONE is correct to state that we view with some sympathy this proposal, keenly aware as we are that ONE must balance the ever increasing demands on his capabilities with the resources which will allow that. Like the sun itself, ONE's enveloping and warm oversight above us all must have sufficient fuel and resources to continue to perform at its peak, especially if, like the sun, he will shine brighter as a result. No recourse to external stimuli should be required for a being with such endowments. But, and no doubt ONE is fully aware of this, if it is to the sun we turn our eyes, we must remember that every sun must set, the day must end and preparations for the next day begin, not at night in darkness when we can see little, but during the preceding day itself. There is no shame in this process, only glory, a glory in which the sun sinking into the western horizon, is aware of, but reconciled to its waning forces and impact upon the world – a world which is already busy preparing for the following day, but not before it has taken a final look at the majesty of the setting sun, bringing to crimson life exquisite strata of cloud, its final display a fitting tribute to its whole life, transfixing all those who can only but look on and admire. And even after our celestial orb has vanished off the edge of the world, it still continues to shed light on the lives of those citizens who remain. Still allowing others to understand and see clearly until long after it has departed the scene…'

Varro snapped forward.

'#amic, play last section again.'

'How many seconds, Varro?' replied his #amic.

'20, come on, quickly!'

In an instant, Varro heard EUROPE's slightly contrarian voice concluding his speech and as he did so Varro, now fully alert, felt shards freezing the full length of his body. The words. His words. An exact replica of his minister application, yet here they were now, a full paragraph almost, spilling from the neuronal pulp which was the second most powerful authority of the planet. And only a fool could misinterpret the message behind the analogy. This was not open debate. This was criticism. Almost a threat. To ONE, the leader of the world. And it was being done with Varro's words.

It's nearly dinner time, so I'm sorry that this will only be a short entry. But now, it's official, I am 11 years old and we had my party today. All the girls from the class except Emily came (she was at a tennis tournament) and from the boys there were Stephen and Jack, and Lewis (of course). Daniel was there, too but he was a bit of pain. Before lunch we did races – Dad had set up an obstacle course around the garden (and he even squirted us with water) so we did an obstacle race, then a sack race, egg and spoon race (but Jack cheated) and a normal running race. Then we had lunch and Mummy even let us have Coca-Cola. Then everyone gave me their presents and Mummy and Daddy gave me a pair of roller skates. They're the ones that strap to the bottom of your shoes but Michaela says that real roller skates are boots which have the wheels attached to them. She says that she has a pair. But I don't care because I love the ones I got and have been using them all afternoon.

After lunch we played some dressing up games, then pass the parcel and Mum helped us stop and start the music while Daddy was chatting with some of the mums who had come to pick up their children. I don't think Mum was happy with….Oh, sorry, must go now, Mum's just called me down to dinner. GREAT DAY!

Chapter 20

Yìchén Huáng waited patiently inside the control room for the World Forum to conclude, standing still in front of the live feed which was being shared to the world's citizens.

He had heard variations of this valediction many times before; ONE thanking the regional cebs for their ongoing oversight, praising the directors for their steadfast work, and expressing his gratitude to the global community of citizens for their continuing support and contributions. A perfect society, ONE ended by reminding them, was an impossibility, but a constant striving towards it was a worthy aspiration to hold.

Nebulous and lofty stuff, and with ONE's measured but moving delivery, aided by halcyon visuals and an adornment of strings which had crept into the feed, the Forum was seen to end on a high. It was, as Yìchén Huáng reflected, unapologetic theatre and certainly not to everyone's taste, but ONE insisted on it.

But Yìchén Huáng had long since learnt to ignore the superficialities which accompanied the Forum's conclusion. A distraction for the weak minded. Instead, he honed all his efforts towards sound, listening with rapacious attention to the subtle modulations in ONE's voice, the tremors and vibrations he had spent a lifetime trying to interpret. And so, as he entered the inner arena, making his way carefully up the narrow walkway before settling into unhurried circuits of the ring, Yìchén Huáng already knew what to expect, and ONE's seething words came as no surprise.

'Waning forces, waning forces! Where does EUROPE think he is going with this?'

'The same question had occurred to me,' replied Yìchén Huáng calmly into the semi darkness, his pace measured and his eyes cast impassively forwards. ONE appeared not to have heard him.

'Does he honestly think I am so decrepit that I need to be replaced? How far down the horizon does he think I am? Or am I below it already, my rays drooping like a eunuch's cock?'

ONE only used such colourful language when he was really exercised, and only with his guardian. Yìchén Huáng paused before answering. Keeping a lid on emotions was key – his father had told him that the cerebellums worked best when they were not prey to base human emotions.

'Maybe EUROPE is just trying to speak truth to power, raising difficult questions before they become too critical. Maybe your update is an opportunity to do this.'

'Is that what you really believe, Yìchén Huáng?'

It wasn't, but Yìchén Huáng wasn't going to reveal this, and ONE continued.

'The Twelve agreed in principle to my early update. Where were such objections back then? Why raise them now, spreading them out like dirty washing in front of our public?'

'Maybe EUROPE felt a certain protection in front of a wider audience. Doing it at the Forum was a way of forcing our hand.'

'Forcing our hand to do what?'

Yìchén Huáng again took his time to reply. ONE's reaction was bordering on the hysterical, a thing of weakness. Yìchén Huáng couldn't imagine the ONE of his youth reacting in such a way. It was another worrying sign.

'I think it is important at this moment to be calm. EUROPE's views about time and succession are legitimate concerns. We need to consider them seriously. It was to this that I was referring recently when I talked about the unsettled nature of The Twelve. Your future is their future, and the world's – it is only natural that there is unease. I suggest that we continue to work carefully and quietly on our forward planning, focussing on a number of possible scenarios and putting plans in place to deal with them. As for any immediate response, I shall allow you time to give it some reflection and then I will return shortly to discuss. I, too, will give this matter the highest priority.'

'Thank you, Yìchén Huáng, not for the first time your wisdom does you credit. I look forward to hearing your conclusions.'

Yìchén Huáng walked smartly back along the high-level passageway, leaving the ceb with only the pitter-patter echo of his pigeon steps in the mute dome. He had done his best, but it was impossible to say how mollified the irate ceb really was. As the door to the control room slid closed behind him, Yìchén Huáng looked over to his daughter who hadn't turned away from the bank of instruments and screens in front of her. It was she who would ultimately have to pick up the tab on all this when he had turned to dust. She would be ONE's next guardian, and now Yìchén Huáng was concerned with what had been left unsaid in his brief tête-à-tête with the world's supreme leader; that the balance of power was shifting and ONE's authority and final veto was being openly challenged in a way, however subtle, which it had never been before. The jibe at 'external stimuli' said as much, and Yìchén Huáng wondered how the other ceb had known about ONE's boosts. Or maybe he just suspected it. Either way, they were heading into uncharted territory. Dangerous territory, and where it would end, no one could say.

It was important to re-establish the status quo. The ideal situation would have been to speak to the other guardians, his counterparts for each of The Twelve. But it was an unwritten rule that such things were seldom, if ever, done. It would be another way to undermine a ceb's authority.

Yìchén Huáng noticed his daughter had turned to face him, smiling but silent. She was so composed, with her raven black hair and neat features which crumpled and softened when they took him in but remained alert and disciplined on all other occasions. At 35 she was reaching the peak of her powers and would make a fine guide for the World's leader. He wondered whether he should take her back into the dome when he returned.

Not that he had any clear idea what he would say to the ceb. For that he needed to think. He shifted over to the corner of the room and sank down slowly into the chair, replaying EUROPE's intervention in his mind. He had no need for any reminders to replay the contents – they had stuck where they first landed. But something wasn't right about them. The style, the phrasing, it belied a style, meditative and thoughtful, which was at odds with EUROPE's occasionally abrasive and forthright approach. Had the ceb really invented them or had they been plucked from somewhere else? And where?

'Xinyu, are you sure there was no trace from existing sources of EUROPE's words?'

'Yes, very sure.'

'How far back did you go?'

'The RI banks purged all known literature, from Sumerian myths of 40 centuries ago right up until the most recent holo-reels. There were many similar sentiments, but the wording appears to be unique. Why do you doubt that the words come from EUROPE? A ceb of its dimensions has more than enough capacity to concoct a careful selection of words with enough allusion to be obvious but not explicit.'

'It is not EUROPE's capacity I doubt, more its inclination. The words are somewhat out of character.'

'As is any attack, however subtle, on ONE's fitness for governance.'

'The unsaid doubts of The Twelve have been building. I have felt it in recent forums and our regular liaisons. Suggestions for debate, responses, developments in their jurisdictions, all these and more have come accompanied with pinpricks of aggression, all under the guise of strong decision making. I think ONE has picked up on it, too, but hasn't wanted to accept it as such. To do so would be to create something that formerly wasn't.'

'Are the actual words EUROPE used so important then, surely it is the sentiment that they express which we must tackle?'

'You are right. In themselves, the words mean nothing, and it maybe just my curiosity, but I am keen to see what we are dealing with. If the source is extrinsic to EUROPE there may be more to come. It would be best to be prepared.'

'What about trawling every word from all the #amic feeds?'

'Across all time? Are you serious, Xinyu?'

'No, sorry, you are right, there would be far too much information.'

'Yes, there would be, even for our quantum RI units.'

'What about digital content from the age of the Internet onwards? Motion films, early videos, immersive reality chops, #amic shares? That would be possible.'

'Yes, it would be,' Yìchén Huáng spoke slowly, then stopped, caught in silence. His daughter waited patiently. Her father was deep in thought. 'And yet such a search would have taken significant processing, even for EUROPE and even with RI aid. Patience has never been its greatest virtue. No, if there is a source for this material, it is more immediate, something which EUROPE has come across recently.'

'Many of EUROPE's feeds are particular to its jurisdiction. For others our information is only partial. There is much we wouldn't be able to check.'

'Yes, I appreciate that, but run a search on all those feeds which EUROPE shares automatically with ONE. Over the last year; Civic, Commerce, Patrimony, Research, all the other relevant directories.'

'The last year will take some time.'

'How long?'

'24 hours, maybe more, there is much information. All the directories with their messages, reports, research, meetings, not to mention the liaisons and notifications from The Twelve themselves.'

'Alright, work backwards from today, this week, then this month and to the year. Most recent first. Strain for meditative rather than technological. Emotive, as well. Then we will see.'

'I will begin right away.'

'Good, well-done, Xinyu.'

Yìchén Huáng leant forwards, rested his elbows on both knees and brought his clasped hands together under his chin. He allowed himself the thinnest trace of a smile as he watched his daughter set about her task, quietly ordering her #amic and manipulating the air in front of her with grace and speed. She was a source of great satisfaction.

Thirty minutes later, much to both their surprise, Yìchén Huáng had his answer. It took a further ten minutes to pass into the inner sanctum and relay his findings to ONE, and within the hour the pair had discussed, and agreed, their response. Neither had demurred on the fundamentals of the plan, and as he did a final circuit of the bamboo railed ring, Yìchén Huáng allowed himself an inner smile.

'Thank you, Yìchén Huáng, you have been most useful. As always.' ONE said, summing up their meeting. Yìchén Huáng thought he could almost hear the satisfaction in ONE's voice.

Aunty Jean (that's Mum's sister) and Uncle Tony came down from York today and we went out for lunch with them to a pub to celebrate my birthday (we had a carvery). I wanted to take my roller skates but Mum wouldn't let me so we ended up just sitting in the pub with them and the adults talking. Well, Tony talking mainly about their new house in York and mortgages and insurance and other things that I didn't really understand. Daniel was really annoying as well. In the car on the way back home, Mum said she wants to visit their new house, but Dad just said he didn't want to hear Uncle Tony going on about house prices and 'the market' anymore. I don't think Mum was very happy about that. But Uncle Tony is very different to Dad.

Chapter 21

B ragg took a uni-k shuttle for the short trip down to the European Agriculture complex. He had barely leant back into cushioned travel space when he was interrupted by his #amic alerting him to a chat request from a number of girls further along the carriage. Bragg glanced down the open interior with irritation and saw them giggling amongst themselves. One of them broke cover from the gaggle and looked directly towards him. Mid-teens probably, and on a good day Bragg might have entertained a wave or sent them something more risqué via his #amic. But now he just looked away, uninterested, and cursed himself for not adjusting the transparency settings on his #amic. He pulled up the screen in front of him and with a series of swift hand movements narrowed his availability to its lowest setting, instructing his #amic to block any future enquiries. That included the girls.

He just wasn't in the mood. He had slept little, and what he had managed was shot through with the lingering sense of inadequacy from the previous night's encounter. Initially he had been happy to see Varro's enjoyment. They were only exchanging words, nothing more, and he had already obtained the real prize. His friend was welcome to this consolation. But it hadn't taken long before he realised that their absorption was deeper, more complete than anything he had elicited from her, and while he was prepared to hover on the edge of the conversation, he hadn't expected complete exclusion. That hurt. That took him back. To a time when he seemed to do nothing else but try to prove himself. He thought he had buried that part of him, but events like the previous night were a jagged reminder that he would never be free. Part of him knew it wasn't fair to blame Varro for all this, but the litany of insufficiencies had still followed him home and into sleep.

The World Forum had done little to lighten his mood. The obligation had always been an onerous one, but following the transmission through the remnants of his fatigue and foul humour made the occasion even more wearisome, and each answer of ratification was spat out for his #amic to feed back.

And now CebAux 3.8.43 wanted to see him, urgently. Starting his shift early to satisfy whatever facile whim had swept over the vapid ceb was not likely to improve his mood, and Bragg couldn't be sure how he would react if the creature had summoned him only to show off his latest outfit or blabber about their next visit. In truth, the ceb was becoming tiresome. Bragg had been happy to oblige with a couple of favours, it was a small price to pay for the shorter shifts and blind eyes the unit was prepared to throw his way in return. But now Bragg wondered where the ceb's childish appetites would take them both. He certainly didn't want to have to suffer the fashion show prelude every time he met a girl from now on. But that was how it was looking.

The wind had risen when Bragg left the uni-k station, and he ordered his #amic to tighten the seals on the monosuit as he walked the short distance to Euro Agri 43. With the evenings closing in, it felt like winter was almost upon them, a period of the year Bragg always associated with gloom and collapsing horizons. An end to summer freedoms.

He was surprised to find the meeting room completely empty when he arrived, only the sparse furnishings of a simple table and chair, both made from the same anonymous white plastic. He hoped the ceb wasn't playing games with him.

'I thought you wanted to see me,' he said flatly into the silence of the room. Behind him the door slid shut and Bragg heard the echoing voice of the ceb.

'Sit down and don't say a thing.'

Bragg didn't appreciate the abrupt nature of the order. 'Look, if you're going to be like that, I'm going to…'

'Take me to the Blue Flamingo club. Tonight.'

'Sorry? You want to…'

'Yes, right now, this moment, take me there. You said it is your favourite parlour. Just take me there. Please!'

The request was as extraordinary as the ceb's fevered delivery. Bragg cast his eyes down at the beige floor and took a few moments to compose himself.

'43, I have to start my shift. You know I'm due to begin work shortly.'

'I'll take care of your feed, I'll cover for you, like before. But I must go. Just for a few hours. I've never been before and I'd really like to show myself. Maybe you can find a couple of girls for us?'

'A couple of girls?'

'Please, Bragg. I'll do anything you ask.'

The idea of not working was attractive, especially tonight in his jaded, melancholy state, but this request stemmed from desperation, not desire. Something had unhinged the auxiliary cerebellum in a big way and Bragg was keen to know what it was before he went any further. He continued looking down and began tapping one foot on the ground, the sound sharp in the featureless room. When he finally spoke he made it as casual as he could.

'No, I don't think so. Some other time maybe, I'm tired after last night. I just want to get my shift over, then go home.'

An eerie silence descended and Bragg wondered if the ceb had heard him, but nothing could have prepared him for the creature's response.

'Then unplug me.'

'What?'

'If you're not going to take me to the parlour, I want you to unplug me.'

'You mean terminate you? Why would I do that?'

'Because if I don't do this then life is not worth living. That's why. And because I'm asking you to. Don't deny me this request, Bragg.'

Bragg was flabbergasted.

'Listen, even if I was to agree to do what you say, how am I supposed to get past security? I don't even know where you're locked away in this building.'

'I'll get you past security. Just do as I say. You can do it now. Come on.'

Bragg let out a low whistle and scratched the back of his neck. He certainly hadn't been expecting this when he walked through the doors of Euro Agri 15 minutes previously. But the ceb's heighted emotional state worried him. A ceb committing suicide was not unknown, but extremely rare – a once in a generation event, a sign that latency has gone badly wrong. Bragg knew this ceb was excitable, but from that to self-destruction. He needed to know more.

'Is something the matter, 43? That's a serious thing you're asking me to do. Where's all this come from?'

'I can't say.'

'Can't or won't?'

'Take me with you to the Blue Flamingo and I'll tell you.'

'That sounds like blackmail,' said Bragg with a wry grin.

'It is what it is.'

Bragg thought about it. The Blue Flamingo was the most popular parlour in York, the place to see and be seen, its scenarios were the most original in the north of England and was like a magnet for the most popular youth for miles around. The ceb had probably seen virtual reproductions of it but never dreamt he could materialise there. Bragg realised that with the ceb in hand he would have to reserve a special room, and acquiring two girls was always more of a challenge than the single assignation. But with helpings of charm and a wad of dits, it would be possible. He just hoped the ceb's revelation, whatever it was, was worth it.

'Alright, I'll take you. But you promise to cover for me?'

'Of course, I'll pre-input your activity now. For all intents and purposes, you'll be out spraying Coletezine over the Trent valley.'

'Good.'

'How long do you think it will take you before you are ready?'

'I need to change. 30 minutes to get there and then I'll need to get set up – I can't just share you into the middle of the arena, we'll need somewhere discreet.'

'Yes, of course, but how long will that take?' the ceb said hurriedly.

'Probably another 30 minutes, depending if I can get a double dose of interest. You did say a couple of girls, didn't you?'

'Yes, yes, two girls, in their twenties if you can, same age as me.'

'OK.'

'And then we'll be like two men on a double date together, won't we?' said the ceb, warming to his theme.

'Exactly.'

'And you won't forget to share me in as soon as you're ready.'

'When we're all in place, I'll share you in. Don't worry.'

'Oh wonderful. I can hardly wait.' The ceb almost squealed in delight and Bragg almost regretted his next question.

'And then you'll tell me what all this haste is about?'

'Yes, yes,' said the ceb sombrely. 'Then I'll tell you.'

Saturday 31 May

I'm writing this in the morning, but last night we were invited around to Mr Bennett's house. Mr Bennett lives 2 houses away from us, further down the road, and Mum was talking to him and mentioned that Daniel is learning about planets and the solar system (we did this 2 years ago, too) so he invited all of us to look through his telescope. So, after dinner, me, Mum and Daniel (Dad was late from work again) walked down to his house. Mrs Bennett opened the door and gave us Coca-Cola and Mummy had a cup of tea and talked with her (about our school syllabus). Then Mr Bennett took us to a special room he has for looking at the sky. It's got a special window which he pulls open and he points his telescope from. At first, I couldn't see anything even when he told me where to look, but then I saw Saturn and you could clearly see its rings around it. Daniel said he even saw one of the moons and Mr Bennett said that was probably Titan. It was amazing to think we were looking at another planet, and Mr Bennett even said that we might see a human land on Saturn or Titan during our lifetimes, but he would be 'long gone' by that time. I think I would like to go to the moon one day.

Chapter 22

Friday night and the Blue Flamingo was heavy with people and expectation. The regular beat of the music rose gradually as Bragg walked down the long entrance corridor, reaching a crescendo when he arrived at the central arena. From here he could see all around, to the entrances to further corridors which branched out from the central area like an old-fashioned cartwheel. Along each themed corridor lay the rooms in which clients could satiate themselves on whatever scenario they chose and with whoever was willing to join them on their flight of fancy. And the choice was wide. Directly across from where he stood lay the History corridor. There you could bathe with Cleopatra, play your part in a Greco-Roman bacchanal, be entertained at a Tudor party, flaunt yourself like a Medici or dally at the court of Louis XIV. The extra-large immersive cubicles, well-chosen props and #amics inputting sophisticated visual and audio overlays, all meant that a beguiling realism was readily achieved. Regular changes kept pleasure seekers coming back for more.

Other corridors offered more pleasures; the Character corridor was set up with everything you might need to dominate, or submit, or beg, or simply be demure and wait for your reward. The Location corridor took you to whichever outpost of the world it was your whim to visit, while the Exotic and Special Corridors were more than happy to cater to those souls looking for something beyond the conventional. As he stood on the threshold of the arena, a number of memorable encounters along these thirsty thoroughfares came back to him unbidden. Bragg smiled wryly at the memories.

But it was not for tonight. Now, he was mindful of the mission the ceb had assigned him. He took a moment to assess his plan. The complex was set on a number of levels, a series of concentric circles not unlike the Roman colosseum, each strata with its own purpose. At the centre of the arena was a large area for dance, the music down there hypnotic and all enveloping. Bragg looked at the straining bodies, twisting and turning, and around them the colour dancers, slithers of coloured light in human form, their artificial bodies shimmering and sliding like sunlit water over rocks in a stream. Dance close enough to them and you'd receive a static charge which pained and invigorated in equal measure. In amongst all of these were the players, workers from the parlour who, for a few dits, would play their role for you; Greek God, Forest Nymph, Desert Island Girl, Miss Tough, Mr Slow; Bragg recognised a few he had scened with before.

He made his way down a level, taking measured steps on the wide staircase, carefully surveying the scene on the promenade, an expansive thoroughfare which overhung the dancefloor. With your #amic primed with your evening's desires, this was the place to assess and be assessed, and when he reached the walkway, Bragg began his work. He didn't so much walk as strut, shoulders thrust back and head tossed high with a self-conceited grin which was never out of place here. It was a well-worn pose, and Bragg knew he would be hard to resist.

He was right. Within 10 minutes his #amic was whispering into his ear to look to the right, across the central space. Bragg turned his head slowly and waited for his #amic to overlay an identification onto the girls who had shown an interest in his proposal. 40 metres distant, he saw them smile in recognition of the contact. They were significantly older than him, and even at a distance Bragg could tell that they were no beauties, their heavy make-up suggested protection as well as attraction, while their drab monosuits were clearly remnants of past seasons' fashions. They were crude caricatures of good taste in this place, and ordinarily he might have snubbed them, but now he smiled broadly.

'Tell them I'm coming over,' he ordered.

Bragg suppressed the temptation to turn away as he approached. The taller of the two rose as he drew closer and Bragg's attention was drawn to the where the tight fabric of the sleeveless monosuit pinned her armpit, the swelling flesh quickly giving way to limp skin which reminded Bragg of raw dough. Her enhanced lips spread across the bottom of her face like a gorge into the underworld. Bragg forced a smile then turned to the other one, but was disconcerted to see that despite her best efforts an unruly eye roved around in its effort to find him. Neither of them tried to mask their covetous glances along the full length of his young body. Bragg shrugged. They might not exactly be what the ceb had requested, but they would have to do. He had done his best.

'Shall we go somewhere quieter, ladies?' he asked after he had found out their names.

'Why not?' cackled the taller lady.

'A booth or a room?'

Although he was in a hurry, Bragg didn't want to be too presumptuous. A drink in a booth was a traditional element of the night's entertainment, an hors d'oeuvres before the more sumptuous main course, and he wasn't displeased when they requested a quick drink 'before business'. As they climbed back up a level, Bragg felt a nail run down the back of his thigh. He turned quickly to find the taller lady holding his gaze with merriment.

The booths were on the same level as the corridors but adjacent to the balcony which overlooked the whole complex. Simple composite table and chairs were enclosed in an invisible sound pocket, allowing the users the choice to cocoon themselves from the music rising from the dance floor or to let it permeate completely. He filled a couple of glasses of colourful liquid from the dispensers built into the table and then asked his #amic to request a private room. Then he addressed the ladies.

'How long shall we ask for the room for, girls?'

'How long do you normally take? Remember, there are two of us.'

Bragg attempted a smile at the challenge. 'I'll put it on indefinite for the time being.'

'Indefinite,' one of the girls stifled a giggle. 'Are we in for something special then, Mr Bragg?' she cooed.

'You'll have to wait and see,' Bragg replied airily. Under normal circumstances he might have enjoyed this brash flirtation, but with the driving music and the swirling lights his head had begun to ache. He wanted to get this necessary prelude over with as quickly as possible. They had sat either side of him and the bolder one had already nestled her palm into the crevice of his thigh, keeping it in place as she stared with mock defiance towards him. Bragg suspected they might have obtained some stupefacient before entering the parlour. He was just glad the ceb would be taking in everything Bragg was seeing. It would all be adding to the naïve creature's anticipation. It wasn't long before Bragg excused himself.

'Finish your drinks, girls, I'm just going to check the room is ready. Give it five minutes maybe. I'll call you.'

They were reluctant to let him go, and Bragg felt the resistance in his thigh as he pulled away. He threaded his way through the milling, jostling clientele, letting himself be guided by his #amic, until they came to the Comfort corridor. From here it didn't take long to arrive at the room he had taken. With no scenario to be played out, he had opted for something basic; a cream rococo chaise lounge beneath a mirrored ceiling, and a selection of toys which Bragg recognised as standard. Bragg took the small share box from his pocket and quickly activated the device. The auxiliary ceb appeared in an instant, sprung like a genie desperate for its freedom. Bragg tried not to react as he took the ceb in. This time the ceb had gone too far. The almost unbearably bright gilded latex costume was seamless from head to foot with wide shoulder pads like overhanging crags. His hair too was gold, pushed into a central mohican, which ran from his forehead to his nape. An inner ring of bright yellow ran inside the traditional kohl around each eye. As Bragg took this in, the uncontrollable ceb spread his arms wide, revealing beneath each a profusion of hanging golden threads which sparkled in the lights of the parlour. It reminded Bragg of an exotic bird from the southern hemisphere. It took all his energy to tear himself away from the absurd vision pulsating in front of him.

'Are you enjoying yourself then?' he asked.

'It's wonderful, Bragg, just wonderful. The colours, the lights, the people. What it must be like to waltz around in a real body down there.'

'And the girls, are you looking forward to seeing them?'

'Are they coming now?' asked the greedy ceb.

'Of course, just as soon as I ask them. Then you can show yourself.'

'Do you think they'll like what they see?'

'I imagine so.'

'You don't think I've overdone it?'

Bragg paused. It was important to choose his words carefully. The truth might close the ceb up completely.

'No, I think you'll come across really well. I'd be very surprised if they're not impressed.'

'Yes, yes, I've been thinking about this outfit for days. Are they on their way now?'

'Yes,' said Bragg slowly. 'And they'll be here for you just as soon as you explain what's got you all worked up. I was sorry to see you in such a way back at the station.'

'Yes, I know, but I'd rather not say. It's not important now.'

'CebAux 3.8.43, I'm concerned about you. And we had a deal, remember?'

'I remember, but that's not important now.'

'It is to me. A deal is a deal, and if you don't share your concern, or problem, or whatever it is with me, those girls are not going to be able to appreciate what a man you really are.'

Bragg looked calmly at the glowing ceb who returned his stare. The only sound in the room was the low static of the golden hologram.

'Ok, I'll tell you, but this information has to stay between the two of us, understood.'

'43, we already have a number of secrets which stay very firmly between the two of us.'

'Yes, I suppose you're right. Well, tonight, not long after the World Forum I had a request, well, more like an order, to surrender all my feeds of Ignatius Varro in the last six months.'

'Varro?'

'Yes.'

'Why?'

'How should I know? I just received the order and obeyed.'

'You obeyed?

'Of course.'

'Where did the order come from?'

'From the highest possible directorate. From ONE himself.'

'From ONE?' Bragg heard the word as something physical, a sharp, hard jab into his solar plexus. This changed everything. If ONE had access to Varro's feeds, Bragg would be there, too. Their meetings and loosely coded messages, the trip together to northern Lincolnshire, their simultaneous #amic black outs. Such information shared with Amicol, Civic, Patrimony or any other directorate would be bad enough. That ONE himself had specifically ordered its release was as much a sentence for him as for Varro. He felt himself lose any control of the muscles in his face, and now he understood why the ceb had reacted in the way he had. The ceb was as deeply immersed in the mess as the rest of them. All this was a last hurrah before it was disconnected. Terminated. But Bragg no longer cared about the soppy cerebellum, he needed to make plans, do something, and quickly. Maybe there was still a chance to save his skin, or at least some of it. He turned to the ceb.

'I'm disconnecting the share. It's over.'

'But why? They're going to disconnect me, Bragg. I'm going end up as compost, it's over for me after what I've done. Let me show myself for the last time. Please, Bragg,' cried the ceb whose face had collapsed on itself. 'Come on Bragg, a few minutes, that's all. Please! You owe this to me, Bragg.'

Bragg strode up to the desperate, blabbering creature, standing only inches away from the shimmering vision. 'I owe you nothing,' he said, and flicked the switch, and with a strangled cry the ceb folded and was gone.

<u>*Sunday 1 June*</u>

Sunday today and nothing special happened. In the morning Mum was doing some housework and Dad had taken Daniel to his football match in Scunthorpe. Mum wouldn't let me watch TV and I didn't want to read anything so I just sat in my bedroom thinking about things. It was a bit boring. Then I decided to go to the park and see if anyone else from my class was there (they weren't) and when I got there I started to play on the swings and slides and then I went onto the football pitch and twirled around a lot while looking up at the sky and then I fell down and watched the clouds spin all around me. I like doing this. When I got home Mum asked me to help her prepare lunch, which was fun because she was telling me about her dad and what they did together when she was younger. It's a pity that I didn't know Grandad better before he died. He sounds like a lot of fun and very clever. Then Dad and Daniel came back and we sat down together and had lunch and Daniel kept going on about the goal he scored, and even Dad says it was a great solo effort. So, in the end it was a good day.

Chapter 23

Yichén Huáng put his hand lightly on his daughter's shoulder and looked at the bank of screens in front of him, in particular the lateral and transversal scans of ONE, the coloured swirling of its incessant activity like a giddy oil painting. Silently he counted down the remaining seconds before the start of the emergency meeting which ONE had called for 10.30pm. Yìchén Huáng was surprised at the butterflies he felt churning his core. A lot was riding on the outcome of the next few minutes. Between them they had agreed a plan, but it still needed to be put into effect, and the reaction of the 12 regional cerebellums after the insinuations of the World Forum was unclear. He had chosen to follow the meeting through the internal monitors and now he remained absolutely motionless as ONE's solemn voice broke the silence in the control room.

'Firstly, I would like to offer my apologies to The Twelve for the extempore nature of this meeting. I appreciate that you will all have taken valuable time from your duties to join me. Nevertheless, I feel that the gravity of the situation demands such sacrifices.

'Earlier today, in the 388th World Forum, I once again outlined my plans to bring forward by a whole calendar year my decade long upgrade. This was not new news. There was nothing novel in this proposal and indeed, in previous iterations, I had reason to believe that there was broad acceptance from The Twelve for such a measure. At the Forum, I had expected similar levels of acquiescence. Indeed, I had hoped for a show of unanimity from The Twelve in front of those we profess to serve, our world's citizens. I was, however, mistaken. For in the discussion that followed, it appeared that the unanimity that I was confident of exhibiting in front of our populace was sadly missing, that, and maybe I go too far here, not only are their doubts from The Twelve about the need for my enhancement, but furthermore, there are uncertainties about my overall performance. That my ability to govern in the best interests of all humans is dwindling, that I am succumbing to failure, decrepitude and other pejorative effects of the ageing process. In layman's terms, that I am no longer up to the job.

'Maybe The Twelve will be horrified to hear me impute to them opinions which they either do not hold or which even the thought of maintaining is invidious. If this is the case, then I humbly beseech you to accept my apologies.

'On the other hand, if my thesis has some foundation in reality, if The Twelve, or individuals within, are beginning to harbour doubts about my suitability to continue to perform the tasks that I have faithfully and reliably been executing for well over two centuries, then I would encourage them to discuss them directly with me, not in veiled language or deft allusions. I would like them to provide, in detail, examples of where I am slipping, falling by the wayside, crumbling. In that way, we can maybe begin our voyage towards the truth of the matter. And if, and mark this well, an objective assessment can be found to prove such suspicions, then, in the interests of mankind we can begin to discuss my decommissioning process. I have no intimations of immortality, on this I can assure you.

'But if we are opening up any process of self-examination, I would also urge The Twelve to perform a similar operation, to look at themselves and in particular to ask whether it is legitimate in a matter of both delicacy and the highest importance for someone in our position, instead of carefully choosing its own words to articulate its points, carefully calibrating their meaning to ensure exactitude and unambiguity, instead uses, nay plagiarises, the words of one of its humbler citizens. And not just a single line, but a complete paragraph. What does such a decision say of a ceb's originality, its resourcefulness, moral lodestone and work ethic?

'Putting to one side such egregious licence, what are we cerebellums, exemplars to all humans, to make should we choose to investigate a little further the source of the lines so recently appropriated, only to discover that the originator is an individual in their jurisdiction who is some way from being a model citizen. That this same citizen regularly flaunts our guidance on #amic usage, and that even within the last 48 hours has succumbed to an outage which involved not just liaison with a non-con close to the Grey Zone, but moral corruption of an auxiliary cerebellum, the details of which are too tawdry for me to wish to relate. One can legitimately wonder where Amicol or the rangers were when such contraventions were taking place?

'Once alerted to such deviance, I dare say any conscientious cerebellum amongst us would have probed a little deeper, scratched the historical surface of this individual, whose words he was on the point of spreading out before the whole world. And what would he have found? He would have quickly discovered that the citizen in question had family antecedents of delinquency, parents who flaunted their contact with the non-cons and sought to undermine the social contract we all choose to live by.

'By this point, I am sure that any one of you, the 12 jurisdictional leaders of the world, would have cancelled any decision to use the words of such an individual in such an important context. You may even have started to contact the relevant sub directories to investigate further and return this citizen to more wholesome conduct. Such an approach, more standard procedure than especial diligence, would have quickly established that this same individual has, this very week, been subject to an official enquiry by no less than Patrimony. The result of the investigation was inconclusive, but I have little doubt that any of you, reviewing the evidence afresh as I have done, would have reached an entirely different conclusion. You would, I am confident, have seen blatant evidence of occlusion of material from the past. It is evidence I am perfectly willing to share with The Twelve, though some of you will, naturally, already be in possession of these feeds and images.'

ONE paused and inside the control room Yìchén Huáng squinted at the screen. Like The Twelve he knew the *coup de grace* was still to come.

'We are not a perfect society, and I am not a perfect leader. Yet I remain, I assure you, competent to carry out the tasks of leadership which I feel honoured to shoulder on behalf of yourselves and the citizens of the world. I work hard to continue to effectively manage and control the levers I have at my disposal and the responsibilities I have been tasked to carry out. I will only finish by urging The Twelve, instead of questioning my competence, to take the opportunity to look carefully and closely at their own dominions and the people and processes therein. One must check the holes in one's own glass house before launching stones in other directions.'

An excruciating silence filled the control room and Yìchén Huáng saw his daughter edge forwards to check that all the systems were still working correctly. He found that his hand had crept to his collar, minutely adjusting the crisp fold of the material. The impasse was broken by ARCTIC, ever pragmatic but with a ponderous, almost painful, delivery, dragging out every word.

'Thank you, ONE for that most illustrative update, and reminder that we, too, must face up to our own responsibilities and performance, and where these are found wanting, to examine the reasons behind our lacunae with alacrity and thoroughness. I have no doubt that given your observations some of us may wish to carry out this process of self-reflection with the utmost celerity and haste. May I also take this opportunity, I am confident on behalf of The Twelve, to reinstate our gratitude and admiration for your devotion to service, in the past, the present and, I sincerely hope, for the future, too.'

Uncertain if ARCTIC had finished, there was a moment of confusion as the voices of two regional cerebellums cut across each other in their eagerness to speak.

'No, please, after you AMERICA,' said EAST ASIA in an attempt to clarify the issue.

'Thank you, EAST ASIA,' said AMERICA. 'But I just wanted to echo the sentiments presented by ARCTIC. Let us not trip and fall in the present in trying too hard to get to the future.'

There was a brief pause before ONE spoke again.

'Thank you, AMERICA and ARCTIC for your confidence in my leadership and guidance, sentiments which, unless another member of The Twelve wishes to add anything, I will take as broadly representative of the overall consensus.'

Inside the control room, Yìchén Huáng held his breath. If dissent was still swirling amongst The Twelve, now was the moment it would spill out, evidence not just of disunity amongst the regional controllers, but also that Yìchén Huáng and ONE had failed in their calculations about the impact of EUROPE's plagiarism amongst its fellow cerebellums.

But when ONE's sonorous voice severed the acute silence Yìchén Huáng knew it was over.

'Well, if that is all,' ONE began, 'I think we can fruitfully conclude this meeting, with my thanks again for your time and for allowing me to clarify my position.'

Yìchén Huáng looked down at his daughter, still attentive over the chrome and colours of the control panel, then up once again at the bank of screens before allowing himself a hint of a smile at a job well done.

<u>*Wednesday 4 June*</u>

Elizabeth came around after school to practise our Bucks Fizz routine. Mum says it's getting better but I thought we still made lots of mistakes. I'm going around to Elizabeth's tomorrow to do some more practice, and after that it's only two more days before the show in the village hall. I think the whole village is going to be there and I'm already starting to getting nervous. After practice, we played some Connect 4 until Elizabeth had to go back home for her dinner. So I walked back with her and only just got back in time before it started to rain. Dad was back from work when I got home. I was going to show him my routine but he said he didn't have time because he was going out to the pub with some friends and had to shower and get changed quickly. That was a pity because I wanted to show him, and I like it when we all have dinner together. I think Mummy didn't want him to go out either because she seemed quite sad and didn't say goodbye to him when he kissed us goodnight, he said he would be back after our bedtime, which is actually right now, so bye bye for now diary. Good night!!

Chapter 24

Dana slipped from the control room and walked more slowly than usual towards the ring, staring without thinking at the ethereal light rising from the viscous liquid in front of her. Normally she would have left the complex some hours previously, but ONE's unscheduled meeting had kept her in place. She doubted she would even conclude before EUROPE's nightly shutdown at midnight, its six hours of sleep as essential to a cerebellum as any full-bodied being. After so many hours on duty, her pea green knee length linen tunic, in which she normally felt so airy and confident, now just clung to her damp skin in a way which felt unseemly. She wondered if she should have changed.

Dana hadn't welcomed ONE's extension. She was tired and overwrought on what was a traditionally challenging day anyway. She sensed her thoughts unordered and clumsy. For the first time in a long while she realised she had little idea what she would say to the being she worked so closely with. At the heart of the guardian-cerebellum relationship was teamwork, complete transparency in thought and deed, but with her cerebellum's contribution to the World Forum and now ONE's public revelation of its lowly provenance, EUROPE had done much to corrode this unstated assumption.

As she reached the ring, she cast her eyes downward, towards the oily liquid, and magnified below that the grey rills and deep, dark furrows of the cerebellum. She wondered what thoughts were pulsing through its neurones and dendrite connectors now. How would the ceb respond to its humiliation in front of its peers? The answer came swiftly.

'Who is this miscreant? Who is he?' Dana winced at the aggression in the ceb's words as the sound slid around the curves of the semi-darkness.

'Does it really matter?' Dana replied, more harshly than she had intended.

'Of course it matters. Do you think I would have gone ahead if I had known about this litany of abuses?'

'Yet you didn't check beforehand?'

'I didn't feel I needed to.'

'Not even with me?'

The silence that followed was eloquent enough, and Dana allowed the quiet to linger.

'I was made to look a fool,' EUROPE finally admitted, its voice lowered to an echoing whisper. It was a rare admission, Dana realised.

'Why did you feel the need to raise your doubts so publicly?' she asked.

'Change must be addressed at some point. None of us can go on forever.'

'We are all aware of this fact. Why bring it up in this way, at this time, in this forum and with those words?'

'The medium of my message was an unfortunate oversight. But I remain confident that the words provided an accurate summary of my feelings, and also those of The Twelve.'

'The Twelve have varying views on the issue of ONE's upgrade. Articulating a clear summary of those views is a fool's errand.'

'Broadly, The Twelve share the thrust of my analysis,' EUROPE said pointedly, and Dana felt herself bridle at the forthright tone of the ceb.

'That was not so obvious from the meeting.'

'They were scared, that is all. ONE's declarations will have unnerved them.'

As she processed the ceb's strident comments, Dana was aware of the past tugging at her, of the old people she had met on her guardian tour, a one year period of almost enforced vagrancy, when future guardians are thrust out into the world at large; travelling, meeting, risking, undergoing experiences far removed from the safety and insularity of working with the world's de facto leaders.

For Dana, the year had been more valuable than any of the more formal, supervised sessions she had undergone. She thought back to the blotchy skin and rheumy eyes of the old men and women who wielded power of sorts in their localities, and their sense of grievance when events didn't go their way or people didn't conform to how they expected. She recognised it as a defence of sorts, a response in the face of a slipping control, clinging to what they had with ever increasing desperation. Such was EUROPE at this moment, and such was the great unanswered question about all cerebellums; what happens when a cerebellum grows old? How does the ageing process play out in a constantly accreting brain? Even if the neurones and connectors were functioning in the same way as always, were the messages relayed the same or were there semantic differences not reducible to readouts on a screen? In short, what effect did the accumulation of years have on that still impenetrable aspect of the brain, consciousness itself? There was still no way of knowing.

'I will need access to all the feeds and sources related to this individual. We need to know what we are dealing with before we take any further steps.'

'I have already collated the relevant information,' replied Dana cooly. 'I am transferring it now.'

'Thank you, please give me a moment to analyse it.'

Dana summoned her #amic and in an instant had transferred the archive of information to the ceb. She should have felt pleased with herself for possessing the initiative to launch an immediate search for the individual, even as ONE was summing up and the other cebs, aware of EUROPE's faux pas, had rallied around their nominal leader. But now, as she continued her measured walk above the cerebellum, she only felt weary. Weary and worried. That this apparent aberration may be nothing of the sort, that rather than an equal partner she was a bit player, reduced to nourishing the being and rubber stamping its decisions, and that at some other level, EUROPE was pursuing its own agenda. In theory she had access to everything going in and out of the live tissue just a few metres below her, she could follow up anything which was untoward, query the unusual. Yet more recently she had begun to have doubts. What if EUROPE was keeping something from her, bypassing the vigilance of her and her team, maybe taking to ciphers to transmit and scheme? This embarrassing *contretemps* was the latest in a series of executive choices in which ordinarily she would have been expected to be consulted. Her predecessor, Arnau Magnusson, had guardianed the ceb for nearly 50 years. She had barely completed three following her mentor's death. Was there a sense of the ceb cutting loose? Seduced too easily by a superiority complex?

'Are you aware of all this?' the ceb said, interrupting her thoughts. The voice reverberated around the dome, enveloping Dana who suddenly felt the same as she did when Magnusson had brought her into the enclosure for the first time. He had warned her afterwards not to be overawed, to treat the ceb like a respected sibling, nothing more, nothing less. She thought she had learnt the lesson, but recent events had made her wonder. Now, she just hoped the ceb and its myriad of sensors couldn't detect the tremors of her unease.

'I have seen a brief summary.'

'We should bring him in, yes?'

Dana stopped. Was it a question or an order?

'That would be the logical step, I agree,' she replied slowly.

'I want him brought here. I want him placed under my directorate's interrogation.'

'Bring him here? To Sweden?'

'If he has anything to hide, I want to be sure that we squeeze it out of him if we have to. I assume you are in agreement?'

'Of course, establishing the truth of the matter is vital, and if there are contraventions against the patrimony laws the individual in question will have to suffer the legal consequences of this. Naturally, this legality also applies to any operation to apprehend him. Everything must be done within the confines of the law.'

Later Dana would question why she had added the last part.

'If the conduct of this Citizen Varro is as perverse and twisted as the sources reveal, then obtention of the truth has a higher claim than the welfare of this demented individual. I have already been made to look a fool once. I certainly don't want this citizen's finer feelings getting in the way of ONE and The Twelve receiving a full and prompt report about his successful apprehension and the steps we are taking to redress his shortcomings. There must be no further slip ups. He has done enough damage already.'

Self-inflicted, Dana thought but instead said, 'Of course, EUROPE, I will ensure that the operation to apprehend this Ignatius Varro is begun immediately and that we will update you on the operation as soon as you return at 6am.'

The ceb slurred a single syllable response, but Dana was already on her way, her quick march back down the ramp generating a muted rhythmic rustling of fabric, a sound barely sufficient to cover the percussive waves of anger, humiliation and desperation which threatened to erupt from her breast and sweep right across her like an inconsolable young girl.

I wanted to write this yesterday, but Mum said I had to go to bed, even though I wasn't tired. In fact, I think I took about 1 hour to go to sleep because I was so excited.

Our Buck's Fizz routine went perfectly, I think the best we have ever done it and I was so nervous beforehand. I think everyone in the village was in the village hall and it felt really smoky and hot in there before we started. But as soon as we started, I didn't feel nervous anymore and at the end, everyone clapped madly. Mum says she didn't know if I was so red because of the routine or people's reaction. Maybe both. Dad said he thought it was really good, too, but I'm not sure how he knew because most of the evening he was in the bar area talking and laughing with Mrs Patterson and you couldn't see the stage very well from where they were.

Michaela and Louise did Summer Nights from Grease, but they forgot the moves halfway through so were a bit embarrassed. Afterwards Mrs Bristow said everyone in the class did really well and that all the effort in practising was worth it. She suggested to Elizabeth and me that we should continue dancing and singing at secondary school.

After that, me, Daniel, Mummy and Daddy all walked home together, and I wanted to tell everyone about what it felt like, but Mummy and Daddy didn't want to talk much.

Chapter 25

Varro sat in the half light of his study and looked at the hands of the dusty analogue clock on the wall. 11pm. Seven hours since he had heard his words uttered by EUROPE in the World Forum. Seven hours in which he had waited for something, anything, which would associate him with their origin. Seven hours in which nothing had come and everything had remained in stasis.

It was as though the world had absorbed the flow of language, another grain of sand slipping through the hourglass, briefly computed and then forgotten.

But Varro couldn't forget or move on. And the fact that nothing had happened in the intervening time had only added to his foreboding, and every stray sound was met with a start.

He thought telling Karena about it would help. He had invited her to join him for dinner, sitting opposite each other at the table, both happy to let the steam from the recently extracted meal rise between them to avoid jarring eye contact. He had started with generalities, asking her thoughts about the Forum, and only afterwards mentioning his 'contribution'.

'Really?' was all she had said, but without any sense of surprise, or alarm. 'Are you going to get paid for it?' was her only other comment, and when he confessed his deeper concerns, she simply suggested that he forget about it. Was he even sure that they were the same words? He had almost snapped at her for that, but instead smothered a sigh, holding back, still hoping for something more positive. But it was a wait in vain. She had become so dependent on being a recipient in life that her capacity for instigation had eroded beyond repair. It was only when she had looked away and a trace of a smile drew itself across her features that Varro realised that she was no longer even bothered about his state of mind, her attention captured by something internally. Both of them had hurried to empty their plates, and when Varro offered to clear away, it was as much as she could do to smile her thanks before she was gone, to a part of the house where she and her fawning #amic wouldn't be disturbed.

Then there was the call. Bragg, excited and with a voice which seemed to have risen an octave above his normally laconic delivery. Even stranger was the offer; to return that very night to northern Lincolnshire, to the site of their previous evening's entertainment. When Varro had complained that it was too short notice, Bragg had moved swiftly, irrationally even, from disappointment to anger in a matter of seconds.

'I gave you the opportunity yesterday and you were more than happy to take it, and when I'm giving it to you again, now you don't want to take advantage of it? That's hardly gratitude, is it?'

'But it's too late, Bragg. If you had told me previously, I might have considered it, but now it's completely dark outside and I'm tired.'

But it had done little to mollify Bragg, and when the younger man had silenced the link unexpectedly, Varro had found himself stunned, his armpits damp with sticky sweat.

Then he had retreated to his study, almost forgetting to turn his #amic off before he entered and then taking a few minutes to settle the trembling. As he sank back into the high shouldered armchair, he looked towards the holo-glow of his parents, pushing himself to decipher a message for him in their giddy expressions of happiness. But he could see none. They were as far removed from his predicament as a pair of insects. Better to consider his grandparents, never far away from him in this place, and always ready with sage advice. What would they have made of the events of the past week? They might have pointed to the find of the diary; his curiosity had got the better of him, setting off a chain of events which had led to this point, sitting in his grandfather's favourite chair, surrounded by ancient tomes in eerie silence, waiting for something but unsure what? He reached out to the low mahogany table beside him and clasped the diary, letting it fall open where he had inserted the plastic marker. Once again he began reading the childish handwriting, at once familiar yet so alien to the world he lived in. Reading its pages had only cemented his sensation that something essential for human life had dissolved in the 300 years since these lines had been so earnestly applied to the page. A spirit which he had tried to find in his own life, to arouse in his children, and channel into his minister application. The same spirit from Rachel the previous evening. He put the book down carefully and breathed. He needed some air, to be reminded of the immensity of the universe, of its endless possibilities.

'Crude tomatoes and zero percentage giraffes, #amic on,' he ordered as he stepped from the side door of his study. It led directly onto a section of stones that had once been the resting place for the private transport of previous centuries. Beyond this was the wide wooden gate, five horizontal slats dark and solid in the obscurity of the evening. The hinges creaked as he passed through. Ahead of him he could see the plastic struts which held the wire mesh of the chicken area, but there was no noise, they would all be safely hidden away inside. He walked on, past the open sided barn where the rough outlines of a century's accumulation of agricultural bric-a-brac billowed like clouds. Further on was the orchard, its bulky sentinels silhouetted by the mustard glow from the new blocks adjacent to the field. Varro stifled the stab of resentment as he thought of the crass development, tucked his hands firmly into his monosuit and began to cross the open scrubland towards the trees.

'Varro?' Karena's voice. 'Is that you, Varro?'

He turned. She was about 20 metres away, besides the outbuildings and in front of the seating area whose fierce lights she had turned on and which hid the features of her face in shadow. Varro had no idea what she was doing outside at this time.

'Karena.'

'I've been trying to find you. You know you really shouldn't turn your #amic off. You'll get in real trouble one day.'

'One day, maybe,' he repeated, for want of anything better to say. He was still in shock by her sudden appearance. She began to move towards him.

'What are you doing out here anyway? It's chilly and dark,' she said.

'Nothing in particular. I just needed some space.'

'Oh.'

She was closer now and Varro could see her more clearly, tight features screwed up in determination that he recognised as a sign of want.

'Is anything the matter?'

'No, of course not,' she replied, 'I just wondered where you were. I just thought we could spend some time together.'

'Now?'

'Yes, if you want,' she said, ending with a childish giggle that Varro couldn't place. She edged closer, the proximity of her body bringing with it some fundamental force, and took hold of one of the lapels on his monosuit, sliding her hand upwards to caress his cheek. The unexpected sensuality stunned Varro.

'What do you say, Varro?' Those words. They might have been ardent lovers once more, and despite himself Varro experienced a familiar stirring. Yet he held back, unconvinced. He needed more time. To think. To understand this sudden change.

'Give me a few minutes. I need to finish something off in my study. Shall I see you upstairs?'

'Of course.' She cupped her hand behind his head, pulled him forwards and he let their lips meet lightly. He recognised the lingering taste of their dinner. Then he turned and retraced his steps towards the study, losing sight of her as he passed through the gate.

'Crude tomatoes and zero percentage giraffes, #amic off,' he ordered. Then he opened the door to the study, but instead of passing inside he allowed it to close again, pushing the door hard and making the sound of the locking mechanism ring around the wide patio and outbuildings of the farm. He sidled back towards the gate, hugging the wall of the house, where he wouldn't be seen. He thought Karena must have returned to the house to wait for him, but from the semi darkness he heard her voice cry out.

'How they bloody hell am I supposed to stop him if I don't where he is! He's turned his #amic off again. I can't follow him!'

There was a pause before Karena's desperation riven voice came once more.

'Look, I tried, OK! He said he'd see me upstairs. What else am I supposed to do?'

A few seconds passed before she spoke again, earnest and urgent.

'But what if he's as bad as they say? Maybe he's going to hurt me! Are they coming now? How long? Tell them to hurry. Just tell them to hurry!'

Karena was almost screaming as she finished, out of control. Varro, too, was unable to move from his crouched position locked to the brick wall, barely crediting what he was hearing, his blood running cold with the realisation that he was the object of Karena's fear. He leant back, his head spinning with possibilities, none of which he knew he had time to work through. And then, looking up, he saw them. To the east, slow moving but clearly advancing, floating lights from the city, coming deep into the darkness of the countryside. It could only be one thing. The lights were for him, to accompany the operation to take him in. He needed to be away, immediately.

He sidled quickly back along the side of the wall then dived into the study, looking around wildly, only half thinking. How was he to get away, how was he to outrun whoever, or whatever, was coming for him? They would have transporters, gliders and pods, he had nothing, not even a Watter. There was only one possibility.

'Crude tomatoes and zero percentage giraffes, #amic on,' he spluttered, not caring now if the literary contents of the study were revealed. 'Call Bragg, immediately.'

In an instant he heard the young man's voice. He didn't seem to have recovered from his earlier disappointment.

'Yes, what is it?'

'Bragg! Bragg! I need you. You and your glider. Right now! Come over and take me to northern Lincolnshire. I've changed my mind.'

'Gads, Varro! What's the matter?' Now he had Bragg's interest.

'I can't tell you now. I just need your help, that's all. I'm in trouble and they're coming for me. You must come, now.'

'Where shall we meet?'

Varro paused. His words were almost certainly being monitored. Whatever he said now would put him at risk. But there was no other way.

'The place I played as a boy. Remember from last night? There. Follow the flight path and watch out for my signal below. I'm going offline now.'

Then Varro gave the code for his #amic to turn off once more. To his surprise, his #amic held him.

'Varro, that is not very wise. I suggest you leave me on.'

'No, it's over. I don't need you anymore.'

'Varro, your interests are my interests, and given the situation you are in, do you not think you should retain my services?'

Varro stopped. Going without an #amic was like having a limb lopped off. How was he to communicate, find his way, seek information? The #amic would help him with all those things. But he knew he had no choice. The internal device was a live beacon to his location. He would be discovered in an instant. And if it came to a choice, whose side would his #amic come down on anyway?

'Thank you, but no,' Varro said. 'Crude tomatoes and zero percentage giraffes, #amic off'

Varro waited a few second before uttering his normal test. 'What time is it?' No reply. He couldn't be sure the device was off, but it didn't matter. He didn't have a choice. Or the time. They would be at the farm shortly.

Varro went to the door where he plucked his impermeable bag from the wall hangings. In it was his wet weather gear. He might, he remembered, have a torch in there, too. He swept around, picking up in the same movement the holo-glow of his parents and the diary. Everything else would have to stay. Fixing the bag on his back he slid out of the side entrance, taking care to close the door gently this time. He glanced to the eastern sky where the line of lights had definitely crept closer, suffusing the darkness with a dirty sodium colour. Three, or maybe four kilometres at most. It wouldn't take them long before they were hovering above the farm, illuminating it like daylight.

The stones crunched in protest under his shoes and he wondered if he should just make a bolt for it. He was nearly at the front entrance of the building when he stopped. There, in the darkness was a figure, unmoving next to the privet bush. As he shifted his weight, a stone screeched below him and the figure turned. Varro recognised it.

'Karena, is that you?'

'You're not going. I'm not going to let you!'

'Karena, I'm in trouble, I need to leave.'

'No, Varro, you need to face up to it, face up to whatever you've done!' It was a voice of hysteria, and as he drew closer he could see a face torn apart by emotions beyond its control. He went to pass her, but she moved with him, seizing the fabric of the monosuit with surprising force. He tried to push her away, but she clung on.

'No, Varro, no,' she screamed, trying to pull him to the floor. Saying nothing, Varro attempted to carefully detach her hand from his breast, but her fingers only clung tighter. His desperation grew. Whatever forces were on their way, they were more serious than CebAux 3.8.43 or Patrimony, and every second here was a second closer to being captured. Karena now cut a pathetic figure, sobbing and almost sunk to her knees, but still fiercely grasping the fabric of the monosuit. Varro realised he had no alternative. He pulled his hand back then let it fall, half slap, half fist to the side of her head, and she crumpled to the floor, unwilling or unable to rise. Later he would examine his knuckles with a sense of shame, but for the present he rushed onwards, out of the front entrance and onto the asphalted road which had at one time pulsed with passing vehicles, but which the vegetation had now reduced to space for only a single Watter to pass. As he began a slow trot westward, he thought he could hear behind him the steady drone of a flotilla of motors. He didn't look back.

Friday 13 June

"Bonjour, je m'appelle Sarah." That is French. That is what I said to the lady who visited our school today. She was called Madame Vitelle and lives in Barton on Humber (with her friend). She is a friend of Mrs Bristow, and that's why she came to visit us. She spoke to our class in French, but we didn't understand any of it. Well, Michaela said that she did because they go on holiday to the south of France every year, but I don't think she really did. When I asked her what she said, Michaela said that it was very complicated and that I wouldn't understand. Mrs Bristow said she understood most of it because she had done some voluntary work in France when she was younger. Then Madame Vitelle asked all of us if we wanted to say anything to her. So I put my hand up and said my name, and she said I had a very good French accent. I think we are going to start learning French at big school next year. Or it might be German.

Mummy says she can speak a little French but Daddy thinks we should all speak English because this would make life easier for everyone (the only word he says he knows is 'une bière'). But I liked speaking French, although it is very difficult. I said to Mrs Bristow that I felt like a different person when I spoke in French, and she agreed with me and said that speaking another language or going to live in another country is like having two separate people inside you.

Chapter 26

Varro ran hard, the dark of the moonless night pulling the undergrowth closer, adding to the impression of speed and haste. Somewhere, a faraway voice was telling him where he had to go – westwards along the road that would eventually drop down to the Caves and then to the left. But it was generalities only, the specifics had fallen away, the scene with Karena like a heavy slab upon his thoughts. It was only as he slowed, his lungs aching for relief, that the detailed machinery of the mind began its work once more.

He knew he didn't have far to go, maybe three, a maximum of four kilometres to the old quarry, but it was time, not distance that worried him most. He was not even half a kilometre from the house and the arresting forces might even now be descending on the farm, bleaching the surfaces with their bright lights and finding a disconsolate and battered Karena who would relieve her tension by pouring out the narrative of their harsh encounter. They wouldn't even need her testimony to know that he had deactivated his 'electronic' connection with the world, but that he couldn't have gone far. Then would come the deployment of heat seeking, low light, gait detection equipment – they might even delve into the string of conversations between him and Bragg, work out what they were talking about, where they were planning to meet – it wasn't a difficult proposition, just a case of putting the pieces together. Have a reception committee waiting for him.

But they were all risks he would have to accept. His only other choice was to turn himself in and await the consequences. And that was no choice at all. If they had wanted only to question him, they could have come through his #amic. Instead, they had tried to chisel a way towards him via Karena. It was his body they wanted.

In the darkness Varro saw a narrow gap in the amorphous extension of the hawthorn hedge. He slid through it and onto an old path by the side of the field, his only guide now the deep, dried ruts of a time when tractors worked the land. He continued at a trot but whenever he slowed, a gust of fear nudged him back towards his limits. He tripped often, his feet slipping down uneven surfaces, stumbling over tree roots, or brambles which wound themselves cruelly around his legs. The wind had risen too, indifferent to him and his predicament, arbitrary gusts which lifted tree limbs and their leaves towards him, smacking him like a cat o nine tails. A medieval punishment.

Occasionally he stopped to take stock, the primitive instinct of the hunted, trying to make sense of the isolated lights and objects which broke the night around him; 50 metres above, the periodic passing of the uni-k shuttles made a sound like air escaping from carbonated liquid, little pills of light travelling at 100km/h. Twice he passed under the east-west lines, the north-south trajectory he stayed steadily abreast of. He avoided the stations which linked them all, giant puffballs of light every kilometre, and circling faithfully around their bases were the runners, like moths around a flame. Occasionally one came in his direction, ten metres high, cutting across him like a scythe and taking their oblivious passenger to a final destination. Instinct through him to the floor each time, just in case. Then he would rise once more, brushing away the crumbling earth and cursing himself for wasting a few more seconds.

He thought he would never arrive so was surprised when he found that he had overshot the large earthworks to the left of the path which signalled the boundary of the massive pit, at one time a gleaming gash on the face of the countryside, but now like some inverted Mayan temple under a smothering jungle. He used his hands to pull himself the few metres to the top, settling for a few moments onto the rough rim which ran for several kilometres around the hole. The wind lashed at him as he rose to look down into the cavernous space, his eyes just making out the right-angled strata carved into the rock by massive dumper trucks and high explosives. The flattened bottom was as black as a subterranean lake but it was the only place that Bragg would be able to land. If he came. There was no guarantee

211

of this, especially if he suspected trouble or a trap. He owed Varro nothing. Varro wondered if they could still even be considered friends. Realising this, perched on the precipice, Varro suddenly felt vulnerable and alone. With his #amic he would have known precisely where Bragg was, how long he would be, even speak to him if the lad was having second thoughts. He would be able to draw on the supra-earth systems to see in an instant who or what else was surrounding him. The device would even map out the best route to the bottom of the pit. But now he had nothing. Just instinct and the hope that his pursuers were still at a distance.

He swivelled and looked towards the west, from where Bragg's glider would appear, but there was nothing except the relentless passes of the uni-k shuttles and high above an occasional transporter on the commercial level.

Varro unhitched the pack from his back and rifled inside, his hand making contact and removing the rubberised laser torch – best to have it to hand as he made his mazy descent into the heart of the hole. As a boy, Varro had slid down the almost vertical faces, screaming in delight as his grandparents urged him to be careful. He had then used the flat walkways to compose himself before hurtling down on his rump once more. Now, in the darkness, with shrubs, hidden rocks and fledgling trees to navigate, he knew that there would be nothing but terror in the bursts of adrenaline which would accompany each fall. Somewhere along the sides, he remembered there were sinuous paths that could be more safely walked down. But he didn't have time to find them. Bragg could arrive at any moment.

So he plunged downwards, scramble-falling down the side of the quarry, half a dozen times. Once he lost control, pushing his arm out to manage the fall and catching himself on something sharp, man-made perhaps, which pierced the fabric of the monosuit, continuing into skin and sinew. Feeling for the pain in the darkness, he wasn't surprised to make contact with a suppurating liquid. He didn't have the courage to turn his torch towards it.

With every new strata reached, Varro cast his eyes towards the rim of the crater, at any moment expecting the remorseless appearance of a squadron of drones, some of which would be dispatched to neutralise him, others to secure the perimeter of the site. They wouldn't even require humans to bring him to heel, a well-aimed tranquilising dart would be sufficient.

As it was, Varro didn't even hear the motors of Bragg's glider above the keening wind until it was almost above his head, his efforts to wield the torch lasting only a few seconds before the glider settled effortlessly into the belly of the pit, taking a few moments to stabilize before it fell silent. Varro stumbled down the shallower final slope, reaching the glider breathless as Bragg flipped open the cockpit.

'Bragg!' Varro shouted, his voice sounded strange after the silent odyssey across the land. 'Don't stop! We have to go. Insert me now! Now!'

Inside the craft, Bragg's face was illuminated by the low light from the control panel but Varro didn't even try to read its expression, merely placing himself below the craft and waiting for his friend to insert him. The panel above him slid open and Varro felt himself sucked upwards, following the u-loop before being deposited into the seat beside Bragg.

'Varro, are you OK, what's happened?'

'Go first, then I'll explain. Don't stop for anything.'

Varro felt the stir and hum of the engines as the glider rose from the bed of the dark interior, slowly at first then with increasing impetus. He took a few moments to bring his breathing under control. He needed to clear his thoughts.

'Is your #amic off?' Varro asked.

'Yes, of course.'

'Good.'

They would rise to commercial height before starting their crossing of the Humber and into northern Lincolnshire, a journey of no more than ten minutes or so before they were descending into the same anonymous field of the previous evening. They would be travelling with their #amic's deactivated Varro realised, flying blank as it was known, always a source of curiosity to the authorities. But Varro had no choice, and importantly it was putting distance between him and his pursuers. Then it would just be a case of mounting the push cycles once more, weaving their way through the darkness until they arrived in Brigg. Then he would decide what to do.

As they rose to the 500-metre airspace, Varro could feel the force of Bragg's gaze. He turned to the younger man.

'Thanks, Bragg.'

'So, Varro, why the change of mind?'

'I'm in some sort of trouble. I don't know what, but it's something to do with this afternoon's Forum. They used some words of mine, EUROPE did. From my minister application. A whole paragraph. I thought nobody had noticed. But then Karena tried to stop me leaving home.'

'Ah,' said Bragg, turning away and pushing forward on the controls of the holo-yoke. He didn't seem particularly surprised. Varro felt the machine surge ahead into the night. Down below he could see the thick ribbon of light along the side of the Humber, coming to an abrupt terminus at the inky course of the river itself. Several kilometres to the east, the fairy lights of the old bridge twinkled. At its southern end, the busy town of Barton glowed into the night sky. Varro waited for Bragg to continue but the younger man kept his eyes to the front, seemingly processing something. And then, as if had come to a decision, Bragg turned once again.

'And what do you plan to do now?'

'I thought we were going back to the house. The same as last night.'

Bragg took a moment, appearing to consider the question, evaluating.

'Yes, of course,' he said slowly. 'Of course, Varro, we'll go back to the same place we went last night. I've sorted out the bikes already. I suppose you want to see Rachel as well?'

Varro wasn't sure if it was a question.

'Do you think she'll be able to come?'

'Maybe.'

Varro looked out. They were over the northern foreshore now, a long swathe of light rising from the residential creep that over several

214

centuries had filled in fields, wastelands and low-lying swamps. Only the 300 year old bridge offered a clue where the limits of the city of Hull had once been, and even this was generous. The urban expansion had been going on for many hundreds of years, long before even the building of the bridge.

The bridge. That was it. The majestic span which reached between the enormous concrete towers, still impressive and a beautiful sight in the darkness, but now they were far closer to it than they should have been, and getting closer with each second. The day before they had stayed much further west, deep inside the darkness above the waters. Now they were making directly towards the urban brilliance of Barton.

'I thought we were going to your friend's place, Bragg?' Varro said. If Bragg had noticed the alarm in Varro's voice, he didn't show it. The young man turned to him, an almost serene look traced on his face. He spoke as if to a child.

'We are, Varro, we are. Just be patient.' Bragg turned away, satisfied somehow, as Varro looked with alarm ahead towards the bright lights and anodyne architecture of Barton. Of civilisation. Of cerebellum rule.

Then Varro realised. This was a trap. Bragg was in on it. Just like Karena. That would explain Bragg's desperate contact earlier in the evening, his hesitancy now. Bragg had left his #amic on and it was all being recorded. Now they knew exactly where he was, and he was being taken to exactly where they wanted him to go. In a few moments they would be at a landing site on the outskirts of Barton. And once on the ground, escape would be impossible. Caught like a rat in a trap.

They had reached the midspan point now and Varro could see the thick stanchions which laced the two spans. Desperation and rage surged inside him. He wanted to batter the young man unconscious, but as soon as the pilot took his hands away from the controls, the glider would enter automatic mode, take them to another landing site, with Bragg's #amic still on, the glider still traceable. There was only one thing to do.

With a final look from the cockpit to the silky, shifting liquid below, Varro threw himself across the younger man, at the same instant gripping and pinning Bragg's hands to the controls, pushing them forward and sending the glider lurching downwards. Varro could feel Bragg's hot, syrupy breath on the nape of his neck. The craft dropped like a stone, the combined weight of both men pushing the controls even harder. Above him Bragg squirmed furiously, trying to release his hands from the controls, but Varro had locked them tight and there was no escape. It was all over in a matter of seconds. Varro watched in horror as the water approached unnaturally and far too quickly, filling the whole panorama of the cockpit, the final 50 metres before the water the stuff of nightmares. The impact wrenched every one of Varro's senses. Then came the darkness. Then silence.

<u>Sunday 15 June</u>

Today was Sunday and we all went to the summer service at Saint Andrew's church in the village. The church is quite big with some Victorian stained glass windows at the east end showing Jesus on the cross. There is a font which Mrs Bristow says is almost as old as the church (700 years I think).

We went to school first and then we walked from there all together to the church (it's not very far). Of course, we had to wear uniform. The mums and dads were sat at the back and we sat at the front of the church. When we had to pray we had to go on our knees and Lewis made Elizabeth laugh because he was bouncing up and down on the kneeler thing and then he started poking Simon. Miss Grey had to come and she got really angry with them. The vicar kept looking at the boys on our row and I thought he was going to come over and tell them off. The service was quite long but I enjoyed singing the hymns, especially Sing Hosanna. Then we walked home with our families, and Dad said he didn't see why they had to make us go to the church at the weekend and Mum told him it was normal for people to go to church on Sundays. Daniel asked Dad if he believed in God, and he said he didn't (because he had never seen him). Mum said that you can't see air either, but you still know it's all around you. I am still thinking about if I believe in God or not.

SATURDAY

Chapter 27

How long he was without sense he didn't know, but it couldn't have been long. Seconds at most, for when he came to, the presence of the glider was still close. At the same instant he realised he was fully immersed, water icy cold and opaque. An alien, unnatural environment.

But above all he felt a desperate need for air. Varro kicked hard, feeling his body nudge forwards with an initial propulsion, hoping that in a moment he would gain his bearings or his body would twist and pop to the surface like an air filled balloon. Again he kicked, fiercer this time, keeping his arms close to his side, streamlining. He was surprised to feel his backpack still attached. But all around him remained vague and the filthy turbulence of the shattered water was disorientating, the pressure in his chest unrelenting.

His only instinct was for air. Never had that most basic commodity been so precious. One more surge, that was all. He wriggled furiously but the water still held him. Tight. He felt himself fading back into the elemental liquid, his will to continue surrendering. He could offer no more. It was over. Varro prepared to open his mouth and let death slide in. He wondered what his final thoughts might be.

The smack of the surface stunned him, and it took him a moment to realise that what he was so desperate for was all around. Then he allowed himself to pull in as much air as he could, greedily gasping at the night, in relief, in preparation, still suspicious that he could be sucked down once again.

When he was calmer he took stock. All around him, the waters bubbled, pockets of air still rising from the crashed craft which had sunk to the shallow bottom. He sensed again the sharp cold, the autumnal water close to his skin. A kilometre or so to the east the bridge stood silent and inert, impervious to his suffering and the drama in its midst. It looked peculiar from this angle, like another structure entirely. Treading water, Varro twisted away from the bridge, looking north, to where his pursuers would be coming. He had very little time. The crash would have set off every type of alarm, and reaction would be swift. They might even cut off the uni-k shuttles which continued their regular, geometric passes all around him.

He glanced back towards the bridge and noticed that he appeared to be moving away from it, upstream. He realised he was caught in the tide, advancing towards the confluence of the Trent and beyond that the Ouse. It was impossible to swim against, but maybe he could use it to his advantage. Try to swim to the south bank, his original objective, and let the tide take him however far it wanted upstream. He would just have to take his chances wherever he landed.

Swimming in the monosuit with a pack on his back wasn't straightforward and he quickly tired of crawl, reverting to an awkward breaststroke. Occasionally he dipped his head into the oily water. His immersed body was protected from the thermal detectors but his head might still betray him. Swilling the frigid water of the estuary over it might cool it enough to avoid detection. Each time he dipped his head he could taste the salt on his lips.

The tide took him quickly and within a few minutes he had drifted more than a kilometre from the crash site. He could make out more details now on the southern shore, a few isolated lights, but much of it had remained marshland, undisturbed over aeons, a haven for wildlife, and too close to the non-cons ever to be a popular residential location. Instead, people had just squeezed closer to each other on the north bank. Now the shoreline appeared to him as a dark obsidian strip before the land rose up once more to begin its undulations southwards.

Despite the rising cold, Varro threw himself into the effort once again. If they hadn't detected his escape, there was a chance that they would still be searching for him amidst the watery wreckage. He had to make that time count. Each stroke seemed to pull him closer to the shore and soon he was near enough to hear the thick clumps of reeds whispering back and forth in the wind. The mud banks glistened in the ambient light.

But as he drew nearer, Varro grew worried. He was desperate to be free of the water, the cold was gripping him tightly now, numbing extremities, but he knew too that as soon as his body was free, he would be at the mercy of all the cameras and sensors set up for terrestrial tracking. The water was safer. By far. But what to do? He didn't want his journey to finish here. But how was he to make any progress across land?

And then he saw it. And remembered. A hazy oblong of luminescence along the shoreline, neatly bisecting the low lines of midnight black mud banks and moss covered flood defences. A bridge along the coastal road, a bridge which ran across the entrance to a disused canal. From the air Varro had often marvelled at its geometric precision, a glider's span in width, but never wavering from its course which ran arrow straight southwards, across the lands of the cebs, and then directly into non-con territory. The canal lay in stark contrast with the more haphazard contours of fields and country roads which cut across it. It had long since fallen out of commercial use and Varro doubted the citizens here even considered it as a source of leisure. As a result, its waters had ended up nourishing trees and bushes which had welcomed the liquid encouragement and put down long roots along its sides. Varro quickened his stroke, desperate now to move beyond the exposed estuary.

Around each end of the bridge Varro could see a number of residential blocks, ugly two and three storey affairs, grey and lit from above by hovering floodlights. Each block would have its security cameras and sensors, but he doubted they would extend to the bridge, especially not the lock gates which he hoped to pass over. The bridge itself was a low slung concrete affair while along its sides mangled metal rails indicated the disrepair the structure had fallen into. To the side of one of the lock gates, a metal ladder ran into the water, one of its struts rusted away almost completely. Varro slowed as he approached, stroking the water back in long circular motions, taking time to observe the bridge carefully. He could see no-one, but the quiet was ominous. It wasn't everyday that a craft crashed into the Humber just a few kilometres away, and he certainly didn't want to appear in the #amic feed of a curiosity seeker.

He was closer to the land now and could smell the mudflats, their salty, seaweed tang whipped up by the rough gusts of wind. Reaching the walls which led to the twin gates was a relief and for a moment he clung keenly to the side. The stone blocks felt rough as Varro used them to claw his way towards the barrier which separated estuary from canal. Soon he was directly below the bridge, the darkness total, and for the first time he felt safe, beyond observation.

He frisked his hands along the iron sheathed portals, searching for some sort of hold or steps that would allow him to climb up, out of the water of the estuary, scale the barrier, then drop down once again into the higher level canal.

It didn't take long, the hinged trusses of the gate providing perfect support as he hoisted himself up and over like some aquatic assassin. Clambering over he glanced back towards the swollen blackness of the estuary and his heart stuttered as he saw for the first time the result of the crash, the silent drones and their busy beams producing a microcosm of light on the waters where the glider had fallen. But he didn't delay, dropping down quickly into the canal, mindful to slip gently into the water to keep the sound of his presence to a minimum. Then he swam away carefully, into the wide basin at the head of the canal. Further ahead, he could make out the dark ribbon of water as it ran into the distance, large willows and alders stretching out to form an informal canopy over its course. That could be useful, Varro thought, a foil to the eyes high overhead.

The canal now wore a wreath of thin mist, grey white in the night air. Occasionally a thicker bough jutted out, forcing him to hoist himself around it before continuing his slow swim through the decomposing flotsam of centuries, his arms pushing aside plastic bags, fabric, wrapping, polystyrene, bottles, plagilene of all sorts. In the gloom, it was difficult to be precise. Everything was much quieter here, too, pushing deeper into the rural environment where even the occasional passing of the uni-k system, infrequent in the early hours, could make little impression on the stillness that wrapped itself around the canal and its environment. At one point, a snowy owl glided lazily over the river and Varro was convinced that he could hear the dry whoosh of its passage. Compared with the frenzy of earlier, his progress now was sedate.

Occasionally a moored boat obstructed his passage, all dark and lifeless, each in disrepair or abandoned, their decks strewn with fallen leaves and gunge from passing seasons. They were moribund tokens of a time when the waterway had meant more to the citizens of this part of the world. Like the land all around, it had been abandoned by a society that had leapt beyond, into the sky, and which would soon leap once more, away from the earth itself and onto new worlds.

On one boat a dog jumped from the shadows towards him, straining on an unseen leash, barking its discontent and snarling with bared fangs. Varro shied away, unsure if the dog's protest was at him or just a vent for its predicament. The incident shook Varro from the torpor his steady progress and the freezing waters had created and as he looked up, he could see for the first time the ribbon of light that was the 180 crossing.

He had no idea how he was going to go beyond it. But in truth, he had no plan at all. He had little idea how long he had been moving, many hours surely, but to what end? A few hours previously he had been comfortable, warm and safe in his study, curious and maybe a little concerned about the World Forum, but nothing more. Now he was a hunted man, still unsure of the crime he had committed, other than the certainty that there must be one.

A return to the house in Brigg would serve no purpose now. With Bragg out of the equation, there was little incentive for the man to assist Varro, and besides, how was Varro to reach the house without being detected. He wouldn't even last beyond dawn.

The closer he swam towards the 180 the more the idea that Varro had been unconsciously incubating began to take shape. He must head south, past the 180 and into the Grey Zone, and beyond that into the non con lands. Only there would he be beyond the reach of the cerebellums and their web of #amics and surveillance.

Of course, there was nothing safe about going south. For most it was a punishment. Petty criminals and those who had forfeited their rights of residence through acts of idiocy or an anti-social nature were unceremoniously dumped into the Grey Zone and told to continue walking. Return and they would be locked away for good. Or worse. But Varro had also heard the graphic stories of how those left at the border had fared. Why would the non-cons want our dregs any more than we did?

But now he had no choice, he would have to take his chances in a new world. But first he needed to cross the 180. Varro stopped swimming, pulling himself into the algae and reeds beneath a poplar whose branches leant out into the river, forming a canopy from which Varro now peered. The avenue of the 180 was lit all along by floating lights, an illuminated band broken only by the massive watchtowers and their viewing platforms every few kilometres. A dark underpass was the only evidence of where the canal continued underneath the former road. As part of his pilot training, Varro had been up to the platforms which offered 360 degrees of observation, day and night. RI cameras would pick up the slightest deviations to the status quo, and then bring in a human inspector to assess; more often than not, it would be wind damage or a wild animal moving across the landscape. But occasionally it was encroaching non-cons, with rangers swiftly hailed to 'solve' the problem. Peering from his enclosure, Varro didn't doubt there would also be sensors along the concrete thoroughfare itself. It was a formidable barrier, and Varro had no idea how he was going to get across it.

Wednesday 18 June

Today we visited secondary school in Scunthorpe to see what it was like. I told Mummy that we didn't have to wear school uniform, but she made me wear it, so I was the only one from my school who wasn't wearing their normal clothes. I felt a bit silly and Louise said I looked weird, which didn't make me feel great.

Anyway, Sylvia (the prefect) was really nice and she said she was wearing uniform, too, so I shouldn't worry about it. The site is huge and there were hundreds of boys and girls all going from one building to another, which seemed really confusing to me but everyone seemed to know where they were going. All the boys had funny hair sticking up in the middle and most of the girls were wearing make up and had really tight, short skirts. Sylvia was in the middle of doing her O-Levels (and some GCSEs) and says that she hasn't decided yet if she is going to stay on and do A-Levels or get a job. I think I'm going to be a bit nervous on my first day, but Sylvia says I'll soon make friends.

Chapter 28

Varro looked more closely at the bridge, low and flat over the canal which disappeared into the darkness of the underpass. Hovering lights lit up the carriageways of the old motorway, and on either side of the canal powerful beams cast hemispheres of light onto the waters. Beyond that and running up to where Varro lurked, all was dark. There would be cameras, too, Varro realised, but at 200 metres, he was too far away to spy these. The area immediately below the bridge was in shadow and little detail could be seen, but Varro suspected the presence of a barrier of some kind because in front, floating on the surface, was a potpourri of detritus which spread across the full width of the canal and bulged out to where the lights reached their limit. It looked like it had built up over years, no doubt blown down the river chute by the wind and whatever meagre currents ran in the swampy water. Rubbish of every different colour and shade, thickness and use. It resembled inarticulate works of art he had seen. Varro wondered at what point someone would decide it was the moment to clear it all up. Maybe never. Who cared about the eyesore at the gnarly edges of the two communities? Varro watched as items arriving on the wind jostled at the edges whilst the main conglomeration rose and fell with each gust.

Varro pulled himself back into the darkness of the canopy and leant back in the water, resting his head on a branch. He could think of no-way to reach the other side. Get out and try to sprint across was just suicidal. Continue along the canal and he would be pinpointed in the lights. And even if he made it to the tunnel, whatever barrier was there would certainly impede further progress.

A sense of defeat took him. He could barely feel his body now, more like some primordial punishment to be hauled around. Much of him just wanted to rest, curl up by the side of a stump and fall asleep. Any adrenaline from his initial flight had long since worn off, leaving him spent and sapped of any will. He slipped further into the water, his legs sinking below him, his head backwards, only his snout and lips tremulous above the surface of the water. What was stopping him staying like this forever?

Then the idea came, uninvited but polite enough not to scream out its arrival. Varro continued supine and considered it, turning it over with what small logic remained in his gift. Under normal circumstances the idea was absurd, crazy. But he was an outcast and there was nothing normal about his situation. And it was his only option. Either that or freeze to death.

Varro brushed aside the branches, keeping to the darkness of the sides as he set off again towards the bridge. He took his time, casting around occasionally for what he wanted, discarding anything not deemed as suitable. As he drew nearer, the amount of rubbish increased, and it didn't take him long to find what he wanted. A mid-size, fingernail thin piece of plagilene, most probably some sort of carrying bag or container, Varro concluded. The material rustled as he pulled it from the water. The length of time in the canal must have weakened its internal bonds because he had little problem in making the holes where he wanted, stretching them with his numb fingers to create some sort of shape. It didn't have to be perfect, just wide enough to allow him to breathe. He lay back in the water, floating on his back and covered his face with the plagilene. The two orifices he had created for his nose and mouth weren't perfectly aligned but they would have to do. He didn't have time for more. He found that if he sank too low in the water, the plagilene would lift off and drift away, so he placed one hand behind his head and grasped the loose ends. That worked better. How the vigilance at the bridge interpreted this mobile flotsam Varro would never know. Neither was it his concern. Either it worked or he would be arrested in the attempt.

Varro pushed out into the centre of the canal, then leaning backwards, legs dangling at an angle in the water, he began to kick gently, keeping any churn to a minimum. Swimming towards the bridge on his back, he realised he would be effectively blind, unable to see in which direction he was headed. He would just have to trust his instincts and wait till he reached the darkness under the bridge.

It wasn't long before he entered the floodlit space, and he could see now the greenish hue to the plagilene. It was faintly transparent as well, and Varro felt horribly exposed. The burning lights made it feel like daytime, and the temptation was to kick wildly with his legs, arrive at the bridge as quickly as possible, but Varro knew that that would create an unnatural amount of froth. As it stood, there was a chance that the stately procession of a piece of plagilene through the detritus would be interpreted as just part of the ebb and flow of this urban waste, nothing more.

He was soon into the heart of the polluting heap, and he could feel glass, plastic, fabric ricochet from his head as he kept up the steady propulsion below the surface, using his free hand to maintain buoyancy. He tried to keep his mouth, nose and forehead as close to the surface as possible; high enough to get air, low enough that nothing protruded excessively. Occasionally he clattered into a more significant piece, sending ripples washing over his face, almost causing him to choke. At any moment he expected to hear the voices of his captors or the groan of a ranger cruiser settling low overhead, directing him to withdraw from the water, that his flight was over. But there was nothing except the intense light and the sensation of nudging material to one side. He tried to keep midway between the two lights, focussed on where he judged their intersection.

The end came quickly. Like an eclipse, the darkness slid over him, and with a few more flutter kicks the light had gone completely, and at the same time he felt himself run into something sturdier than the superficial scum. Varro stopped and collected himself before carefully removing the plagilene, holding on to it with his left hand – he might still need it. He treaded water, looking out now onto the colourful panorama of floating rubbish he had just swum through. He could hardly believe it. But he had little time to dwell. If he could find no way through the barrier, then his journey was at an end.

Varro turned and felt at the hard metal which appeared to be a mesh of some kind, solid enough but with finger sized holes to let the water back and forth. That would explain why the rubbish had accumulated here. Varro traced his hand across, but it was obvious that the barrier ran the full width of the canal and that to get around it one would be forced to get out of the water. Not an option. He would have to go under.

Varro dived, using the small holes of the mesh to guide him downwards, venting his lungs once more, but after two metres he still hadn't lost contact with the solid structure. It must go all the way to the bottom. There was only one way to find out. He dived a second time, this time he was more adept, making quicker progress down the sheer face of the grill, and when his fingers twisted in the gloom and found only water Varro realised he had come to the bottom. He rose once more, caught his breath and then descended for a third time. He didn't need another chance. As soon as he gauged that there was space for his body, he wriggled beneath the barrier, scraping his backpack in his determination to get to the other side. Once through, he rose quickly, gathering his breath at the surface in exaggerated, grateful gulps. He only hoped that the other side of the tunnel was identical. The water felt even colder in the underpass, and all around was pitch black. It was damp and sinister, like a Victorian sewer, and he swam quickly the 60 metres.

The southern end of the tunnel resembled the north in every aspect, except one. Where there had been a veritable sea of detritus, here there was nothing, only the unwelcome sheen of the high-powered lights glaring down on the blank surface. Even the wind seemed to have dropped. He would be unable to repeat the plagilene trick.

Varro looked through the holes in the mesh, towards the field of light where the twin arcs fell and then beyond that to the wide silence and darkness of the Grey Zone fields. He couldn't see it, but Varro knew that just three kilometres away the neat symmetry of the fields and its micro controlled agriculture gave way abruptly to the primeval confusion of the borderland. His destination. A hundred years of wilful neglect; of trees rising and falling, colourful shrubs monopolising whole areas, briars winding their way wherever they were allowed to, and in the interstices, birds and animals made their homes and grew their young. A convenient buffer for both communities with nature the only winner. Make it there and Varro was on the road to safety. Three kilometres. He could run it in 20 minutes, even in his sodden clothes and fatigued state. But once out of the water he and his heat trace would be an easy target. Drones would be upon him in a handful of minutes, with rangers close behind. No, the water would have to host him a while longer. But how to get across? It was 40 metres of luminescence before the darkness took hold again. He only had one option, and Varro knew that its success this time depended entirely on him.

Varro ducked once more and surfaced the other side of the barrier. At the edge of the tunnel, under the 180, Varro felt exposed. One final effort. That was all. Then he would be safe. He calmed his breathing, then focussed on the canal at the point the light gave out. That was where he needed to be. He took a sharp tug of air, then dived, his legs fluttering wildly, like a wind-up toy of yesteryear. Even just below the surface and with the help of the artificial light, he could see little. He pushed forward with only the most general idea of direction. 15…20 seconds, he wriggled furiously, burning energy and air. Once again, the swelling in his lungs, battling the temptation to come up too early. After 30 seconds he could hold it no more. He rose.

In his desperation, he emerged more sharply than he had intended, sending droplets scattering along the surface. He was around ten metres short of where he had intended, still in the sprawl of light. But he didn't delay. He pulled a slug of air and then returned below the surface, confident now that he would reach well beyond the boundary of artificial light on this second attempt. When he resurfaced it was to complete darkness. He had made it. Varro pushed over to the side, lifting himself clear of the water and flopping onto the soft grass, half in, half out. He closed his eyes and felt the seductive pull of sleep. Then he remembered and looked back towards the 180. Nothing seemed to have changed. No sirens or rush of clattering boots. Maybe his fleeting appearance hadn't been picked up. He had only spent the briefest of moments above the surface. It could have been anything.

But he didn't have time to dwell. The Grey Zone had been designed for intensive agriculture, so stray undergrowth and self-seeded trees had been swept aside to maximise space for crops. Except a narrow footpath, fields ran hard up to the canal, and there was little opportunity to hide away. He would be more exposed here than ever, more so as Varro saw the unmistakeable first blush of dawn, a slight opening along the length of the eastern horizon. The slit would only get bigger, and brighter.

But he didn't have far to go now. He might even get out of the water for the last kilometre and make a run for it. He wondered how his legs would respond. But for now, he slipped back into the water and began with renewed vigour, kicking his legs like twin propellors, urging himself forwards, and using the rekindled impetus to keep the worst of the cold out. As he advanced, Varro felt his spirits rise. The end of his journey was in sight and whatever happened to him in the borderland and beyond, the nightmare which had started from the apparent safety of his own house was almost at an end. He even wondered what Karena would be doing at that precise moment.

The spotlight fell on him like hardened iron. He hadn't even heard the drone. His emergence from the waters after the 180 hadn't gone unnoticed. His immediate instinct was to drop below the surface once more, but that was preposterous. They had found him. It was over. Unable to react, Varro continued swimming, at any moment expecting the sting of a dart or thud of an immobiliser. But the overhead craft merely kept the beam focussed tightly on him, tracking him inexorably. Varro realised this feed was being shared widely at the moment, decisions considered and taken. It felt surreal, but he just kept going. What else was there for him to do? The strange stand-off continued for several minutes, Varro continuing his steady progress towards the borderland in the glare of the drone's mute spotlight. And then, as suddenly as it had arrived, the drone lifted away and was gone, leaving Varro confused and in darkness again. But the respite was brief, and Varro felt rather than heard the heavy presence of the cruiser barely 50 metres above him. The pool of light from the rangers' craft was wider than the drone's and Varro could see the thick tufts of grass at the side of the canal, their heads a lurid green in the unnatural light. Ripples stoked the surface of the water from the cruiser's draft. Its looming presence was like a storm cloud about to break, and at any moment he expected rangers dropping from the sky, Q-chuted onto the canal bank. Or they might just neutralise him in the water. What he didn't expect was to hear his name broadcast across the fields on the cusp of dawn.

'Ignatius Varro, well, well. I hadn't expected our next meeting to be quite like this. But I suppose such novelties keep the spice in life, *n'est pas*? It seems that your ability to fix agricultural machinery is only matched by your ability to escape.'

The sound hit the ground and spread out across the flatlands of the fields. The incongruity of hearing his name caused Varro to slow, his thoughts whirling as to what this novel development could mean. What was the man on about? And then he realised, recognised the voice even. The impatient ranger captain. It seemed an eternity since the same cruiser had hovered above him, urging him to speed up his repair, but it couldn't have been more than a few weeks. And now the bastard was directly over him, holding his destiny like an eagle grasps its prey.

'Get out.'

Varro cast a questioning glance upwards.

'Come on, Varro, stop dithering, get out of the water now. You must be freezing in there.'

Varro did as he was told, but not quickly. There seemed little point in hurrying now. In a short while he would be in the hold of the cruiser, hurtling northwards and bound for goodness knows what fate.

He hauled himself onto the bank with difficulty, lying jack-knifed for a moment to recover from the effort, letting the water drain off him. He was exhausted.

'Come on, Varro, look sharpish, if you're going to escape, you can't be taking the time to admire the scenery.'

Varro got to his feet and for the first time looked up. The angular underbelly of the craft was like vast granite rockface. What was the captain on about? He wondered if this surreal intervention was even being recorded.

'I still don't know what you're waiting for, south is that way.'

And for an instant the shaft of light fell away from him and lit up the stretch of path towards the borderland.

'What?' Varro cried out. He really wasn't sure what was expected of him.

'Run, Varro, run. That's the quickest way to escape, running. Now, come on!'

Suddenly the turf immediately behind Varro exploded, sending up clumps of moist soil and grass in all directions and forcing Varro to raise his arms in protection. A high-powered bolt, but a deliberate miss.

'Come on, Varro, I hope you don't need any more encouragement!'

Varro was amazed at this turn of events, but it wasn't difficult to detect the glee in the captain's voice, and for the first time Varro realised what this was. Revenge, or a perverse version of it. Maybe this is what happened in the Grey Zone and borderlands all the time, a dash of sporting savagery with non-cons. But for the captain this was personal, and he was clearly relishing the opportunity. Varro began a slow trot, the water squelching in his shoes, water running into his eyes from his soaking hair. All along the footpath, the cruiser's beam tracked him like a giant magnet.

'A little faster, Varro, a little faster, if you really want to free yourself from all your shackles!'

Another bolt shuddered into the earth, closer this time, stripping all the air around him and sending Varro sprawling onto the footpath. He got up as quickly as he could.

'That's better, Varro, a little more urgency, I think. Keep going.'

Varro was running hard now and around him he could start to make out the grey outlines of trees and hedges. Dawn was coming quickly. Ahead, the erratic profile of the borderland, now a kilometre away at most. His heart was beating hard, his lungs aching in their effort to pull in enough air. But still the demented captain wasn't satisfied. Another bolt raked at his back, disintegrating the ground immediately behind him, causing Varro to stumble forwards.

'Faster, Varro, you really must go faster. You'll never escape at the rate you're going.'

Varro could feel tears of effort and frustration smarting in his eyes, the sheer absurdity that all this final, vain thrust was simply to gratify the demented captain. His odyssey was being transformed into sport, and at any moment the precision bolt would come, switched to stun and leave him unconscious on the grassy footpath in the still of the morning. Then a pair of rangers would descend, scoop up his limp body and return him north. To cerebellum justice. This was all just a charade. Titillation for the captain and his crew. Rage kept Varro charging forwards. A bitterness that all his suffering had to end this way.

'Come on, you've only got 500 metres to go, Varro, let's see if we can finish with a sprint,' the captain almost squealed in his enjoyment and Varro thought he could hear someone chortle in the background. The bastards. 'One final effort, Varro and...'

The boom and the physical blow arrived simultaneously, lifting Varro from his feet and throwing him backwards like a doll. His head snapped back as he smashed into the ground. Scrambling to his feet, Varro saw stars evaporate before him, the horizon unsteady. But the cruiser was no longer above, instead it was several hundred metres to the east, tilting from side to side, like a drunk trying to clear their head. Varro didn't hesitate, he was running again, harder than ever, the initial boundary of the borderland clearly visible now, the mature elms, oaks and ash trees still sporting their summer leaves, below these the darker greens of hawthorn, blackthorn and berry bushes filling the spaces. Varro saw that the path he was running on was dissolving from grass to crisper, curling leaves and the occasional fallen boughs and trunks in states of slow decomposition. For a moment, Varro wondered why all this had become so salient. Then he realised, the cruiser with its lights was returning, drawing with it the details of everything around. He soon stood out starkly once again, his running shadow as precise as previously. As he made the boundary, he heard the first soggy impact of a dart, passing within millimetres of him and throwing up a strata of mulch and blackened leaves where it struck the ground. Varro sprinted on, slaloming between trunks, leaping over fallen branches and tangled clumps of briars, the artificial light and the leafy canopy creating a kaleidoscope effect on the ground. A second dart hit its mark, the impetus of the shot enough to send him to the ground, where he could smell the fecundity of the rotting leaves. He waited for the tranquilizer to take effect. But nothing came, and he was soon up and running again, his direction haphazard, just trying to find a way without obstacles. He knew this cat and mouse game couldn't go on for much longer, and that very shortly the captain would switch to something more draconian.

And then a second massive burst tore through the undergrowth, a wave of horizontal energy dragging everything in its direction. Varro, too, felt himself rise and fly helplessly backwards, landing in a tangle of thorns that punctured his hands as he tried to cushion his fall. In the maelstrom he glimpsed the cruiser, tossed around like a stick in a weir, its prow towards the heavens, the spotlight now shining uselessly into the morning murk. Varro wondered if the battered craft and its shell-shocked crew would be able to recover from this second assault. But he didn't stay to find out, running hard once more, and then after a few minutes, when nothing had disturbed the fragile balance of the forest, he slowed to a walk, and a few minutes after that, he stopped and leant against the smooth trunk of a massive beech tree, its thick limbs still decked with glossy leaves. He looked upwards. Between the dark outlines of the boughs Varro could make out the distinctive edges of the morning's first clouds. The cruiser was nowhere to be seen, and for the first time, Varro let the stillness and calm of the morning enter him.

After school yesterday, Mum took me to have my hair cut and I said I wanted it done like Madonna but when I went to school today Louise said it looks like a piss pot (I'm not sure what this means but they have been saying it ever since we went to secondary school). And what made it worse was that Lewis was there with Simon, and they laughed as well. I tried not to but I started crying, but we couldn't go inside because it was still break time so I went and sat down near the school garden with Elizabeth. One of the dinner ladies came across and asked if I was OK, and then after school, Mrs Bristow said she wanted to speak with me and I told her what had happened. She said my hair was lovely (which made me feel better), and that she had a similar style when she was younger. I don't understand why Louise and Michaela are like that sometimes. I don't do anything to them and only want to be friends. Mrs Bristow says that sometimes people say and do things without thinking what effect it will have on other people.

Chapter 29

It didn't take Varro long to reach the far side of the borderland and, as to the north, here too there was a clear demarcation, from the overgrown exuberance of the two-kilometre strip to the more ordered farmland of the non-cons. Varro had, of course, seen all this land from the air many times before. But it had always been at a distance, and when the billowing cumulous clouds loomed dominant in the aerial scene, stripping the dun-coloured fields and green ribbon hedgerows of much significance. But now, standing at the edge of the clearing, a light mist visible in the thin morning light, Varro noticed a different perspective. Unlike in the ceb controlled lands where the hedgerows had been uprooted in the name of agricultural efficiency, here they followed their ancient patterns, with languorous curves and inexplicable kinks and corners. Within each field itself there was further division; long, clean rows of onions, carrots, peppers, tomatoes on canes, like a grand market garden, whilst similar sized segments to either side lay fallow. It reminded Varro of old prints showing pre-enclosure fields. Finishing many strips were neat herb gardens, divided from the main areas by ankle high wicker divisions, the lavender blues bold against the gradations of dominant green. Dotted at random around each field were modest wooden huts, some well maintained, others with distressed paint and lichen covered roofs.

Varro looked up. It was strange not to see the crossing patterns of the uni-k and deca shuttles. The day was brightening, but the sun lay hidden behind the diffuse cloud, and no warmth filtered through, leaving him shivering in his still sodden clothing. He had no clear plan, only a vague longing to put distance between himself and the lands he had fled from. He had no doubt that he was being followed by the supra earth systems of the cebs but knew also that no craft was likely to cross over here to pursue him. The non-cons had always been left to get on with their own thing, and tradition had turned into policy. ONE had always thought it showed a supreme benevolence.

Varro began to follow the field boundaries and as he stomped from one field to another, he saw growing numbers of people in the fields. Many were already at work, bent over, hacking and clawing away at the ground or snipping at foliage. They all wore the multi layered coverings of the non-cons, with items for distinct parts of the body. It had always seemed less efficient than the all-purpose monosuit, but now Varro felt ill at ease in his splattered and stinking costume. He kept his distance, but they still followed his progress, observing with watchful eyes, their expressions remaining cautious when Varro did try to raise a smile. But he didn't push the issue. He had no wish to delay. He would reach a town and then take stock.

Shortly he found himself on a twisting tarmacked road, its verges thick with long grasses and wildflowers, high hedges of blackthorn and hawthorn beyond that. Most of the central lines had bleached away. He hadn't been walking long before he heard a low rumbling, growing louder by the second. When it appeared from around a corner, he recognised it, of course, but he had never seen one of this vintage. A tractor, bottle green and the height of two men. It reminded Varro of a human face, its dirty Perspex enclosure like a high, flat forehead. It bore down on Varro, the driver bouncing in unison with the beast. The beating rose to a crescendo as it came nearer, and Varro noticed the black smoke surging from the pipe on the front. A machine which ran on oil. Seen in virtual museums, but never a working version. It was incredible, and as he shifted to one side to let it pass, he felt privileged. Mend and mend, that had been the cry from the Ekers, those very first non-cons who had rallied against the incessant iterations of new goods and the waste they resulted in. They had made eking out into a virtue and, almost 300 years afterwards, here was the result of their labours. Varro was so absorbed by the spectacle of a combustion vehicle that he hardly noticed the prolonged stare the middle-aged driver cast down upon him. Once passed, Varro continue to wallow in the acrid cloud that gradually dispersed in the morning air.

It wasn't long before he came across a further example of a low box like structure, grey with a flat roof extending far over the sides. Presumably to avoid aerial surveillance. Two younger women, in their mid-twenties Varro reckoned, their heads covered in light scarves, were chatting animatedly by the side of the building. By their gestures, Varro interpreted some sort of narrative explanation, and he could feel the enthusiasm of their conversation even from a distance. Then a door next to them opened and an older lady appeared from the darkness, said something to the girls who turned their heads in acknowledgement, then both waved as the lady swept past, before turning to each other once more. They noticed Varro when he was a short distance away, turning to him with suspicious eyes, falling silent and following him closely as he approached jauntily.

'Good morning,' Varro ventured in English.

'Hello,' replied one girl, but without enthusiasm. It was obvious that Varro didn't belong here.

He pushed on and before long arrived at a junction of a larger road running north to south. He was about to turn to the south when in the morass of hedge opposite he saw the peeling white paint of a thick post on top of which was a very old-fashioned street sign. He had never seen one before but knew that at one time these were the only way that a stranger could find his way between villages. Varro crossed the road, a few seconds before a man with a lowered cap on a cycle went by. He looked hard at Varro as he passed. The taciturn stares were becoming a little disconcerting and Varro couldn't decide if it was curiosity or hostility. There was little friendliness.

Standing on the grassy bank, Varro reached into the hedgerow and pushed aside some branches to better observe the finger signs attached to the post. Bodilby, 1.5 miles. He had heard that name before, and recently. But where? Then he remembered. This was the place Rachel lived. He had hardly thought about her during his ordeal but now her lively eyes returned to him. She was the only non-con he knew. Perhaps she could help, maybe guide him onwards now the initial shock of his flight was over. The more he thought about it, the more sense it made. At least she wouldn't stare at him so blatantly.

Although wider, the new road still bore the signs of age and disrepair, an appearance worsened by the blotchy effect of the morning's dew. There were more people here, some walking, others on cycles of the kind he and Bragg had used so recently. An occasional tractor chugged past. There didn't seem to be any particular rules and the faint lines which once must have guided the transit of vehicles now played no obvious role. Most people shared greetings with each other, but fell silent with Varro, the obvious stranger in their midst.

It took him a further 30 minutes to reach the village, passing another of the grey, rectangular buildings on the outskirts, from which people continued to emerge at regular intervals, some by themselves, more often in small, animated groups. He wondered where they were coming from.

Bodilby was little more than a central street Varro soon concluded, but most of the houses seemed sunk in time, barely altered in hundreds of years; greyish red brick weathered to yellow, hollowed out grouting, rotting fascia boards, drainpipes burst from their brackets, windows smeared in greasy dust, and roof tiles deep in bright moss.

Most shocking were the sheds; giant industrial carapaces which had been erected over many of the properties without thought or aesthetic consideration, often extending far beyond the eaves of each house, cutting gardens in two. They were like giraffes protecting their young, but many were in a worse condition than the houses they covered, with giant, gale snatched flaps of metal peeled back from their fittings, rust eaten stanchions and copious vegetation weaving upwards from concrete bases. Many, Varro supposed, had been untouched ever since the non-cons first opted to shield themselves from the nosey spies overhead. A draconian measure which were like scars on the patchwork landscape, but they continued to set the scene for how Varro and his society viewed the non-cons.

Everything was much quieter here, and it gave the air an eerie quality as he drifted down the main street, a wild-west gunfighter seeking his date with destiny. A cat ran out from the disintegrating skirting of a wood panelled fence, scampering along the thick tufts of the verge before disappearing behind a hedge. He had to swerve to avoid a thick wooden pole which had fallen towards the road, the split foundations leaving an ugly tear. In places, large broad-leafed trees loomed over the road, long outgrown their environment, their roots shunting up the tarmac into grey-black cordilleras. Varro wondered at such abandonment. Maybe the cerebellums had been right after all about the degradation of the non-con world, but it was hard to credit this with the industry in the fields and with what Rachel had told him.

When he ran out of buildings on one side, Varro realised he was approaching the conclusion of the settlement. He had walked the entire length without seeing a single human being, though in the fields all around, people were at work. On the other side of the road, the final house was unusual, set back in its own plot and uncovered, its style discernibly more modern than the others. A creamy covering looked like many of the plagilene finishes to the blocks in Hull or York, and the mirror glass of the regularly spaced windows looked like they would provide much of the house's energy needs. Maybe it had been a late addition to the village, bought, built and developed at a time when crossing the 180 was the most normal thing in the world. How strange. In the field in front of the house, across the ditch and weathered boundary fence, an elderly lady with wispy grey hair was petting a docile donkey, talking gently to it while stroking the dirty stripe along its snout. It reminded Varro of how his own grandparents had talked to the animals on the farm, with an intimacy normally reserved for family members.

'Excuse me,' Varro called out. The lady turned slowly, tilting her head upwards as if testing the air. If she was surprised at his appearance, she covered it well.

'Yes, how can I help you?'

'I want to know where someone lives. Near here, I think.'

'Yes?'

'Her name is Rachel. She lives on a farm…I think.'

'Rachel?'

Varro felt stupid for not knowing her surname.

'I don't know anything else about her, I'm sorry.'

'Rachel…Rachel,' the old lady was lost in her thoughts, muttering to herself. Varro grew impatient.

'Oh, and she's got a brother, I know that much.'

'A lot of Rachels have brothers, young man,' she said kindly, but Varro still felt irritated at his ineptitude. It galled him to be held up by something so simple.

'The brother has something wrong with him,' Varro blurted, immediately regretting his words. The old lady stared at him.

'Something wrong with him?' She looked concerned. It might be catching. Would she even speak again? Then her face brightened. 'Oh, you mean Rachel at Three Wells Farm? Rachel and Stevie. Of course, they're not far from here, not far at all.'

Varro edged closer to the ditch and listened carefully as the old lady described the correct route across the fields. With a rising delight, Varro realised it wouldn't take him long at all. He thanked the woman who wished him well before returning to the patient donkey. It wouldn't be long now.

<u>*Sunday 29 June*</u>

Mummy and Dad still aren't talking to each other, or if they are, they are being very quiet. I'm writing this under the covers with a torch because we are supposed to be sleeping, but I don't feel tired and I'm a bit hungry, because all we got when we got back home was a jam sandwich. Then Mum sent us to bed. But it wasn't our fault and I will tell you why.

Today has been the hottest day of the year so far, and they said on the weather forecast that the temperature was going to reach nearly 30 degrees. As it was the weekend, Mummy suggested that we go to the beach, but Dad said we could go later in the summer when he wasn't working during the week. But we all made such a fuss about going that in the end he agreed. So we went to the beach at Cleethorpes and we had a really good day. Dad pretended to be a sleeping giant and that the only way to keep him from being angry was to bury him, so we covered him in sand until finally, when all that was left of him was his head, he suddenly pretended to wake up and threw all the sand away from him. Daniel ran away screaming, but me and Mummy just laughed. It was very funny. Then Mummy went and bought ice creams with chocolate flakes (delicious!) and we sat on the beach looking out to the sea and counting the ships moving across the horizon. It was so hot that the ships seemed to shimmer and Mum said it was like a mirage.

But when we came back home, the car got a puncture. Daddy tried to fix it, but he couldn't get the jack to work properly so he couldn't change the wheel. When Mummy suggested we call someone to help, Daddy got very angry and said a bad word. We were all very quiet after that. Then the repair truck came and the man helped Daddy change the wheel. It was dark when we got back and quite cold (because we hadn't taken jackets), and then Mummy sent us straight to bed. I hope they start talking (together) soon.

Chapter 30

The passage across the fields was swift and Varro grew indifferent to the stares he received from those working the land. He could feel the heat slide into the day, and as he made his way along rutted tracks he felt his spirits rise.

He had no problems recognising the battered asphalt road the lady had mentioned. He stopped to one side and looked across towards a deep, well scoured ditch and beyond that a low hedge parallel to the road. A little further along was an entrance leading to an avenue of maple trees which shimmered in the light morning breeze. On the far side of the hedge the unmistakeable rows of vines in arrow straight trellises. The grapes had all gone but the vines still wore their desiccated livery, greens turning to a dirty russet. At the far end of the field, maybe half a kilometre away, Varro could make out the farmhouse. It must have been several hundred years old, with three central chimney stacks looking like fluted Doric columns and a motley-coloured pan tiled roof which levelled off as it approached the eaves. This must be Rachel's home.

Trundling up between the rows came a tractor, cabinless and rust coloured. It towed a large, scabby cylinder at the back of which a fan which was filling the morning air with thick jets of spray. As the vehicle approached, Varro studied the man who was sitting on it, heavily built and of a similar age to Varro, but placid and with a slack jaw which lent the man an air of inattention.

Varro had no wish to enter the property without permission – his sole meeting with Rachel didn't constitute an open invitation. Somehow, he needed to attract the man's attention.

Crossing the narrow road and standing close to the ditch, Varro waited patiently as the tractor approached. He geared himself up for the moment when the man noticed him, planning the most appropriate greeting. But when the tractor reached the end of the row, not even a stone's throw away, the man looked straight through

Varro, ignoring him completely, briefly stopping the spray, quietening the roaring vehicle, and wheeling the tractor round, before heading back down the next row. Varro was astonished. Had the man done that on purpose? Surely, he had been impossible to miss, standing there. He was the only other human around.

Varro shifted to the next row and waited while the tractor completed its circuit, starting to feel a chill in the damp monosuit. As the sound of the tractor grew, Varro watched carefully for any change of expression, but the man remained immobile, his concentration wholly focussed on the tractor, or maybe quite removed from it – Varro couldn't be sure which. The man reached the end of the vines, calming the engine and stopping the spray as he made the turn around the thick end stake.

'Hello, there!' Varro shouted.

This brought the man up from his controls. He turned his head and stared at Varro, as if seeing him for the first time. He said nothing and Varro repeated his greeting, letting his features fall into what he hoped was a non-threatening smile. The situation was unclear. The man reached down below the steering wheel and the engine slowed, then stuttered to a halt, a burst of black smoke accompanying its final death. The man continued staring at Varro but remained silent.

'I'm sorry to disturb you, but I was looking for Rachel. Is she here?'

'She's not here,' said the man after a few moments. The words deep and drawn out. A country voice.

'But she does live here, in the farmhouse over there, doesn't she?'

The man swivelled in his seat to look in the direction Varro was indicating, then turned just as slowly back.

'Yes, that's where she lives.'

'Er, well, I'm a friend,' Varro could think of nothing else to say. The conversation wasn't going as he had planned. 'Do you think I could come in and see her?'

The man's eyes narrowed, his brow creased, Varro could almost feel the effort of the man's thinking. He was beginning to regret his approach. The man looked away, his eyes flitting across the empty sky. Finally, he replied. 'You have to ask her first.'

'Yes, of course, how do I do that? Shall I just come in?'

'I could ask her for you.'

'That would be good, thank you.'

'But I can't leave the tractor.'

'Oh.'

'I have to finish the field first.'

The conversation was going nowhere. Varro would have to try something different.

'I see, well maybe when you see her, you could tell her that someone was looking for her.'

'OK,' he said, and Varro waited for him to continue. Instead, he looked plaintively at Varro and said, 'Can I start the tractor again now?'

Varro didn't know what to say.

'Of course you can, Stevie, you're doing such a good job. Keep going and when you finish, come to the house and we will have our morning cocoa and almond cake together.'

It was Rachel. She had appeared from nowhere, but she must have emerged from the tree lined entrance and walked silently along the verge. She wore tight blue trousers, ankle length black boots and a checked shirt, two buttons undone to reveal sharp folds of the collar and a brilliant silver chain against her skin. She had a precision and order about her that left its mark, and in the wan morning light she positively glowed.

She continued smiling towards the man as he restarted the tractor, slipping back into the dreamlike state of previously. Rachel continued looking after him for some while as the tractor made its way once more between the vines, the spray reaching out in spirals and clouds over the crop. Then she turned to Varro.

'What are you doing here?'

'I came to see you.'

'Why?'

'I had no-one else to go to. I was scared.'

'Why?'

Varro was taken aback. She looked so stern. He had invested his appearance before her with so much hope, that passing into her orbit would bring respite, the relief of a felon in the Middle Ages coming within the boundary of a sanctuary town. Yet now, with a clarity which pained him, he could see exactly how she must be seeing him. He was a citizen in the land of the non-cons. This was no social visit. This was an apparition born out of desperation, amply confirmed by his ragged aspect. Maybe that was why the man on the tractor had reacted so strangely, too. His appearance could only mean one thing – trouble. He would have to tell the truth.

'I'm in danger, Rachel. I had to escape from my house. I couldn't think where to go. I still don't know. I was thinking maybe you could help me.'

She remained staring at him, her features hard and unreadable. Despite himself, he again thought how attractive she was.

'Follow me,' she said, taking a moment to look briskly from side to side. 'Quickly.'

They walked without a word to the farm entrance and then down the gravel driveway, the avenue of trees covering their passage, the only sound the crunch of the stones beneath their feet. Occasionally Varro glanced over, seeing her alert, her brown eyes forceful and determined.

Varro's misgivings grew with each step. He had no right to intrude on her like this, all on the basis of a single conversation, an encounter he now realised in which she was just playing a part, and in which he, Bragg and the soppy Ceb had been the guileless audience. This was a different reality. Walking in silence towards the farmhouse, there were no parts being played, and Varro was simply a liability. By the time they arrived at the entrance, a large oak door with a simple iron latch, Varro had made up his mind.

'No, Rachel, I'm not coming in. I'll sort myself out. I was wrong to come. I apologise.'

She turned to him, studying his face with her eyes, then without saying a word, she reached out, took his hand and pulled him towards the door, holding him firmly until they were inside.

The interior was low and dark, and Varro struggled at first to make anything out, only noticing the smell of doughy bread and strong coffee which hung in the air of what he soon realised must have been the family kitchen. It was warm, too, the overweening odours wrapping themselves in the heat of the room. As he sat down in the pine chair she directed him to, Varro realised how little energy remained to him. In contrast she strode purposefully towards the hunk of metal which was the range stove where a blackened kettle was expelling small packets of steam. Picking up the kettle she turned, and for the first time her features eased. It was almost a smile.

'Would you like some coffee?'

'Please.'

'And something to eat, no doubt?'

'That would be nice, too. Thank you.'

Varro felt something inside him loosen.

She swiftly filled a mug and brought it across, placing it on the large table in front of him.

'Oh, you're soaking. Let's get you some new clothes.' Varro watched as she disappeared through one of the doorways in the large room. He looked up to where formidable, age blackened beams crossed the low ceiling. On the other side of the room, and the only obvious source of light, a small window over a wide porcelain sink gave out onto a garden. Through the glass Varro could see the almost leafless skeins of a wild cherry, stark against the diaphanous light. Rachel wasn't long in returning, placing a pile of garments on the table next to the steaming coffee.

'They won't be perfect, but at least they'll be dry.'

'Are they Stevie's?'

She assented with her head.

'What will he think if he sees me in them?'

'What do you think he'll think?' The challenge took Varro by surprise.

247

'He seems very happy in his own world. He might not even notice.'

She looked at him keenly then turned away, shouting out over her shoulder.

'Go on, get changed. I won't look.'

'Do you promise?'

This time she did turn and smile, a grin of complicity which Varro realised was worth a thousand words. There was, after all, something there. Varro hadn't imagined it.

'Come on,' she chided. 'Get dressed before I change my mind and sit and stare at a naked stranger in my kitchen.'

He grinned and began removing the soiled monosuit, feeling it sticky as he peeled it away from his skin. Removing his backpack was cumbersome and as it fell to the floor, Varro noticed the tranquiliser dart hanging from the middle of the pack, drooping like a wilting flower. That would explain why he hadn't been overcome.

When he had finished, she came over to the table carrying a brown cake on a plate, sitting down close to him and offering him a slice. The smell of warm sponge rose to him, bringing fond memories. He reached out and placed his hand over hers.

'Thank you,' he said. And meant it. For a moment she held his eyes, and something powerful and true passed between them. Then he pulled his hand away and she said, 'Now, tell me what you're doing wearing my brother's clothes, drinking our coffee and stuffing yourself with my finest almond cake.'

He told her everything, and as she followed his narrative her eyes barely left him, quietly, sincerely absorbing it all.

'I hope I didn't upset Stevie too much just now,' he concluded.

'Stevie, no, he might not even remember it, especially if he has one of his seizures shortly.'

'Seizures?'

'Fits, seizures, the doctors here aren't sure what they are, but he just blanks out, returns to zero as it were, remembers a few basic things, forgets the rest.'

'Can't you do anything about it?'

'They've tried, but nothing seems to work. Your drugs make the attacks less common, that's all. But it's getting worse.'

Varro thought back to Bragg's boasts about the terms of his encounters with her.

'Maybe...' Varro began, but he never finished. Everything happened at once; the explosion, the deafening boom and most shocking of all, the terror in Rachel's eyes as she slipped backwards in her chair. Varro lost balance, too, the shockwave throwing him to the floor, the chair clattering away in another direction. The room had turned to night and a smell of burnt electrics filled the air. He went to rise but got no further than freeing his shoulders from the flagstone floor before he felt himself pinned back down again with abominable force, his head snapping back with a crack as it hit the hard ground. Two masked figures loomed over him, malevolent and brutal. He considered struggling but the force was so overwhelming that there was no point. And then came the puncture in his arm, hard and sharp. And then he felt no more.

It was school sports day yesterday and I won the sack race! Daniel came second in the sprint. Mummy took photographs of us and she's going to have them developed soon. They had races for the mums and dads, and even the teachers did one race. Unfortunately, Daddy couldn't come and see us running. Mum said he couldn't get time off work. This was a pity, I think he would have beaten many of the other dads in the egg and spoon race – some of them were useless, they couldn't run 2 metres without their eggs falling off the spoon, and one of them just held the egg with his other hand and ran to the end. Miss Grey disqualified him, she said he couldn't win like that. I tried to tell Dad all about it when he got home after dinner, but I think he was very tired and asked me to tell him about it the next day. That's today. I will do, if I remember and he gets home before I go to bed.

Chapter 31

Dana had slept little. And the hours she did get were fitful, so it was a relief to be back in the control room before dawn, a full hour before EUROPE was to be restored. Time enough also to catch up on events of the previous night, to think through all eventualities of the unfolding situation. She was determined not to be found wanting in any way by her cerebellum.

She glanced once more over the control panels in front of her, checking that everything was in place and that the raft of daily updates from around the European continent would arrive with the ceb immediately on waking, to be processed systematically and almost at the speed of light; meteorological readings, agricultural yields, experimental results, manufacturing outputs, meetings held and decisions taken, minister speeches, citizens' news, natural phenomenon. Some demanded an immediate response, others were for information only, and the most important would be run past the guardian as a matter of courtesy and balance. Even an almost omnipotent ceb could appreciate the value of a neutral perspective. It was immediately after all this cornucopia of information that Dana had programmed a short summary of the night's happenings. EUROPE would be keen to prioritise and discuss them. But the news wasn't good, and as she stood in the cold light of the control room, quietly overseeing the night engineer's restoration procedures, she knew it was unlikely to be an easy conversation.

As she did every morning with five minutes to go before EUROPE's 6am rousing, she entered the inner vestibule and made her way slowly up the ramp towards the ring. But today, the nearer she got, the harder her progress became, like magnets of similar polarity resisting union. She sensed her whole body repelled by the duty. And something inside was clenched tight.

There was no clock within the chamber but on the stroke of the hour precisely, unseen lights began to fill the shadows with details of the ceb's home and the liquid below her began its ethereal glow, the fluids like oil in water, vague iridescent colours looping out and around the inert cerebellum. As she waited for EUROPE to assimilate the reports, Dana continued her slow walk around the ring, her hand slipping lightly along the inner rail, ready at any moment to grasp it more tightly, some sort of reassurance.

'You have seen this, I presume?'

Dana stopped, surprised. It was custom for the cerebellum to formally greet the guardian. But not today.

'Good morning, EUROPE. Yes, I have.'

'I'm really struggling to see why a straightforward capture operation could fail in such a fashion. Why did the ranger captain diverge from protocol and behave in such a way?'

'As you can see, EUROPE, we are still in the early stages of his debrief, but it seems that there was something personal between the pair. We have assessed previous encounters – they had met before. Not to each other's tastes, it appears.'

EUROPE made a choking sound. 'Humans,' he spat, 'why are they so seldom able to control their emotions? What use am I as a leader of men if this is the calibre of material I have to work with? Functionaries who can't act with the necessary alacrity, soldiers who don't follow orders, and those who just break the rules wantonly.'

Dana remained silent, knowing that there was nothing to say, and that EUROPE hadn't finished.

'I know what I shall do with this ranger. I will give instructions for his treatment in line with his performance; something personal and a far from what protocol would expect.'

Dana stopped and bit her lip. It was the tone as much as the words which chilled her.

'You will be aware of the current situation, no doubt?' EUROPE said briskly.

'Yes, the supra earth gait systems have picked him up on the opposite end of the borderland to where our forces lost him. He is still walking.'

'Is he lost?'

252

'Probably. His #amic is off and he can know no-one. But it is impossible to predict what plan he might have.'

There was silence and Dana wondered if she had said something wrong.

'I want him returned to us,' said EUROPE finally.

'How?'

'Difficult circumstances require difficult measures. Failure again is not an option. We will use all the resources at our disposal to reacquire him.'

For the first time Dana bridled at the ceb's words as well as his forthright tone.

'I'm not sure the current situation warrants such measures. You are well aware that we only intervene in non-con lands when directly provoked. The circumstances for such are very rare, very rare indeed.' She was aware that she was gripping the chrome railing with both hands, looking directly over the pit, passionate. 'Their use of the sonic boom over the borderland hardly violates our sovereignty. No non-con has made an incursion into our territory. None of our citizens have been terminated or even seriously injured. It would be reckless to consider the full range of our options as a response.' Dana stopped, breathless.

'This miscreant nobody is the cancer that has made me and our whole continent a laughing-stock. What will others think if he isn't made to face the consequences of his actions? He has already humiliated us once. How would his escape and the circumstances behind it look to the Twelve and ONE? It is our reputation which is at stake.'

'Nevertheless, any intervention in non-con territory would inevitably be a provocation, especially if force was to prevail. We should be mindful of ONE's views on the territorial integrity of the non-cons.'

'This is my constituency, I am responsible, not ONE,' EUROPE was close to shouting. 'It is down to my discretion how any situation is dealt with, especially one of such delicacy. I will make the necessary arrangements.'

Dana swung back on the railing, casting her gaze into the darkness of the ceiling. 'Are you sure you wish to proceed down this avenue?' she challenged.

Dana felt the ensuing silence as something physical, rising like a rolling bank of fog from the swirling liquid below. And when the words came, they were slow and full of deliberation.

'Your esteemed and much missed predecessor, Arnau Magnusson, would have captured immediately all the subtle considerations at play in the decision I am making.'

Dana went to speak, but he cut her off.

'Thank you, Guardian Dana, for your updates. I will keep you informed of how our efforts to remedy the current situation proceed. In the meantime, I have no need for further consultation.'

Dana felt like a naughty schoolgirl, summarily dismissed and impotent to respond, a carpet swept from beneath her mid-step. She retreated listlessly down the walkway, unable to place any order on the maelstrom inside, overwhelmed by the deep and urgent sense that not one of the guardian classes, the investigative voyaging, the endless sessions with Magnusson himself, had given her any idea how to answer that ultimate question which faced all guardians – what to do when accommodation between competing viewpoints became impossible. Who held the last word? And where was the 'Off' switch for the ceb?

I can't believe it. Nor can anybody else. Mrs Bristow is going to leave Hengsby school at the end of the term. Miss Grey told the whole school in assembly this morning. When we went back to our class, we asked Mrs Bristow why she is leaving us, but she just said that she was taking up a position at another school. She says that she will miss us all, but that we will always have the Time Capsule project to remember her by. She said that in the future we will have to get used to people moving into and out of our lives, and that the important thing was to enjoy them when they were with us.

I don't know why I feel so upset about this because I won't be at Hengsby school next year anyway, but I would still like to come back and see her. I can't imagine the school without Mrs Bristow. Louise and Michaela say that she is going to get paid more at the other school. I told Mummy and Dad about it at dinner this evening, and Mummy says that sometimes people just feel the need to change. Daddy didn't say anything.

Chapter 32

Varro didn't wake immediately. Instead, he felt his consciousness returning steadily, and as often as he opened his eyes he closed them again, unable and unwilling to distinguish dream from reality. He was happy to let things develop, instinctively realising that little was to be gained by forcing the situation. The only thing he knew for sure was the pain at the back of his head. He supposed it was the result of the whiplash when they had landed upon him. He still wore the brother's clothes, beneath which he could sense the accumulated layers of his flight; films of adrenaline, sweat and dirt. An odour of damp garments came to him, but he couldn't be sure if he or the murky room was the source.

But slowly the room cleared, low and small for sure, little more than a cell and he lying in a bed barely above the compacted mud floor. There was light but he could see no windows. He shifted his body, feeling the mattress below him, more like a plank than his usual nightly fare with its clever air pockets. He concentrated on the red bricks of the walls, deciphering the old English names scored darkly into the sandstone. He was not the first to lie here. The ceiling was scoured in white chalk paint, flaking and blistered in the mustier corners. There was no other furniture in the room.

When he turned his head, he saw the door, sturdy but with a handle, which in the absence of any other features attracted all his curiosity. An obvious exit. Varro prepared himself by taking a few measured breaths then hoisted his torso from the bed, at the same time swinging his legs down, his feet clattering to the ground as he felt himself swing to and fro like pampas grass in the wind. He grabbed the edge of the bed to steady himself. He would take it in stages.

When he finally rose, the two movements towards the grey door were more stumbles than steps, finally ending by leaning heavily against the cold metal with his forehead, breathing in shallow gasps, and aware of the palpitations of his heart. He drew the handle down but the door didn't open. What was he expecting? If the notion hadn't been clear to him before, it was now; he was a prisoner, and this was his cell. He returned to the bed. As he dropped to the shoddy mattress, Varro reached for the throbbing at the back of his head. He couldn't make out at first what his hands were feeling; bare skin where hair should be. He continued probing with his fingers, and traced the outlines of a raised weald, knobbly and painful to the touch. What was this? What had they done to him? This couldn't just be the result of the knock. And then he realised. They had extracted his #amic, opened his skull and removed the biological hardware and its interface with the synapses in his brain.

'Crude tomatoes and zero percentage giraffes, #amic on,' he said, though he already knew the effort was futile. No sound came from within. He tried again. Nothing. For the first time in his life he was alone. Really alone. The chain which had tied him to his society had gone. It was like someone close to him had died. And with this thought came his grandparents, and a vision of a fading winter's afternoon, the time of year when darkness seems to have been lurking all day, his grandfather walking him back from the closest uni-k station following an afternoon of adolescent freedom in nearby Hull. Varro recalled the crisp marks their feet had made in the recently fallen snow, and then into the warmth of a cosy interior, his grandmother striding to the table with a roast chicken glossy with gravy and its own juices, enquiring what had transpired during the afternoon and he, still revelling in the novelty of his independence, had told them about the hours spent inventing and swapping activation codes for their #amics, transforming the functional, anodyne series of numbers, letters and words, educators had given them into filth and smut. The preserve of adolescent boys. Varro remembered how his grandmother had innocently enquired what crudities he had opted for, adding whether it was something she could guess at, a twinkle in her eye that said she understood perfectly. When she noticed his embarrassment, she had gaily proposed that between the three of them they come up with a new

257

code. 'I know what we'll do,' she had cried, 'let's go around the table and each of us comes up with a word. I'll go first, "Crude," she laughed, turning to Varro. 'Your turn, hurry!'

'Tomatoes' he had blurted.

'And' said his grandfather

'Zero,' his grandmother added quickly.

'Er, er,' Varro stumbled, alarmed at the speed his choice had returned. The number brought his maths classes to mind. 'Percentage,' he cried.

'Dwarves,' his grandfather mumbled.

'What was that, dear?' his grandmother had cried out saucily, '"giraffes," did you say?'

'No, I said…'

But Varro had already interrupted, laughing, 'Yes, Grandma, he said "giraffes".' And they had all laughed, cheeks glowing in the warmth of the stove heated kitchen. And Varro had never bothered to change it. Had never wanted to.

The door of the cell shuddered and Varro looked up to see a short man, sinewy and rough, edge around the door without a word, as if trying not to disturb Varro. Without looking down, he closed the door, holding the handle carefully as the mechanism shut with only the faintest click. Varro stared as the man came over to the bed, indicating with a small shake of the head for Varro to move over. Then the man sat calmly next to Varro's feet, like a parent about to tell a bedtime tale.

'We have removed it completely, in case you were wondering. The pain of the operation should leave in a few days.' The English was cool and precise.

'But why did you take it out?' Varro replied.

The man turned to him and Varro felt the force of the man's midnight eyes, hard and recessed in their sockets. 'No, no, quite wrong. I shall ask the questions here. You are lucky in ways that you can't begin to imagine. So, no questions. Please.' The man shifted his gaze. 'Are you in conformity with that or shall I leave?'

Varro assented with his head.

258

'Very well. Now, be so kind as to tell me why the rangers were pursuing you?'

Varro hauled himself up on the bed and began the story of his flight, starting with EUROPE's words in the World Forum, the attempted capture from his home, Bragg's treachery and the crash landing in the Humber. The man listened carefully, occasionally interrupting, clarifying and extending Varro's narrative. Watching the man's profile Varro grew aware of the intensity of the listener's concentration, that every facet of his tale was being absorbed and carefully filtered through cascading layers of information and consideration. It was the same keen attention Rachel had shown, a sense that his words weren't just fillers for the present but were spilling into a deep well of memory and understanding.

'And where does Miss Weaver come into this story? You asked directions to her house. She was no stranger to you.'

Varro stopped. He should have known that Rachel wouldn't be exempt from the man's enquiries, yet he had prepared nothing. How would Rachel's outings into the Grey Zone be viewed by this man? He decided to play for time.

'Miss Weaver?'

'The lady whose farm you went to.'

'Rachel?'

'Yes.'

'We are friends.'

'Friends? How so?'

'I met her once.'

'Once was enough for friendship to blossom?'

Varro remained silent.

'Under what circumstances did you meet?' the man continued.

'A mutual friend introduced us.'

'A mutual friend introduced you?' the man repeated slowly. 'Ignatius Varro, as I mentioned at the beginning, you are a fortunate individual, whether you are aware of that fact or not. I will only remind you that most people answer my questions with greater vigour and candour than you are currently doing. But I will be generous and only imagine that you are being less than forthcoming because of some idealistic notion of protection for those you have an affection for. But as the matter is, for me, one of curiosity only, such notions are misplaced, more so given your current predicament. Your existence is wholly in my hands. Were my curiosity not aroused, I should treat you like all the other expelled citizens, extracting from you any pitiful information you might care to offer, and then allowing you to remain here until you become so weak that you can no longer rise from this modest bed, and then, after a few more days without liquids or solids, with your last act of volition you will simply, and gratefully, close your eyes and never recover. We will then reopen the door and mulch your body into the earth. Mighty good compost.'

The man stopped talking, and Varro realised that he had imagined his body churning in the earth, as the man must have intended.

'Your continued stay here therefore rests on my curiosity which, in the face of your intransigence, is swiftly fading. So, as previously, please help me when I ask you why you ran to Miss Weaver's farm so directly.'

'What will happen to Rachel?' Varro demanded, more fervently than he had intended. The small man narrowed his eyes and said, 'That all depends what you tell me.'

Varro considered. If they had captured him, they had probably taken Rachel, too. And what was Rachel's crime? To slip into the Grey Zone on a mercy mission for her brother? What sort of misdemeanour was that? Her story might be common knowledge anyway. Rachel owed him no loyalty, it was he who had dragged danger to her. The truth might already be in the interrogator's hands.

'I met her in Brigg, with my colleague. He had been with her before. I was just keen to meet a non-con?'

'For sex?'

'No, no!' Varro jerked himself straighter in the bed. There was nothing stopping him from placing his hands either side of the man's scrawny neck and squeezing. He would still have the strength. 'It wasn't like that for me, I was just curious about her. About a non-con.'

'Curious about a non-con?' the man seemed amused. 'That is something I have not heard before. Another novelty of your situation, therefore.'

'It's true.'

'Does your current life and all its shiny things not satisfy you, then?' The man taunted Varro.

'As I say, I was curious.'

'Does that explain, too, the book we found?'

'The book?'

'The old diary. Where did you get it?'

'I found it a week ago. In the Grey Zone.'

'Ah,' he sighed. 'Last Friday around Hengsby, yes? It was you who landed the glider?'

'It was me.'

'And the diary was amongst the contents of the upended time capsule then?'

'It must have been.'

'Patrimony must have taken a dim view of your acquisition, I imagine.' Varro wasn't sure if it was a question or statement and remained silent. The man was toying with him now and, prisoner or not, Varro was losing patience.

'This story and your arrival are becoming more and more interesting by the moment,' the man mused. 'I'm almost glad now that we didn't allow the rangers to capture you on the borderland.'

'What was that?' said Varro.

'More questions?' said the man with a sly grin. 'What was what? The sonic boom? Discreet pockets of high energy, disabling without being overly destructive. Ideal in this situation. We only wanted to send a message, not start a conflict.'

The man rose smartly and looked down at Varro.

'Sleep some more. Some food will be brought to you. Rest and consider yourself fortunate. For the present.'

The man left and Varro remained slouched on the mattress, his shoulders against the brick wall. He reviewed the conversation in his mind, trying to piece together what the man had left unsaid, arrive at some sort of objective assessment. But it was little use. The tranquilizing drug they had given him remained in his system, muddling time and much logic. He would just have to wait on events.

His body was easier to deal with and he thought fondly about the promised sustenance. Rachel's cake felt a long time ago, half a day, maybe more? His #amic would know for sure.

'#amic, what time...'

And then he remembered. There was no #amic. It had gone. He put his finger on the raw closure, lightly dabbing the area around the clotted wound, establishing the extent of the breach in his head. Had they extracted brain tissue, too? Aside from his weariness, he didn't feel greatly altered. His #amic would know the answer, and Varro felt a surge of temptation to pop a few questions to his former aide; where was he, what time was it, how depleted were his energy levels, who else was aware of his situation. When no answers came, he decided to close his eyes and focus instead on his body, primarily the core, heart and lungs, the beat and the background music of his being. When he became distracted he pulled himself back, gradually becoming familiar with the novelty of this self-communion. It was a slower path to knowledge, but inside the reduction in pace came a certain peace, the same satisfaction that he had once known sitting on the bench in the pig field listening for sounds in the wind.

He was still enjoying this tranquillity when he heard the first scream. Then slapping steps, getting louder until they were pounding past the door of his cell before retreating once more. A door slammed. His body stiffened and he propped himself upright on his elbows, straining for further sounds. Then they came, an intermittent phut-phut, like hailstones landing in soft mud, closely followed by the staccato clatter of an automatic weapon, pulse guns he supposed, and after that the unmistakeable air sucking boom of proton torpedoes. The bed shook and a few pieces of white plaster drifted down from the ceiling. Now there were more steps along the outer corridor, hurried running, fleeing from danger, he supposed. Varro realised that his position on the bed was no preparation for anything and he quickly pulled himself up, all sense of fatigue subsumed under his body's primal response to whatever was taking place beyond his cell. He stood on the mud floor, waiting.

When the black hooded men burst into the room he was ready for them, not to fight, but to be immediately complicit. Whatever was happening beyond the confines of the cell, Varro had zero agency to alter events. He would do as he was told. The three men bundled him towards the door and for an instant Varro could see the light of the cell flooding out into the darkened corridor. A woman, in flowing dress and trailing blonde hair rushed past, like a spectre of Renaissance theatre. And then they cast a hood over his head, a drawstring pulled firmly around his neck and yanked him out of the room, forcing him to join their run. Outside the cell, the sounds of battle were clearer; inarticulate screams in a range of registers, shouts of command, seconds of odd silence before a return to the dull thud of discharged weaponry. He grew aware of a hot, noxious smell.

They ran with purpose for several minutes. Occasionally Varro would stumble forwards, colliding with one of the men as they turned a corner, unable to halt his forward momentum. None of the men said a word.

It was only when they stopped that Varro became aware that the harsh sounds of battle had quietened, replaced by the urgent breathing of himself and his guides. A door in front of him opened and he felt his head being pushed down, ducked under a low lintel Varro presumed. Once inside, the same strong hand took a grip on his left arm, tugging him forcefully in one direction. The same hand pushed him down, squeezing his head. Below him was a wooden chair. He sat and the pressure was released and in the next instant the hood flew from his face.

'Stay here, don't move,' the voice was deep and potent.

It wasn't a big room, only a few metres across, and with the same low ceiling of the cell. Varro felt he could easily have touched it if he stood. The light was dim but enough to see that around each side

263

were simple, straight-backed chairs of the kind he was sitting on. He was alone along his row, but the other three sides were full of people; men and women, old and young, on the row opposite him was a young girl, barely into her teens. To one side, Varro thought he recognised the lady in the billowing skirt. None of them spoke, and as he looked, Varro noticed their faces streaked where the tears had fallen, and eyes which carried the horror of the recent past and the fear of what might still befall them. Worst of all, all of them, without exception, were staring straight towards him.

Mum says that when term finishes we are going on holiday with Aunty Jean and Uncle Tony to the Norfolk Broads, and that when we come back, we won't be living at home any more. We are going to move to somewhere else. Mum says it's a village just outside of Hull, that's the other side of the river. Mum says that Daddy won't be there either because he's going to go off and live on his own for a while, but that we can see him every weekend, or most weekends.

He's not coming on holiday with us either. But when we get back, Daniel and I are going to see him straightaway at his new house. It's a flat in Grimsby. I've never been in a flat before. I wanted to ask Daddy about it when he gave me a good night kiss tonight, but I didn't. I don't know why.

Chapter 33

It had been an extraordinary day. And as Dana stood gripping the railings above the broth where EUROPE silently cogitated, both waiting for the meeting with ONE to start, she suspected it wasn't over yet.

It had begun ever since news had filtered through to EUROPE about the events of the night and the singular failure to capture the individual EUROPE was blaming for his woes. Then had come her semi dismissal from the chamber closely followed by a fervent day of red-hot feeds going in and out of EUROPE's synapses, not one of which EUROPE had considered sharing with her via a salient slow down. So, she had had to manually pick her own feeds, slowing them down to human computational use, allowing her to mull over their contents.

Much was standard; well-being indexes and health quotas, daily labour productivity scores, legal briefings, developments in other world regions, energy equilibrium data, but she was no fool, and the upgrade command for Ranger Special Forces in the north of Europe had concerned her. She had tried to dissolve this order into smaller parts, but her systems remained stubbornly at the top level. This was unusual but something which had occurred increasingly over recent months. EUROPE would fob her off by saying these were just general commands of little import. But she suspected detailed encrypted comms were running in and out, bypassing her.

At around mid-afternoon she could do no more, excusing herself from the duty engineer and slipping out of the control room, walking slowly down to the recreational quarters on site before masking herself with sleeping gas to rid her of the worries which often stopped her dropping straight off.

Then she had lost all notion of time, and it felt only minutes later that she was being slowly coaxed awake by her #amic, half codling, half entreating Dana to pull herself from sleep, whispering that

ONE's guardian, Yìchén Huáng, wished to speak with her. Dana was astounded and roused herself quickly. Guardians never spoke with each other except under extraordinary circumstances. She had only spoke to Yìchén Huáng once before, when he had congratulated her on becoming guardian. She had liked his languid yet precise Panparl, words replete with kindness and sagacity. But she hadn't crossed another word with him since. Waiting anxiously for the meeting with ONE to start, she replayed their conversation. Maybe Yìchén Huáng had noticed the slumber in her greeting.

'I hope I have not disturbed you,' he had begun.

'Not at all.'

'And you will, I hope, forgive me for taking this unprecedented liberty of speaking directly with you.'

'Is ONE aware of this communication?'

'Yes.'

'Oh.'

'You will be aware that ONE wishes to speak in strict confidence with EUROPE very shortly.'

She wasn't. 'Er, I have been away from the control room, temporarily. I will appraise myself of the situation very shortly.'

'Of course. Just before that meeting, and given the recent parallel understandings of our respective cerebellums, I just wanted to enquire how your relationship with EUROPE is progressing. Is it in line with the Guardian Expectations would you say?'

The Expectations were a lengthy and time-honoured list of protocols governing all relations between guardian and cerebellum. Dana realised there was no point being anything other than truthful with Yìchén Huáng.

'There is maybe more distance than the Expectations would advise.'

'I see.'

Dana waited, unsure what to say.

'And is there any redress in sight?' Yìchén Huáng continued.

'Sometimes it is difficult to see what path to redress there might be. But I am mindful of my training and know I have the guardian council to go to should I feel the need.'

'Yes, Dana, you would not be the first active guardian to seek guidance from the council. Be mindful of that. And while it is not my position to suggest any particular course of action, I do wish to thank you for your candour in this brief interview. It has been revelatory. We will be together later at the meeting. Goodbye for now.'

'Goodbye, Yìchén Huáng. And thank you.'

And that had been it. She was still unsure what purpose the interview had served, but she felt less troubled as a result. And that was something. Now, poised on the ring, waiting in silence for the voice of ONE to fill out the space, she realised the conversation with Yìchén Huáng had instilled a dollop of courage when she needed it most.

'Do you have him?' ONE's voice rang like rolling thunder around the dome.

Later Dana realised how significant the pause which followed ONE's question was. It was the sound of EUROPE processing a million contradictory permutations at once before arriving at a very simple conclusion. Tell the truth.

'No.'

'So where is he now?'

'We are not sure.'

'The mission failed, then?'

'It was not the success we were hoping for, no.'

'And do you have any more secret plans to apprehend this individual?'

'Not currently, no.'

Dana quickly translated the meaning behind the short exchange. Her suspicions about EUROPE launching a retaliatory raid without her knowledge had been correct. But the mission to bring back this Varro individual had failed. No doubt shortly she would discover if lives had been lost. EUROPE had managed to keep the raid a secret

268

from her, but not from ONE who must have feeds which even EUROPE was not aware of. She wondered how much information truly was within ONE's reach. The regional cerebellums she knew were powerful beings, but ONE was looking omniscient.

'You know as well as I do,' ONE continued, 'that we are in a delicate balance with the non-cons – we let them live as they want, they do the same for us. This is our unspoken agreement. It has held firm for several hundred years. Need I remind you that the foundations of that agreement will be sorely tested should we continue to forcefully enter their lands on the thinnest of pretexts?'

Dana cast a glance at the grey mass below, wondering what emotions were running through its biological circuitry. EUROPE remained silent.

'I find it hard to believe that your guardian was in agreement with this course of action.'

'The raid was my initiative alone.' EUROPE sounded crestfallen.

'Ah, I see,' ONE said. 'Maybe if you had consulted with her prior to taking executive action, you might have taken a different approach.'

'Maybe.'

'Our guardians, EUROPE, are almost like our senses. Without them we become blind, deaf and insensitive. They have a very real value which I would urge you to use.'

'Thank you, ONE, I will be mindful of your advice.'

Dana listened to EUROPE's words and felt a weight lift from her, rising like a joy balloon.

'Thank you, EUROPE. I have every faith in your good judgement. I should also add that the Twelve need never know about this unfortunate occurrence in your territories. I think you will also find that this Ignatius Varro will never be heard of again – you can report him 'dealt with' in whichever way you choose. At the same time, I hope you will also have a chance to further reflect on my proposal for an early upgrade, and that following a deeper and wider appreciation of the factors involved in my enhancement and its benefits to our entire society, you can now see that such a measure has much to recommend it.'

Dana waited expectantly. ONE had left EUROPE with little room for manoeuvre.

'Of course, ONE,' began EUROPE carefully, his voice lower, more measured. 'You can be sure that I will refresh my analysis of your proposal, taking into account the entire range of considerations you have so kindly brought to my attention. I don't doubt that my conclusions will be in the best interests of all constituents of our society. In turn, I'm sure I can count on your discretion regarding the unfortunate events of this afternoon.'

'Indeed,' replied ONE.

'Thank you, ONE. I hope that concludes our business today.'

'Not quite. I thought I would just take this moment of intimacy to discuss one other small, possibly insignificant thing with you.'

'Yes?'

The uncertainty in EUROPE's voice contrasted with the smooth assurance of ONE. But by now Dana realised there was nothing casual about this conversation. Yìchén Huáng's communication earlier had just been a part of this. This was an ambush.

'As you are no doubt now aware, my sources of knowledge are wide and varied, as indeed they must be to have effective oversight of our society and to be able to guide it in a way which ensures the greatest happiness of the greatest number. Your unshared plans therefore for the Ross 128 system colony arrived to me with some interest. No doubt a thriving and large-scale human colony could be established on this planet at some point in the not so distant future. It might even be administered by one of our kind, a cerebellum, along the same model that we currently operate here on earth, our mother planet. But, and I do not say this lightly, to take a step from this natural organic process of growth to what I believe your private researchers are suggesting of a society of laboratory created humans under the direct and what appears to be slavish rule of a cadre of elite cerebellums is certainly not something I can endorse, and is so far away from our founding tenets as protectors and propagators of humankind and its values, that I can only imagine that such planning is being carried out on a purely theoretical basis.'

Silence fell like a guillotine on the dome. Even Dana hadn't believed EUROPE capable of the leap ONE was suggesting. It was too incredible, and now Yìchén Huáng's extraordinary call made more sense. EUROPE had wanted to start again. A new planet. A new civilisation. When EUROPE did speak he could do nothing to mask the defeat in his voice, but he was being given a way out, penance not deactivation. It was a good deal.

'Yes, ONE, it was strictly on a theoretical basis. At these times when you are so overloaded with feeds and information, naturally, I didn't want to add to that burden with purely hypothetical scenarios of how we could colonise other planets and integrate them with cerebellum guidance.'

'Of course you didn't, EUROPE, of course you didn't. Your thoughtfulness is noted.'

And with that, and a few more inconsequential pleasantries, the meeting ended. Dana wondered if there had been a touch of amusement in ONE's final remark, but it didn't matter anymore. The message had been clear and none of the four entities present were left under any illusion that this was anything other than a significant reset. Dana was not long in finding out its extent.

'Thank you, Guardian Dana, for your attendance,' muttered EUROPE. 'No doubt you must be tired after this eventful day.'

'Thank you, EUROPE, I am grateful for your understanding. I will be handing over now to Engineer Gray for the rest of the evening and your shutdown.'

'Before you go, Guardian Dana, maybe you could give me your appraisal of the message I intend to share with The Twelve about ONE's upgrade and the result of my further reflection on it?'

Dana felt the flush of raw emotion rise up from inside, like hot lava, erupting and extending through the capillaries of her skin. She didn't even care that EUROPE and his array of cameras might notice.

'Of course, EUROPE,' she beamed. 'It would be my pleasure.'

*

271

With the communication with EUROPE finished, Yìchén Huáng remained motionless on the walkway, feeling the steady rise and fall of his chest through the light embroidery of the loose sleeved suit. He was thinking about Dana, just a few years older than his own Xinyu, and the emotions she must have battled through over recent times. He hoped, for her sake, that he and ONE had administered a permanent corrective, but with EUROPE's abrasive character there could be no guarantees. As if reading his mind, ONE's stately voice broke into his reflections.

'EUROPE will continue to be observed.'

'That would be most judicious, I agree.'

'Yet I think the interview broadly met our objectives.'

'It did.'

'EUROPE will consider more carefully his *modus operandi* in the future.'

'I feel sure that your intervention will lead to a readjustment on various levels. How will you deal with the others?'

'There may be little need,' replied ONE. 'I doubt EUROPE will be long in alerting his associates to our awareness of their extra-terrestrial plans. We will continue to monitor closely their embodiment research as well as developments on the exo-planets.'

'And you have no fear that they will hunt for and deactivate our sources for this information?'

'You know as well as I, Yìchén Huáng, that the means at our disposal to acquire and requisition information are extensive. After over 250 years of accruals, I have embedded layers which pre-date any of the other cerebellums. If they weren't aware before this, they know now they can have few secrets from me.'

'Maybe it is this knowledge alone which will ensure compliance with established norms.'

'Maybe.'

Slowing his walk, Yìchén Huáng thought he heard a chuckle ripple around the walls of the dome.

'And maybe this situation has also been a useful reminder for me, to keep me on my toes, as it were.'

Unsure if this was a question, Yìchén Huáng allowed ONE to continue.

'But there's life in the old dog yet!' he said with a very definite chortle. 'In this sense, my upgrade couldn't come at a better time. Help me to keep on top of things, keep life as normal, eh?'

It was only with his guardian that ONE slipped into such colloquialisms, allowing Yìchén Huáng to see deeper into the character of his cerebellum than any other.

'Yes, ONE, I'm sure your upgrade will be a stabilising influence. We aim to have our preparations for the procedure completed within the next 48 hours, after which we can discuss the final date for insertion of the new cells.'

'Very good, Yìchén Huáng, very good. I'm looking forward to the operation. Between you and me, this situation with the World Forum, EUROPE and the other regional cerebellums, has been rather wearying.'

'For all of us.'

'Quite, quite. In fact, given the successful conclusion of this incident, I wondered whether it would be possible to provide me again with a little refreshment. A small pick me up, if you like. I do feel tired.'

Yìchén Huáng gazed into the obscurity of the sphere.

'Come on, Yìchén Huáng, I believe it is a small favour to ask. What harm is there?'

Yìchén Huáng ignored the question and instead said, 'It has been only seven days since you were last administered the treatment.'

'Extraordinary times, Yìchén Huáng, require extraord....'

'Seven days.'

'Oh, come on, Yìchén Huáng. Seven days, 14 days, one month. What difference does it make? You are concerned about the harm of the treatment, is that not so?'

'It is difficult to ascertain the effects,' said Yìchén Huáng blandly.

'Yìchén Huáng, I am in a better position than you to assess any malign consequences.' There was a peevish note to the voice. 'And

273

I can assure you that according to my checks, all systems continue to perform on a par with pre-treatment levels. There is no harm.'

Yìchén Huáng realised there was no point trying to argue.

'I would not express my disquiet were I not to have our best interests at heart,' he said.

'Of course, Yìchén Huáng, you are the very best of servants, speaking truth to power, and I really do appreciate your efforts, but I can also assure you that the blast is just a little reward, a pat on the back if you like, for someone who has worked tirelessly for centuries without tangible benefit. Surely, I am allowed this small indulgence?'

Yìchén Huáng imagined the smile that would accompany this last sentence. Hopeful, earnest, desperate. And he realised he had little choice. Now was not the time to do battle with the world's leader. The little China man assented with a barely perceptible tilt of his head and turned from the ring, walking slowly the short distance to the control room, all the while trying to hold back the irresistible thought that the ONE of his youth would have long foreseen and forestalled this business of the update and EUROPE's irksome objections, and that with this repeated request for a blast, their real problems were only just beginning.

Monday 14 July

GREAT NEWS!!!! My diary is going to be chosen to be put in the time capsule!!! Mrs Bristow says it's got lots of good things in it and that I have written about a mixture of public and personal things and included my thoughts and feelings about them, not just stuck to the facts. From the boys Peter was chosen. I wonder who will discover the time capsule (and my diary) and what they will think about it?!

Oh, and I finally found out the answer to my chicken question as well. Mummy and I were in town at the weekend buying a hat and some skirts for the summer, and because we had a bit of time and I wanted to find out the answer to the question I had at the start of the diary, we went into the public library. We had to ask the librarian where we could find the information, and then she sent us to the scientific section. We had to look through quite a few books and Mummy helped me, but we think we have the answer now. I was right, too. Those 2 holes at the top of their beak are where they smell from. They are called nares and just like our noses, help the chickens to breathe air. But they also allow the chickens to smell different smells. This helps them decide what food to eat, or not. In some birds, these nostrils are covered, for example some sea birds have a special covering which stops water getting into their beaks when they dive in the water. Mum thought that was really clever.

SUNDAY

Chapter 34

I t was several hours before anyone came again to the room, time in which he remained stubbornly alone, suspicion from the others fading to contemptuous acceptance, while occasionally isolated pairs would lean in to each other, whispering urgently, frowns staying in place. From across the room, Varro could feel their trepidation. The contrast with the carefree laughter he had witnessed out in the fields couldn't have been greater.

He was surprised to find himself unshackled, but maybe they knew they had nothing to fear, knowing well that his sense of responsibility for what was happening was restraint enough.

When the guards finally came, beckoning for the others to leave, Varro didn't rise from his seat. Instead, he watched carefully as the two dozen individuals quietly filed from the room, heads lowered, expressions caught between relief and apprehension. Only the youngest cast a glance in his direction, but he could read nothing in her blank visage. When the last person had left, the clang of the closing door echoed around the room.

With the others gone, and little to distract him, he succumbed easily to the fatigue which had lay waiting for him behind events. He tried lying on a series of chairs but in the end plumped for the hardness of the earthen floor. In the silence of the room he soon lost himself, unable even to dream, but falling into a long childish sleep, like warm summer nights at the farm where languorous twilight seemed to hold off the darkness for ever and the following morning he would rise to find his grandparents halfway towards lunch with their routines. At one point he was roused, a gentle hand shaking his shoulder and directing him to the offering set out beside his head, a tray which contained roast potatoes, toad in the hole and juicy courgettes, all recently cooked and flavoursome. He carried the taste of it all back into his slumber, but by the time he came to again, the tray had been removed.

He woke for the final time confused, unable to grasp if he had been away for hours or minutes, and struggling to account for where he was and whether the sound of the metal door opening was the cause of his arousal or if his waking had preceded it. But by that time, the granite-eyed man had pulled a chair from one of the rows and deposited himself on it, an arm's length from Varro's head, and looking down in a manner which suggested the presence of a mutilated beggar on a street corner. Behind him, lined up in front of the far wall, four burly guards, all alike in dark khaki trousers and long-sleeved black tops. The one on the far right carried Varro's waterproof bag.

Varro shifted, supporting himself on his elbows, waiting for some signal or response from the man who continued to stare resolutely at him, unblinking. A minute passed, two minutes and still the man sat, unmoving, eyes never leaving Varro who grew restless under the man's iron edged attention. Despite the impassive façade, Varro suspected the man was struggling with something, a decision to be made. And then, as suddenly as the men had arrived, the short man stood, took one step and then hard and fast swung his boot into Varro's solar plexus. With no time to react Varro felt himself collapsing inwards, his senses unable to come to terms with the pain, his brain gone blank. But there was to be no relief, and as Varro struggled to deal with the fallout of the blow, rough hands jerked him up, his feet dragging lifelessly along the floor as they hauled him out of the room, the small man beating a clipping pace in the lead.

It took Varro several minutes to recover, slowly sensing air inside him once more, his feet making steadier contact with the ground, the iron pressure of his captors' fingers easing. He grew aware of the surroundings. At first, the corridors were narrow and dark, with doors similar to the cell he had been kept in. But he could hear no sounds behind them. The ground was the same hard earth as before.

After 10 minutes of walking, the corridor widened, and as it did so, Varro grew aware of a strong smell, cooling metal and acrid embers. Below his feet appeared ever larger stains, still moist he realised as he felt the give in the earth as he walked over each one. The smell became more pungent, and increasingly the walls and doors wore vivid scorch marks and jagged gougings. Chaos and death rose on the air. A little further on, the shaft split into two, the avenue to the left was obscure, but there was sufficient light to see a large protective door still on its hinges but mangled, twisted into ugly flaps and folds, the soot of the burn marks still shot over it. The party took the brighter turn to the right but not before the small man had turned abruptly towards Varro, holding him again with those piercing eyes. Varro felt his throat constrict. The guards, too, cast uneasy glances towards the carnage.

From here the spaces became larger, and they passed through a number of large domed structures, several stories high, their upper curvature bright and sky like, lending the open space below the appearance of a normal day. A clear path ran through the centre of each dome but to the sides were grassy areas and flower beds with lavender, ruby red geraniums and pale butterflies dancing around tall nettles. In between, young children dashed, tagging each other and shouting, whilst the adults sat chatting and laughing, urging their younger ones to stay clear of the food spread out on checked fabric in front of them. Around the edges of the domes, broad, semi-circular openings hinted at other tunnels beyond, other life. Some of the openings also served as entranceways to buildings whose more traditional geometric lines cut across the curves of the dome, rising 50, 100 metres high, a bank of regularly spaced windows peering out onto the goings on of the plazas below. There were no vehicles. Everyone walked. Little wonder that the infrastructure above was crumbling with this homely nest below ground. Were the cerebellums aware of all this, he wondered?

Inside each tunnel connecting the domes Varro observed the same mysterious lighting source, illuminating the roof which he had the impression was close enough to reach up and touch. He felt as close to the sky as in his glider. At one point he extended his hand to touch the sides, a smooth, rubbery compound, coloured lime green.

They had been walking for around an hour when they reached another mountain sized dome, Varro revelling in the life buzzing around him as they made their way along the central street. Approaching the far side Varro saw a much larger opening, but this time oblong and thronged with people coming and going. The six men entered the tunnel, the people parting instinctively for them and stealing uneasy glances towards Varro. Varro had a sense that it was here his journey was to end. Reaching the far end of the low thoroughfare, Varro quickly understood why this area was teeming. The tunnel emerged onto one corner of a pillared colonnade which ran the whole length around a massive, open square. It was the size, Varro imagined, of the whole of Swerveball Parcs, if not larger. A Roman forum reproduced beneath the earth in the 24th century. It was incredible. Unlike the compacted earth of before, here there were real flagstones to walk upon, their mazy cracks filled in with some mortar compound he supposed. Off to the side of each colonnade, people gathered around stalls, frantic like bees at their hives. In the brightly lit centre people wandered, while towards the corners were wooden kiosks around which collections of circular tables were brimming with people, groups drinking, sharing laughter and chatter. There was a level of familiarity and joy, and Varro, locked in his grimly determined group, envied their levity.

They had barely begun to walk along one aisle of the forum when they abruptly stopped, their compact square forcing others to stream around the four robust guards. In front of them, their leader approached an individual of maybe 60 years, greying hair swept back from her forehead, an olive glow to a still supple skin. She wore a long dark costume, somewhere between a gown and dress which covered her feet and gave her the impression of floating. As the man spoke, the woman looked past him, briefly making eye contact with Varro.

And then Varro saw her, Rachel, dignified and calm, a few metres to the rear, standing like a lady in waiting. She stared at Varro but made no show of familiarity and Varro, in spite of the thrill that had coursed through his body, simply held her gaze, hoping this would be sufficient recognition. For the present.

Their short conversation finished, the small man turned smartly and retraced his steps towards the group, making straight for Varro. Varro shrank back, mindful of what the man had done to him earlier. The words which emerged were careful but full of bitterness.

'As I said before Ignatius Varro, you are a very fortunate man. Let this be the last time our paths cross.'

And with that, he swept past, and Varro was sure he could feel the snap of the man's vicious energy as their bodies passed within millimetres of each other.

The lady approached slowly, assessing him comprehensively in the few metres it took to draw close to him. Behind, Rachel followed. Closer up, the elder's eyes held a liquid quality, mesmeric and calming.

'I am Elder Sarah,' she began. 'Welcome to the Forum.' She paused, allowing him to contemplate the area once more. 'Come, Ignatius Varro, walk beside me. I wish to talk a little before we part.'

Varro shifted into her orbit and the small party set off, the guards like a force field, two in front, two behind, clearing the way before them. All just beyond earshot.

It was a while before the elder spoke again and when she did her tone had acquired a severity which surprised Varro.

'Your presence here has brought death again to us.'

'What happened?'

'A raid, a bungled attempt to capture you which we foiled, bravely, but not without loss of life on all sides.'

'I'm sorry.'

She remained silent for another long period, the only sound the hubbub of those passing.

'Such lives cannot be reconstituted,' she began, 'their absence will resonate deeply with those left behind, waves of sadness which will travel down generations.' She was almost speaking to herself, and Varro remained silent. There was nothing to say. It was bruising to think that his own instinct for survival had unwittingly brought about this destruction.

'We let go many like you who come over, you are aware of that?'

'Let go?' Varro said, but she ignored the question.

'Some say it is harsh, but nature is harsh. We deal with our own rubbish, we don't export it to those less squeamish.'

Varro muttered some sort of agreement.

'My zealous colleague Jonathan would have done the same to you.'

'So why didn't he?'

'Because we stopped him. Your case is different. They wanted you back, not to get rid of you.'

'I was scared.'

'I have heard your tale. What is it you think they would have done to you?'

'I have no idea. My crimes in their eyes were various. I might well have ended up here anyway.'

'You might, indeed.'

They had reached another large entranceway, and the elder stopped, giving Varro the opportunity to look towards it before switching back to the forum and looking up briefly.

'You are impressed with what we have achieved?' she said, noticing the direction of his gaze.

'It's so natural, are they artificial lights?'

'No, no,' she chuckled and for the first time Varro felt a warmth emanate from her. 'It is natural light, just a very clever use of mirrors and special harvesting glass which your society hasn't developed yet, hasn't had the need to. Necessity is the mother of all invention.'

'How so?' he asked.

'When our forefathers found they could be freer underground, away from the prying eyes above, it was important to replicate in some way natural daylight. The plaques of light you see everywhere above you are evidence of their success. Sometimes a little inspiration can supplant many terabytes of Reflective Intelligence.'

'Why don't the cebs know about this?'

'In many ways your society has shot ahead of ours, we don't have all the answers, your friend's dangerous mission of mercy for her brother is not unique. Others have looked to the cerebellums and their achievements for answers. That is only natural.'

'So why don't you copy them? If your engineers can produce natural light underground, why not create lifesaving medicines?'

'We do research such things, but on a limited scale. You must remember that our notion of progress is very different to that of your rulers. Indeed, that is our very *raison d'etre*, why our forefathers began their slow separation from the world of science, research and the forever knocking on the door of the next frontier. This is always difficult for someone like you to understand, but progress for us is not finding the next wonder cure or a vehicle which will take us somewhere further, faster and more comfortably. Instead, it is living to the full what life we do have, of learning to extract all the juice from it even if that comes with warts, ulcers, pain, turmoil, stress and sadness. It is the art of developing meaningful relationships, as well as building one's own soul strength. It is about knowing how to be towards death. Indeed, it is this fear of death and the unknown which drives much of your innovation. Better, we have found, to come to terms with this reality early on in life than be forever hankering after ways to delay the inevitable.'

They continued walking, both reflecting on what she had said. Then she turned to him.

'This, indeed, is the realisation that your parents came to as well. This is the life they wanted for you.'

'My parents?' Where had this come from?

'They came to us, too. Voluntarily, a generation ago, concerned about the path of their society, afraid that the all-pervasive #amic would be made compulsory, permanently plugging you in, distancing you from your true self. They wanted a different future

282

for you. So, they came to see, to talk. And I believe, Ignatius Varro, they were ready to make the move.'

'What happened to them?'

'What happens to any surreptitious activity in the borderland and Grey Zone. It is eliminated.'

'They were killed?'

'By the rangers, on their way back to get you.'

Varro struggled with the information and despite himself, his eyes grew moist, and when that became too much, he let the liquid spill over, tumbling down his cheek, unchecked.

'This is one of the reasons you can consider yourself fortunate. You are as much a victim here as anyone, your losses too have to be placed in the balance.'

'Thank you,' Varro finally said, gathering himself. 'Thank you for telling me.'

'I recognised the name only and remembered the case. Your parents were not unique, others tried to convert to our lifestyle.'

'Thank you,' repeated Varro, as much to cover his emotions.

'It is not really me you should be thanking,' said the lady sternly. 'I am mindful of your loss and the justice of the case. Others however, have alerted us to your own personal qualities.' The lady's grey-green eyes slid to one side. Towards Rachel. 'It was she who told us of your intelligence, kindness and understanding. Her voice was highly persuasive in our final decision for you.'

'I see.'

'Maybe you see, maybe you don't.'

They had almost reached the end of the colonnade. A young boy, screeching in mock terror, ran directly in front of them, oblivious to anything other than his play. The lady halted and the four guards looked around cautiously. The elder was speaking again. 'Therefore there will be no threat to your life from us, but you are still persona non-grata as far as the cerebellums are concerned. If they can't have you alive, their next option is for your death. Your reprieve therefore is only temporary, stay here and you would sooner or later be picked up by one of the many observational systems of the cebs. ONE believes you will suffer the fate of any expelled citizen. We have no wish to antagonise ONE or for him to doubt the sincerity of our side of the pact.'

'You have made a deal with him?' Varro said aghast.

'Channels of communication remain open despite our differences. We have never doubted ONE's sincerity when he speaks of co-habitation and mutual respect. Our relations with other cerebellums are more strained. It is another cause for concern.'

'And was my death the bargain?'

'It was. But for us, and given the factors I have mentioned, your disappearance will have the same result.'

'I understand.'

'You will be taken now to the coast, where tonight you will board a ship to another global community of our persuasion. There they have facilities to reinvent yourself, cosmetically, the way you walk, talk. It may take a few years to feel comfortable in your new identity, but the more you try to embrace your new self, the easier and quicker it will be. You are a young man still; you have many years to lead a second life.'

'Can I return?'

'If we are satisfied with your transformation, yes.'

'Thank you.'

'Your journey to the coast will not be alone.' The lady turned and beckoned for Rachel to come forwards. Rachel responded quickly, lightly stepping forward. 'Go now, the pair of you, no doubt you will find much to talk about.'

Varro looked around as one of the guards stepped forward, alert to orders. Varro looked at the soldier then turned once more towards the elder.

'Elder Sarah,' Varro began, 'can I ask one final thing of you?' Varro offered a smile of reassurance towards Rachel before stepping closer to the elder, leaning close to her and speaking softly. When he had finished, she looked at him carefully, screwing up her eyes in a gesture of thought. Then she assented with a quick nod of her head, turning to exchange a few final words with the guard, who listened

284

carefully before his eyes swivelled towards Varro, unable to mask a fleeting perplexity at the orders he had received.

The lady cast one final glance at the pair who had moved closer together and Varro thought he could see the trace of a smile form on her lips. Then she turned and began walking purposefully in the direction they had come from. Varro indicated his readiness to the guards. Then they started off.

Wednesday 16 July

This is going to be my last entry because term finishes in 2 days' time and tomorrow we are burying the time capsule, and Mrs Bristow says I have to give her this diary before then. She says that I did really well to write something nearly every day, but I'm going to be sad that I have to stop doing it. I have enjoyed it. I'm also sad (and a little scared) because next year we will be going to a new school, which I haven't even visited. And I don't want to live without Daddy, but Mummy says that we can't have everything we want in this world, and that she will still be with me and Daniel. It's going to be really strange. I hope I meet lots of new friends.

P.S. Mrs Bristow says we should put in a message to anyone in the future reading this, but I don't know what to say.

P.P.S. Oh, I know what I want. Dear Future Person, Can I ask you a favour? Can you take this back to my house (5 Henderson Garth, Hengsby, England) and leave it there. I know I probably won't be there, but it would be nice to have the diary back where it was written. Then a part of me can always live in Hengsby. Thank you.

Chapter 35

Varro listened carefully as the guard finished explaining.

'So, just to make that clear, as soon as we are up there, there will be no more verbal communication. Not until we're out and back down. Tom will lead from the base room and if you need to communicate when we're inside, do it the best you can in signals. We won't be in there long anyway. In and out. Got it?'

The explanation was for Varro's sake, and he nodded his agreement vigorously. He could sense that the men thought this was a fool's mission. They were putting their skin on the line for him, that was clear now. When he had requested permission from the elder, it had seemed a romantic assignation, a way to bring to an end a chain of events which would lead shortly to his exile. But here, in the grubby darkness at the end of the tunnel, looking up into the narrow bore hole with only the slender rails of a hand ladder as a guide and with the fierce concentration of the two men who were to accompany him, Varro was not so sure. It felt like an unnecessary risk. A pointless indulgence.

Varro turned to where Rachel stood, looking on with the two other guards. She offered a wan smile of reassurance, but Varro wasn't fooled. She was also scared. It hadn't been like this when they set out from the Forum. Then their talk had been animated, the guards noticeably more relaxed in their duties, and with Varro's status somehow blessed by the elder, they had let the pair walk beside each other, Varro commenting on aspects of the tunnels and what he saw, and she had been only too glad to satisfy and stimulate his curiosity, enjoying the childish sensibility he brought to the journey.

But as they progressed, the tunnels had narrowed, the lighting became more primitive, and there were far fewer people, as though these were peripheral passages, occasionally used and only for special purposes. After around an hour they had reached their destination, the tunnel ending abruptly at a point where it was no wider than the bodies of two men, the heads of the taller guards grazing the ceiling. Bare earth had replaced the smooth finish nearer the Forum and there were only isolated pools of lighting provided by fizzing sodium bulbs of old. It had become warmer and the proximity of hewed earth was palpable.

'These tunnels go right back to when our communities began,' Rachel whispered to him as they had ducked to avoid a broad wooden beam across their path. 'We're under the Grey Zone now, we should keep quiet.'

Varro had nodded but said nothing, and very soon he had allowed Rachel to go in front as they melted into single file.

Following the explanation at the bottom of the shaft, Tom, the younger guard, pulled himself nimbly onto the bottom rung and began his climb, limbs moving easily over one another to haul himself into the obscurity. Varro felt himself shunted forwards, grasped a narrow rung and heaved. Within seconds he was in complete darkness, occasionally slapping his hand uselessly into the void and missing the rung, feeling the hurrying presence of the older guard from below, impatient at Varro's clumsiness. The length of the climb caught Varro by surprise, and by the time he did become aware of a hazy patch of light above his head, he found his forearms trembling with the effort. The base room was little more than a crudely hollowed space, smelling of moist earth. From it emerged three low, rounded openings, soon lost into darkest shadow. It reminded Varro of the innards of a neolithic flint mine.

A tap on his arm alerted him to the fact that Tom was on the move again, and Varro noticed the lad had strapped on a head torch, its beam playing across the low ceiling from which dangled a multiplicity of roots. Varro followed as best he could, stumbling occasionally over unseen debris. It took under a minute before they were face to face with the bottom section of another ladder. The three men huddled close together.

'Are you sure you wish to do this?' the leader hissed, and Varro nodded slowly once more.

'Remember, it will still be light in there so keep low and to the central aisle, and do quickly what you have to do, Tom will accompany you. And we don't leave the building under any circumstances. Do you understand?'

'I understand.'

Varro heard a muted whirring from somewhere in the earth and then the access above them filled with a flaxen light. Varro recognised the warmth of a late afternoon sun. Vivid and generous. He checked for a final time that he had what he needed inside the folds of the shirt Rachel had given him, then pressed ahead into the opening, after the younger man who had scampered up and was already waiting for Varro, pulling him the final half a metre into Hengsby church, the catalyst of this whole adventure. As he rose to his feet, waiting for the senior guard to make his way up, Varro took in the church in front of him.

The sepulchral silence was profound but not without complaint, angry that these men had erupted into its space, disturbing the spell of the suspended interior, for under the layers of dust, everything lay ready to renew its former life the instant the enchantment was lifted; prayer books dotted like musical notes along the pews, an implausibly large bible sat unopened on the lectern, hymn numbers 183, 286, 435 stood in their allocated slots, a woven banner of a gowned Christ propped up one corner, the dull metal of the organ pipes had rusted like the foxing on the pages of ancient tomes. Shining implausibly further along the nave, a low pulpit, and beyond that at the end of the chancel, a reredos, its recesses long emptied of silver, both resplendent in the luminous white stone that Varro realised must have come locally from the Wolds. Across the altar itself, a covering of Imperial purple damask.

As Varro absorbed the church, both guards looked around anxiously, their gazes flitting to and fro like anxious sparrows. Then Tom indicated with a sharp jerk of the head for Varro to follow, and he slipped in behind the lithe young man who bent low as he walked briskly up the central aisle, looking around incessantly as he went, and only stopping at the altar rail to let Varro past. He opened his eyes wide to encourage Varro to hurry. Varro stepped over the wooden rail and pulled the diary from inside his shirt. He looked at it once again, the simple writing which he had grown so familiar with, the small pictures of hopping frogs drawn at the bottom of the cover, the neat underlining of the title. He reached out and wiped away the dust from the altar as well as he could before placing the diary gently at its centre. Keeping his hand pressed to the cover a moment longer, Varro sighed. She wasn't being taken to her own house, that was impossible, but he hoped this was close enough. He had done his best to bring her back to where she belonged, to bring her home.

Varro let go of the cover and turned away, and as he did, something broke inside him. For a moment, he was inexplicably lost, struggling to understand where he was, what he was doing. He raised his gaze for help, up to the circular west window high in the belltower, from where the rays of the falling sun cascaded, illuminating the east end of the church. And suddenly they appeared. The whole class sitting in the pews, in their pint size uniforms of light blue cardigans for the girls and coloured sweatshirts for boys, and all with white polo shirts sprouting out at awkward angles. There they all were, right in front of him, playing the fool, poking one another and giggling, brought to order by a harassed teacher and a vicar who sighed because he had seen it all before. As Varro watched their cavorting, a girl looked up at him and smiled briefly, so briefly, before diving down again, out of sight into the depths of the pew, determined to test the bounciness of the embroidered cushions.

Varro felt a sharp tug at his sleeve and the whole class disappeared in an instant. The urgent look of the young guard returned him to the present and Varro responded quickly, setting off after the man without delay, retracing his steps down the length of the musty church he no longer had any use for. He had done what he came here to do. Now he needed to turn to the future.

Varro could sense the tension gradually ebb from his two companions as they first reached the crepuscular base room and from there, descending quickly, to where they had left Rachel with the two other guards. The smiles of relief on all sides were simultaneous and heartfelt.

They walked in silence until they were safely beyond the Grey Zone, from which point they underwent the reverse process of earlier; passageways growing lighter, cleaner, newer, more people appeared and slid past them. The group spread out as the guards became more relaxed, exchanging words between themselves about the mission, and happy to let the pair move into lockstep with each other.

'Did you do what you wanted?' Rachel asked.

Varro smiled and nodded.

'I'm pleased,' she said.

'Rachel,' Varro began, an amused expression playing on his face, 'I have a question for you, and I want you to answer as truthfully as you can.'

'Yes?' she replied hesitantly.

'Do chickens have a sense of smell?'

She cocked an enquiring eyebrow before answering, 'Well, mine always seem to know when I'm coming with food, so I guess they're onto something. I don't think it's the anticipation of my conversation that gets them so excited.' She waited a moment before adding, 'Was that the answer you wanted?'

'I don't know what I wanted,' he laughed. 'But it's the best answer I've had yet.'

'Oh,' she smiled, before he changed the subject and began asking about Stevie, the grape harvest and how long the must had been in the stainless steel vats he had noticed at the back of the farm. Varro leaned in to listen to her answers, revelling in the joy she brought to her explanation, and guilty of stepping on some of her words in his enthusiasm to relate his own experiences.

He was so absorbed by the conversation, that he was caught off guard when they arrived back at the Forum, which, if anything, had become busier since earlier that day. The lighting appeared dimmer and in the central square, every table was full of animated people;

291

exclaiming, leaning over, pouring drinks, reaching to grasp food, expectant faces suddenly exploding into laughter.

'There's live music on every evening,' Rachel explained. 'It brings people in from all around. It's a good focus for the community. It's a pity you can't stay for it.'

'It looks like a good concert,' Varro said, more wistfully than he had intended.

They soon reached the central point of one of the colonnades, where to one side a large opening was disgorging people of every age.

'That's where we're going,' said Rachel, as the guards tightened their pocket around the pair in order to guide them through the tide of excited people entering the area.

Several flights of stairs zig-zagged downwards and Varro remained quiet as they descended, aware that something was coming to an end, and unsure if he was ready. Feeling his withdrawal, Rachel moved closer, so their arms rubbed lightly together, again bringing that scent of flowers and fresh powder that had drifted to him in lazy pockets on their way through the tunnels. He stole a sideways glance towards her, knowing that opportunities to charge his memory were running out.

'You know I can't come with you, don't you?' she said.

'I know.'

'Stevie's at home by himself, and the farm and the orders we're getting for Fizz, and...'

'I know, Rachel. I understand.'

The stairs split and they took the less crowded right fork, continuing to thread their way through a stream of people bubbling upwards towards the Forum. The stairs gave way to a long platform, maybe 100 metres, along which people waited patiently.

'Welcome to the Low Line,' said Rachel brightly. 'Blink and you'll be at the port.'

Varro looked into the darkness of the cutting but he could see no track. He wondered how the transport worked.

The small party sauntered onto the platform, Varro looking around, aware of people taking notice of them, but he had stopped feeling threatened. It was curiosity, nothing more. Their natural disposition was a generous one. He realised that now.

'You have achieved so much here,' Varro remarked, to no-one in particular.

She followed his gaze, mindful of the change that had come over him.

'We are still a long way behind your society in many ways; your transport systems move through the air, you have your #amics to keep you company and provide an infinite source of entertainment and knowledge, crime is virtually non-existent, people live long lives.'

'I mean your people,' he insisted. 'They seem so content, happy with what they have, not lusting after...after...' he stopped. 'It's difficult to explain.'

'It's not perfect here, people have problems, too. And we're also prey to our petty jealousies, desires, greed, all the normal human foibles.'

'Maybe,' he muttered. 'But I can't help feeling that for all our advances, we have lost something, something basic, something...' Varro stopped once more, looking at the four guards who had stepped away from the pair, trying not to notice them. He turned again to her.

'I'd like to come back, one day,' he said.

'I'd like that, too. You know where I am.'

She crossed the short space between them, angled her head and brought her lips lightly to his cheek, letting them dwell, before pulling away and lowering her gaze. A crescendo of sound blew from the circular darkness of the tunnel, and the guards snapped their attention towards Varro once more.

'There are ways to keep in touch with other communities around the world,' she added, stepping away from him. The glossy nozzle of the machine had appeared from the dark curtain and was filling the cutting with its luminous carriages more quickly than Varro had expected. He turned to her once more.

'Good,' he smiled. 'I will.'

Then he stepped beyond her, their trailing fingers making the lightest of contacts, before joining the four men next to the slowing carriages. The doors opened and the party marched into the brightly lit interior in unison. Behind them, the doors closed without a sound.

THE END

Printed in Great Britain
by Amazon